Acclaim for t

"Powerful, honest, and emotionally gripping. I read it in one sitting!"

—CJ Redwine, author of
Defiance (for *Broken Wings*)

"This is one of my favorite series! Dittemore has accomplished a rare feat with *Broken Wings*: she's written a sequel that's as good as or better than book one. Beautiful, romantic, and fascinating. I couldn't stop reading this enthralling page-turner. I'll be the first one in line for book three."

—Jill Williamson, author
of *By Darkness Hid*,
Replication, and *Captives*

"A gut-wrenching plunge into the supernatural, *Broken Wings* reveals Dittemore's skilled, elegant prose and her prowess with compelling characters! Tangible fear and violent beauty collide in this page-turning sequel in the Angel Eyes Trilogy. Simply unputdownable! Tear the veils from your eyes—*Broken Wings* is one of the best YA novels out there!"

—Ronie Kendig, award-winning
author of the Discarded Heroes
series and *Trinity: Military War Dog*

"The author has spectacularly designed a supernatural setting filled with charismatic characters whose gifts are worth noting."

—*Romantic Times*, 4½ stars
(for *Broken Wings*)

"Stunning. A captivating read with all the intensity necessary to keep me turning pages well into the night."

—Heather Burch, author of the critically acclaimed *Halflings* (for *Angel Eyes*)

"*Angel Eyes* has everything I look for in a novel—gorgeous prose, a compelling heroine, humor, and an intriguing plot—and two things I dream of finding—permission for brokenness and the promise of hope."

—Myra McEntire, author of *Hourglass*

"*Angel Eyes* is a fine debut. A touching and exciting romance with celestial implications."

—Andrew Klavan, award-winning author of *Crazy Dangerous*

"Shannon Dittemore gives us a classic tale of good versus evil with an authentically contemporary feel—and the assurance that beautiful writing is back."

—Nancy Rue, author of the Real Life series (for *Angel Eyes*)

". . . teens who like paranormal, edge-of-your-seat drama with a strong Christian message will enjoy this second installment in the trilogy."

—Ragan O'Malley, Saint Ann's School, Brooklyn, NY

DARK HALO

DARK HALO

Book Three in the
ANGEL EYES TRILOGY

SHANNON DITTEMORE

THOMAS NELSON
Since 1798

NASHVILLE DALLAS MEXICO CITY RIO DE JANEIRO

Published in Nashville, Tennessee, by Thomas Nelson. Thomas Nelson is a registered trademark of Thomas Nelson, Inc.

Thomas Nelson, Inc., titles may be purchased in bulk for educational, business, fund-raising, or sales promotional use. For information, please e-mail SpecialMarkets@ThomasNelson.com.

Publisher's Note: This novel is a work of fiction. Names, characters, places, and incidents are either products of the author's imagination or used fictitiously. All characters are fictional, and any similarity to people living or dead is purely coincidental.

Library of Congress Cataloging-in-Publication Data

Dittemore, Shannon.
Dark halo / Shannon Dittemore.
pages cm -- (Angel eyes trilogy ; book 3)
Summary: Will Brielle choose demon Damien's dark halo and the ignorance that comes with it, or will she choose to live with her eyes wide open and trust the Creator's design—even if it means a future without Jake?
ISBN 978-1-4016-8639-0 (trade paper)
[1. Supernatural--Fiction. 2. Angels--Fiction. 3. Demonology--Fiction. 4. Love--Fiction. 5. Fate and fatalism--Fiction.] I. Title.
PZ7.D6294Dar 2013
[Fic]--dc23

2013011841

Printed in the United States of America

13 14 15 16 17 18 RRD 6 5 4 3 2 1

For Sharon & Stephanie,
who held my hands when the world went dark

A Note from the Author

You are picking up the third and final book in the Angel Eyes Trilogy. Reading Books One and Two first would be ideal, but if you're determined to jump right into *Dark Halo*, there are a few things you should know about this story.

In *Angel Eyes* we were introduced to Brielle, a talented ballerina who'd been away at boarding school for the past two years. A couple of months into her senior year, her best friend, Ali, was killed, and Brielle returned to her hometown of Stratus, Oregon, to get away from the memories that haunt her.

While she was away at school, a new boy, Jake, and his guardian moved in next door. But Jake's guardian is no ordinary caregiver. Canaan is a Shield, an angel sent to Stratus to protect Brielle. In his possession are two supernatural items.

He has a chest cut from onyx. Occasionally the Throne Room of heaven delivers items to Canaan by placing them inside the chest. Just before Brielle returned to Stratus, a diamond engagement ring appeared there. Engraved on the band was the phrase *From hands that heal to eyes that see.*

Canaan also has a halo, a crown that was given to every angel who did not join the rebellion of the Prince of Darkness eons ago. When Jake was young, Canaan gave the halo to him. The halo comforted Jake, something he desperately needed as a child, but it also gave him the ability to heal. In an attempt to help ease Brielle's devastation, Jake passed the halo to her. Not only does the halo provide Brielle with the strength she needs to cope, it gives her the ability to see through the terrestrial veil and into the celestial realm—a realm usually seen only by angels and their kind.

In *Angel Eyes* Jake and Brielle used their gifts to dismantle a child trafficking operation and dispatch a fallen angel, Damien, who desired to corrupt their gifts.

Jake and Brielle thought they were free of Damien. But when the engagement ring disappeared from the chest only to be replaced by Damien's bloody dagger, Jake didn't have the heart to tell Brielle they may not be as safe as they think.

In *Broken Wings* Damien was commissioned by the Prince of Darkness to capture and bring Jake and Brielle to him. Damien wanted the halo as well and enlisted the help of a human named Olivia Holt to track it down. But heaven had other plans for Stratus and sent another group of angels, the Sabres—whose worship has the capacity to tear through the terrestrial veil—to the tiny town with just that purpose.

Unwilling to have the celestial realm revealed, the Prince of Darkness retaliated by sending a legion of his finest warriors, the Palatine. As *Broken Wings* closed, a heavenly war was ravaging the skies over Stratus. In the midst of the chaos, Damien snatched Jake from the safety of Canaan's wings. Brielle could do nothing but watch as they disappeared into the sky.

—SD

I will ascend to heaven and set my throne above
God's stars.
I will preside on the mountain of the gods far away in
the north.
I will climb to the highest heavens and be like the
Most High.

—The Prince of Darkness

1

Brielle

Jake's gone.

His absence races through my veins like a bomb destined to explode if it stops or slows. That's how I feel: that the truth of what happened here yesterday will kill me if I stop moving.

So I don't. I keep dancing. I keep praying. Moments of peace find me, sprinkled like cinnamon onto a poisoned apple.

For the thousandth time I yank my mind away from dark things and back to the Creator, who brought Jake into my life. Back to the beauty of the Celestial. The Celestial that is coloring this grove of trees red. I open my eyes and take it in. Our neglected apple orchard, full of brittle gray wood, snarled leaves, and cobwebs, is lit up around me. Reds of every shade grace the branches and the rotting fruit below. Dead trees are transformed. Light and life expand from their center, reminding me that reality as I know it is not all there is.

Another sprinkle of cinnamon . . .

Jake's been gone for eighteen hours now, and still the Sabres sing. Still they fight. Their presence has thinned the terrestrial veil here in the orchard, and it can't be long before their worship tears through. I just . . . I don't know what that means.

For me. For Stratus.

My chest heaves with exertion and my body is slick with sweat when a gigantic silver angel comes into view overhead. My celestial vision has been erratic for the last few days, but as I watch, the battle remains visible for a solid minute, if not more. It's long enough to pull me from my dance anyway, to force my gaze through the tangle of branches above.

A Sabre hovers there. I can't tell if it's Virtue; this angel's been fighting for hours, days maybe, so his skin is too bright and his wings too fast, moving like an orchestra of bowstrings. Wings that I know are made of hundreds and hundreds of blades. They blur, sending music—sharp and staccato—into the sky. Tendrils of royal blue fill the orchard—the incense of worship. They wrap around me, lifting my arms. I breathe in the Sabre's worship. It smells of the ocean, of briny wind and sand. The fragrance fills my chest, and I let my body mimic the ribbons of worship.

I try not to take my eyes off the scene above for longer than a second or two, because thirty paces beyond the Sabre a gaggle of demons dodges and leaps, avoiding the shards of white light ricocheting off the Sabre's wings. Like a well-aimed spear, lightning slices through three of them, and they disappear in a burst of ash.

The Sabre's music picks up and I dance faster, yellow incense joining the blue. Smelling of salty sunshine, it wraps around my legs, one after the other. The incense guides me; I stretch and spin, my face craned to the sky, watching. Always watching.

A single demon moves closer, slinking past his brothers. He jabs with his crooked sword, his mouth moving in a strange animal way. But I hear nothing of it. The song of the Sabre drowns his cry. I curl into myself, backing deeper into the grove. The demon is way too close.

The Sabre must think so too.

He spins, ducking and then arching in one swift movement. The demon tries to evade attack, but he's nowhere near fast enough. Wings of blade hack at the fallen monster, and I watch as with a sputter of fire and sulfur the thing is shredded. I turn slowly, embers falling around me as the remaining demons are dispatched with one graceful spin after another.

The Sabre's dancing too, I think.

It's strange. Wonderfully strange to be dancing with an angel.

The Sabre turns toward me, his wings slowing, his music softening. He's wrapped in tendrils of green now and he's still far too bright. I can't make out his features, but when I hear his voice in my head, I know it's not Virtue, but one of his kin. This voice is more bass than tenor.

"Your worship blesses me."

I've done little more than cower and dance. But before I can voice my thought he speeds away, a white smear across the red sky. I roll back onto my heels and stare after him. The green tendrils diffuse as he distances himself from me, the blue separating from yellow. He takes the blue with him, a vibrant tail splashing across the sky. The yellow tendrils are left with me in the orchard. They curl around this tree and that.

My eyes retrace the path of the yellow ribbon as it snakes through the trees. Around the limb of an elm—one of many that are trying to reclaim this orchard—and through the tall grasses that surround me, right into my chest.

I push to my feet and breathe deeply. Virtue said my song had power, that I could use worship against the Fallen. I just . . . It's strange seeing it. I shouldn't question what I see anymore. After everything I've witnessed, I shouldn't be surprised.

Still, who knew these skinny arms could fight?

2

Marco

Marco hasn't slept in days, but it's not for lack of trying. Memories sit like sand beneath his eyelids, scratching away at the tenderness there whenever he closes his eyes. He's never been a great sleeper—even as a kid—but once Ali died, sleep lost its appeal entirely.

The worst of the nightmares are the ones that swallow him whole, the ones that make him forget he's dreaming. And since the moment in Jake's house when he put that Tron-disc-looking thing on his head, the dreams have only gotten worse.

Brielle called it a halo, but there's nothing angelic about what it did to him. Since touching the thing, his dreams have grown to include memories from his childhood. Memories that had been long forgotten. Dreams of his and Ali's early days are often interrupted by images of Marco's elementary school burning, Brielle burning with it.

But the Brielle in his dream is too old, too sickly, too out of place. He tells himself it can't be real, says it again and again, but still the dream comes round like a dark horse on a carousel of pink ponies, blighting everything. And carved into all of it, like it's been branded to his retinas, are the words from Ali's gravestone.

There is special providence in the fall of a sparrow.

Providence.

The word frightens him.

Alone, he straddles a chair on Olivia's veranda, his knuckles white as they grip the porch railing. The view from the West Hills is one of the most sought after in Portland, but for Marco it's like looking at snapshots of a funeral. All the bad that happened in his life happened here. In this city. On those streets.

Liv's lawn is an overgrown mess of tangled grasses as it slopes away from the million-dollar home and disappears into the evergreens that separate her property from the world-famous Rose Gardens below. Beyond the gardens, downtown Portland sprawls like a leggy spider, its bridges stretching from one side of the Willamette River to the other, Mount Hood in the distance lording over it all.

Marco grew up not far from here. Not here in the West Hills; even when his dad's pockets were at their fullest, his family couldn't have afforded a house like this one. But the neighborhood he grew up in, the playgrounds he haunted, the elementary school that burned with Liv's mom inside—none of it's far. Just down the hillside, past the gardens. Maybe a five-minute drive.

For hours now he's been trying to figure out why Liv doesn't take her money and run. Her mother died here, in that school. Why not leave? Get away from this cursed town, away from the past that destroyed her family. She could get a job anywhere. Staying makes no sense to him.

It's been a day and night of restless nothing. Olivia's house is by far the grandest place he's ever slept in. Hardwood floors run throughout the residence, and intricate millwork decorates the archways and moldings. Marble accents add an extravagant touch Marco could never get used to, and the state-of-the-art wine cellar pushes the whole thing over the top. Everything is dark and fine and very, very Liv.

He recalls the first time he saw Olivia Holt. It was summer then also, and the city was warm. His dad was perpetually jobless, so his mom had taken to babysitting every stray kid in the neighborhood for extra cash. Marco had escaped the whining and the crying by climbing out the window and settling in on their fourth-floor fire escape. Ten years old, a stack of X-Men comic books on his lap, he stared at his own reflection in the window, trying to imagine what he'd look like if he shaved his head like Professor X. But he was too thin, too gangly, too pale. The squeal of brakes and the idling of an engine pulled his attention away from the dirty glass. A moving truck sat parked in front of the building across the street.

Low-income apartments lined this road, but the one across the street was the nicest: a brick building with little planter boxes full of roses outside the ground floor windows. His building was nothing but a converted hotel with chipping stucco and shaky fire escapes. Neither structure was glorious, not like the homes a few blocks over, but he was very aware that his was the worst of the bunch.

He closed the comic book and watched as a woman climbed from the cab of the truck. Tall, thin, and curvy all at the same time. She reached her arms up and lifted a girl from the cab.

Liv. She was the first beautiful thing he'd seen in a long

time. Creamy copper skin and thick brown hair, braided back. Mother knelt before daughter, right there in the street, and spoke something in her ear. Her words were too quiet for Marco to hear, but he shifted anyway, leaning closer. The movement sent a comic book slipping from the pile in his lap, through the iron bars of the fire escape and skittering to the ground.

Over her mother's shoulder, Liv's eyes found Marco's. Embarrassed, he fought the impulse to look away, but even then the actor gene was strong, and with an audience below he couldn't resist. He stood and waved.

"You dropped your book," Liv called, stepping around her mother.

Chivalry attacked him then. Perhaps the first bout of it he'd ever had.

"You take it," he said. "It's a good one. Wolverine saves the day."

With a light shove from her mother, Liv crossed the street.

"Who's Wolverine?" she asked. She was directly beneath him now, picking up the comic.

He knelt, ignored the bars that creased his knees, and pushed his face to the grate. "He's a mutant. He's got retracting claws and a healing factor that keeps him alive even if you shoot him a million times."

"That's gross."

"It's not gross. It's cool."

She flipped a few pages. "It doesn't look cool."

"What are you talking about? Now you *have* to read it."

"I don't *have* to do anything."

"Sure you do."

She tipped her face to him now. "Why?"

"Because I dare you to," he said.

She shook her head. "Mom says dares are never a reason."

Girls! "I double-dog dare you then."

"You're weird. You know that, right?"

"I triple-dog dare you," Marco said, the grate scratching at his lips. "And now you *really* have to."

"I already told you. I don't *have* to do anything."

"But that's how a triple-dog dare works. You can't back down. Not ever."

She closed the book and pressed it to her chest. "All right then," she said. "I'll read it. But it still sounds gross."

Even now, he can feel his face stretching like it did that day. She crossed to her side of the street and sat down on the curb. Her mother was busy sifting through the cab, dropping blankets and pillows and bags onto the sidewalk. Liv turned her eyes on the neighborhood then, examining it, twisting the comic book in her hands. Even from his perch on the fourth floor, Marco could see the disappointment on her face. He couldn't blame her. She looked like she was used to something better. She deserved something better.

Something fine.

Something just like this place, he thinks.

She had a bedroom made up for him when they arrived yesterday. He was tired. Frustrated at his last encounter with Jake and Brielle. Angry at them for reasons he had trouble naming. So he didn't argue when Liv insisted he rest. Shades of burgundy and brown, deep and rich, filled the room with warmth, but when the French doors were closed behind him and Marco climbed into the gigantic bed, the sheets felt like shackles, the lavish room a cell.

He could think of nothing but Henry Madison. A pedophilic old man who was directly involved in the child trafficking operation that got Ali killed. The last time Marco laid eyes on him, the monster was disappearing into thin air. It's something that continues to plague him. Just days ago he learned that Henry was Liv's grandfather. Her grandfather! After her mother died, he was made her legal guardian. The thought of what she suffered at his hands is enough to turn Marco's stomach.

But Liv promised to take him to Henry. That's why he'd followed her here. That, and the need for distance. Just a few short days with friends had proved too much for him. After the psych hospital, Stratus was filled with too many loving, caring people. Too many pats on the head and hugs from less tortured souls.

And Brielle.

Her scrutiny was all too knowing. "You're not going after Henry?" she'd asked, but she couldn't understand how badly he needs this.

According to the authorities, the investigation is still ongoing. Several traffickers have been arrested, including the madam and the child pornographer who were found at the warehouse. But Henry disappeared that night and has not been pursued by law enforcement. Marco is determined to make him pay for the part he played—not only in Ali's death, but in the pain inflicted on those children.

Marco needs this.

He needs revenge.

But it's not the only reason he followed Liv. Ever since he'd tried on the halo at Jake's house, the nightmares have been coming. He thought putting some distance between himself and the halo would bring a reprieve, but the opposite seems true. Since leaving Stratus, the images have grown. They arrive with more frequency and in more detail. And even more content.

It's not just Brielle disappearing into the fire anymore.

He's reliving memories of Ali. His precious Ali. Good memories. Their first date, spent wandering the very Rose Gardens that sit beneath him. In his dreams the memory is recreated in staggering detail, conjuring moments he'd forgotten. Like Ali hopscotching down the brick walkway honoring the Rose Queens crowned at the yearly Rose Festival. Tiger's blood snow cones from the snack shack, sugary juice staining their lips red. Ali standing on a bench in the Shakespeare Garden reciting sonnets in her mother's British accent. Laughing so hard at her effort that he almost impaled himself on the sundial there. The memories slice into a heart that's not yet healed.

Even thinking about the dream now turns his blood cold as it races through his body. His hands shake, and all he can think about as he stares at the city below is that he wants to murder one of its residents. If distance from the halo won't stop the dreams, perhaps avenging Ali's murder will.

Guilt flickers in his stomach, but he snuffs it by repeating aloud the only words that seem to calm him: "Henry deserves to die."

And if anyone deserves to serve him that death, it's Marco.

His hands slip against the banister as he turns that thought over once again. The truth is Liv deserves it more. He wipes his clammy hands on his jeans. It doesn't matter. None of it matters. Liv brought him this far. She'll make sure he gets an audience with Henry.

At least that's what he thought last night. Image after image attacked him as he lay in that sumptuous bed—Brielle consumed by flames, Ali laughing at his Sean Connery impression, ten-year-old Liv being hauled away from the burning school on a stretcher. Henry disappearing from one nightmare and reappearing in the next. Over and over they'd played on the insides of his eyelids, on the ceiling of the room, on the underside of the thick, stifling comforter. He'd flipped and turned, fighting the images as best he could, but he was helpless against the onslaught. He couldn't avoid them in the darkness. He needed light.

He'd crawled from the bed and onto the stone hearth of the fireplace in the corner. His bag was there, in the way, so he pulled it into his lap, holding it to his chest like a toddler with his favorite stuffed toy. He slammed his fist into a button on the wall, and the fireplace sparked to life. And then he curled sideways on the stone, his bag beneath his head, and stared into the fire.

He wished his seeing eyes would blister and scar, but all the brightness did was fan the memories into a frenzy. The emotion they evoked held him there, staring, unable to move as they played out before him.

Ali's blood on his hands, her scent in his nose. Accusations ringing loud that he'd killed her, that he'd pulled the trigger. And then memories of his time in prison rose from the flames. Memories of the night he escaped. Of his last appointment with the prison doctor and the unconscious guards at the checkpoint, of his armed escort passing out mid-step.

He saw something in the flames then. Something he'd forgotten, or maybe never known. But there in the distance, at the end of the hall, a flash of auburn hair appeared. He stopped, afraid to approach, afraid he'd be blamed for the unconscious guards. And then she was right in front of him. So close he couldn't breathe without inhaling the heat off her skin. Her silver eyes entranced him, and he heard her voice in his head.

"There's a car parked two blocks over. On Clay. Are you listening? It's yellow, fast."

She pressed a ring of keys into his fist, her tiny hand burning his, and then she disappeared, and Marco sprang into action. He found every checkpoint empty, every door between him and freedom open. Every prisoner, guard, and staffer asleep.

This memory looped and looped until another took its place: Ali bent over her journal, sketching images of sculptures at an art gallery, Brielle blushing at a nude sketch. It was the day he met the two of them, the day he fell in love with Ali.

With more willpower than he'd ever exerted, he forced himself upright, unwilling to have that memory tainted by whatever sick thing the halo had done to his brain. The image didn't leave, but instead of a sharp, stabbing wound, it became a bruise behind his eyes, in his chest. He stumbled from the hearth and flung open the door, leaving his bag there by the fire.

But all was silent. Adrenaline racing, he stormed through the massive house—all three levels of it—calling Liv's name, pushing himself into rooms he had no business invading, but all he found was a note on the kitchen counter.

Be back soon. —O

He decided then that he didn't need Liv. He could track down Henry without her. But her computer was password encrypted and her drawers were empty of address books or personal effects. She probably kept everything on that phone of hers. He considered calling a cab, but his lack of cash stifled any further attempt to head down into Portland alone.

So he sits here and stares at the city that killed Ali. He tries not to think. Tries to avoid the word that stirs in his chest, prodding him, scratching at his insides.

Providence.

It's more than a word, isn't it? It's a concept. It's the idea that something, no, *someone* has already determined his destiny. Had guided Ali to hers.

Does such an evil exist?

3

Brielle

My feet tangle in the long grasses and I stumble forward, my arms splaying to catch my fall. Arms catch me, but they're not mine. These are thick with muscle and sweltering in their embrace.

Canaan.

I've been dancing for hours now, and my legs ache. It's his grip alone that keeps me upright.

"Thank you," I say.

He stands before me in a pair of dark jeans and an army green button-up, but here in the orchard where the veil has all but thinned away, I see glimpses of his celestial form. Cords of light wrap his arms and legs, his broad chest bare. White wings emerge from his shoulder blades, swooping like an inverted scythe away from a head of silver hair. They've seen battle. I can tell by the ruffled feathers and the gaping holes where some have been torn away. I can't see his inner wings, the sinewy, almost reptilian ones, but I know they're there. I know because he's tucked me safely inside them before, held me upright. Like he's holding me now.

But all these things are simply details. Even his war-torn wings don't concern me as much as they usually would. Today I notice only that he's alone.

I feel the fear wrap me, slow me, silence the questions ravaging my gut. I didn't expect him to return without Jake, and I take a step back. But Canaan doesn't release my arms. His face is sadder than I've ever seen it.

"I'll find him, Brielle."

Some questions don't need to be asked, I guess. They hang on you, weigh you down like chunks of rock within the mud of fear.

"I'm asking you to trust me."

But trust might be too much to ask right now, because I've been here before. I know the Father's plan sometimes includes death. It includes hard things.

I don't want Jake to be just another hard thing I have to survive.

"I want to go with you," I say.

"No." He doesn't think about the response. He doesn't let me beg. He just shakes his head. Very curt. Very final. "You're brave. You don't have to prove it."

"That's not why I want to go. I want to be with him," I say, choking on the words that terrify me most, "wherever he is."

"Even if your presence will make his fight harder?"

The answer, honestly, is yes. I want to be with Jake no matter what. But as I stand here, Canaan's silver eyes threatening to swallow me like some bionic nightmare, I know how wrong that answer is. I know it won't earn me sway with Canaan either. More than that, I *want* the answer to be *no*. I want to want Jake's best more than mine.

But before I can lie to my Shield, he stops my lips with a warm finger.

"I know, Brielle. I can't say I understand what you're feeling entirely, but I know you want to be with him. He'd want the same thing. He said as much yesterday when we were attempting to breach Stratus."

"What did he say?" I'm desperate for any word of him, even if it has no bearing on the *now*, even if it's voiced only to make me feel better.

"He said being with you was all that mattered to him, even if it meant Damien taking you both."

My laugh is strange and wet, tears soaking it. The thought is sappy and romantic, but it isn't true. Jake doesn't think that way. "He's such a liar."

"Mostly to himself, I think, but yes, sometimes." Canaan's smile reaches his eyes now. It's a small thing, but something about it stirs hope. It's still there; it's just buried beneath the fear.

He takes my face in both his hands. Heat rushes up his wrists and through his palms, bathing my face in warmth. I can't help but think of Jake. How he'd hold my face, how he'd kiss my lips. How his touch became the most important thing in the world.

Now I keep my eyes wide open. If I close them, if I blink, I'll get lost in those memories, and I can't afford that.

"I am sorry to leave you here," Canaan says. "Truly. But I won't let Damien use you against Jake. Take confidence in that; I won't let anyone use Jake against you either. Not if it's within my power to stop."

I tilt my chin down and step back. I try to make the movement smooth, like an overzealous nod, but the truth is his grip's too familiar, too like Jake's, and my heart is confused with the clashing of fear and hope. He lets his hands fall to his sides. If he notices my discomfort, he says nothing.

"Besides, getting past the Palatine is not an easy thing. I did not make it through unscathed. I can't guarantee your safety."

It's a funny thing to say, and despite the tears pooling in the corners of my eyes, I bark a hollow laugh. "Can you ever guarantee my safety?"

His glorious face creases. "No, I can't. But this time there's an army of demons hovering overhead ready to haul you to the Prince should you fall into their hands."

The world speeds up, my feet unsteady. "Is that where Damien's taken him? To the Prince?"

"Not yet," Canaan says, taking my hands in his. Heat roars up my arms, spreads across my chest, and sinks to my belly, warming me, relaxing muscles I didn't even know I'd clenched. "Not yet, anyway. The Commander's sent Pearla on ahead."

"The little black angel?" I ask, remembering the tiny winged thing that distracted Damien yesterday. Her wings bought me just enough time to slip free of his grasp.

"Yes. She's a spy of the Cherubic order. She was there in the Prince's stronghold when Damien received his orders. Unless things have changed, we have until tomorrow."

Damien's words make sense now. Yesterday, just before he took Jake, he said something about the Palatine arriving early. Something about having two more days.

And now there's only one.

"What happens tomorrow, Canaan?"

"Damien will deliver Jake to Danakil."

I rack my brain for any former utterance of this word. So

many new terms to keep straight: Palatine, Cherub, and now Danakil.

"What's Danakil?"

"The Danakil Depression. It's a desert, a wasteland of salt flats and volcanic activity—the hottest place in the world."

So strange that Jake, the boy with flaming hands, is being taken to the hottest place on planet Earth. "Can he survive . . . Do people survive there?"

"Certainly. The nomadic Afar people inhabit it, mining the salt there by hand. They carry it across the desert on great caravans, camels marching nose to tail. But it's a cruel place. Some say it's the cruelest place on earth."

The idea of Jake being stolen from me, abducted from the air, makes me ill, but that he'll be taken to a cruel and violent place to face a cruel and violent Prince feels like more than I can handle.

Canaan rubs a hand down his face. He's tired. He fought his way through the Palatine following Damien, and now he's fought his way back to me. He needs time to mend. I'd tell him so, but first I need to understand.

"Why Danakil?"

He lowers himself onto a stump, shaking his head. "It's a place the Prince has always been drawn to. He's waged battles there before. I've turned it over in my mind trying to work it out, but I can't say exactly why it appeals to him so. With the exception of the nomadic peoples who have always inhabited the place, Danakil's one of the least populous places to stage an attack. It's home to the lowest point on the earth's surface, it's inhospitable in every way, and it's marked by violence. All things that could appeal to the Prince for various reasons."

"But it's hot—the Fallen hate the heat."

"Celestial heat, celestial light, Elle. The temperature of the Celestial is consistent whether you're in the depths of the ocean or the Danakil Depression. In the Terrestrial the Fallen can withstand much more than the average human. Danakil will not be nearly so hard on the Prince as it will be on Jake. Still, it's not the heat that should concern us."

Images of Damien assault my mind. I've no idea what the Prince looks like—what the great dragon appears to be in either his celestial or terrestrial form—but Canaan's right. He's far more terrifying than anything this earth can throw at Jake.

I shake the thought from my head, needing to act. Needing something to do.

"We have a day, you said. What can I do, Canaan? How can I help?"

"In a very specific way. I have a favor to ask."

"Of course," I say. "Anything."

"I need you to monitor the chest. Every few hours, if you can. The Throne Room knows I'm not the only one who checks it these days. They know Jake has been nearly as active with their instructions as I have. And they know you're aware of it as well. They may choose to communicate with you that way. We can't afford to leave the Throne Room out of this battle, you understand? We must respond quickly to whatever instructions they send."

It's not nearly the kind of favor I was hoping for. The kind that requires movement and skill. Something that allows me to do more than just sit. I almost argue, but I can tell by the urgency in his voice that it's important. This is what he needs.

"Okay."

"And, Elle, you need to keep fighting here. Jake's been taken—there is nothing you can do about that. He has his own battles to fight now. Yours is here."

Fighting sounds a lot better than sitting on my butt staring into a chest. But how?

"I don't—"

"The Sabres did not come here to protect the two of you. That's not their job. They were sent by the Creator to tear the veil. The Palatine will try to stop them, and since they can't . . ."

My brain spins. "They can't?"

Another smile that reaches Canaan's eyes. "No, and they know it. But they will do everything in their power to repair the damage once it's torn. They can't afford for humanity to see the Celestial. For humanity to see them disrobed."

"But Michael? Michael and his forces will fight."

"They will. They're here, fighting already. With the Sabres here in Stratus, they chose to attack from above. But we must hold the ground here. You must fight here."

"I'll do anything, Canaan. Anything. But how?"

"You keep praying. You keep worshiping. You keep fighting the fear your celestial eyes show you. Because it's growing, Elle. Fear is all over Stratus. Your friends and neighbors don't have your gift; they can't see the war brewing overhead, but many of them can feel it. Soon there won't be a soul in this town unaffected. And so few know how to fight. Most of them don't know they have the ability to contest the terror that descends from above. Your prayers, your worship—they help more than you know." He stands now, his face alive, his body radiating the importance of what he's about to say.

"There's something else, isn't there?"

"The people of Stratus have begun to dream," he says.

Everything about that sentence is confusing. "They're having nightmares like I am?"

"Your dreams were just the firstfruits, I believe. Others are dreaming as well. About the past. About the future."

"Like Marco," I say. "But I thought it was the halo that made him dream."

"It certainly sped the process up, didn't it?"

"You should have seen it, Canaan. It was crazy. As soon as he put the halo on his head . . ."

"Yes, I think Marco's a dreamer. Many in Stratus will dream for a time because the veil is thinning, because the invisible feels closer to them than it has ever felt. But I don't think time or distance will strip Marco of his dreams now that they've begun. Just as I am certain nothing could ever take your sight."

He smiles, but the thought isn't altogether comfortable.

"At least my nightmares will fade," I say.

"They *may* fade, Elle, yes. But I know this: for now, for as long as they're given, you must allow yourself to dream."

I know the dreams are important. The Throne Room wouldn't have sent them otherwise. I just hate the nightmares. Hate that they feel so real. Hate that I never seem to be myself in them, that I have to watch through someone else's eyes, feel someone else's pain.

But others are dreaming in Stratus. There's a measure of comfort in that. That we're all in this together. It seems I'm just one dreamer in a town haunted by a past we can't piece together.

The Celestial comes into view again, and I watch as Canaan's wings flutter and sag.

"You need to heal," I say.

"I know. I will. Brielle, how much of the Celestial are you seeing?"

"Bits and pieces still. Sometimes more."

"What about now?"

"I see your celestial form, but the trees, most everything else I see with my terrestrial eyes. There's a demon in the treetop here, but he's small." I cock my head. "And blind, I think."

"A Vulture," he says, glancing at the thing.

"What?"

"They're Vultures. Most have no official assignment, having been out of touch with the Prince and those in command for centuries. Simply put, they've been left too long in the celestial light."

I step closer, unafraid of the strange bat-like thing before me. He has no muscle to speak of, his legs curled and useless beneath him. His wings are nothing but a warped skeletal frame, the charred remains of feathers clinging like melted wax to black bone. He grips the uppermost branches of the tree with talons that are brittle and cracked, his nose sniffing at the air. Like Damien's, his body is coated with fear. It drips down the branches of the tree. With my celestial vision coming piecemeal, it looks like he's melting in the sunlight.

"This is what Damien feared he'd become," I say.

"Precisely."

"Why is he here?"

"Because Darkness has gathered. It's thick here, a canopy of demons caging the town in. One thing that's fairly certain is just how scared humanity is of the dark. Vultures feed on fear, spread it if they can. But mostly they're trying to survive. There will be others, Elle. They will carry terror to the citizens of Stratus, tainting the dreams they've been given, turning them dark. Fear will spread like the disease it is."

"It's hard to believe he was once an angel like you."

I watch the Vulture a moment more. His weak, pained form might conjure sympathy from another, but I see him for what he is. He's a parasite. A leech.

"Do you know what your name means, Gabrielle?"

I turn away from the sickly demon. "It comes from Gabriel, doesn't it? One of the archangels. He is a messenger," I say. "A Herald, right? He appeared to both Mary and Joseph. And to the shepherds the night Christ was born. Good tidings of great joy and all that."

Canaan's eyes sparkle down at me. I'll take that over a gold star any day.

"Gabriel is your namesake, yes, but it means 'God is my strength.'"

I imagine that phrase as a tattoo inked onto my shoulder blade, as the etching on a shiny Roman breastplate I'd wear into battle.

"Let God be your strength, Gabrielle. You cannot do this alone. We don't have time for you to try."

"I won't," I promise, feeling every bit of that responsibility.

He pulls me against his chest, and I'm surrounded by six and a half feet of angel. He smells of fire and sky. He smells of promise.

When he releases me, his terrestrial form is gone. He's transferred to the Celestial. His lips are still, but I hear his voice in my head.

"It never occurred to me that I'd come across another human I could trust as much as Jake. I thank the Creator that I have you. I'm honored to fight alongside you, Brielle."

His white eyes stir, as though a wind has brought a fresh supply of oxygen to the twin flames there. All four of his wings spread wide. The inner ones are sinewy, visible mostly in the way they smudge the world as they flutter. The outer wings are feathered and bright, the color of morning clouds. They're sliced through in places—all four of them—but with more effort than I've ever seen Canaan dedicate to flying, they lift him from the ground. He unsheathes the sword of light at his waist, and with a flourish cuts down the Vulture clinging to the tree above. Ash spits down on me, and I blink against it.

I've lost sight of Canaan already.

4

Jake

A chunk of sandy brown hair hangs in Jake's face. He tries to raise a hand to brush it away, but pain flares through his body. Something's wrong with his arm, but he refuses to move again; his breath is nothing but gasps and spit as he stares at the gray floor beneath him. And that's when he realizes he's been lashed to a chair. Green duct tape wraps his chest; his hands are tied behind him with some kind of cord, and his ankles are strapped individually to the metal legs. He shakes the hair from his face and blinks.

Pain has made his focus lazy, and it takes a minute for his surroundings to come into view. They do not inspire confidence. Aged and crumbling walls of faded brick contain him. A rectangular window, high and narrow, is cut into the block on his right, its glass thick and dark. The light that makes its way through is dirty and succeeds only in coloring the room in shades of shadow. A metal staircase is screwed into the wall opposite him, a flickering bulb swinging on a chain above it. The stairs seem to curve slightly as they make their way up, but he can't be sure;

everything about the room feels misshapen. Still, he's fairly certain he's being held in a basement.

Teetering racks line the wall to his left, but even the shelves are sparse—a canned good here and there, everything thick with dust. The place smells of mildew and rot, and the thing that roused him moments ago: it smells of doughnuts.

Cinnamon and sugar twists. He's almost certain.

His stomach aches with hunger, but for the first time in his life the sweet smell makes him sick. His body arches against the ropes that hold him to the metal chair and he dry-heaves. The chair tips to his right and he falls—the chair with him. Pain forces away thoughts of food as his body contorts.

He gasps and tries to shift off his side, but it's useless. His arm is broken or his shoulder dislocated. Maybe both. It's impossible to tell with the chair on its side and his body tied this way. The pain seems to be coming from everywhere, but he's got to get out of here.

He kicks against his binds, but the action does nothing except send slivers of sweat-inducing pain through his chest and arm. He kicks harder, panic growing. Memories build like black water behind a dam as he flails. They threaten to break through, to drown him.

He and Brielle in the red orchard, her hair spilling over her shoulders as he warns her about Damien, tells her how dangerous the demon's new eyes have made him. Dirt smearing from his fingers to her face as he wipes the tears away.

And then she was gone.

The panic he felt in that moment rivals what he feels now. Was it friend or foe that took her from him? He didn't know. Not until Canaan pulled Jake into the Celestial. Only then did he see that it was Helene who had taken Brielle. It was Helene who held her safely.

And then demons. Everywhere demons. Canaan fought hard, but there were too many. Razor-sharp daggers sliced a gaping hole through the wings that held Jake tight to the Shield's chest, and he fell.

That's the last thing Jake remembers.

Falling.

"I enlisted once. US Army."

Jake goes still. Fear wraps his arms and legs, holding him tighter than any rope ever could. He opens his eyes, and though his face is pressed against the floor now, he does his best to peer around the room. He sees no one. The basement seems just as it did before: quiet, vacant. But it's a lie. He knows the voice snaking into his head. Knows it. Hates it.

Damien's here.

"*Enlisted* may not be the correct word," the voice continues, "but you understand. I learned a lot during my time with the Special Forces. It's amazing what you can do with a little duct tape, nylon cord, and a couple zip ties. No, I don't imagine you'll be breaking free of that chair anytime soon." Damien's voice is confident, cocky even, and for a demon who doesn't talk much, he seems anxious to say what's on his mind. "Haunting the army gave me access to . . . well, to boys just like you. Warriors who think they fight for noble causes. Children broken by war. Soldiers who think they can fix this world."

Pain flares through Jake's body again. He smells Damien's breath—sulfur and decay—feels it on his brow. And then the demon materializes in front of him. His knee presses into Jake's shoulder, his human face scrubbed clean and shaven, his terrestrial body clothed in camouflage fatigues.

"Good soldiers." He spits the words now, running a finger over the Special Forces tab on his left sleeve. "Brave. Bent on helping others. On healing the broken. But like you, they lack the ability to heal themselves."

Damien grabs Jake by the neck, lifts the chair, and slams it down upright. Metal rings out against the concrete floor, and the once-sturdy chair wobbles. Jake cries out in pain, but he makes note of Damien's mistake, pressing his foot against the leg of the chair. He hears the grind of the screw. It's loose now.

"Why do you think that is? Like me, you can heal others. I've seen you do it. But here you are, bent and bleeding." The demon crouches before him. "My body heals itself. Why doesn't yours, Child of God?"

There's something in the question. Something of need. Something of ignorance. Jake blows air through his teeth in an effort to control the pain and rage bubbling in his stomach, a dangerous chemical reaction that will yield nothing but more of the same.

"Because . . ." Jake's first attempt to speak produces only scratches. He clears his throat and tries again. "Because we need one another."

Damien's black eyes widen. Like a dog who suddenly understands human language. *No, it's more than that*, Jake thinks. This dog doesn't just *understand*. He remembers.

"You've forgotten what it's like, haven't you?" His lips are dry, cracking with the effort. "You've been working on your own for so long, you've forgotten that you can't do this alone."

Damien barks a laugh and stands. He disappears and returns before Jake's had time to blink. The army uniform is gone now, replaced by black cargo pants and a gray T-shirt stretched tight across his broad chest. A gun is strapped to his waist. He looks unstoppable, unbreakable, but Jake knows better.

"*What* can't I do alone?" Damien asks.

Jake runs a dry tongue across his lips. "Win," he says. "You can't win."

The right side of Damien's mouth curls like a villainous mustache, but his black eyes have lost their shine.

"I'm not the one bound hand and foot," he says.

"Aren't you?"

Damien kicks the leg of Jake's chair, sending him spinning into the wall. He rams the brick sideways, the shoulder of his injured arm taking the brunt of it, his head colliding next. Concrete crumbles rain down, filling his eyes. He slams them shut, but the crumbles scratch and bite at his corneas and he's reduced to a blinking, coughing mess. He sees the basement like a bad home movie, flickering and wobbly. Damien towers above him, and between spastic eye twitches he sees the demon raise his elbow. Before Jake can flinch, the massive elbow is dropped.

Jake's world goes black.

5

Brielle

The sun is an overripe grapefruit high above when I step into the field between Jake's house and mine. Today's about as warm as it gets here, mideighties probably. With the Celestial bleeding through, it was warmer in the orchard. Out from beneath the red trees, Stratus feels almost big, the sky too vast, everything too blue.

I catch the occasional demon swimming through the ocean of air above. Their warped bodies are foreign and out of place in the terrestrial sky. If I look hard enough I fear the Terrestrial will peel away altogether and I'll see the entire demonic legion above. I don't want to see the Palatine. Not right now. I told Jake once that I had a problem with blind faith, but right now it doesn't sound half bad. Seeing is harder than believing.

I search the sky for Canaan, picking through it carefully, not looking too hard at any one spot, but I don't expect to find him. He's healing somewhere, I hope. I wonder how far he had to travel to find a safe place. Did he have to pass through the Palatine to find one?

I check my cell phone again out of habit, but there's no

missed call from Jake and nothing from Helene. I jam it into the pocket of my jean shorts. Clutched in my other fist is an envelope of pictures. They're old pictures, taken when I was young, when my mother was in the hospital being treated for cancer. They were taken over the course of several months, and they show Mom in various states of health. In some she's smiling and laughing, genuine joy spilling from the glossy print. In others the pain is evident, though she seems always to have a grip on her smile.

There are pictures of Mom and Dad. Pictures of the three of us. There are even pictures of Miss Macy and Pastor Noah, of the pastor's wife, Becky—all of them visiting Mom at the hospital.

At Good Samaritan Hospital in Portland.

Why she was being treated there instead of at Stratus General or at any of the hospitals between here and there is just one of the many questions I have for Dad.

The other questions revolve around the presence of Olivia Holt in my mother's hospital room. The same Olivia Holt who blew into Stratus like a breath of fresh air, latched onto my dad long enough to encourage his drinking habit, and then left with Marco and the halo.

I know she's working with Damien. It's a piece of intel Helene's been able to glean from the Commander and his Army of Light above.

I have to keep reminding myself that there's an Army of Light above.

That their commander, Michael, has surrounded the Palatine. I wish I could see the fight from their side, from heaven's side. I wish I could see what the angels of light look like in battle. It's miserable to be here, on the earthly side. With the exception of the Sabres, my intermittent celestial sight picks up mostly the demonic: the rear flank of the Palatine. The stragglers, the Vultures, the ones stupid enough to engage the Sabres on this side while an entire army readies their attack from above.

Even after hours of worship, the sight of these stragglers hovering so near reminds me just how much stands between Jake and me. Not just distance, but demons—actual demons—thousands of them. I've faced a demon before, several actually, but this? This is . . .

Impossible.

It's impossible.

I'll never see him again.

The thought carves out a place in my chest with a spade so sharp I barely feel the cut. And before I know it, the impossibility of it all is the only thing filling my mind.

Fear is shoveled in with the very spade that hacked me open, and I feel it now. I feel the fear chill my insides. My heart fights back, beating fast. I can see the fear now. It drips from my fingers like motor oil. I have to blink twelve, thirteen times before the sight is swallowed by the Terrestrial. I clench the pictures more tightly in my fist, forcing the tremors in my hands to slow.

It doesn't matter how far Jake is from me. Doesn't matter what fills the chasm that separates us. It only matters that he can't be separated from the love of the One who has the power to save him. And as painful as it is to admit it, that's not me.

I can't save him.

But I can fight.

The Sabres worship on this front, fighting in their own way. Canaan and Helene too are doing what they can. And even Jake. Somewhere Jake is fighting, I know that.

It's time for me to do my part.

Wiping the sweat from my brow, I make my way up the front steps of the house Canaan and Jake share. Affectionately: the old Miller place. My feet are bare and dirty. Ignoring the smears of red dirt they leave on the stairs, I push through the always unlocked door and into the living room.

It's not as hot in here as it usually is. It's no wonder, with all that once warmed it taken from Stratus . . . just another thought I have to fight to replace. I push toward the bedroom and through the memories of the last evening I spent here with Jake.

It started off so well, so peaceful. A bucket of ice cream and two spoons. And then the two of us sorting through old bulletins, reading news reports, researching the spiritual history of Stratus. It was late when Marco returned for his stuff, when he left with Jake's bag and the halo. I can't believe he did it on purpose, won't believe he took it at Olivia's bidding.

And then a photo appeared in the chest. Just the back of some guy's neck and the two words inked there. *Jessica Rose*, it said. Jake's mom. Stamped on the back of the photo were the words *Evil Deeds Tattoo Parlor* and an address. Jake took that picture and headed into Portland, hoping to find out more information about the parents who had abandoned him.

But not before we fought.

Because he lied.

That's not entirely accurate, I know. But it felt like a lie. He let me believe my engagement ring was still in the chest, let me think everything was okay, when months before the ring had disappeared only to be replaced by Damien's dagger.

Jake should have told me.

But I should have understood why he didn't.

I was awful.

I move quickly down the hall and into Canaan's room, where the fear that ate at me that night is too much to push through. I back out of the room and lean into the wall. The angry words I threw at Jake scream at me from the silence, and I'm not ready to face them. I turn away from Canaan's room and take six steps before turning into the room at the end of the hall.

Jake's room.

As always, it's a mess. The floor is covered with all the little details that make up Jake's day-to-day life. T-shirts and jeans cover most of the floor, but there are books, too, and CDs. I've been trying to convince him to upgrade to an mp3 player, but he doesn't see the need.

"What would I do with all my CDs then?"

What indeed.

With my toe I carve my way toward his dresser. By far it's the cleanest two square feet in the room. There's a picture there, on the corner. It was taken in early May, I think: Jake and me in our climbing gear getting ready to rappel off Crooked Leg Bridge. Jake propped the camera on the railing and set the timer. We must've posed a billion times to get the exact shot he wanted. Both of us leaning back in our harnesses, his lips on my cheek, my blue eyes staring at the camera. He's digitally enhanced it so that all the colors are ultra-real. Everything's too bright. But it's exactly how that moment felt. I can almost see the Celestial in the work he's done.

I run my index finger along the frame, and a tiny cloud of dust gathers beneath my nail. I turn away and promise myself that we'll do that again. Jake and I. We'll spend a day rappelling and taking stupid pictures of ourselves. Pretend we're great outdoorsmen.

But pretending makes me tired, and I fall onto Jake's bed, tummy first, careful to keep my dirty feet off the sheets. He has my permission to be a slob, but I can't quite give myself the same courtesy.

I press my face to his pillow and breathe it in. Coffee. Sweet and robust. I slide both hands beneath the soft pillow and burrow deeper. My fingers connect with something hard, something square, but before I can flip my hand to grab it, I've knocked it to the floor.

I scrabble off the bed, hoping I'll be able to identify the culprit amidst everything else on his floor. Careful not to put my knee in a cereal bowl he's stored beneath an old camera bag, I press my face to the carpet and peer beneath the box spring.

Ironically, the floor under Jake's bed is nearly as clean as the dresser. And there, wedged between the frame and the wall, is a thin, square box. I have to stretch to reach it, but I succeed.

The box is wrapped in brown paper with a piece of black twine holding a tag of sorts. I flip the tag over and read: *Brielle.*

Jake's taken pains to write neatly, something he's not known for. I run a finger over my name and wonder if this is the surprise he never got around to giving me. With Mom's empty grave being unearthed and the Sabres showing up in Stratus, with Dad stumbling into an old addiction and my world imploding, I'd forgotten. The box is too thin to be the missing jewelry box from the chest, but I'm intrigued nonetheless.

I twist my finger in the twine and pull. It snaps in half, and I dig at the tape with my fingernails. Eventually it comes free, and I unfold the gift within.

Another photograph.

At first glance I think it's of Jake and me, but it's not.

And this picture wasn't taken with a camera's timer; this one was taken by a bicyclist that Ali and I nearly plowed over on the waterfront. After we apologized profusely, we begged the poor guy to take our picture.

In it, we're dripping wet, Ali's on my back, her cheek pressed to mine, a tangle of bridges crossing the Willamette River in the background. With her hair slicked back and her lips curled into a crooked grin, it's no wonder I first took her for Jake. Tanned skin and hypnotic eyes, the two of them have a charisma that transcends the lens. It's that camera-ready stage presence so many have to hone.

I run my hand over her face and sort of laugh-cry at the memory. We'd spent the day walking around Portland, snapping shots, wasting film. And when the day was done, we celebrated with a little romp through the Waterfront Fountain. We regretted it thirty minutes later when the sun set and the night turned cold. But it was a fun half hour, and the picture is gorgeous.

"Thank you, random bicycle man," I whisper.

The picture is from a roll of film I asked Jake to destroy. The very first day I met him, actually. I pry the brown paper away from the edges of the frame, and an envelope jostles loose.

I lift it from my leg and open it. Inside is an index card and a rumpled film strip.

The very same film strip I thought I'd never see again.

I leave it in the envelope and withdraw the card. Jake's handwriting's not nearly as neat here, and it takes me a couple tries to get each sentence decoded. Once I have it, I read again just to relish the sound his silent voice makes in my head.

I was going to destroy this film strip, Elle, I really was. But curiosity got the better of me, and I had to have a look first. Once I saw the film, I couldn't do it. Your life is full of great shots. I hope you know that. Forgive me for breaking my promise.

I slide the index card back in the envelope and withdraw the film. I lift it to the light and run my finger down the silky strip. It bumps here and there over the crinkles, but the strip's not too bad. Most of the pictures can be salvaged, I'm sure.

I whisper a quiet thank-you to Jake. I'd give anything to throw my arms around his neck and thank him in person, but that'll have to wait. I tuck the strip of film back into the envelope and look once again into Ali's face.

"I don't know what I'm doing, Al. You should have been the one with this gift, with my eyes. You would have known what to do with them. You would have been brave. But I'm not brave. Canaan thinks I am, but I'm not. I'm scared all the time. Of what I'll see. Of what I won't see. Of not understanding what any of it means. And I'm scared of losing everyone before I figure it out."

I have to put the picture down on my knees because I'm crying again. I dry my face with the corner of my shirt, then rewrap the picture in the brown paper. The twine is split now, so I just slide the rectangular package under Jake's pillow without it. I press my face to the mattress and pray that he'll make it back here. To his messy room and the surprise he's kept under his pillow. I pray he'll make it back to me.

When I'm done I stand, grabbing what I can of the courage Ali's image left lingering in the air, and I make my way out of Jake's room, back down the hall toward Canaan's. As pristine as Jake's is disastrous, white-and-black decor contrast everywhere.

With stalling steps and a tremulous prayer shaking my lips, I make my way to the chest at the foot of his bed.

If it weren't for the desperate need I have to find Jake, I don't know that I'd open this chest again. I'm not sure I've forgiven the Throne Room for taking my ring, the ring Jake planned to propose with. But it doesn't matter now. None of that matters. Finding Jake is the only thing that's important, and the Thrones can help with that.

Like Canaan, they're loyal to the Creator. They've been assigned to His Throne Room where they dispense instructions to Shields positioned throughout the earth. Their work brought Jake and Canaan to Stratus. So I guess I do owe them something for that.

I crouch before the chest and shove at the lid, my whispered prayer louder now. My ears full of it.

"Tell me what to do," I pray. "Tell me how to fight."

But my prayer remains unanswered. The chest is just as it was before. Damien's blood-crusted dagger there at the bottom—nothing more.

6

Marco

Liv starts the car in silence. A fancy thing. Red, like her lips, like the heels she's wearing. Marco tries not to notice these things about her, but everything about this woman reminds him of what life was like before all the pain. Before Ali. Sometimes that's a sweet escape.

She walked in the door five minutes ago, and true to the chairman-of-the-board persona she's adopted, demanded his presence in her car. Her tone irritated him, but after waiting for hours, he elbowed past his pride and complied.

They speed through the West Hills, her car hugging the turns, earning her a shout from a stroller-wielding soccer mom. When they pass the entrance to the Rose Gardens, and the reservoir below it, Marco's stomach tightens. It's not excitement. Killing a man is nothing to be excited about, but there's so much adrenaline blasting through his veins, he's light-headed at the thought.

Everything about this neighborhood is familiar, and memories stretch their spindly arms out to him as Liv navigates each turn. Marco turns his head away from her and closes his eyes, hoping for some small reprieve, but the fire burns brightest beneath closed lids, and he has a hard time pulling away from the sweet memories that attack him. A few minutes later the car jerks and instinct pulls Marco's eyes open.

Liv's going the wrong way. She cranks the wheel hard, gunning it up the ramp and merging onto the highway.

"Whoa, whoa!" Marco cries, one hand bracing against the door, the other against the dash. "Why are we getting on the highway? Henry lives here. In Portland. That's what you said."

"That's what I said."

"So why are we leaving the city?"

She drags blood-red fingernails through her hair but doesn't answer.

Marco slams his palms on the dash. "Liv!"

"Change of plans."

"What? Why?"

"You could use some sun," she says. "You're getting pasty."

His hands twist in the seat belt. "You promised me Henry."

Her brows lift. "You get Beacon City instead."

"Beacon City? Are you kidding me?"

She grabs her phone from the console and scrolls through it with one hand. With the other she steers the car away from the embankment.

"You like that girl, Brielle?" Her voice is calm, her posture relaxed.

"What?"

"Forget it. I'm not going to talk to you when you're all tetchy like this. I'm heading to Beacon City and I'd like you with me. But if you're going to be awful company, I've got the radio."

She drops her phone in the console and flicks it on—talk

radio, some kind of political soapbox channel. Marco grits his teeth and slams his back into the seat. Clenching his bag tight to his chest, he turns his face away and watches the trees fly by. Patches of shadow and light roll over the car. Shadow. Light. Shadow. Light. It's disorienting to be pelted by one after the other.

Twenty minutes pass before he's calm enough to look at her again. Tired of hypocritical rantings, he reaches forward and turns down the radio.

"How can you listen to that guy?"

"I was just trying to outlast you."

In the console between them, her phone beeps. *Keith Matthews* flashes on the screen, but she slides her finger across it, ignoring the call.

"What's with you two?" Marco asks.

"Keith? Nothing. He's interesting, I guess."

"You're such a liar."

"What? You don't like him?"

"I don't dislike him, but he's not interesting. Not to someone like you."

"You haven't seen me since we were kids, and you somehow know what I find interesting. How's that?"

"I just do," he says.

"You're full of it."

"I do. Liv, I know you."

"You don't know me."

There's a bitter edge to her voice, and it silences him.

"What about you?" she says, shaking the hostility from her face. "His daughter, Brielle. You think she's interesting?"

"She was Ali's best friend," Marco says, "and between her

and Jake I never went more than two days without some sort of call or doughnut-laden care package while I was holed up getting poked and prodded like some kind of science experiment. She's beyond interesting. She's family."

"But she can be a bit much, right? Her intensity level's off the charts."

Marco smiles. "Yeah, she's a lot like this other girl I know."

"What, me?" she says, feigning surprise. "I'm intense?"

"You are intensity defined."

"Yes, well," she says, fumbling for something in the console. "I've got grown-up responsibilities. Some of us are paid to be intense." Her shoulder slides out of her silky blouse as she jams a cigarette between her teeth. It trembles.

"You want a light?" he asks, punching the cigarette lighter.

"Nah. I don't smoke. I just, you know . . ." She pulls the cigarette from her mouth and puts it back in.

He narrows his eyes. "No, I don't think I do."

"Oh, come on," she says, her laugh hollow. "You're an actor. You pretend all the time. It's cathartic being someone else for a while, isn't it?"

"So the cig helps you pretend."

"Sure. Like a prop."

"Like a prop?"

She rolls the window down and lets the wind suck on her hair while she chews the end of the unlit cigarette.

Marco watches her for a while. Finally curiosity gets the better of him, and he calls loudly over the wind, "Why are we going to Beacon City?"

She glances at him then, pulled from whatever thought had her miles away. "You ever been there?"

"When I was a kid. My mom took me. Ice-cream cones and kites on the beach. Water too frigid to swim in."

"That's right," she says, nostalgia written all over her face. "You remember the Bellwether?"

"Sure," Marco says. The Bellwether Lighthouse. It was decommissioned years ago. "We used to climb the rocks on the cliff there. Why?"

"'Cause I bought it."

The highway grows dark as the road narrows, trees growing up on every side. Through the shifting light he watches her, confused.

"You bought a lighthouse?"

"Well," she says, lifting a piece of tobacco off her tongue, "the foundation bought it."

"Does the foundation make a habit of acquiring assets that technology has made outdated?"

"Only since I've taken over. Henry would never have allowed such a thing."

Henry's name sits between them. It festers like an open wound for a solid minute before Marco regains enough of his composure to speak in measured tones.

"I hate him, Liv. When you stormed into the house today and said 'Get in the car,' I thought that's where we were heading."

It's another painful minute before she answers him. "You're not the only one who hates Henry, and you're not the only one who wants him dead. But I'm not taking you to him."

Marco explodes, measured tones forgotten. "Then why am I here?"

Unfazed by his frustration, Liv flicks the cigarette out the window, and with the press of a button the wind is closed outside. "Let me tell you about the lighthouse, okay?"

He's angry and confused, doing his best to not think about all the crazy that's found him since the psych hospital gave him a clean bill of health. But it's the gleam in her eye, the excitement there—about a lighthouse, of all things—that does it. Girls have always been his Achilles' heel. Beautiful, passionate girls. He deflates, settling against the seat once again.

"Go ahead. Tell me about your bouncing baby lighthouse."

She smiles. The first real one he's seen since they stumbled into one another at the lake last week.

"Well, about a decade ago this old couple cashed in their retirement and bought the Bellwether. They converted the lightkeeper's house into a pastry shop. Adorable little place. A rock garden out back, sea spray on the air, and the best chocolate tarts you've ever had, I swear."

She removes a hair tie from the emergency brake, and with both hands pulls her hair into a ponytail. The car veers slightly left.

"Geez," Marco says, moving to help with the steering wheel. She swats his hand away and steers with her knees as she continues to talk.

"It wasn't long before the unthinkable happened."

"The economy tanked?" Marco guesses.

"Yes, and this poor old couple went belly-up. Their life savings, retirement fund, children's inheritance, everything."

"Sucks," Marco says. It does suck, but it's a story heard 'round the world these days.

"So the Bellwether sat on the market for months. I watched it, watched the price drop. Finally, when it dropped far enough, I jumped in and snatched it up. I'd like to use it one of these days."

"Use it for what?"

"Here's something I bet you didn't know about Beacon City. It houses one of the largest group-home programs in the state. Thought it'd be a great work project for them . . . if we could get it up and running. Teach the kids to cook, teach them to run a business." She shrugs. "I paid next to nothing for the place. If it fails, it fails. But if I can turn it into something, it'll be great press for Ingenui and a great pick-me-up for a seaside town in desperate need of some help."

He's still annoyed but kind of impressed. "I didn't know you were such a bleeding heart, Liv. Thought you were all business."

"My heart bleeds a bit."

But Marco can tell this is more than just a side project to her. He knows what it is to dream, to put yourself out there and cross your fingers that it all pans out.

And he knows what it's like when the foundation your dream is built on crumbles.

"It's a kind thing to do, Liv. A great idea. Really."

"Yeah, well. Don't go all sappy on me. For now that's all it is. An idea. The board doesn't even know I bought it."

"Don't you need permission?"

Another shrug. "I do what I want, and the board usually backs me. It's when projects go astray that they leave me high and dry."

"Happen often?"

"No," she says, a wicked little smile curling the right corner of her mouth. "Not often."

"So that's where we're heading? Bellwether? Why?"

She stabs at the radio, snapping the nail on her index finger. She curses and jams the injured finger into her mouth.

"Liv, why are we going to Bellwether?"

"I'm letting the old couple rent the keeper's house back from me for now," she says, her voice muffled over the finger. "Mostly because I'm in love with their salted caramel truffles. You're going to die when you taste them. Gosh, that hurts," she says, withdrawing the finger and prodding it with her thumb.

"Liv . . ." He takes her hand in both of his. "Why Bellwether?"

"Your hands are clammy," she says.

"Liv, please."

"I have a business meeting, okay?" She tugs her hand away and cranks the radio up, stabbing at it until she finds an obnoxious hip-hop station.

Marco shouts over the music, "And you need me there because . . . ?"

"I don't," she calls. "But road trips are more fun with a friend. You are my friend, right?"

"Liv . . ."

"Let it go for now, Marco, okay? I'm driving. I want you with me. Can't that be enough?"

She's used to being in charge. He can tell that by the set of her jaw, by the tiny lift in her brows. She'll do whatever it takes to get her way too. It's the seductive pout of her lips that tells him that.

"You promised me Henry," he says, turning the radio down.

"Henry's dying, Marco. Take me instead."

A thrill slides up his spine. The curve of her cheek, the bright caramel of her eyes, a bare shoulder that has to be softer than the silky shirt she's wearing. It would be easy to take her instead. Instead of bitter memories. Instead of the guilt that visits him nightly. Instead of seconds and minutes and hours of pain and sadness. Instead of the ache he feels every time he opens Ali's journal. It would be easy, so very easy to let her drive for a while.

"I'll go with you to the lighthouse, Liv. But that's it, okay? I made a promise."

She laughs, a tiny strain of cruelty in it. "You made a promise? To who?"

Marco slides his bag beneath his head and closes his eyes.

"To Ali."

7

Brielle

When I walk into the kitchen, Miss Macy's still here. Her hip is pressed against the granite island, a dish towel thrown over her shoulder. Good. I was counting on her sticking around. What is a little shocking is the presence of Pastor Noah. Dad's not a fan of the guy, and this makes twice in the past week the pastor has braved my kitchen. His wife, Becky, is here too. Tall and lean, her brunette hair curling under at the shoulders.

Dad squints at me from a barstool. His head is wrapped with a clean bandage. One hand holds a steaming mug of coffee, and with the other he pops a pill.

"Close the door, baby," he says. "That sunlight's a killer."

I close the door and let the dim kitchen light settle around me. I'm sure Dad's headache is a result of several things: the alcohol he managed to down yesterday before I trashed what was left in the fridge, the wound he sustained when Damien flung him into the television, the talon he took to the shoulder, and the Sabres' worship that, for reasons passing understanding, Dad can hear. He's allowed a little grumpiness, I guess. I glance again at the coffee cup. At least he's sober.

"We'd like to talk to you, Brielle," Pastor Noah says.

I drop the pictures on the island next to Dad's elbow. The envelope's a little worse for wear now and it opens, the snapshots spilling across the granite.

"Good. 'Cause I'd like to talk to you too."

"What are these?" Becky asks.

"Pictures of you all," I say. "And of Mom."

The kitchen turns into a chorus of oohs and ahhs as they pass around snapshots that are a decade and a half old. After dancing for hours in the heat and light of the Celestial, I'm exhausted, but impatience battles for dominance over my drooping eyes and throbbing legs. I'm short on time and need answers.

And I've got to keep moving.

I start to interrupt, but they've got their system down now, passing the pictures in a circle like they're steaming sides at Thanksgiving dinner. With the big toe on my right foot I scratch at the mud on my left; I drum the island with my fingers and sniff like I'm coming down with a dreadful cold, but they're immersed. I decide to give them a minute while I search for caffeine. The fridge is nearly empty after my little confrontation with Dad's beer yesterday, but there in the back behind a splotch of ketchup is a lone Dr Pepper. I crack it open and lean against the counter.

"Brielle, baby, are you okay?" Dad asks.

I didn't realize I'd closed my eyes. I open them, and though I view the room through glossy, wet teardrops, I've made my decision.

"I'm such a crybaby," I say, yanking the collar of my shirt up and wiping my eyes. "I'm not going to cry anymore. I'm not. I'm just . . . not."

"You can cry," Becky says. "Tears are healthy, they're real. They're—"

"Constant," I say.

She smiles. "Sit, okay? We just want to talk to you."

Miss Macy leans across the counter. "And I'm sorry about the timing, sweetness. I know you and your dad have had some"—she glances at Dad—"happenings here, but I've got to haul some of our girls off to dance camp, and I wanted to be here for this little chat."

"It's okay," I say. "I'm glad you're here."

"Good, then," Miss Macy says, patting my hands. "Go ahead, Pastor."

Pastor Noah flushes red, but clears his throat. One look at him and I understand he really does have something he needs to say. I guess that makes two of us, but curiosity gets the better of me and I let him go first.

"Right. Brielle, I've been wanting to talk to you for a while now. Since Christmas, actually. If your dad's okay with it, I'd like to tell you some things you may not know about your mom."

"About Mom?"

Dad sniffs, his mustache bristling. "Tread lightly, Preacher."

"Okay then," Pastor Noah continues. "Back when Hannah was a member of our congregation, we had a lot of interesting happenings going on ourselves."

"Interesting happenings?"

"Well, healings and such. It wasn't just business as usual, if you know what I mean."

I don't say anything, but I do know what he's talking about. At least I think I do. Jake found some old church bulletins online the other night. The year Mom disappeared was a year of extraordinary and miraculous things here in Central Oregon.

"It all started with your mom, Brielle. She was sick. You

know that, of course, but you may not know just how hard the church prayed for her. We prayed and prayed and prayed, and then one day she was better. The treatments started working, and the cancer seemed to be leaving her body. It spurred us on, in a way. We don't see many miracles in our day and age, and we were just certain our prayers had helped in some small way."

Dad buries his face in his mammoth coffee cup.

Pastor Noah plows on. "So we got brave. The people did. They started asking for prayer for all sorts of things. Not for earthly gain, mind you, but for things they may have been too proud to ask for before your mom. We prayed for everything. We prayed all the time, it seemed. And the craziest thing, Brielle . . . our prayers were being answered."

I've seen Jake heal. I've seen Canaan and Helene do it. I've read about it in Scripture, but I haven't heard much about it happening at the church here in town. In fact, I haven't seen a single person healed there in the seven months I've been going.

"And then your mom got sick again," Noah says. His voice catches and Becky moves to his side, picking up where he left off.

"We kept praying," Becky says. "We prayed day and night, but it just didn't seem to do any good."

"I'm sure it did," I say.

"No, Elle," Dad says. "It didn't."

The fridge buzzes and the clock on the wall ticks away the time, but other than that the room is quiet. No one dares to refute Dad's claim.

"When your mom . . . disappeared," Miss Macy says, blushing at the lie she kept hidden, "the praying all but stopped."

I blink at the words. Two, three, four blinks. "I don't understand. You stopped praying for my mom or . . ."

"We stopped praying for the sick," Miss Macy says, her lips set in a thin line. "We stopped believing for miracles."

"I'm sure individuals continued to pray, Elle. Certain of it," Noah says. "But Hannah disappearing wasn't common knowledge; *I* didn't even know until you mentioned it the other day. We all thought your mother died, and that almost killed our little congregation. At the very least, something broke that day. Something changed."

I turn the words over in my mind, swishing them around, trying to make sense of them. I think of Virtue's presence on my mom's last day in Stratus. I think of him in that flame-ravaged school. I think of him here, in Stratus, with eleven others just like him.

"Miss Macy," I ask, "when did you stop going to the church here in town? You drive into Bend, don't you?"

"I do," she says. "It was just too much after Hannah died. And then the praying stopped, and I all but shriveled up here. I'm a flower, love. I need to be watered."

I glance under my lashes at Noah; her words are sure to sting. But Miss Macy—ever vigilant Miss Macy—catches me peeking and pats Noah's hand.

"Noah here was just a young buck back then. He wasn't our fearless leader, Elle."

"I wasn't," Noah says, "but I'm not sure I'd have done much better. The leaders, they did what they could, but we were all lost after your mom died."

My mom's been dead for as long as I can remember, but I hate that Noah assumes it's true. Especially since the only thing we're actually certain of now is that she was really sick when she disappeared.

"It shook us," he continues. "Down to our foundation it shook us. A lot of things fell away when we couldn't explain the loss. But after years of mulling it over, I think we just stopped believing."

"In God?" It's Dad, the incredulity in his voice nearly comedic.

Pastor Noah sighs. "Well, we believed He was there, certainly. But that He knew best? I think we stopped believing that altogether."

Dad mumbles something that sounds an awful lot like, "Could've told you that," but I don't reprimand him. I'm tired and don't have it in me.

"Why tell me now?" I ask.

"I tried to tell you the other day. The day your mom's grave was desecrated," Pastor Noah says. Well, that explains his awkward presence here that day. "Miss Macy thought it was time."

I glance at my ballet teacher, my mentor. She sips her coffee with something of a satisfied grin on her face. "I'm glad the truth is out there, Elle. You needed to know."

"But I'm also here because I owe you an apology," Pastor Noah says, looking around. "*We* owe you an apology."

"I don't think—"

"No, Elle. We do," he says. "We owed your generation more than we gave. We should have showed you what faith looks like when dark and inexplicable things happen. All we had to offer was disillusionment and grief."

His words sit with us. So intimate. So real.

"It's understandable," I say, wondering just how different Stratus would be if they hadn't stopped believing. If they hadn't stopped praying.

"Perhaps," he agrees, leaning forward on his elbows. "But it's not acceptable."

The room is quiet now. The ice maker dumps another round of cubes into the bucket with a mechanical *clink*. Becky reaches past her husband to pick up another photo off the counter.

"Where'd you get these, Elle?" she asks.

"Dad," I say. "Well, Jake, actually. Dad dropped the film off at Photo Depot but never picked up the pictures. Jake asked me to pass them along."

"Where is Jake?" Pastor Noah asks, looking up from the photo in his hand.

I glance at Miss Macy. She knows something happened yesterday. Something violent. One look at the destroyed living room and the blood leaking from Dad's head and her inner detective kicked in. She bandaged Dad up, peppering us with a zillion questions. Dad mumbled incoherencies that I'm sure she chalked up to a hangover, but I said nothing, escaping to the orchard as soon as I could. I'm not sure what Dad has told any of them, but I can't imagine Miss Macy let him off the hook after I left.

I let my eyes settle on him.

"He'll be back soon," Dad says, pulling me next to him. "Right, baby? He'll be back."

My heart swells at—Is it faith Dad's showing? I think it is, and there aren't really words to describe just how big a deal it is that he thinks Jake will just turn up. Especially since Mom never came back. Mom, who was also taken by invisible forces. I pry my mind away from that train of thought. It's not helpful, not in the least.

I'm tempted just to let his answer be, to lie to my friends and neighbors, to convince myself I'm protecting the Celestial. But everyone in this room knows full well there's an invisible world. Dad may not like it, but that wound on his head and the Sabres' song he's trying to hide from even now isn't letting doubt take hold.

Helene and Canaan. Jake. They're all gone, and I can't do this alone.

I need these people.

"Jake was taken," I say.

"Taken?" Pastor Noah asks. "What does that mean, *taken*?"

Before I answer I tug the pictures from their loose grips and close them away. Then I climb up on the barstool by Dad and take his hand. I can do this. I can.

"Last December, when Kaylee was kidnapped," I say, looking around the room, making sure my audience is following along, "the man who orchestrated the child trafficking ring wasn't just a man. His name was, er, is Damien . . ."

"Read that in the paper," the pastor says, tapping a rogue picture against his chin, "but last I heard they couldn't locate a last name or any information on him."

"That's because he's a demon."

Nothing. No gasp. No tears. No panicked expressions. Just eight saucer-like eyes staring back at me.

I try again. "Damien's a fallen angel. They aren't going to find a last name. They aren't going to find him at all. And really, it's better that way."

"Elle, sweetie, you can't . . ." It's Becky. Her beautiful face is screwed up tight with the dose of common sense she's about to dole out.

"She's telling the truth," Dad says, taking my hand in his. "Damien was here. Yesterday."

"Keith," Miss Macy says, "you can't believe—"

"He did *this*," Dad continues steadily, gesturing to the bandage on his head and then yanking his T-shirt aside to expose the wound on his shoulder. "And this."

I haven't seen Dad's shoulder since he interrupted Jake's attempt to heal it. It's no longer bleeding, but there's a silver marking where Damien's talon punctured his skin. Icy like the scars the demon Javan left on Olivia's arm.

I'm angry again. Angry that the Fallen have hurt so many in their tirade of rebellion. Angry that my loved ones have suffered. Angry at Darkness.

"I'm asking you to believe something without seeing it," I say. "I know that's hard, but I wouldn't ask this of just anybody. You're people of faith. If anyone can believe that what I'm saying is true, it's got to be you guys."

Pastor Noah takes his wife's hand in one of his and Miss Macy's hand in the other.

"Go ahead, Brielle," he says. "We believe you."

I glance briefly at the others. Becky looks like she's been splattered with pie, Miss Macy's brow is tied in a million knots, but Pastor Noah? Pastor Noah looks like he's ready to fight a dragon.

Good.

We may need to do just that.

I tell them everything. Well, not everything. I tell them about Canaan and the halo, but I don't tell them I took a knife in the stomach last December, because that means I'd have to tell them about Jake's gift. And as much as I need their support, that's really Jake's to tell. I hedge a bit when it comes to my gift as well. I tell them Canaan's wings and the halo give me celestial sight, but I don't mention that I've started seeing the invisible on my own. I just really, really don't want to talk about that right now.

But I do tell them about Damien's pursuit and his defeat at the warehouse. I even tell them about Virtue and Mom's grave. This part is harder for me to explain because it means telling them about my dreams. It also means confirming Dad's worst fears: that the singing angels are responsible for Mom's disappearance. I try to soften the blow by telling them how Mom saved Olivia. I tell them about her too, about her involvement. Dad weeps through all of it. The others shed tears as well. I stutter a bit when the fear starts to flow. When it trickles from the pastor's nose and slips down Miss Macy's arm. They're scared, but I think that means they believe me.

I've seen too much, I know too much for my story to be a lie.

I need to get back to the old Miller place, but my audience has a lot of questions, and it's another hour before they settle into a thoughtful silence. Dad leans his head against mine, a forehead high-five. It's something we haven't done in years. I think maybe I can do this. If my dad believes in me, maybe I really can be strong.

Becky steps behind me, her hands kneading my shoulders gently. "I'm so sorry about Jake," she says. "And I'm sorry we didn't believe you. What can we do to help?"

I swivel the barstool around and find on her face the same desperation I felt in Canaan's room just a little over an hour ago.

"You can start praying again. You can start believing that miracles happen. Because we're really going to need a few."

8

Jake

The pain is worse than before, a trickle of blood leaking from Jake's mouth. He's been unconscious for who knows how long before he wakes. His eyes and nose are crusted with a disgusting mixture of concrete, snot, and tears. But with his arms bound, there's precious little he can do about it. He leans forward and spits the grainy debris from his mouth.

Damien's gone, but he can't be far. If he's left Jake here, he's got to be biding his time; he must be waiting for something.

"I thought"—the room spins—"thought you were taking me to Danakil?"

His cry bounces off the walls, and from its echo Damien's voice crawls. It slinks back into Jake's mind, cold and numbing.

"What do you know of Danakil?" The demon's words coat Jake's mind, icing over his vision. The room crystallizes before him. "What do you know of that place, boy?"

The cold slows Jake's reflexes. Slows his mind. Exhausted, he leans into the wall.

"Nothing," he admits. "I know nothing."

A low chuckle vibrates in his ears. Gritty. Toxic. Damien

rematerializes in the far corner of the room, standing in the shadows at the foot of the staircase.

"Soon, boy. When I'm done with you, you'll go to Danakil. You'll meet the Prince."

Jake's stomach flips. "When you're done doing *what* with me?"

Jake's expecting an answer, needs an answer, but the demon pulls a cell phone from his pocket and snaps it to his ear.

"Where are you?" he growls into the phone. "Then come down. We're waiting. Yes, *we*."

Damien slides the phone into his pocket and leans against the corner, all but disappearing into the shadows.

Jake asks again, "When you're done doing what?"

But the sound of a door squeaking open is all the answer he gets. He turns his gaze to the staircase, where a pair of red heels step into view. Two very long, very lean legs follow. Behind them, dark jeans and stone-washed Toms. With the clamor of stilettos on steel, Olivia Holt makes her way down the stairs, Marco moving silently in her wake.

And then Marco's not so silent anymore.

"You!" He pushes past Olivia, dropping his bag and lunging at Damien, the man responsible for Ali's death.

"Marco!" Jake yells, wincing at the pain flaring in his shoulder.

Marco's face turns toward Jake, but forward momentum propels him into Damien's chest. The demon shoves him to his knees.

"Jake?" Marco says, still seething. "What are you doing here?"

Jake doesn't answer. He's too busy watching the exchange between Olivia and Damien.

"You have it?" Damien asks.

Olivia's face is hard, harder than Jake's ever seen it. Her eyes bounce from Jake to the demon before her. "Why is *he* here?"

"I asked you a question," Damien says. "Where is it?"

Olivia stoops to grab the bag Marco dropped—Jake's bag. "It's in here," she says, handing the bag to Damien. "Take it."

"Untie him," Marco demands, moving closer to Jake. He looks first to Damien and then to Olivia. But no one's listening to Marco.

Damien tips the bag onto the floor. A collection of clothing topples out, along with a few personal things. A wallet. A leather journal.

"What are you doing?" Marco asks. "Looking for my fifty-eight cents?" His fingers grasp and slip against the cords on Jake's wrists. "I can't do this. I need a knife. Cut him free."

But he's ignored.

"Where is it?" Damien asks.

"Check the pockets," Olivia says, slinking toward Jake. "I'm sure it's there."

"You told me you had it," Damien charges. "You haven't checked the maggot's bag?"

"Didn't need to. It's there. I can hear the thing."

Jake's so consumed by the conversation that he forgets the pain in his arm, his head.

"You can hear it?" Damien asks, echoing Jake's thought.

"You can't?" she asks with a flip of her silky black hair.

Damien pulls at the many zippers on the bag, one pocket after another, jamming his large hand into each one before moving on.

"It's in the front one," Jake says, his voice cracking, his eyes moving back to Marco's. "Unless you removed it."

"Removed what?" Marco asks. Jake watches him for signs of

a lie. But his gift isn't sight, and if this actor wanted to lie to him, it'd be only too easy.

"The halo," Jake says.

Marco looks to Damien, who's finally found the front pocket of the bag.

"I didn't know . . . didn't realize it was in there," Marco says, his eyes huge, the look on his face leaving little doubt of his ignorance. "How?"

Jake takes pity on him. "When you came by the house for your stuff, you took—"

"The wrong bag," Marco finishes.

"Yeah."

Olivia stands behind Marco now, her hands on her hips, scrutinizing Jake with those caramel eyes of hers. "I still don't understand why you took the boy," she calls over her shoulder. "What do you intend to do with him?"

But Damien's preoccupied. His fingers fumble with a jammed zipper. He curses and yanks harder, splitting the zipper and sending the halo tumbling to the floor. Jake flinches as it lands on the concrete with a metallic *chink*. They all turn to look. All except Olivia.

"I thought I'd put distance between me and that thing," Marco says, his voice quiet. "But I'd just strapped it to my back, hadn't I? Why does he want it?"

For the first time since Marco entered the basement, Jake looks him over, considers him. He looks awful, tortured, his green eyes ringed red. His face is pale, and despite the extra clothing in his bag, he hasn't changed since the last time Jake saw him. And that was what, a day ago? Two days?

"I don't know why he wants it, Marco."

They watch as Damien steps from the shadows and tosses the bag aside. He kneels and with careful fingers lifts the halo off the floor. Jake half expects it to burn him like the halo burned Elle when Olivia touched it, but the demon registers no pain. Strange, considering the supernatural heat the halo is known to give off. But it seems only Damien's celestial form is affected by heat.

He turns it in his hands, its glow lighting his olive skin, brightening his black eyes. When he speaks his words are laced with adrenaline and purpose of the darkest kind.

"What happens when one of us wears the crown of the faithful?" he asks, stepping closer. "Aren't you curious? What happens when a demon wears a halo?"

Marco inches closer to Jake. "What is he talking about?"

But Jake shakes his head. "Damien—"

The demon's eyes are frenetic now, staring at the halo as it molds from crown to cuff and back again. He's mesmerized. "I want to know if its power can be wielded. If this golden halo can be used to instill gifts at will. At *my* will."

"It was made by the Creator, Damien. You think *you* can corrupt it?"

Damien pushes Olivia and Marco aside and leans into Jake's face. "*I* was made by the Creator, and it took very little to corrupt me. So, yes. If it can be corrupted, I will figure out how."

Jake feels the blood drain from his face and watches the confused halo morph back and forth in the demon's hand. Cuff, crown, cuff, crown. Damien's words are true.

Is it possible? Can the halo be used for evil?

Jake refuses to believe it. "You're an idiot," he spits.

"And you're my prisoner," Damien says. "My guinea pig.

Only . . ." His eyes move from Jake to Marco and back again. "Ms. Holt, find me another chair."

Olivia laughs, but it's hollow, forced. She's as confused as the halo. Whatever she agreed to, it wasn't this.

"I got you the bracelet. You do your own legwork from here on out. Come on, Marco."

She reaches a hand out to her old friend, but faster than humanly possible, Damien is on top of her. He slams her against the barren shelves, pressing her against them with his massive arms and chest.

"What the—" Marco tries to intercede, but with a well-placed elbow Damien throws him backward. Jake watches Marco for signs of distress. He groans, but his chest rises and falls. Jake turns his attention back to Olivia.

In one fist Damien clenches the halo, in the other a handful of Olivia's hair. She flails against him, but Damien is not deterred. He sniffs at her face and neck, growling with delight.

"You wear fear well, Liv. Can I call you Liv?" He grabs her chin and yanks it up and down. "Good. 'Cause I'd like us to be partners. You'd like that, wouldn't you? Partners, like you and Javan."

She squirms against him, terrified gurgles coming from her throat.

"There it is again, the fear. I can smell it on you. I can taste it on the air you stir. Like an old friend, you've grown comfortable with it, but I'll share a secret with you, Liv. Fear answers to me."

She shakes her head from side to side. Jake knows she's doing her best to shake off the fear, to free herself from its grasp.

"Oh yes, it does," Damien coos. "It answers to me. With just a little direction fear itself would squeeze you tight. I could suffocate you, collapse those lungs of yours, without laying a finger on you. Did you know that? Fear would do it for me." He grins. "That puts you in my debt . . ."

Olivia rips her arm free and drags her nails across his face, but within a second he has her hand slammed against a splintered shelf.

Her lips curl back. "I am not. In your debt."

"So independent," Damien says, pressing his face closer to hers. "You think you're free? Think again. Every one of us serves one master or another. I've spent eons dwelling on just how unfair that is. But it's true."

"I don't even know what that means." She tries to pull her arm free, but he holds it tight.

"It means you're mine." His voice is flat, matter-of-fact. He's just laying it out for her now. "Javan made promises to you, but he's gone now and his promises mean nothing. I've moved in. I own you. Every decision you've ever made, every deception, every crime, every wayward passion of the heart—they've all ensured your loyalty to Darkness. You couldn't be free of us now if you tried."

"That's not true, Olivia," Jake says. "There's a way. There's always a way."

But Damien's captured her attention. "And those wounds Javan promised to rid you of, those are mine too. Mine to exploit."

Olivia swallows. "There are just so many. Which ones are you claiming?"

Jake watches in horror as Damien's hand slides to Olivia's wrist and yanks it forward. He turns it so the soft flesh of her inner arm faces out. She screams and thrashes as an invisible claw carves three lines into her skin.

Jake yells out, but Damien just smiles.

"Keep your eyes on the pretty lady, boy. I'm not done yet."

Olivia gasps. Her knees buckle and she falls forward. Even strapped to a chair, Jake tries to catch her. But the attempt is useless, and Olivia smacks the concrete floor hard, knees first and then face. Her legs curl and shake, her expensive shoes scraping against the floor before working loose and falling away. Jake watches in horror as the backs of Olivia's legs blister and burn, an invisible fire melting the skin away.

"No!" Jake yells. "Damien, stop! Please! Stop!"

And then Olivia's legs scab and scar. In just seconds the body's healing process has completed itself. It's not as tidy a job as Jake's hands are capable of, the skin puckered and pink, but her screams of agony fade to whimpers, and Jake sags against the chair.

Damien grabs Olivia under the arms and lifts her to her feet. She's trembling, head to toe, her face streaked with tears. He tips her chin up and then dusts the dirt from her hands and face in a motion that is almost tender. Bile fills Jake's mouth.

"Now, Liv, go get me a chair." Damien eyes Marco. "I like the idea of having two guinea pigs."

Olivia gives a spastic little nod and gingerly walks toward the stairs. With a lacquered finger she strokes the silver scars on her arm. Bare feet and scarred legs . . . it's not hard to imagine Olivia as the singed child from Brielle's nightmares. Jake's heart breaks for her. For the life she's lived. Even with the ability to heal, there's a soul sickness his hands can't touch. There are wounds he can't heal.

"Olivia . . . ," he tries, his voice weak. "Olivia, you don't have to—"

"Oh, but she does," Damien says, silencing Jake with a look. "Go on, doll. Get me what I need."

Fear burrows deeper and deeper into Jake's heart as Olivia climbs the stairs and opens the door to the floor above. Cinnamon and sugar sneak in, wafting through the dank basement. Jake's stomach threatens to turn again, but he forces the muscles to relax.

There's something beyond that door, Jake thinks. *This cellar isn't all there is. I just have to find the way out.*

Because there's always a way out.

9

Brielle

"I brought Oreos."

Kaylee's standing in the doorway of the old Miller place. She's wearing a Snuggie with monkeys printed all over it and her Tasmanian Devil slippers.

"Aren't you hot?" I ask.

"A little," she admits. "But I'm cozy!"

"What are you doing here?"

"I told you, I brought Oreos." She shakes the bag in front of my face. "Hot boy better have milk." She steps inside, tugging a bedazzled rolling backpack behind her. "I did bring my Justin Bieber collection, though, so I didn't forget everything."

I'm still staring at the backpack. Surely that's not what she plans to take when she leaves for the Peace Corps.

"Are you under the impression that I'm throwing a sleepover?"

"No, you're waiting and praying," she says—air quotes around the waiting and praying. "Did I get that right? I'm the one throwing a sleepover."

"Kay . . ."

She closes the door and adopts that doe-eyed innocence she

wields so easily. "Let me do this, okay? Let me make this better for you. Please, please, please. You need me."

I love her, that's true, but *need* is such a specific kind of word.

"Come on, Elle. I want to be here. I want to help."

She looks so eager and so not scared.

"It's just . . . it's dangerous," I say. "And you're wearing a Snuggie."

She points at me with a sparkly blue fingernail. "Don't knock it till you've tried it. And dangerous? Dangerous like the crazy demon who stabbed your dad and chucked him into the wall? I was there for that, remember. And I think I helped a bit. Right? I was helpful?"

"You were awesome, Kay, but being close to me right now, tonight, it's just . . . it's not safe. I don't want anything awful to happen to you."

"Funny you should say that, 'cause the only way I could get out of massaging Aunt Delia's feet for the rest of the night—yeah, awful—was by telling her I promised you a night of juvenile frivolity. If she asks, you and Jake are having problems, which is kind of true. I mean, missing is kind of a problem. So really, by letting me stay, you're saving me from something awful."

She slides the plastic tray out of the cookie bag and offers me an Oreo.

"Don't worry. I washed my hands." She waggles the cookie in front of me. "Go on, take it."

I do. I take the cookie. How can I not?

"You're—"

"Incorrigible," she says. "I know. Delia makes sure I know."

"I was going to say *amazing*, but now my mouth is full."

She beams, her chest out, her eyes sparkling. "You're more than welcome. You just have to promise to tell me if you see any more of those demon guys, okay? And if Damien comes back, I fully expect you to throw yourself between the two of us all dramatic-like. Really show off that superhero vision you've got there, okay?"

"Okay," I say, a smile undoing me.

Kaylee looks around the living room for the first time. Sun streams through the windows, lighting the furnishings. A pair of Jake's dirty socks are still on the floor. His work schedule sits on the coffee table.

I'm scared for him. So scared it hurts.

"Now, where are we setting up camp?"

"Canaan's room," I say, blinking back tears.

Kaylee gestures grandly. "After you."

I have half an Oreo stuck in my teeth, so before we head down the hall I fill two glasses with milk and hand one to Kaylee.

"So, this is Canaan's chest?" she asks, stepping into his room. "I mean, obviously it's not his chest, chest, but it's his chest? And what does it do exactly?"

She's been here for four minutes and I already have milk shooting out my nose. I wipe it away and try to explain. "This is how the Throne Room communicates with Canaan. It's where he gets his assignments from."

"Like you," she says. "You're an assignment?"

I nod.

"And this is where your engagement ring just appeared. All magical and stuff."

"It's not magic, Kay." But I really, really don't want to talk about the ring right now. It's gone anyway. There's not much more to say about it.

"Well, it's nifty." She tilts her head, staring at the chest. The lid's still on. I don't have the heart to open it and show her the dagger. That's another thing I'd like to avoid for the night. "I kind of want to climb inside. You think I'd fit?"

"Let's not find out, okay?"

"You're the boss." Kaylee busies herself with all sorts of sleepover rituals. I do my best to pray silently, and I monitor the chest every few minutes, opening the lid just wide enough for me to see inside. But so far there's been nothing.

"We need music," Kaylee says, rummaging through her bag. "You pick: Justin or Taylor?"

"Taylor," I say.

"You said Justin, right? I heard Justin." She leaves, heading for Jake's massive stereo in the living room.

I sneak another peek inside the chest. There's nothing new, just the dagger and a chill that latches onto me before I can stop it.

"I'm starved. What do you want for dinner?" Kaylee hollers over the music.

"Whatever," I say. "You want help?"

"Nah. Get to praying. Canaan's got a microwave. I'll be all right."

Rubbing my bare arms, I step out of Canaan's room and into Jake's. I'm not cold, not really. But getting lost in a sweatshirt sounds nice, and anything in Canaan's room would swallow me. Gingerly I make my way through the chaos on Jake's floor until I'm standing in front of the closet. I pilfer through it, finally settling on a navy blue hoodie with a gigantic pocket in the front. The seams are frayed and the drawstring is missing, but it smells like Jake.

I wander back to Canaan's room and crawl onto the bed. I draw my legs up under the sweatshirt and wrap my arms around my knees. Canaan's window looks out across the highway. Somewhere the sun is setting—I can't see it directly, but the sky is a bruise of darkest purple. Pink and orange striations ripple through it. It's beautiful, but I close my eyes on it all, on the beauty and everything hiding beneath it.

I pray. Silently, of course. The words are more eloquent that way. No stumbling over them, no shame when I can't get them just right. In my head I'm very articulate. I pray for Jake. For Canaan and Helene. I pray that Jake will walk through the door and that this nightmare will be over. I pray that fear wouldn't find a permanent home in Stratus. That the dreams finding their way into the minds of my friends and neighbors wouldn't be tainted by darkness. I pray that Dad would choose God and love instead of hate and doubt. I pray for all kinds of miracles.

When I open my eyes, Kaylee's there, sitting on the floor with a tray of s'mores and marshmallow all over her lips. I crawl down beside her, rolling the sleeves of the sweatshirt up over my wrists and grabbing a square of graham cracker heaven.

"You did good, Kay. This is the best dinner ever," I say, staring at my s'more and trying to decide just how best to bite it.

"All they have in the fridge is, like, a hunk of cow and some spicy hot wings." She swallows and continues, "There's got to be something in that Bible of yours about an angel eating hot wings. I mean, come on!"

I laugh, a hand clamped over my mouth to keep the crumbs inside.

"Tell me I'm not right," she says.

But I can't tell her anything, I'm laughing so hard my stomach aches. Finally, lying on my back, happy tears streaming down my face, a s'more half-eaten in my mouth, I hear it: the sound of rustling paper. It's soft, muffled. And if my ear hadn't been pressed against the chest, I doubt I'd have heard it at all.

I hack and sputter, forcing myself to swallow the bite in my mouth as I sit up and spin around. I lift the lid off the chest and shove it all in one motion. It falls to the ground with a dull *thud*.

A bundle of off-white pages have been added to the chest. I snatch them up. They're folded in half and in half again, the square of paper looking far more docile than the blood-crusted weapon next to it.

"What is that?" Kaylee says.

"I don't know. Pages of some sort. They look like they've been ripped from . . ."

But Kaylee's not looking at the paper in my hand. Her eyes are trained on the dagger. I lean past her and grab the lid. It's awkward with her in the way, but I heft it back in place, shutting the past away.

"Do angels always keep bloody swords in their trunks?"

In spite of the heaviness surrounding us, I snort.

"I guess that didn't come out right," Kaylee says, lacking all of the humor I've come to expect of her.

"It's not Canaan's, Kay. The Throne Room put it there."

Her face goes white. "Why?"

"I think they were warning us about Damien's return."

"That's Damien's?"

I nod.

She picks at the polish on her thumbnail. It takes her seventeen scratches to eliminate every last blue sparkle she'd painted on.

"He said he'd killed you once before. The other day, in your living room, he told your dad he'd killed you before and he wouldn't hesitate to do it again." It's painful watching someone else dissect the events of yesterday, but I let her do it. I know she needs to understand. "This is how he did it, then. At the warehouse. This is how he killed you, isn't it?" Before I can answer, she presses her fingers to her eyes. "I remember . . ."

"What, Kay? What do you remember?"

"Rain. And blood. All over your shirt. All over your hands." She lets her hands fall away and starts picking at her other thumbnail. "But I can't . . . Why can't I remember more?"

"Doubt," I tell her. "Denial. They make us feel better about the things our brains refuse to believe. Once they've taken root, they take on a life of their own."

"You're saying I'm in denial about the warehouse?"

"Not all of it, obviously, but the angels, the demons? Yeah, I'm guessing you chose denial."

She moves on to her index finger, scratching, scratching, blue chips flying. "I believe, though. Now I do."

"I'm glad," I say, pulling her into a hug. "You have no idea how glad I am."

"Do you think I'll remember?"

"I don't know, Kay. Maybe." I wish I had time to sit and really explain everything to her. Wish I could open the Bible and show her the stuff Jake's shown me. Well, really, I wish Jake was here to do that; he's so much better than I am at the Bible stuff. I always forget where everything is. But we don't have time for any of that. We have to figure out what these pages are.

"Okay, bloody swords aside, what is this?" Kaylee asks, swatting at the pages still clenched in my hand.

I think I know what they are, but I'm hesitant to say. Hesitant to hope. I unfold the wad of paper, and now I'm sure.

"They're pages torn from a journal," I say. "From Ali's journal."

"That ratty leather book Marco's always carrying around?"

"It wasn't always ratty," I tell her. "Ali loved that thing."

"So, let me get this straight," Kaylee says, fingering the pages in my hand. "This Throne Room of yours—"

"Not mine."

"—tore pages out of the journal in Marco's pocket and dropped them into this chest for Canaan to find?"

I think it through. It's possible, I guess. Anything's possible, but . . .

"There were pages missing from Ali's journal." I sort through the thin stack in my hand.

"What?"

"Before he left, Marco had Ali's journal out. He was asking me a question about a quote she'd copied down and . . ."

"And?"

"And I noticed a section had been torn out."

"So. Okay. Then someone . . ."

"Maybe Ali . . . ," I venture.

"Sure, maybe Ali, but *someone* tore the pages out, and then an unspecified amount of time passed and the Throne Room snatched them up and delivered them here."

"Sounds about right," I say.

"But why tear the pages out to begin with?"

"Because Ali never carried a purse. I bet she just tore these out and crammed them into her pocket."

"This is all so cryptic. She could have helped us out and been a bit more specific. Do you know what these notes mean?"

"I don't. Ali always joked she was doing top secret research. I never thought she was serious."

"I know what this is though. This is Bellwether," Kay says.

"The lighthouse?"

"Yeah," she says, sinking back next to me.

I look at the page she's shifted to the top and think maybe she's right. On the back of it is a pencil sketch of the lighthouse. Ali's captured it well. I recognize the cliff line behind it.

"In Beacon City," I say. I flip through other pages, looking at their mostly blank backs. One has the sketch of a rock garden on it, but the others are empty. In the top left corner of the page with the lighthouse sketch, Ali's delicate cursive hand has penned a phone number. I recognize the Portland area code. Below it are the words: *just past mile marker 178, 1pm*

"I know that number," Kaylee says, reading over my shoulder. "Gosh, whose is it?"

"Let's find out."

The phone's already in my hand. I dial and put it on speaker.

"If we knew what freeway she was talking about, we might be able to figure out—"

The voice mail on the other end of the line has picked up. My hand goes slack and the phone slips out. Kaylee picks it up off the carpet and ends the call.

"Holy crab cakes," she says.

"Why did Ali have Olivia Holt's phone number in her journal?" And then another memory surfaces. "There was another sketch."

"What?"

"In Marco's journal. It was of Olivia's arm. I didn't know it was her arm at the time, but it was."

"Okay, Dr. Frankenstein, what makes you an expert at identifying arms—especially from pencil sketches?"

"The scars," I say.

"I've known Liv for a while now, and I haven't seen any scars."

"Yeah, but I have."

Kaylee's face is screwed up so tight I'm actually surprised she can blink. But she manages eleven of them before her brow relaxes and her jaw loosens. She looks like she's going to explode with all the questions crammed into her head, but she settles for an easy one.

"She has scars?"

"Yeah."

"And Ali met her?"

"Must have."

"Why?"

"That's not the right question to be asking," I say, jumping to my feet. "We want to know where they met."

"I'm guessing it was a half mile past mile marker 178."

"Me too," I say, dashing out of the room and across the hall into the study. I hit Jake's desk chair at a run. I have to grab both sides of the desk to keep from sliding too far, but I steady myself and pull up Google.

"What are you searching for?" Kaylee asks, following me in, albeit at a much more reasonable pace.

But I can't slow down. I can't stop. I've got a feeling that . . .

"They've turned Bellwether into a pastry shop?" she asks, her eyes on the page I'm clicking through.

"Just the keeper's house," I say. "The lighthouse is up the road . . ."

"Across that creepy bridge," Kaylee says. "I remember."

I click on the link that says Directions and my eyes scream across the page. Looking, looking . . .

"There!" I say, jamming my finger into the screen and reading aloud, "'If you're traveling on Highway 101, we are two and a half miles north of the world-famous Sea Lion Caves and a half mile north of mile marker 178.'"

"Ali met Liv at Bellwether?"

"I think so."

"But why?"

"That's the question, isn't it? What's Ali's connection to Olivia?" I grab my phone from Kaylee's hand and dial Canaan. After four rings it goes to voice mail. Next I try Helene. Nothing. Forcing myself not to curse, I redial Olivia's number. But every single call goes to voice mail.

"Don't you hate that?" Kaylee says. "What is the point of having a phone if you never, ever answer the thing? Delia's the worst. I'm convinced she's just ignoring me."

But I've moved on.

"We have to go to Bellwether," I say.

"What? Why?"

"Because the Throne Room sent us this," I say, holding up the wad of paper. "And it has information that ties Olivia to that lighthouse. And she was working with Damien."

"Something I still have trouble believing," she says. "But I thought we were waiting for stuff about Jake? I thought that's what we"—air quotes around the *we*—"were praying for."

I bite my lip, because if I'm really, truly, completely honest, that's exactly why we have to go to Bellwether.

"Oh," Kay says, sinking back, her eyes wide, her long lashes curling into her brows. "You think Jake's at Bellwether, don't you?"

"I don't know," I say, trying to rein in the hyperactive hope, "but if he is, we need to get moving."

"Why?"

"Because in less than a day, Damien's taking Jake to Satan."

That shuts her up.

"You ready?"

"To try to rescue your boyfriend from a guy with pointy horns and a forked tail?"

"I doubt he has a forked tail."

"Please, puh-lease let me have my delusions for now. Imagining him as a cartoon character might be the only thing that gets me through this."

"Okay," I say, leaping from the chair. "Forked tail it is."

"Sure then. Why not? Delia thinks we're eating Oreos and commiserating. Let's go get Jake."

I grab her hand and drag her toward the door.

"I can bring the Oreos, right?"

10

Jake

Jake watched as Damien tied Marco to a wooden chair. Damien was pretty adamant about wanting a metal one, but Olivia insisted it was the best she could come up with. Yellow with white daisies painted up its legs and on the chair back. Damien strapped him to it, using his zip ties and nylon rope. And duct tape, of course, around Marco's chest. Irritated that he didn't get what he asked for, Damien overcompensated by cinching the binds so tight they cut into Marco's wrists and ankles. He woke screaming, thrashing against the binds, which only made them bleed more.

After that, Damien shoved the halo onto Jake's head and then took five steps backward, like Jake was set to explode at any moment. But when he did nothing but close his eyes and sigh, Damien yanked the halo—and a handful of hair—from Jake's head and shoved it onto Marco's.

Here he arrived at something that seemed to please him more.

Marco whimpered when Damien came toward him with the thing, but he silenced when the halo was dropped into place. For an hour Marco stared straight ahead, his eyes wide, his mouth open. Jake watched, nearly as transfixed as Damien. Occasionally Marco's brow would crease or his eyes would close. Once he sobbed openly and twice he laughed. And then his head bobbed once, swung like a pendulum, and stilled against his chest.

Now Damien sits in the corner of the basement, spinning the halo on his finger.

Jake looks again at Marco. His chair is jammed in the corner of the room; his hands, like Jake's, are tied behind his back. Every now and then a drop of blood falls to the floor. The healer in Jake has been doing everything he can to figure out a way to help.

Even with the metal chair wobbly from Damien's temper tantrum, Jake hasn't been able to work either his legs or arms free. Getting to Marco could be a problem. And then there's Olivia.

What little light slips through the window has changed, adding brown shades to the gray, but Olivia's perch under the stairs keeps her face in shadow. Jake can see her legs plainly enough—crossed at the ankles, her feet still bare. They're strangely still. She drops her hands to her lap and with her right thumb she strokes the scars on her forearm. Reading her is hard. Fear doesn't shake her as easily as it shakes others. Jake would do anything to have Brielle's sight right now.

He closes his eyes and conjures her crystal blues, her red lips. An ache crashes around his chest, heavy like a bowling ball. There's no guarantee he'll see her again. The thought gains momentum, making it hard to breathe, but Jake stares into her imagined face for a minute longer before he forces his eyes open. When he does, Damien's gone. Or at least invisible.

He strains, finally locating Olivia's eyes in the darkness under the stairs.

"Where'd he go?" Jake asks. "Damien. When will he be back?"

She doesn't move, doesn't answer him.

"Olivia?" His patience is thin, his fists balled, his voice insistent. "Olivia, it's important. Where did—"

"Don't ask me questions."

The anxiety Jake's been searching for on her person is finally evident in her words. Her hatred for Damien is obvious, but she's shattered. Bound to him somehow. Not with zip ties or nylon rope like he and Marco are. It's fear that keeps her here.

Jake presses his back against the seat. The binds against his wrists relax, and relief floods his injured arm. It'd be so easy to quit fighting. So painless to sit and wait, to accept whatever's coming.

But physical pain's never frightened Jake much. Other things terrify him, but not that.

"Marco?" he asks.

Marco's chin still rests on his chest, his hair a shaggy mess blocking any view of his face, and the blood continues to drip. He's hurting, and while Jake can deal with his own pain, he can hardly stand it on others. With a glance at Olivia and another one at his suffering friend, Jake decides.

He presses his toes into the floor and leans forward. The injured side of his body flares with pain, but he bites his cheek and takes two tiny steps toward Marco before his calves give out and his chair totters back.

"Okay, Marco. I'm going to walk my chair closer to yours, all right? If you can turn your chair away from me so I can"—he casts a glance at Olivia—"so I can see your hands, that would help."

But Marco doesn't move. Neither does Olivia.

"Okay. Well. We'll deal with that when I get there." Jake cracks his neck and shakes his own hair away from his face. He pushes the pain in his shoulder to the back of his mind and rolls onto his toes again. He leans forward and lifts the chair legs off the ground. Sweat breaks out on his upper lip as he moves toward Marco. He manages a few steps before the pain in his shoulder demands a break. He throws his head back, breathing in the musty air as the pain ebbs. Then he grits his teeth and tries again. It's several minutes before he gets to Marco's side.

"Okay, Marco. I'm here," Jake says. He's drenched in cold sweat now, his hair matted against his face and neck, and still Marco ignores his presence, his effort to help.

And now Jake's done all he can do. Marco's hands are bound behind him; without some help from Marco, there's no way Jake will be able to reach them.

"Marco, my man, can you turn your chair at all?"

Just the *drip, drip, drip* of blood falling to the ground.

Jake tips his chair a bit, knocking his shoulder against Marco's. "Look, man, I know this sucks, but I can help. Really, I can. Look, the halo gave you nightmares, right? Visions? Okay. It gave me a totally different gift. I can . . . my hands . . . I can heal the cuts on your wrists, Marco. I can do it with a touch, but I need to be able to reach them."

Marco's sniffles taper off, but he doesn't move.

"Come on, let me help. I need you better. I need you to *want* to get out of here. Let me help. Please."

Marco's face tilts up, but his eyes are glassy, and though they meet Jake's, they're focused on something beyond him. On something beyond the room. Jake throws his weight against the wobbly chair, and his knees connect with Marco's.

"Hey, listen to me. Whatever's going on in that head of yours, snap out of it. Pay attention. We've got to get out of here."

"He's not here," Olivia says, leaning into Marco's face. "Not really." Jake's been so focused on Marco he didn't hear her creep up behind him.

"Turn his chair for me," Jake says. He doesn't ask. He can see the compassion she feels for Marco. The tenderness. She doesn't want to see him in pain.

She reaches out, but fear grabs hold of her hands and they tremble. Jake doesn't care. He's done giving in to fear.

"Turn his chair, Olivia. Turn him so his hands touch mine."

She stands there, her shaking hands frozen in midair. "I didn't know, Jake. I didn't know he was going to take you."

"I don't care about any of that. Please. I can help Marco, and we can get out of here. All of us."

Her head shakes violently now. "You don't know what he did to me."

"You're right, I don't. But I know Damien."

"Not Damien," she says. She kneads her hands together, her eyes locked on Jake's. He knows that look. Seen it many times. She wants to talk. To confess. She has horrible timing, but if he can get her talking, maybe he can help her too. "Javan. Henry's Javan."

Jake exhales slowly, keeps his voice calm. "He did that to your arm."

She nods. "I was ten when I went to live with my grandfather. My vile, pedophilic grandfather. Javan said he could protect me from him."

Jake knows this part because Brielle's dreamed it, but it's different hearing it from Olivia. It's sadder, more real, when you consider that Elle's nightmares were someone else's reality.

"Did Javan keep his word?"

Another dip of her chin. "Henry never touched me."

"And Javan . . . ," Jake asks.

"Not like that," Olivia says. "Never like that." Her eyes look like Marco's now. Glassy. Far away. "That wasn't Javan's way. I'm fairly certain I repulsed him. That everyone repulsed him."

"What did he do to you, Olivia?"

Her mouth hangs open for a second, the bottom lip quivering. Despite the pain she's obviously in, Jake can't help but appreciate her show of emotion. It's good to know the woman can still feel. She might not be as broken as he thought.

"He crawled inside my head." Her hands fall to her sides, the seemingly ridiculous statement pulling her back to the room. "That sounds weird to you, doesn't it?"

"Not at all," Jake says. "I believe you."

"Do you?" She moves closer now. "He never shut up. He told me whom to befriend, what to dream. He told me which classes to take and which men would pay big for favors. His sick, twisted voice taught me how to seal a deal. And you don't walk away from situations like that . . . unscathed."

"Unscathed?"

She wraps her arms across her chest. "I wasn't quite twenty when Henry's business associate took advantage."

There are a lot of things Jake can help with. A lot of things he can fix, but this isn't one of them. "Oh man, Liv. I'm sorry. So sorry."

"Javan showed up, beat the guy senseless, but it was too late."

"But you survived, and sometimes that's—"

"I'll never have babies, Jake. And it's probably the only thing I ever really wanted. My mom was an obstetric nurse. I used to stare at all those little babies in the nursery and dream of the day I'd have my own. Of the perfect life we'd have." She unfolds herself, the flickering light casting a glow on the silver-blue lines cut into her forearm. "All these scars on my body, and the one that caused the most damage is hidden. Most people will never know how broken I am."

"There's always hope, Liv," Jake says, his heart hurting worse than his arm.

Her smile is slanted. "Who's dreaming now?"

Somewhere close, pipes squeal, and the rush of water quiets them both. Doors open and close on the main floor above them.

"If we're going to do this, we need to hurry," Jake says. "I just want to help Marco."

She stares at him for a long time. "If you leave, he'll hurt me."

"He's already hurt you, Liv. Look at your legs." Jake works hard to keep the exasperation from his voice, but it's not easy. They've got to move.

"No," she says, turning so Jake can see the wounds on the backs of her legs. "These, I've had these for years."

"But they'd healed."

She shrugs. "Sort of. A gift from Javan. I worked hard to have these scars removed, but in the end it didn't matter."

The sentence confuses Jake. She was scar-free. How can that not matter? But it's Marco who voices the question.

"Why?" he asks, his head lifted, his face a torrent of emotion. "Why didn't it matter?"

She turns to face them, tears falling like stars from her lashes.

"I could still feel the burns. Not when I ran my fingers over the skin, but beneath. Deep inside I felt the pull of damaged flesh. I felt the stinging chill of an open wound. Sometimes I thought I could smell them burning." She shakes her head. "Having them look healed was worse than when they were gaudy white scars. Far worse. I never should have let Javan *fix* me. So this," she says, "this is nothing. You can just see what I've always felt. Wounds that never stop hurting."

"What about your arm? What is that?" Marco again. His voice is thin, desperate.

And now Jake remembers. Marco's seen a drawing of this, of Liv's arm. In Ali's journal. He must be all kinds of confused.

"Javan gave me these. As a reminder, he said."

"A reminder of what?" Marco asks.

"He used me. He broke me, but he also kept Henry away. And that was all I ever wanted. I saw what Henry did. I would have let Javan drag all ten of his razor-sharp nails down my back to avoid that fate."

Jake can't help the repulsion he feels at that statement. She knew what Henry was? Saw what he did? And she just let it happen?

"Liv . . . ," Marco says, his voice catching. "I would've helped. You know I would have."

"I had help. I had Javan."

Jake weighs his next words carefully. Marco can't take much more, but perhaps honesty will help him see through the chaos. "Javan's worse than Henry, Liv. He's a demon."

Marco's head whips toward Jake. "And Henry's not?"

"Javan is an actual demon, Marco," Jake clarifies.

Marco's face loses what little color it had left.

"I know what Javan is," Olivia says. "I've known for a long time. We had no pretenses between us. There was no reason. My eyes were wide open when I chose what he offered."

"You were a child," Jake says.

"Don't kid yourself. Henry was never far. I chose Javan every day of the week. If I hadn't, he'd have hand-delivered me to the old man."

"Stop," Marco says. "Just stop. What are you talking about? He's a demon?"

Jake looks to Olivia, wonders if she'd like to do the honors, but she just takes a small step back. Jake hates this part. Explaining the invisible and then waiting for the inevitable fallout.

"He's a fallen angel, Marco. Like Damien."

Incredulity crosses Marco's face. "Damien's a fallen angel?"

"Yes."

Marco looks away, his eyes moving over the wall, over the floor. Eventually, he looks back at Jake. "Then the halo really is evil."

"No, Marco. The halo doesn't belong to Damien, or Javan, for that matter. It never did. It belongs to—"

"Canaan." Marco's incredulity is replaced with understanding.

"Does it, now?" Olivia says. "I didn't realize there were so many angels in Stratus."

Marco's eyes settle somewhere near the staircase. He's thinking. Hard, by the look on his face.

"So it's a halo," Liv says. "That explains why it hates me so much."

Jake's never seen a person so backward in their thinking. His eyes wander to the scars on her arm. "I can help you, Olivia."

"Like Javan helped me?"

"Everything about Javan has been corrupted. Everything. His gift, especially. No, Liv, listen to me. He can offer healing, but he can't sustain it. He can deal out death, but he can't make it stick. He can break you—he's been given the power to do that. But, Liv, he can't make you whole."

She laughs at him, but her heart's not in it. She wants to be healed. She wants to be whole. Jake can see it in her eyes.

"And you can?"

"No," Jake says. "I don't have that power either. But I can heal your legs, and I can heal the cuts on Marco's wrists. I can show you that the God who graced me with these hands has carried more pain than you and I could ever imagine and has also destroyed its ability to last forever. He's the only One who can make you whole."

The shadows shift again, the light coming through the window brighter than before. Jake imagines the clouds moving outside, the wind blowing them away from the face of the sun. The three of them turn and watch the elongated window, the light beyond a smidgen of hope.

And then the sound of wood scraping against concrete. Olivia drags Marco's chair sideways, and her eyes meet Jake's.

"Start with Marco."

11

Brielle

We round the bend at the top of the mountain, my knuckles white on the steering wheel. It's dark now, but I breathe a little easier when the seaside town of Beacon City comes into view. It's nestled below us in a shallow valley surrounded by the coastal range here. Cliffs, like the one we're navigating now, line the ocean west of town. There's very little beach access here unless you're willing to navigate the rocks.

Slugger's getting a little old for this kind of driving, and I've made Kaylee swear she'll never tell Dad we drove her out here, but with Kaylee's car on E, Slugger was the best choice. Stopping for gas was the last thing I wanted to do, and even my little Beetle can make it the three and a half hours to Bellwether on a full tank.

The turns here are hairy, the drop-off steep, and I'm more than a little frayed by the time we reach the Sea Lion Caves. There's a bathroom here, and Kaylee's been crying for one for the past hour, so I pull over and we climb out.

"Hurry," I tell her, but she knows. She's running to the small brown building.

My eyes burn. I need to sleep, but it's more than that. I feel a nightmare coming on. Right at the front of my mind sits its preview. An unfamiliar scene has been playing out in the shadows of my mind, but with my eyes on the road and my mind on Jake I've only been able to make out Olivia's face, her pencil skirt, her arms crossed in defiance. Her mouth moves, but I hear nothing. And there's sweet relief in that.

What would I do with another nightmare right now?

I'm walking into the worst kind there is: Jake in Damien's care.

But the cold air feels wonderful on my face. I've not changed. I'm still wearing my jean shorts and over my tank top, Jake's sweatshirt. I force myself to uncross my arms, to let them hang. My fingertips brush the thin fringe of denim hanging below the sweatshirt, the wind off the sea whispering up my legs.

"I can't do this alone," I say to the God of wind and rain. "I need help."

Fog has swept into the cove here, turning everything a milky gray. The wind picks up, pushing against my knees hard enough that I open my eyes. A drop of water lands on my cheek. Rain or sea spray, I can't tell, but it reminds me of Ali. Of a song she sang as Éponine in a production of *Les Mis* during our junior year at Austen.

"A little fall of rain," I whisper into the darkness, "can hardly hurt me now." It's a line from the show, from Éponine's song with Marius. "You're here, that's all I need to know."

The wind grabs the fog and pulls it along, pushing it away, and for the first time I see the waves below. They're calm. Calmer than they have any right to be on this terrifying night.

"You're here," I pray. "That's all I need to know."

"You owe me, Matthews. The door was locked, so I peed behind the ranger station."

"I'm sorry, Kay," I say, turning my back on the ocean and running back to the car. "I just need to get there."

"I don't think anyone has ever made it from Central Oregon to the coast this fast, girl, and considering we're driving a wind-up toy, that's saying something."

"Be nice. Slugger's been good to us," I say, turning the key. "We're almost there."

We turn out of the ranger station, and I push the gas to the floor. Slugger groans, but mile marker 177 comes into view and my heart stammers. One more mile. The curve here is wicked sharp, so I take my foot off the gas, and that's when Bellwether rises in the distance.

The lighthouse is a haze of Halloween colors against the night sky. The Fresnel lens spins, bathing everything in its path with light. Its long neck is stretched against the black sky, the fog swirling about it.

Kay leans forward, her nose inches from the windshield. "Criminy. That's spooky at night."

I'm silent, but I couldn't agree more. And then the trees obstruct our view. Mile marker 178 flies by, and I swallow against the fear that's stuck in my throat. I can't . . . I can't . . . I don't even know how to pray.

A gap in the trees opens up, and the keeper's house comes into view. Like everything else, it's swabbed in a haze of moist fog. The moonlight catches it, transforming the white house into something ghostly. A lawn and white picket fence surround it all, but shadowed as it is, the house is far less welcoming than it was on the website.

And yet there's no place on this planet I'd rather be.

Jake's here.

I'm sure of it.

The house is still several hundred yards up the road, but I pull off the freeway and park Slugger against the mountain.

"You'll have to climb out on my side, Kay."

I stand on a thin strip of dirt between my car and the freeway. All is quiet. The road beside me is empty. Beyond it is a cliff face where evergreens grow out from the rocks, jutting over the sea.

"Hey, Elle?" Kay's sitting in the driver's seat now. "Before we storm the castle, what do you want me to do with these?"

She's holding the pages of Ali's journal in her hands. It's a good question. I don't know what I'm going to find here, and I don't want to carry in a bunch of cryptic and possibly incriminating evidence. "Put them in the glove compartment," I say, kneeling down next to her, handing her the keys. "If this goes, you know, bad . . ."

The moon has painted her face white, like the cliffs here, like the road, and with her eyes wide and her hair pulled into two high knots she looks like some sort of manga superhero.

"Knock it off, Elle," she says. "It'll be fine. We'll be fine."

"Okay, but you have to figure out what those papers mean," I say. "Get them to Canaan if you can, or Helene, but if you can't—"

"I promise to do my best Sherlock Holmes impersonation, okay? But let's talk about now. I don't think we should go in all guns blazing and stuff. We need to have a plan."

"Yeah," I say. "I thought about that."

"And?"

"Well, I don't have one. I mean, what do we know? Nothing. It's really hard to come up with a plan for nothing."

"Okay, well. We don't know anything, but what are you

thinking? That he's at the bakery here or up the road at the lighthouse?"

"I don't know," I say, feeling very, very unprepared. "There's no way to know."

"What about those eyes of yours? Can't they help us out a bit?"

"I don't know," I say. "Without the halo, I don't have any control over what I do and don't see, but . . ."

"But you could try."

"Yes, I could try."

"Okay, then that sounds like a plan," she says, stepping out of the car. "I'm good with plans." She closes the door quietly, but when she steps away, her Snuggie tears. It's gotten caught in the door. "You know, maybe I should leave the Snuggie here?"

"You know, maybe you should."

She strips it off and leaves it on the driver's seat, closing the door once again with as much silence as she can muster.

"All right," she says, taking my hand. "I'm ready."

We start up the road, staying off the freeway as much as possible. After fifty yards or so, the trees and rocks on our right give way to a grassy, unkempt stretch of land. We rush through it toward the picket fence lining the keeper's house. Crouching there, my pulse leaps and jumps, my heart skipping to catch up with it. Blood pounds against my eyes, and my hands go cold. I'm scared. And hopeful.

But mostly I'm scared.

The house is larger than I remember it. Two sets of stairs service the porch, one on the right and another on the left. Six steps up either takes you to the front door. Over it hangs a wooden hand-painted sign that says Bell's Baked Goods. Through the branches of trees and over the awning on the porch the lighthouse burns bright, its lens favoring us with its beam every few seconds. But the house itself is dark. No light in the windows or on the porch. The place looks empty. Abandoned. And suddenly I'm all doubt.

What if I was wrong?

What if we read the pages wrong?

What if I misunderstood the Throne Room?

Maybe I should have stayed.

What if the Throne Room sent something else after we left, and we just drove to some abandoned lighthouse on the coast?

"Elle!" Kaylee's voice is a hiss coming at me from down the fence line. She's sneaked to the back and is waving me over. Staying low, though I'm not entirely sure why, I run to her side.

"What is it?"

"Olivia's car," she says with a nod of her head.

"Oh." Parked at the back of the property is a red BMW.

"They're here, Elle," Kaylee says. "You were right."

"I was." I kneel now and press my forehead to the fence. Between the slats I have a good view of the house and I focus. Hard.

And then I pray.

"God, help me see," I say. Kaylee's hand finds mine, and she squeezes. I focus harder.

And then the wall before me thins away. It doesn't change colors, it doesn't glow, but I can see the dark room inside. Tables and chairs and a counter—everything wrapped in shadow.

And empty.

"Do you see anything?"

I'm not used to seeing through walls without the celestial light. It's weird. But maybe if I get closer. I throw my leg over the fence and make for the front door. If Jake's in there we have to be sure.

Kaylee follows, though with a smidge less grace. Her Tasmanian Devil slipper gets caught on a loose board and she barely catches herself before her face connects with the ground.

I reach down and pull her up.

"Sorry, sorry. I thought we decided not to march in," she says. "What did you see?"

"Nothing," I say. "I mean, I saw inside, but it's . . . Let me try from up here." I walk to the foot of the nearest staircase and try again. "Please," I pray. "Please."

The front wall disappears almost immediately, but all I see is that the entryway and seating area are empty. I turn my attention up, through the ceiling of the converted living room and into the bedrooms above. Gorgeous Victorian-style furnishings, but completely vacant.

"I don't think there's anyone here, Kay."

And then a cruel chuckle shakes my insides. "Oh, but there is."

Kaylee screams, but I'm too shocked to make a sound. Before I can move, Damien's hand knots in my hair. He lifts Kaylee, screaming and flailing, and tucks her under his arm like a football. He doesn't bother keeping her quiet; he likes the fear. He yanks me by the hair, pushing me before him, up the stairs and through the front door.

Despite the aged, Victorian feel the house gives from the outside, the inside is a mashup of cozy and modern. Crisp, square tables in oak are surrounded by bright yellow chairs and spaced evenly throughout the room. Damien pushes us toward the counter—a glass display case with empty trays and fancy index cards marking them for what they hold—as my mind flies through options stupid and implausible.

I could run. Try to get away. He has Kaylee, and it would be hard for him to keep track of us both. Hard, but not impossible. Still, I could do it. I think I can. And if I can get away, I can come back with help. Unless the angels are too busy to answer their cell phones. Again.

It's entirely possible, even likely. Neither Canaan nor Helene has returned a single call or text Kaylee sent on the way here. There's no guarantee they would be available now. And even then, I'm certain Damien sees more value in me than in Kaylee. He's stupid like that.

There has to be another way, but unlike Damien, I can't think with Kaylee screaming. Her terror heightens mine, and it's all I can do to keep moving. Damien knees me in the back, and I stumble forward.

I can't believe I let him catch me. If Canaan's right, and he's always right, my captive presence can only make things harder for Jake. Make his fight more painful, more costly. What would Damien do to me to make Jake cooperate? A tremor runs through my body, because I know exactly what he'd do. He'd do whatever it takes. Even now, with my hands trembling and anger at myself seeping from every pore, I wonder how much it would take to break *me*. Very little, I think. Any kind of pain inflicted on Kaylee or Jake, and I don't know if I'm strong enough to allow that. Even for a higher call. Suddenly I'm willing to risk the fallout of trying to escape. Whatever the cost, I can't be used against Jake. I won't be an arrow in Damien's quiver. And I won't let them be used against me.

But I've got to act now. The counter is just in front of us, and beyond it a room swallowed in darkness. Who knows what I'm walking into?

I throw myself to the left, losing a hunk of hair in the process. I actually think my scalp is bleeding, but adrenaline keeps me moving. There's a table and four chairs between us now, but I don't look back. There's a side door here, an emergency exit sign glowing above it. Looks like a wheelchair ramp on the other side. I hear Damien yell, I hear Kaylee scream louder.

I think she's cheering me on.

But my feet tangle in something and I fall toward the door, my palms smacking the bar and propelling the door open. The cold night air, thick with salt, rushes inside, making room for me out there. If only I were standing on my feet! I clamber as fast as I can, trying to get upright, but my lip is bleeding, my chin scraped, and for a moment all I see is stars.

Behind me, something akin to war is breaking out. Kaylee's not just yelling, she's screaming like a feral cat. I hear open hands colliding with flesh, again and again. The demon curses and Kaylee yells. I turn for her, but she waves me away.

"Get out of here, Elle. Go!"

And then she's screaming again. I want to go back for her. I *have* to go back for her.

"Brielle! Get out of here!"

Agony tears through my chest at the thought of leaving her behind, but if I go back now everything will be so much worse. If I can get free of this building, maybe, just maybe, he'll let Kaylee go and come after me. Maybe she can work magic with that phone of hers and find help.

So many maybes, but I crawl out the door and roll off the handicap ramp. The fall is farther than I thought, and when I land, it's like the air is vacuumed from my lungs. Still, I keep moving. I stand, grass and mud on my face, dampening my knees. The fog is thicker now than it was before, but a blast of light strikes me in the face. And then it's gone. Through the trees, I see the lighthouse silhouetted against the foggy night. In a move that is probably more symbolic than wise, I run toward it.

And then I hear wings overhead. If I can hear him, experience says I can see him, but I don't look. I just duck my head and run faster.

"Please, God. Please, please, please."

In front of me, out from the fog, emerges a wooden bridge built to fill in a gap left by sliding rocks. It's old, the wood peeling, trees invading it. Blood runs down my neck and chest. I spit it from my mouth, but still I run toward the light. The blinking, spinning, very alive, very real light.

And then his voice crawls inside my head.

"What will you do when you get there, girl? What will you do when you get to the light?"

The world around me threatens to ice over. The trees, the road, the railings on the bridge, they all take on a glazed look. I blink and blink and try to will his words away, because he's right. There's nothing beyond the bridge. Just rocks that fall away into the sea. Just a cliff. Just ocean.

How far down is it? Do I know? Is that a piece of information I have locked away in my memory somewhere? Maybe, but as my feet pound against the bridge, I can't recall it. I stumble, his words making my feet slip. I press on, straightening up and refusing to fall.

I can't fall now.

Because I finally know what I have to do.

On my right an outer building passes by and then another, both of them as white as the dove on Canaan's wall. The fog encases them, turning the small buildings into tissue-wrapped gifts, but I fly by, my eyes on the swanlike neck of the lighthouse. And then I'm below it, its thick trunk a phantom reaching into the heavens.

Damien's still talking.

"Where are you going? What are you doing?" He asks the same things over and over again, a hint of amusement in his voice.

He's toying with me, but that's okay. It buys us time. And that's what I need to give Kaylee. Time.

My hands, my hips smack a wooden rail. It's meant to keep tourists off the cliffs below. Meant to keep people away from danger, but I throw my legs over. I slip and slide down the cliff-side, Damien laughing inside my head. Rocks cut my hands and tear my clothes, but eventually I slide to a stop. I'm still much farther above the water than I'd like. Below, it crashes on the rocks, sending up a spray that freckles my face and legs. But I don't stop to ponder the distance.

I just jump.

The sky spills around me, stars and inky blackness, wisps of fog, and at the corners of my vision, everything icing over.

"How do you like falling, little dancer?" he asks. "It's still the best feeling in the world."

Damien roars with delight. The writhing wall of water grows closer and closer, and everything in me screams for the lighthouse above.

"God, I need wings." My prayer is strange and garbled, but without wings I'm helpless. Without wings I can't fly. Without wings I will surely drown.

And suddenly I'm snatched from the sky.

My prayer is answered in the least desirable way, but relief floods me nonetheless.

Still laughing, Damien slams me against his body, frozen and covered with the sticky tar of fear. I've most likely traded one death for another, but I can only hope I've given Kaylee enough time to call for help.

12

Brielle

My eyes are wide open when Damien tucks his wings and falls into a dive. Crushed against his frame, I shiver uncontrollably, but my celestial vision is clear and concise. It doesn't come in pieces. It's complete and as reliable as it ever was with the halo.

Below us, the keeper's house is swathed in the red flames of violence. The flames throb against the night sky, ominous and chilling, but they beat out a healthy rhythm and I take solace in that. Wherever Kaylee is, whatever she's doing, she's still alive.

But there are far too many flames flickering below to account only for the wounds Damien inflicted on Kaylee and me. It's the first sign I've had that there are multiple people inside the building. Is Kaylee one of them?

Is Jake?

My stomach is already in my mouth when we tumble across the sky and through the roof. My glimpse of the bakery is brief, but I see no sign of Kay. And though I'm wrapped in the tar of fear, both mine and the demon's, I find that hope again—the hope that's been buried deep beneath the fear. It surfaces.

As long as one of us is free to call for help, we still have a chance.

Damien twists hard and fast, past the counter and into the kitchen beyond. And then he opens his black wings and we stop. It's abrupt, painful. The wind is knocked from my chest again as his inner wings tighten around my body. I struggle for breath as we descend. Through the floor, it seems.

There's a basement?

Of course there's a basement.

I refuse to close my eyes as we fall through the floor. The celestial light burns, but I let them water. I don't even blink. Instead, I press my face against Damien's transparent inner wings. Looking. Waiting. Hoping.

When the basement comes into view, my heart falters. The violence, most of it at least, originated here. The room is painted red with it. Splashed on the walls, coating the floors, the flames pounding out several different cadences. The first thing I see within the flames is Olivia. Her back is to us; scars, thick and puckered, have bubbled up on her calves. Scars that weren't there before—not at the lake.

It's unsettling to see what must always have been just beyond the reach of my terrestrial eyes. Would I have seen them before if I'd dared try? I don't know. And that terrifies me. Shames me. I should have tried to see her. To really *see* her.

But there's much to terrify in this room. Beyond Olivia, I see the boys. My boys. Jake and Marco sit back-to-back, their hands and legs strapped to chairs. Jake's hands wrap Marco's wrists and I swell with pride. Even broken, his hands can heal. Even stolen, he seeks the lost.

Unceremoniously, Damien opens his inner wings and I'm

shoved to the floor. He materializes behind me, his terrestrial hand twisting again in my hair, yanking me to my feet. My scalp is already tender, and despite my intention to be brave, I cry out.

More demonic laughter.

And then a wave of confusion crashes over me. I'm no longer wrapped in his wings, but my celestial vision remains entirely intact. In another place, in a peaceful room, this might be inspiring, but here, with crimson stains of violence surrounding me, the hues spinning and glowing, I try to blink away the Celestial, baffled by its totality. Two more quick blinks and I realize I'm not the only one confused. Olivia spins at my sloppy entrance, and Marco curses in surprise.

I want to explain. Tell them I'm here to save the day, but Damien kicks the legs I've locked in defiance and my knees buckle, my face inches from Jake's.

"Your girlfriend's here," Damien says.

I don't know how many seconds pass, but in all of them I let my eyes devour Jake. First I sweep them over his body, looking for injury, looking for pain and fear. Something's wrong with his right shoulder, I can see that immediately. Violence bubbles there, red and angry. And his arm, even tied back, juts at an unnatural angle. His head and face have lacerations. The one on his temple is deep, so deep I wish for the millionth time that I had his gift. That I could heal.

But I can't.

I can see the pain but I can't fix it.

And now my eyes find Jake's. The same twin flames I saw in the Stratus cemetery the day I first saw into the Celestial stare back at me. They're white-hot with love's greatest expression. If he had celestial eyes, I know he'd see the same pure love in mine, but the idea of it is enough to make me ill. This bond, this choice, this promise, it's exactly why we can be used against one another.

I want to close my eyes on him, like I've done so many times before, pretend demons are mythological nonsense, that angels only appear in freaky paranormal novels, but I refuse to lie to myself. Damien's presence makes the lie hard to swallow anyway. If his plan holds firm, we're meeting the Prince soon, and I can't help but wonder how much darkness it would take to dim the lights in Jake's eyes.

What would the Prince do to me to force Jake's compliance? How hard would it be to corrupt the gift in his hands? I don't know. Jake is stronger than any one human ever should be, but the fire burning behind those black lashes says he'd die for me if he could. He'd take a bullet for me, or a knife. He'd throw himself on a grenade. He'd hang so I could walk free, but is there anything the Prince of Darkness could do to me to force Jake, a boy raised by an angel, to choose corruption?

I don't know, and the not knowing is a pain I can't tolerate.

I cry out, wrenching myself from Damien's grip and falling into Jake. My knees land on his thighs, our faces colliding. I taste blood, but I kiss him anyway. He winces, but I don't pull back. I'm selfish. I need this moment because we're not guaranteed another one. And then I'm talking and I don't think God Himself could shut me up.

"I love you," I say. It's not romantic, my declaration. It's too loud, too brusque; there are too many people here. Marco and Olivia do what they can to fade into the shadows, but there's a demon standing behind me, for crying out loud.

I don't care. I have things to say.

"I've never said it to you. I don't know why that is, why I've never said it, why *we've* never said it, but I do. I love you."

Jake's eyes slide to Damien, who is chuckling once again. Apparently I amuse the monster.

"Brielle," Jake says, his voice nothing but a whisper in the storm. Tears, like drops of paint, roll down his face, but the words that have been trapped in my throat for the past two days won't be silenced. They tumble out.

"Damien knows I love you," I say. "My eyes told him that months ago. I don't care who knows. They're going to try to tear us apart—Darkness is—I know that. But your soul, Jake, your soul is far more important than how I feel about you. Far more important than how you feel about me. Far more important than some ring in a chest and a future we were never really promised."

It hurts, this confession of mine. These words that I've needed to say are worse than Damien's dagger slicing into my chest, because with them I give away my heart. But I've been presumptuous, thinking I know best. Thinking I've decoded heaven, that I know what the future holds. That because I caught a glimpse of something that might be, could be, that I'm owed happiness. But I'm not. I'm not owed a thing.

"Don't try to save me," I tell him. "Don't agree to anything that would forfeit your soul. Promise me."

He leans closer, and I'm overwhelmed by a desire to have his arms around me. I grab his shoulders to make it so, but he's bound and shackled. I cry out, angry that I've been denied comfort.

"Fight fear," he tells me. "Never stop fighting."

What does that mean? What does it mean?

He didn't promise. I need to hear him say the words. And now I'm a teary mess. My face clouds with the tears I swore I wouldn't cry, my words spoken through an ocean of them.

"I love you, Jake, more than anything," I say. "More than life. More than death, but please, if you love me . . ."

Damien's laughter is unleashed now, and whatever I had planned to say, whatever possibility there was to conjure a promise out of Jake, is lost in the chaos of his hilarity.

"You love him far more than you should, little dancer."

I tear my eyes away from Jake's at Damien's statement. The man is gone—Marco and Olivia blinking at his disappearance—but before me stands the demon. He towers above us, the tops of his wings pressing through the ceiling above. But his charred wings aren't the thing making fear bubble from my eyes and run down my face. It spews from my heart and coats me with a frigid black tar. Next to the sheath at Damien's waist hangs the halo. My halo. Canaan's halo.

Questions jumble on my tongue, but I'm slow and afraid and my mouth does little more than fall open. I watch as—carelessly—Damien shoves Marco away from Jake. His chair rocks sideways and nearly falls, but Olivia is there. She rights it and steadies her friend, her beautiful face obstructed by the same fear that coats mine.

Damien draws his scimitar. The icy blade smokes in the heat of the Celestial. The stench makes me gag, but I refuse to take my eyes from the curved blade. He could do so much damage with that thing. Not just to Jake and me, but to Marco. To Olivia. And I have no idea where their souls lie.

But instead of inflicting violence, he cuts Jake free.

Jake cries out as his right arm falls from the bind and dangles strangely at his side. I lift his hand into mine, attempting to take the weight of his shoulder. Even now, in pain and misery, Jake's hands are warm. Fear runs down his chest, but I think it's mine. I'm spreading fear. I came to save the day and all I brought was terror.

Jake's grip tightens on my hand, and I follow his eyes back to Damien.

His weapon still clenched in his fist, his black eyes unhindered by the celestial light, Damien's inner wings reach out like strange alien appendages, and he scoops Jake and me to his chest. It happens so fast, I'm not prepared. My knees knock against Jake's, our foreheads too. Somehow Jake's other hand finds mine, and then we're airborne.

I hear Marco yell, but he's far out of my reach. There's nothing in the world but Jake and the white fire burning in his eyes.

13

Marco

"Untie me."

Marco's head has finally cleared. The vision the halo gave him lingers, confusing him. Frustrating everything he thought he knew, but for the moment at least, he can actually think. And he knows they need to move. Now.

"I could use a little help here," he says.

But Liv's eyes are trained on Jake's empty chair.

"Oh my g—" she says. "Do you know what I've done?"

"Yeah. You're awful," Marco says, but there's no conviction to the words. "Untie me so we can get out of here."

Liv is visibly shaken by what just happened. She stares at the chair, her arms hanging lifeless at her sides.

It baffles Marco. "Did you really think you were the only one at risk when you climbed into bed with that guy?" The words are barely out of his mouth when he realizes just how hypocritical they are. "Never mind," he mumbles. It wasn't so long ago that he was tangled up with Damien. He owns a share in Ali's death. Something he tries very hard not to dwell on.

"Where is he taking them?" Liv asks.

"I don't know, but if we're going to help them we've got to get out of here."

She laughs at that. Bitter. Angry. "We can't help them. They're gone. Lost. If Damien hasn't broken them yet, he will."

"Liv! Untie me."

Her eyes clear and she scowls at him, but she doesn't reach for his binds. She turns on her heel and marches to her seat in the shadows beneath the stairs.

"What are you doing?" Marco demands. "Over here!"

She reaches beneath a discarded rag and withdraws a knife. It's a short, stubby thing, a paring knife or something.

Marco stutters and then flashes her his best smolder. "You're going to use that to cut me free, right? Not gut me for chum?"

Her scowl deepens, but she steps behind him and saws through the binds. Relief hits Marco in several small explosions. His head understands before his legs that he's free. But when at last they get the message, he jumps from the chair and sets to examining his wrists. They're red from irritation, blood smeared up his forearms, but the wounds have healed over. He runs a thumb over them.

Liv tosses the knife back into the shadows. "Your friend has a gift."

"And Damien's going to kill him for it," Marco says. "Is that how this works?"

"These guys don't kill, Marco. Not often. Not outright. Killing's too fast. Too clean. He wanted the bracelet."

"The halo," Marco corrects. "And you hand delivered it to him. Why?"

"*We* hand delivered it to him."

"I didn't have a clue it was in the bag, Olivia."

"How could you not know? I can feel the thing a mile away."

The thought cows Marco. "Do you really think it belonged to an angel?"

She shrugs.

"Do you even believe in angels?" He feels a bit like a kindergartner asking the question, but he wants to know. Does Liv believe?

"Believing in demons is easy enough when you've lived the life I've lived, Marco. But if there are angels out there, I've got a bunch of questions that need answering."

"Like . . ."

"Like 'where the heck have *you* been?'"

"Yeah, that . . . that's a good one." But he remembers again that flash of red hair at the prison, keys and freedom jammed into his hand. "Here, let me see that arm."

Before she can jerk it away, he takes her wrist. Soft, kind. He wishes with everything in him that he could show her men can be those things.

"Henry's man did this to you?"

"It was a long time ago," she says, her voice thin. Her lipstick is smudged, her glossy hair rumpled, but her eyes are dry.

"Not so long, Liv."

"Long enough." She covers the scars with her other hand. "Feels like I've always had them."

"I remember a time when you didn't," Marco says.

"That was before. Before my dad died, and then Mom." Liv's chin trembles. "Before Javan."

"I'm so sorry, Liv. You deserved better. You deserved the best of everything."

She shakes out her hair, blinks back the start of a tear. "In some ways, I have the best. The very best."

Marco nods. "Your car, your house. Your job. But in other ways . . ."

"Yeah. In other ways, I got screwed."

Marco can't decide if it's awkward, holding her arm like this. Can't decide if he should just let her go. "At least you weren't accused of killing your pregnant girlfriend."

She stiffens, and then it really is awkward. Because now he's thinking of two beautiful, broken girls. He never should have brought Ali into this. His hand freezes on her arm.

But Liv is fast to recover. "I've done worse," she says. "Things only I can accuse myself of. Things no one knows."

"You haven't done worse," Marco says.

But her eyes are hard, her face set. "I have."

A quick breath whistles across his teeth, but there's no time to discuss it further. They have to get going.

"Let's just . . . What are we going to do about Jake and Brielle?"

"There's nothing to do, Marco." She stoops and picks up a scuffed red heel. "They're gone, and I'm going home. You should do the same."

He kicks at the yellow flowered chair, splintering the wood. "You can just walk away? After Jake . . . after everything? We have to do something."

She puts her hand on his shoulder, looks him straight in the eye. "I'm sorry for them. Truly. I didn't know Damien was going to take Jake. Or the girl. He hired me to find the bracelet, and now that he has it I can go home, get back to work."

But there's something in the way she says it. "Hired you or blackmailed you? What does he have on you, Liv?"

Her hand slides away, down his shirt, over his heart. "Does

it matter? He doesn't need me anymore. If I stick around, if I go chasing after him, I'll just draw attention to myself and to—"

"The chain he has locked around your neck?"

She tilts her head, like her king's just been checked. It's the sadness that breaks him. Liv looks just like she did standing on that street so many years ago. Forced to settle for the lot she'd been given when all along she was meant for something greater. Marco steps toward her, but she moves away, her back pressed into the wall.

"You really think Damien's going to leave you alone? His man killed Ali because she stumbled into his world, and he all but branded you tonight. You're his, and he's coming back for you. Unless we can find a way to help Jake and Brielle."

"I'm missing why they have the power to change anything, but that's beside the point. You planning to sprout wings and fly?" She tries to mock him, tries to laugh, but there's no sharpness to the blade. "My car's going back to Portland. If you want a ride there, it's yours—as long as you keep your fingers off my radio. If you're heading somewhere else . . ."

Thwack!

A heavy *thud* comes from above, echoing around the basement. Marco twists toward the metal staircase. A powdery white cloud tumbles down the stairs—flour by the smell of it. He and Liv curse in unison as two Tasmanian Devils emerge from the fog.

"Jinx," Kaylee says, stumbling down the last two steps. "You two have potty mouths, but you both owe me Cokes. And I could use some caffeine, so I'm cashing in soon."

"Kaylee?" Marco asks. "What happened to your face?"

Her left cheek and eye are a mess. Even in the dank basement light, he can see she's swollen and bruised.

"Damien," she says, working her jaw. "He's got quite a backhand. In fact, I think I'm going to sit for a sec. I'm still kind of . . ." She draws circles in the air with her pointer fingers.

"What are you doing here?" Liv asks.

"Yeah, sorry." Kaylee lowers herself carefully onto the bottom stair. "I really was trying to give you two a minute. At least, it sounded like you could use a minute." She rolls her neck and exhales. Loud. Shaky. "You asked me something, right? Oh yeah. What am I doing here? Easy. I'm here to rescue you." She puts both fists on her hips, wincing at the movement. "Shazam!"

Liv wrinkles her face. "Shazam?"

"Captain Marvel," Marco says.

"Two points to the tall, lanky one," Kaylee says, looking around. "Gah, this place is awful. And kind of mysterious." Her eyes light up. "It's like something out of *The Goonies*. You think?"

"Maybe," Marco says, a reluctant smile pulling at his face. "I guess."

"Sloth's not tied up down here, is he? *Hey, you guys!*"

Marco glances sideways at Liv, but she's sliding her other shoe into place. "Kay, do you have a car?"

"Yeah. Slugger's parked just past the bridge."

"Well, look at that," Marco says. "I guess I do have a ride."

"And with a Goonie, no less," Liv says, straightening up. "How did you find us, Kaylee?"

"Some supernatural freaky stuff, that's how." She twists her arm, trying to get a good look at her elbow.

Liv cocks her head, clears her throat. Kaylee's eyes move from Liv to Marco and back again.

"You want details. Okay, well, some pages from Ali's journal showed up in that chest of Canaan's. Okay, not his real chest, you understand, but that black shiny thing at the foot of his bed, you know? You don't know. Okay. Don't tell Elle I said that. It's hard to keep track of what everyone knows and, well, doesn't know. Anyway, we found these pages *somewhere*, and on one of these pages Ali had sketched a lighthouse. Bellwether. And then we found Liv's cell number on one of the other pages—"

"From Ali's journal?" Marco asks, turning to Liv. "You knew Ali?"

"How could I?" But Liv's response is too fast, too quipped, and Marco remembers.

"Your arm," he says. "Ali sketched your arm."

"Yeah, that's what Elle said too," Kaylee says, removing her slippers, shaking out the dirt.

"You knew Ali." Marco's not asking now. He knows. His brain shifts into rewind. "She saw your arm, before Javan healed the scars. She drew it."

"What are these scars everyone keeps talking about?" Kay asks.

But Marco's locked away with Liv. It's just the two of them, his dead girlfriend, and three jagged scars.

"I don't know what you're talking about, Marco. If she sketched my arm, she did it without my knowing. I never met Ali."

He almost believes her. He considers arguing, demanding the truth, but thus far that hasn't worked with Liv. He lifts her arm again. "But these scars weren't here before. When did Javan . . . heal them?"

She rolls her neck, kneading the muscles with her other hand. "Javan didn't heal these. The scars on my legs, yes. As a reward for . . . good behavior, he made those disappear. But these? These disappeared when he did."

Marco shivers. "And now Damien's brought them back." He didn't know his hatred for Damien could burn any hotter, but it does. Tonight, it does.

"From one taskmaster to the next," Liv says. "It's like you said, I'm all but branded."

"But you can break free of this," he says, grabbing her shoulders, turning her toward him. "Like Jake said. There has to be a way."

"Maybe if I kill Henry," she says, her voice flat, her eyes like flint. "Maybe that'll make me better."

Her words sting; a lemon squeezed into a heart that's been cut open and laid bare. Is that all he's been doing? Trying to feel better?

"Look to your own chains, Houdini, before you cough up the key to mine." She turns to walk away, but Marco grabs her elbow. She jerks free and slips into the darkness beneath the staircase.

Marco can feel the tears burning his eyes, the sob tearing at the back of his throat. He coughs to clear it away, but all it does is settle a little lower, in his chest. Next to the hole Ali left.

Kaylee pushes herself off the bottom stair and steps toward Marco. She wraps her arms around his middle and squeezes. "I'm sorry, Marco Mysterioso," she whispers.

He clears his throat again, harder this time. "Here, let me look at your face."

Marco moves her onto the stairs, under the single bulb where he can see everything a little better.

"I finally got hold of Canaan," Kay says while he pokes and prods at her cheek.

"Did you tell him about Damien?"

"Ouch. Yeah. He's on his way."

"Here?" Liv asks, stepping out from beneath the stairs, her shirt straightened, her hair pulled into a low knot.

"I think this is just a bad bruise, Kay. And a lot of swelling. You're lucky he didn't break your eye socket."

"Canaan's coming here?" Liv tries again.

"Oh no, not here," Kaylee says. "He's on his way to Danakil."

Marco pulls back. "As in the Danakil Depression?"

"If by 'depression' you mean desert, then yes. That's where Damien's taking them. To the desert to meet Satan. Terrifying, right?" But she doesn't look terrified. She looks . . . exhilarated. "All righty, Marco, if you'd like a ride, you're more than welcome. Liv, you can drive yourself home. No offense, but until we know we can trust you, you'll have to stay out of Stratus."

Liv snorts. "Oh, sweetie. You don't have that kind of power."

"No, but I do." Helene appears in the center of their little circle. Kaylee jumps, Liv squeals, and even Marco gasps at her sudden appearance.

"You too?" Liv asks. "Use a door or something next time. Climb a stair."

Helene's wearing a long, pale dress that reminds Marco of a toga. Her auburn hair is braided and twisted into a circlet atop her head. But he sees so much more than her appearance when he looks at her.

"You broke me out of jail," he says.

"You're fighting the doubt." Her eyes are bright, her smile wide. "That's good."

"But why?" He can't comprehend it. "I was accused of murder. Why free me?"

"Providence. Those things are God's call, not mine."

Providence. The word that won't die. It crashes through

Marco's mind like a rhinoceros, wreaking havoc, turning everything over.

Helene shifts her gaze to Liv. "I'll be staying with you for a while."

Liv shakes out her shoulders, her carefully maintained composure all but gone. "You wanna drag your claws down my arm too? Mark me? Stake a claim? You're a little late for that."

"No claws," Helene says, her eyes tender. "Just me. Shielding you."

Liv huffs. "Any way I can talk you out of that?"

"Sorry," Helene says, sarcasm notably absent from her tone. "You don't have that kind of power."

Liv bristles. "Well, just . . . just stay invisible, all right?" She stomps past Marco and Kaylee, her shoes ringing against the stairs.

Marco watches her go, and then Helene steps toward him.

"Be wise," she says. "Be brave." With a nod, she turns away.

"Thank you," Marco says, his words rushed, afraid she'll go before he can say them. "For what you did, breaking me out. You gave me a chance to make things right. To tell my story. If you hadn't come . . ."

"I was the Father's hands and feet, Marco. Nothing more." She's so small, so like Ali. Same delicate face, same tiny hands. "He wanted your story told. He gave you that chance. I just unlocked the door."

She did a lot more than that. He knows she did, and he has questions, so many of them, but with a wink at Kaylee, Helene disappears.

"I'm not a fan of the whole vanishing thing," Kaylee says. "It's very *I Dream of Jeannie.*"

"It's the reappearing part that freaks me out."

"Yeah. That too." Kaylee rubs her jaw, looks around. "There's no way we're going to beat that exit, but are you ready?"

"Yeah. Let me just . . ." Marco stoops to gather up his belongings still strewn across the floor. His bag, a T-shirt, Ali's journal. He runs his fingers over the leather book before folding it in half and sliding it into his back pocket. He zips the bag and throws it over his shoulder.

"You mind if we make a little detour?"

Kay crosses her arms. "Are you plotting, Mysterioso?"

"Not in the slightest."

"You're not going to kill Henry, are you? 'Cause Slugger's a Bug. A Volkswagen Beetle. We'd have to cram the body in the bonnet. The bonnet, Marco. Plus, I'd be the worst getaway driver ever."

A smile's taken Marco's face before he thinks to fight it. "You ever think about acting? Your comic timing is very . . ."

"Betty White?" Kay tries.

"Phoebe Buffay."

"I'm flattered, but no. I fall daily. Cameras would be all kinds of unhelpful. No murder, okay? Promise me."

"No murder," he says. "Shall I pinkie swear?"

Kay's standing two steps higher than he is, and when she leans forward, her forehead nearly smacks his. Her brown eyes rove his face, like two searchlights routing out a criminal.

After a minute she straightens up, turns on her heel, and marches up the stairs, puffs of flour squelching from her slippers.

"All right," she calls over her shoulder. "Detour it is. But if Slugger poops out, you're pushing."

14

Brielle

It's a long time before either of us says a word. I've deflated. The need to talk, to make sure Jake knew how I felt about him, had grown in the hours he was gone. Not just gone—taken. It sat in my chest like an ever-expanding balloon pressing the words from my mouth, forcing my fears into the open air. Now, crammed against one another, shoved against Damien's body, my words have been sucked away by the reality burning in Jake's eyes.

We're going to see the Prince.

Celestial heat presses against Damien's inner wings, warming one side of my body, while the other, the side pressed against his chest, burns with an icy chill.

The ocean shines below us, so bright, so blue it's hard to believe dark waters lie beneath its waves. Fathoms and fathoms of it. Eventually land replaces water, but whether it's hours or minutes that pass, I couldn't say. Jake and I both drift in and out of consciousness. The violent stains of his assaulted body fill the space between us, and when I close my eyes, the red flames seep through my eyelids. I don't dream, and for that I'm grateful. The flames are terrifying enough.

Are we flying over the States? Are we flying across the Atlantic? Are there other avenues open to the angelic that mortals are unaware of? These questions pass through my mind like a train that blunders right through its scheduled stop. I don't know and I don't really care. Not enough to sort out the answers. Soon enough we'll be standing before the Prince. And while there are so many things I don't know, I'm fairly certain about one.

"He'll separate us," I shout over the flapping of wings.

Jake tries to answer, but the fiery red stains pulsing all over his body flare, and he clamps his mouth and eyes shut. The colors lighting his face dim, and he squeezes my hand tighter in response.

His strength is waning, but he doesn't have to answer now. Months ago he told me the way evil would most likely use two souls bound like ours. The Prince will separate us. Divide us. He'll tear us apart and use our bond against us. I never thought love could be used as a weapon. But in the hand of Darkness, I suppose most anything can.

Jake's eyes flutter open and he shifts, pressing his shoulder into Damien. I must give him a strange look because he attempts to smile. "Gigantic ice pack."

"I wish I could fix you," I say.

"I wish you could too."

Damien snaps his wings wide, tilting to the right on currents of celestial air. Wind snakes by, but it's quieter without the beating of wings to contend with.

"When I said 'I love you,' you didn't say it back," I say.

A hint of Jake's crooked smile emerges. "You didn't give me a chance."

"You do. I mean, I know you do. Your eyes say it every day, but you've never said it out loud. I just . . ."

Damien chuckles. Not in our heads. No, he's much more brash about it. He opens his mouth and a demented sort of cackle ripples through the air. A braying donkey. A laughing hyena.

He's listening.

Of course he's listening.

Jake's smile disappears and he presses his face closer, violence coloring him red. He's hurting, but he opens his mouth to speak.

It's wrong. So, so wrong. I don't want to share this moment with anyone. Certainly not with Damien—a monster who's actually killed me, who's stolen and beaten the guy I want to spend every one of my days with.

I press my lips to Jake's, the words caught somewhere between us.

"Tell me later," I say. "When we're back in Stratus."

"Deal," he says, peering at me with half-open eyes. His lips are moist, shimmering like sunset waves. I lean in once more, but Damien wraps his charred outer wings tight against us and we fall into a dive.

Our faces connect, my lip splitting against his tooth. Jake presses the hand of his good arm to my chest, lifting me from his face and steadying me against Damien's inner wing. But the pressure is intense. Damien's wings continue to tighten, and Jake's arm bends. He can't hold me at a distance any longer. The strength in his arm gives out and our faces press together, my lips settling into the soft curve of his cheek, my eyes pushed tightly against his forehead.

And then I hear music. It comes in bursts and fades, but I swear I hear it. It's caught in the wind, but it's there. A voice. Loud, robust. I force my eyes open and tip my chin up, but black feathers are the only thing I see.

"Canaan," Jake says, his voice muffled, his mouth moving against my lips. "It's Canaan."

Jake's arms tighten around my waist, and my skin tingles with the hope his name brings.

Canaan!

If he's here, that means Kaylee was able to call for help. If he's here, she must be safe. Or as safe as Kaylee ever is. But when Damien rights us and his outer wings part like gothic curtains torn asunder, I am wholly unprepared for what I see.

We're still strapped to him, a crusty-feeling platform beneath our feet. Dark forces—several hundred of them—surround us, swords drawn, wings at attention. Ugly, vicious sneers on every face. Some stare at us, salivating. Others hiss at Canaan, who stands opposite us.

Jake was right. He's here, his mouth wide open, song pouring forth. His body bears the marks of countless demonic swords, the icy wounds hissing and smoking on his celestially hot skin. Amidst a field of lime and yellow patches of brittle-looking earth, he stands. As we watch, he's forced to his knees. Tendrils of worship spiral from his chest and mouth. So bright, so fiery orange it's nearly lost in the Creamsicle sky. On either side of him, a demon holds each arm.

But I've never seen demons like this. They're huge. Bigger than Canaan. Bigger than Damien. Their chests are strapped with breastplates that cover the entire abdomen, chest, and shoulders. Interlocking dragon wings have been hammered into them. Each one's head is covered in a distinct kind of helmet, shaped to protect the demon's deformed skull. Their legs are also strapped with armor, like scales wrapping them from hip to ankle, leaving only their massive arms bare.

With talons sharpened to a point, they stretch Canaan's arms wide. Another armored demon hovers above, shredding his wings, flaying white feather from bone. Canaan's muscled body shudders at the abuse as down freckles the sky.

Blood and gore included, this has to be the most violent thing I've ever witnessed. I scream, my throat stinging with the effort. Jake's voice fuses with mine, angry tears ripping down his face.

But as horrific as the sight is, our cries are lost in Canaan's song. So loud. So strong. So vibrant.

Damien opens his inner wings, and we tumble to our knees.

"Canaan," I whisper, looking around.

But the Celestial's gone now. The demonic army is gone. One look behind me and I see Damien is gone. Our Shield, bloodied and broken, has been shrouded by the terrestrial veil. To any other human, it would seem Jake and I are alone in this wretched place, but we're not so deceived. We're not alone, and that fact is chilling even in the sweltering heat.

I stare gape-mouthed at Danakil. Like a torture chamber, a spiked ball and chain, a cat-o'-nine-tails, its cruelty couldn't be more apparent.

The ground bites at my bare legs, at my hands. I expected sand. I expected dirt. But Danakil is unlike any desert I've seen in any photograph. Jake and I kneel on a knotty platform, similar to the one Canaan stood on just moments ago. I say a prayer for him and another. Next to me Jake's words are indecipherable, but I know he's praying as well. I wrap my arm around his waist, trying to keep the weight off his shoulder. Trying to do anything to make this easier for him. But everything here hurts.

The platform below us pricks like coral beneath my legs, but when I scrape my fingernails against it, tiny granules slip under my nails and stick to the pads of my fingers. I rub them against my palm.

"Salt," Jake says, dabbing a finger to his tongue. I do the same. I notice then how stiff my upper lip is. I pull my hand away to see flecks of dried blood. I've split my lip a couple of times in the hours that have passed, but there's no cut now. The scrape on my chin has also healed, leaving behind only a stained face and collar. Being pressed against Jake has many, many advantages.

"There's so much of it," Jake says, crushing the salt between his thumb and forefinger.

"A wasteland of salt," Canaan had said. He wasn't kidding. The salt has formed enormous flat lumps that jut from the ground like trodden mushrooms. They surround us, an army of petrified suction cups spread across the desert. I start to count them, but there are too many.

And while the desert tastes of salt, it smells of sulfur. Of brimstone. It's a smell I will always associate with evil. I tug the collar of Jake's blue sweatshirt over my mouth and nose, willing my stomach to remain intact. In the distance a dark mountain rises. To our right and left, beyond the yellow salt platforms, I see what look like pools of green acid. Some kind of hot spring, maybe.

"I can't believe people live here." Sweat coats my skin now, soaking into my clothes. It has to be at least 115 degrees under the sweltering sun. I release Jake's waist for a moment and strip off the sweatshirt, grateful for the sleeveless shirt beneath. But now the salt in the air mixes with my sweat, sliding into the creases of my elbows and knees, twisting in the beads around my neck. It grates like sandpaper. "This is what I imagined hell would look like."

"It's terrible," Jake says. Sweat drips down his face, turning his sandy hair dark and slicking it to his forehead.

I see fear. It'd be easy to miss—here, in this hostile environment, with so many things to stimulate my senses. But the black stain spreading like spilled ink from Jake's chest reminds me just how much is at stake.

I reach out a hand and press it to his sternum. Jake gasps at my touch and the fear latches on, clamping my fingers. Before it can shake me, before it can make me tremble, I pray. Out loud. Which is hard for me, because I hate looking stupid. I'm not sure I get all the words in the right order, but I know that God promised not to leave us or forsake us. I know, because I read it in Mom's Bible. And I know that He's everywhere. Even here, in the cruelest place on earth where hope has been shredded like Canaan's wing, we can't escape Him. And that means fear can't escape Him. I remind myself of that. I remind Jake.

I remind fear.

And it works.

Hundreds of tiny explosions pop and hiss around my hand. One right after the other, until the fear is nothing but a dissipating fog.

I pull my hand away, but Jake grabs it.

"We can't let fear win," he says. "We can't."

"I know."

And then he's yanked from my grip. Cloaked by someone or something. My heart falters, my courage wanes, but I cling to the idea that it was a power of light that took Jake. That I'll be next. I try to fill myself up with all kinds of positive thoughts.

But as the minutes pass, hope fades, and my fingers hold nothing but air.

When the fear starts dripping from my hair, when it snakes itself around my arm and wraps the very hand I just defeated it with—when I find myself suffocating on the black thickness as it pours from my mouth, that's when I know.

I can't win without Jake.

Without the halo.

I'm not strong enough.

I've never been strong enough.

15

Jake

When he's snatched from Brielle's side, Jake expects to be slammed against something hard and cold. The heavenly body of one of the Prince's underlings. Damien, maybe. So when the heat of the desert gives way to the heat of the Celestial, Jake groans with exhausted relief. He's been scooped up awkwardly and his injured arm only complicates matters, but even as he moves and adjusts he can feel the heat seeping into his shoulder, into his heart, soothing things he didn't know were tender. He can feel his shoulder healing.

"Canaan?"

"I'm here." The angel's voice is strong and steady. The first sure thing that's entered Jake's mind in hours.

"I knew you'd come," he says, his eyes closing. He doesn't have the strength to fight the serenity that surrounds him. He's wounded and exhausted, and the Celestial is beyond inviting. Still, he squirms, trying to find complete comfort.

Canaan's inner wings loosen, putting a few feet between himself and Jake and creating a cradle of sorts. Jake slides to the center and rolls onto his back, facing his Shield as they soar through the sky.

"Hold on, son," Canaan says, his voice stiff, his lips still. "Rest."

Jake lets the fire of healing replace the pain. It nearly lulls him to sleep, the brightness and the colors filling his thoughts, streaking everything with peace. He could revel in this kind of slumber for days, but in the back of his mind he understands there are things to fear. That this healing is only the beginning. And it's only moments before a very real, very terrifying thought wakes him.

"Where's Brielle?" he says, his eyes flying open. "Why didn't you grab her?" He tries to sit up, but Canaan's wings tighten around his arms, keeping him still.

"I tried," Canaan says, his face painfully stoic, golden tears running down his face. They drip from his chin and land on Jake's chest. In all their years together, Jake's never seen him cry—not in his celestial form—and it tells Jake just how desperate a situation Brielle is in. "The Creator wouldn't allow it."

"What?" Like his laugh, Canaan's tears are contagious, and Jake doesn't attempt to stop the ones now running down his face. "Why?"

Another voice, shrill and noxious, slips into Jake's mind. "The Prince has other plans for her."

Over Canaan's shoulder a demon flies into Jake's line of sight. His scimitar is outstretched, aimed at Canaan's neck. A warrior-like impulse overwhelms Jake, and he reaches for the sword of light Canaan always keeps sheathed at his hip. As if he could wield it, even lift it.

But it doesn't matter. The scabbard is empty.

And for the first time since he's been pulled into the Celestial, Jake notices Canaan's hands. They hang loosely at his waist, shackled with chains made of the same icy stone the Fallen use to fashion their blades.

"We're being escorted," Canaan says. He adjusts his inner wings, turning Jake so that he faces outward. "Look."

Jake presses his palms to the transparent wings, looking out over the desert. The world is a show of fire and color, vibrant earth tones dotted with patches of lime and apple red. His arm and shoulder are free of pain, but what he sees brings an entirely different kind of ache.

They're surrounded on all sides by demonic warriors. Thick demons, clad in dragon armor, like the ones he saw mutilating Canaan. Suddenly things don't make sense.

"We saw you attacked," Jake says, "your feathers stripped."

"You saw what the Prince wanted you to see," Canaan says.

It seems Canaan's not closed his mind to their demonic escort. They chuckle and hiss, leaving Jake feeling left out of a very awful, very black kind of joke.

"The Prince manipulates what is," Canaan continues, "and turns it into what isn't. I'm here, yes. I came like you knew I would, but I was outnumbered and beaten. I was shackled. Instead of showing you that, he showed you my destruction. My spiritual flaying. He always starts with what's possible, Jake. His lies are built with light."

It's a terrifying thought. Especially with Brielle suffering alone. She counts on her eyes, on what she sees—especially in the Celestial. With that kind of power to fuel his lies, the Prince could convince her of almost anything.

"But how would he—"

"Everything you see—everything—is based on how the light is filtered through your eyes. Temperature affects that. The chill of fear affects that. When a created being, like the Prince, learns to manipulate the light . . ."

"A mirage," Jake says, sickened. "He made us see something that wasn't there."

"I finally understand why he likes the desert so much."

"Circle back, Shield," a demon hisses. "Someone wants to talk to you."

The demons lift their weapons higher, and Jake finds himself facing the sharpened point of a crooked sword.

"It should be me down there. Damien took me." And then a sobering pain tears through Jake. "Why would the Creator leave her to the Prince?"

"Close your mouth, human, and open your eyes. Maybe you'll learn something." But as the seconds pass, it's not the demon who convinces Jake to turn his attention back to the ground, it's Jake's desperate need to know.

Canaan does as he's told, his outer wings stretched wide, circling. The demons stay within a wingspan of him, haughty looks on their faces.

"Who are these demons, Canaan? The Palatine?"

The Fallen around him huff, but it's Canaan who answers, and this time it seems he's closed his mind to all but Jake. "They're the Prince's Guard. Often they're promoted from the Palatine, but the Guard act as his personal attendants. They're his *favorites,* and they take great pride in that."

Jake wonders if their pride has made them lazy, if their pride has made them weak. If that's why it takes nearly a dozen of these gigantic, armored demons to secure one Shield.

A Shield who's been disarmed, carries a charge, and has his hands shackled.

It's not long before Brielle comes into view. It doesn't look like she's moved. She remains kneeling on the platform of salt, fear seeping from her chest and leaking from her scalp. Fog rises from the muck, obscuring their view momentarily. But as Canaan circles, the fog shifts and he sees her. He's never seen her so bound by fear. If he could take her place he would. But if the Creator willed this, what can he do?

He is forced into inaction, and the stone weight of that presses down, crushing his heart.

If only he had Canaan's ability to communicate telepathically. Surely Canaan has a plan for escape. There has to be something they can do. Something!

Movement catches Jake's attention, and he turns his head. Emerging from the ground just feet from Brielle is Lucifer himself.

The Proud One.

The Great Dragon.

Satan.

Jake's never seen the Prince before, but there's no mistaking him. By all accounts, he's the most beautiful, the most seductive, the most dangerous of all created beings. And this creature lives up to every one of those reports.

His wings move gracefully as he emerges from the ground. Up and down with elegance and poise. And then with a sky-splitting sound, he snaps them wide. Bright white and glowing, their tips stained black. Moments later Damien rises from the ground behind his lord and prince. His improved appearance is nothing to that of his superior's, but as he flies in the Prince's wake, there is something of victory in his posture.

"Damien gave your halo to the Prince," Jake says. Based on what he sees below, he can only assume the Prince received the halo with all the enthusiasm Damien had hoped for. Jake's fist is balled tight, a desire to drive it into Damien's fanged mouth consuming him. But Canaan doesn't seem the least bit concerned about his halo.

"How is Brielle's celestial sight?" Canaan asks. "She doesn't seem to notice their presence."

"Still sporadic," Jake says. "She saw my fear. Destroyed my fear. But I don't know. We didn't speak much."

"The Prince will have a level of control over what she sees here." Canaan drops lower, a prayer rumbling in his chest. "God's will be done," he says.

"Sometimes that's not a comfort."

"I know."

Damien and the Prince fly low, circling the skies above Brielle. They seem to be conversing, their minds closed to the outside. After several rotations they turn toward Jake and Canaan.

Rumors of the Prince's beauty haven't done him justice. Jake would never have guessed he'd be so . . . glorious. His skin is alabaster, his hair midnight, his eyes two pale blue gemstones throwing back the light of the Celestial.

Strange that even the devil reflects God's glory.

Their escort snaps to attention as the Prince's wings pull him to a stop. Everything about him screams winter. The frosty chill that smacks Jake in the face as he approaches, the snow-white skin, the fear that twists down his arm like a rivulet of muddy rainwater.

"Let her go," Jake says, doing his best to stifle every sign of fear. It's not the Prince he fears anyway.

The Prince moves closer, too close for Canaan apparently. His wings tick, moving them back. The Prince closes the distance again, his topaz eyes traveling Jake's body.

"Let her go," Jake says again.

"I think we'll let her make that decision herself," the Prince says. "Unlike some, I would never take that choice from her." His eyes leave Jake's and meet Canaan's. "Never."

"Having choices to make doesn't mean we're free," Canaan says.

"Semantics will always be the mountain you and I can't scale, old friend. But a lack of options certainly can't mean freedom. And speaking of lack," he says, "you seem to have lost something."

And then Canaan's golden halo is there, hovering between them.

"It's Brielle's," Canaan says. "It was given to me by the Creator. I made it a gift to Jake, and he in turn gave it to her."

"And now it's mine."

"Damien stole it to earn your favor," Canaan says. "That does not make it yours. It just proves you're the thief you've always been."

"Thief? Again, semantics. But I'll play by your rules. What if *she* were to give it to me? Would that make it mine?"

Jake feels Canaan go rigid, but his Shield remains silent.

"Oh, come now," the Prince says. "I'm not offended; I know I'm a thief. But if your logic is sound, then you must agree that if she were to give the halo to me, that would make it mine. Yes?"

"It doesn't matter, because she'd never give it to you," Jake says.

"Giving a golden ring to the fairest one of all," he says, grandly gesturing to himself, "sounds like a fairy-tale ending to me. And I'll tell you a little secret, boy"—he moves closer—"pretty girls like happy endings."

"Canaan's halo on your head is not a happy ending. Brielle. Wouldn't."

The Prince crosses his arms, amusement all over his face. Jake balls up his other fist. He'd love to break those perfect teeth.

"And why not? I see you're angry with me, but I want nothing more than a simple answer. I can be very persuasive. Why wouldn't your Brielle give me her halo?"

"You don't have to answer him, Jake." It's Canaan. In his head.

Jake wants to answer him. To hurt the Prince with his words. But he struggles. The Prince is so certain. So confident. "Because that would be, it would be . . ."

"Disloyal? Is that the word you're looking for? Or maybe it's *unforgivable*?" The Prince's eyes narrow at the word. "If Brielle gave away the gift you gave her—to the Great Dragon, of all creatures—that would make her unforgivable, wouldn't it?"

"She wouldn't."

"Shall we make a little wager?" the Prince says.

"No." It's Canaan, his mind open for all to hear. "You don't get to make deals with my charge."

"I wondered when you'd pipe up." The Prince raises his eyes to Canaan's. He smiles then and lifts the halo from the sky. "It's nice," he says. "A magnificent crown. But I'm certain I could do better."

The Prince raises his hand, and Damien moves to his side. "Take them home," he says.

"But, Lord Prince," Damien stutters, "you wanted both. I brought them both."

"And you've been rewarded for doing so. But now that I've seen them, I think I'll talk to the girl alone."

"We're not leaving without Brielle," Jake says.

"Oh, but you are." All hilarity has gone from his face now. For the first time the Prince looks evil. "She'll be returned to you. I don't keep many promises, but this is one you can count on."

"Forget it," Jake says.

"Why drag Jake out here if you're going to turn us loose?" Canaan asks.

The Prince's nostrils flare, but he's silent.

"Ah." There's laughter in Canaan's mind now. It's subdued, but it's there. "You've not been given permission to keep him."

"I don't need permission," the Prince says, but the words are delivered through clenched teeth, and everyone present knows this is a lie only he believes. He turns to Damien.

"Take these with you." The Prince gestures to demons circled about. "I'll keep the rest of the Guard with me." He turns then, flying toward the desert floor. Toward Brielle. Jake fights against Canaan's hold, but it's fast.

Damien barks a laugh. "Even if you could break free, boy, what could you do but fall?"

Canaan intervenes. "Are you to be my jailer, Damien? Is that the reward you get for turning over my crown?"

"One of many," Damien answers.

But as the Prince drifts farther and farther away, the tension in Jake's chest builds. Surely there's something he can do. Something he can offer the Prince in exchange for Brielle's release.

"Take me!" he cries.

The Prince turns, his face radiant. But his beauty disgusts Jake. Canaan's told him how the Prince keeps his appearance so pristine. By giving himself ample time to heal in the depths of his fortress, he's ensured his splendor remains intact. His skin glows white.

White like the light that shines in Brielle's eyes, white like the love she declared just hours ago. She came for him. That's why she's here. He can't leave her. He won't.

"Chivalry. An admirable trait, but you'll have to wait your turn."

And with that, the Prince drifts away.

"Move," Damien says, pressing the flat of his scimitar against Canaan's inner wings. The cold sears, and Jake pulls his hands away. "Do it, or I'll carry the boy to Stratus myself."

Indignantly, Canaan snaps his wings, but he pushes forward. This is the second time Jake's been tucked beneath these wings while leaving Brielle in mortal danger, and it's too much.

"Canaan, we can't leave her alone with him."

Canaan wraps his wings tighter around Jake and picks up speed. The Guard around him does the same.

"She's not alone, Jake. You have to believe that. She's never been alone."

16

Brielle

The minutes pass and I'm frozen here, on my knees. Sweat soaks through my shirt, the salty air sticking to my face. I think of the ocean, of Bellwether. I think of the rain. I'd give anything for a little fall of rain here in the desert. I'd give anything to see another sign of life. Another anyone.

I didn't bother turning my head left and right; I didn't whip around when Jake disappeared. I know what disappearing means. I know it means he's either as safe as a Shield can make him or in mortal danger. I did try to will my angel eyes to return, to let me see through the terrestrial veil, but they wouldn't cooperate, and now as the seconds tick by I'm forced to imagine the worst.

For whatever reason, I can't see the fear now—it disappeared with Jake—but I've learned to sense it. I know what it feels like when it takes me, when it breaks down the walls I've built around my heart to protect it. I know how it chills and bites as it enters my bloodstream, and I know the very moment I'm in its clutches. I try to breathe, to count the salt formations before me, but four little letters interrupt every attempt at distraction.

G. O. N. E.

Canaan's gone. And Jake. Again he's been ripped from my side, and though I knew we'd be separated, I didn't expect to be left here alone. I envisioned a scene with the devil himself, with demons and chains, with pain. But I didn't expect to be abandoned. It surprises me that I'd prefer the company of Satan to the complete and utter aloneness before me. But the salt stretches far and wide. Along the horizon the heat plays with my mind, haunting shapes that stare deep into my soul, smears of unearthly color that mock me.

And then a voice, an intoxicating voice grows from the desert itself.

"I'd ask you to stand, but you're captivating on your knees."

I can't tell if the words are in my mind alone, but with no one else around to hear them, it hardly matters. They're meant for me.

And they're lovely.

I feel the fear gurgle and slow to a trickle. I'm not alone.

I'm not alone.

I'd give anything to hear the strange disembodied voice again. Something deep inside my chest tells me I shouldn't want that, that I shouldn't entertain this speaker, but I do. I want to hear him say other things. My name. Yes! I want to hear him say my name.

"Gabrielle, isn't it?"

I shove to my feet and look left and right. I spin, searching the squash-colored salt platforms. I search the sky. Where? Where?

And then he's before me, standing on the platform adjacent to mine. Human, but most certainly not. Black curls hang around a face so pale I fear the scorching sun will blister it. His face is perfectly symmetrical, a plump bottom lip nestled lightly between his teeth, his eyes the palest blue I've ever seen. He stands there, his fingers twined before him, in a shirt precisely the color of his eyes. The collar hangs open and the sleeves are folded neatly at the elbow. His pants, the same soft color, hang loosely on his hips. His feet are bare and everything about him seems to shine, even to my terrestrial eyes. Another warning trills through my body, but I'm terrified he'll leave me. Terrified I'll be left alone.

I stand and walk to the edge of the platform, my toes sending a shiver of salt to the desert floor. It's only then that I see the danger in his eyes. Beyond anything I could have imagined, he's striking. Like a cobra, like a scorpion, like a crystal goblet full of cyanide.

Like forbidden fruit.

And I force myself to acknowledge what I've been stifling.

This is the Prince.

Not some handsome boy who can be trusted. Not an all-powerful Creator. On the contrary, he, too, is a created being. Like me. He's selfish and arrogant. And he wants to destroy everything I've been given.

Hatred floods me. Because it seems to be the only thing keeping the fear in check, I let it. It makes my muscles throb with a desire to lash out, to kick and flail and scratch at him, this fiend who's stolen so much. I bite back my question—the one my heart screams in staggering little gasps. But I don't ask him where Jake is. I won't. I refuse to discuss the things I love with seduction itself.

But I have to say something to this demon man. I have to say something to this desert snake staring back at me with mirrors in his eyes.

"What do you want?" My voice shakes, and I can't tell if it's from fear or anger. Probably both.

"Ironic," he says. "I was going to ask you the same thing." He's not like the other angels I've met. He's closer to Jake's height than Canaan's and has a similar boy-like charm. His eyes light up when he speaks, his tongue wetting his lips.

"I want to go home," I say.

A broad smile, the contagious kind, drops dimples into his cheeks, and the hatred I'd reined in only moments ago feels less important. I remind myself to hate him. To fear every word he breathes.

"The smell of cows and greasy diner food? That's what you want to go home to?"

"It's my home," I say.

"I thought you couldn't wait to leave Stratus. Perhaps I'm doing you a favor."

"The desert is a favor?"

"Sure. It's exciting. Exotic."

"Smells like rotten eggs."

He laughs, and I can't help the smile it brings on. I've only known one other person whose laugh carried that kind of power. My chest is tight, sick with emotion, and the hilarity hurts. And just like that, it's not funny anymore.

The Prince cocks his head, his own laugh falling silent.

"Offensive odors aside, when did that pinprick on the map become your world?"

He wants me to talk about Jake. But I won't.

"There was a time when you wished for more. You wanted beauty and art. A stage. An audience."

He leans forward, his shoulders squared. His arms are

extended just inches from his sides, but it gives him a look of power, of authority. And when he speaks, I almost believe him.

"I can give you that."

I'm not tempted. I'm not. But he's right. There was a time when our ugly little town nauseated me. When the lights of a city—any city—held such sway I would've given anything to touch them. I turn my face away, looking out over the yellow desert. Things have changed. I've changed. And my goals are different, but I'd be lying if I said I didn't miss that person. The girl who believed that all dreams were within her grasp. That she controlled her own destiny. It's an intoxicating notion, after all. But it's a lie.

"I know that look," he says. "You're writing me off."

"Because you're a liar."

He turns his palms up and shrugs. "Placate me, will you? Let yourself believe, for just a moment, that the what-ifs in this life are attainable. That to reach them, all you need is a little help, a little assistance from someone like me." He spreads his arms wide to match that smile of his. "Imagine this desert is my platter. Imagine that I could craft the very things you most want and offer them to you. What would you ask for?"

I'm done listening. "I want to go home."

"No, you don't," he says with obvious disgust. "You're much too special for Stratus. With all your potential, everything you've seen, you expect me to believe that the greatest desire of your heart is to go home?"

I've disappointed him, and for a fleeting moment I wonder how I could have deigned to fail such a magnificent being. It's a strange thought, an out-of-place thought, but as he continues to speak, it burrows into my mind. "Which of us is the liar now?" he asks.

"What are you talking about?"

"I'm talking about desire. Need. I'm talking about that gigantic hole in your chest that leaks fear."

I look down at my chest. And he's right, the fear's back. Hatred couldn't keep it at bay for long.

"I'm talking about the only way to stop the bleed, the only way to cap the leak. I'm talking about satisfying the monster that keeps chewing free. Tell me what you really want. Because we both know it isn't Smalltown, USA."

I want to tell him. I don't know why I want to tell him. Maybe it's just so I can hear Jake's name, feel it on my lips. Maybe it's because I want someone to tell me it's okay to be self-centered. I don't know, but the need to say it out loud feels like an open blister, every word he says stinging air on the wound. I want my feelings to mean something. I want my need to fit into someone's plan.

But I know it's the magic of his voice. The sorcery of his words.

"You've heard a lot of things about me, I know, and much of it is true. But there are things they've glossed over, things I could help you understand. I'm sure you have questions. About your friend Ali. About your mother."

He's grabbing my emotions, manipulating them like clay. I know he is, and yet I'm chained to how I feel. I don't know how to act against it.

"Gabrielle," he says, stepping toward me. "Come. Sit with me."

His platform is three or four feet from mine. He crouches and then throws his feet over the edge, where they dangle a foot or two off the desert floor. He waits there, looking up at me, a twisted Romeo and Juliet kind of moment. I force myself to step back. It's a small victory, considering how tired I am, how much I could use the simplicity of rest. But every inch I give him is a battle lost, I think. I know I can't barter with the devil.

"I said sit." His voice never rises, his face never reddens, but I am shoved, violently shoved to the ground. I land hard on my backside, my back cracking and my left leg going numb. "Isn't that better? Sitting. Relaxing. I'd just like to talk for a minute, Elle."

"Don't call me that," I say, repulsed—truly repulsed for the first time.

"Your friends call you that, don't they?" he says with a shrug. "In fact, everyone calls you that."

I rub at my leg. "You're not everyone. You're certainly not my friend."

He leans forward, both of his hands curling around the lip of the salt platform. "Then what am I?"

I stare at the mirrors in his eyes. I need to see myself say the words. "You're my enemy. The enemy of my soul."

His smile turns patronizing. "Do you even know what that means?"

"It means you want death for my soul, and I want life. That makes you my enemy."

"Your soul is eternal, gifted one. There's nothing you or I can do about that."

For a minute his words baffle me. "Don't play games with me. I've told you what I want: I want to go home. Now it's your turn. What do you want?"

"You," he says, crossing his ankles as they dangle. "There. I've said it. I've been honest. You can tell me, Elle. What is it you want more than anything?"

I'm silent.

"It's only polite. Come, you may not like me, but I'm not awful to look at. Not awful to talk to. And the Creator's seen fit to let you choose. I won't force you to do anything."

"But you'll try."

"Like Canaan's tried? There's no use denying it. He's tried to convince you to see the world the way he sees it."

His choice of words is ridiculous. "I do see the world the way he sees it, or haven't you heard?"

He ignores me. "I can't blame him. *I'll* certainly try, but the least you could do is be honest. We both know what it is you want, don't we? You wouldn't be telling me anything I don't already know."

That ticks me off. "You don't know anything."

"Well, that's not true and you know it. I know plenty about you. Certainly not everything, but who does?"

"The Creator. My Creator. Your Creator. He knows everything about me. He knows where I am. What I'm doing. What you're doing."

A shadow passes over the Prince's face, his expression growing tighter. "You're deflecting. My point is that I know enough about you to be helpful."

I make a face.

"Oh, but I do. For instance, I know your father's having a rather hard time of it right now."

"You leave my father out of this," I say through clenched teeth.

He sits up and crosses his legs. "But he's right in the middle of it, isn't he? Now, I know you're trying your hardest not to mention your boyfriend, but I assure you I'm less interested in him than you think. Don't get me wrong, as a pair you two ship off rather nicely, but alone he's nothing but a circus act, and trust me, I've got plenty of those. But a girl who can see into the Celestial—now that's something special. That's a gift. That's useful."

"It's *my* gift," I say. "Useful to me and mine. Not you. Not yours."

"True. Very, very true. And like your soul, I couldn't take it from you even if I tried."

His words are silky, confusing.

"But I do have a proposition for you."

"No," I say.

"It's polite to wait until I've made the offer to decline it. Let's try again. I have a proposition for you."

I open my mouth to tell him no but find my lips sealed shut. I start to panic, but I can feel the invisible fingers pressing into my face. It's a solid reminder that I'm not alone with the Prince. That he's brought minions. I find myself wondering again the same thing I've wondered so many times over the past few days: are there really more fighting for me than for him?

The fact that there are *some* steadies me. I might feel alone, but I'm not. I will my heart to slow and stare down the Prince with as much vehemence as I can muster.

"Much better, Elle. You're growing. I like that. Now, here's what I have to offer. You hear me out, give me a few truthful answers, and I will save your father."

I still can't speak. My lips refuse to move.

"He's dying," the Prince adds quickly. "Or didn't I say that already?"

My heart flip-flops and I sputter. My mouth finally opens. "You're a liar."

"Yes," he says, his dimples returning, "I am, but only because I've seen the damage truth can cause."

"Truth sets you free."

"Does it? Do you feel free right now?" He leans forward, his sentences firing fast, giving me no time to respond. "It was truth that kept Adam and Eve locked in a garden. Truth that plunged the apostle John into boiling oil. Truth that exiled him. It was truth that saw your people stoned to death. Truth that had them chained to the floor of the coliseum. And it was the God of truth who fed them to the lions."

"That's not—"

"True? I assure you it is. And right now the truth is your father is dying."

"I don't believe you."

"He didn't take your sudden absence very well. You should have left a note."

"I—"

"The police told him he couldn't file a missing person's report. Not just yet. You haven't been missing nearly long enough, and what with your boyfriend being gone, and your car, well, it looks far too much like a romantic rendezvous."

Tears threaten to spill over, but I don't want to cry. Not here. With the Prince. I pinch my eyes shut, but I feel their coolness on my cheeks anyway. The Prince continues, his words conjuring images that rise from the darkness of my mind. I see Dad. I see his hand wrapped around the neck of an amber-colored bottle. He blunders around, confused, his eyes frenzied. I open my eyes to escape the tragedy of it, but a gust of frigid air smacks me in the face. You'd think it'd be something of a relief here in the desert, but the change is too much, too severe, and I'm light-headed. I fold in half, my hands on my thighs, my eyes on Dad.

He's here.

Over the Prince's right shoulder I see him. I see Stratus. I jab two fists in my eyes, sand and salt stinging, scratching. But I blink them open again and the image is that much clearer. I'm still in the desert, still facing the Prince, but beyond him Dad drives down Main Street, a Vulture demon clinging to the top of his truck. His arm hangs out the truck window, a beer bottle clenched tightly in his fist. Desert sand coats the buildings of Stratus, the streets. It gathers on the sidewalks and in the gutters. More Vulture demons skitter through it, invisible, jabbering craziness as pedestrians cross.

"Before he went out searching, your father threw a couple back. He nearly lost control of his truck as he crossed Crooked Leg Bridge. There's a smear of paint on the railing to prove it."

I watch Dad leave Main, watch as his truck bumps along the highway past Delia's, past the high school. I watch as he hangs a left onto the narrow road that leads out to the bridge. His face is pale and frightened. Fear fills the truck, pouring from the open windows.

The Prince's voice is soft. "He made it off the bridge, but only just."

"So he's okay?"

"I'm afraid not," he says. "My sources tell me his truck slid down the hillside just beyond it. Your father is currently slumped over the wheel in a ditch."

I see it. All of it. The bridge and the truck, the ditch and the overgrown grass there. I want to disbelieve him, but I can see it so clearly. It's there, right in front of me. It's so probable. So likely.

"My source tells me there's been quite a bit of blood loss. You and I both know Crooked Leg Bridge is just far enough outside of Stratus that no one will find your old man until it's too late."

I want to tell him that his words are lies, that there are angels watching out for my dad, but the truth is I have no idea if that's true. Canaan's here, most likely being prevented from healing by his demonic torturers, and I have no idea where Helene is. Maybe Michael? Maybe Virtue? It's possible, but the Army of Light has their hands full at the moment.

"Is this the kind of truth you want?" He's so close to me now, his breath in my ear, on my cheek. When did he cross to my platform? When did he get so close?

And then I realize he hasn't moved. I have. I've climbed across the chasm that separated the two of us. His words captured my imagination, and their very probability pulled me to his side.

"No," I breathe, my exhalation moving the curl at his temple. "I don't want this."

"I didn't think so," he says, those pale eyes so compassionate, so tender. "There's a way to make that truth go away, Elle. There is. A simple command from me, and your father will be back in his bed sleeping off the hangover. I ask only that you listen to me, that you answer my questions honestly. Do that, and I will make this truth go away."

I know Jake will be disappointed in me. He'd want me to trust that regardless of how much it hurts, God's plan is better than any deal I could make with the devil. But I've already been there. I've lost my mom. I've lost Ali. And if the chest at the foot of Canaan's bed is any indication of where my relationship with Jake is going, I'll lose him too. Somehow. Some way. I'm bound to mess that up. Maybe I already have. Maybe that's why the ring is gone.

Maybe we've already lost heaven's blessing.

I bite the inside of my cheek. I can't think about that now. If there's a way for me to keep Dad, I should. It's the right choice, the only choice.

"Okay," I say, looking him in the eye. "Do it."

17

Marco

They've been back in Stratus for less than a day and Marco's dreaming again. In fact, he can't stop the dream that Damien started when he slammed the halo onto his head. It's there when he closes his eyes and it's there when he wakes. He does what he can to appear normal, for Kaylee's sake mostly, but the scene plays out again and again, and eventually he takes to Delia's spare bedroom to analyze it. It's a distraction that leaves a lingering headache behind his eyes, but he almost doesn't mind. It's the first he's had like this. A dream about the future, and it's not terrifying. There's actually hope in the images that stalk him.

And with Jake and Brielle on the far side of the earth, with Liv nursing the scars on her arm and legs, he finds himself clinging to the promise of a better tomorrow.

Because in that tomorrow he sees Jake. Healthy, whole. Sitting on a barstool, strumming a guitar, singing a song Marco's never heard. The room is full—young people, old people—the smell of chocolate clinging to the curtains.

There by the window, just past a square table, surrounded by yellow chairs so similar to the one he was strapped to in the basement at Bellwether, stands Brielle. She looks older, five or six years, maybe. She has a camera propped in her hands, snapping shots of Jake, of the crowd. Kaylee sits at the table, a clipboard and a row of highlighters before her. The sunlight beyond the window brightens her brown eyes, and it's here, in a dream, that Marco realizes how enchanting she is.

But it's when Liv enters the room that Marco understands: what he's seeing is the very definition of hope. Her dark hair is shorter than it is now, brushing her shoulders as she walks. She's swapped out her business suit and red heels for sandals and a strapless dress that does nothing to hide the fact that she's pregnant. Very, very pregnant.

She hands Brielle a cell phone before dropping into a chair next to Kaylee.

"What's this for?" Brielle asks.

"Thought you'd like to call your dad."

"Why?" After seeing the scene countless times, Marco's fairly certain Brielle already knows the answer to her question.

"I just received confirmation," Liv says. "We leave tomorrow."

Kaylee squeaks. "And Marco too?"

A smile cracks Liv's face then. A smile like he hasn't seen on her since she was ten years old. "Marco too," she says.

That's it. Four minutes of a scene that makes absolutely no sense and then the dream fades into darkness, leaving behind the sound of a restless sea. A moment passes, maybe two, and from the ocean surf comes the sound of Jake's voice and the strumming of his guitar. The scene plays out again. And again.

And just when Marco thinks he's memorized every step, every word, every shadow on the floor—when he knows just what to expect—the dream ends and a nightmare takes its place.

18

Brielle

"Done."

Behind the Prince I watch a scene take shape and hover above the salt. From the bed of Dad's truck a demon crawls. Small, chalky. Before his talons can hit the ground he's taken a human form. Old, gray, bald. He pulls a cell phone from his pocket and dials.

Relief blossoms next to the guilt taking root in my stomach.

"The sheriff himself will handle the call, I've made sure of that," the Prince says, taking my chin in his hands and turning my face toward him. His hands are cold, but I've been bathed in fear for hours now and I hardly notice. "They're friends, yes? The sheriff and your father. His involvement should keep this little incident out of the papers. Off the television. I know how you dislike that."

My lips tremble as I speak. "Th-thank you."

"I've held up my end of the bargain," he says. "Now it's your turn."

I owe him. I know I do, so I sit. I'll listen. I'll answer his questions because he saved my father, but that's all. I don't owe him any more than that.

He crosses his legs and sits, our knees nearly touching.

"Now, tell me. What is it that you want?" he asks.

"To spend my life with Jake," I say. Because it's the honest, if selfish, answer. I don't think the Prince minds selfish. He won't judge me for it. There's a sick sort of relief in that.

"It makes sense, you know? Even to me. The two of you are beautiful, gifted, talented above others your age. And more than that, you love each other. I've spoken to him, and I know he loves you. Selflessly loves you. That's uncommon. Even the Creator's seen fit to bring you together for whatever purpose He's working toward." With a delicate finger he brushes away the salt that's gathered on his cheek. "So the question begs to be asked: why are you afraid?"

The answer's an easy one. The seed of it planted by Jake the night I found out the ring was missing. "I think we've messed it up. We've done something . . . or maybe it's me, maybe I've done something . . ."

The Prince looks genuinely confused, and I'm saddled with this need to make him understand.

"Maybe it's nothing that's happened yet, you know? Maybe it's what I'm going to do. He's all-knowing, God is. Omniscient, right?" I'm flustered, talking too fast. "He sees something in my future. Something I'm going to do that will change . . ."

The Prince leans toward me. It's a small movement, but it steadies me somehow, reminds me I'm not alone here. "That will change what?"

I breathe deeply, force my mouth to slow. "Maybe I'm going to do something that will change God's mind." The salt shifts beneath me, and I pull my legs closer to my body. It's honest, what I've said. But the words are out there now, and the silence that wraps them is uncomfortable. "About me. About Jake. About us together."

He's thinking. I can almost see the mirrors in his eyes spinning with the effort. It's another eight seconds before he speaks.

"What made you so certain you had His seal of approval in the first place?"

"The engagement ring." The words are out of my mouth before I've considered the consequences. I've handed him something. A truth he didn't know. A weapon.

He cocks his head, surprise registering. "He made you a promise, then. The Creator."

"It wasn't a promise. Not really."

"And then He took it away, didn't He? The ring."

"How do you know that?"

"I've known Him a long time, Elle. His ways are not so mysterious to me. I bet it was beautiful. But you could be right. Perhaps it wasn't a promise. Just a simple manipulation," the Prince continues, "to get you involved, to see His plan move forward."

"He wouldn't manipulate—"

"Call it what you will, Elle, but letting you two believe you were meant for one another and then taking back the sentiment sounds a lot like manipulation to me. I'm rather an expert in that field."

"I'm sure there's a reason," I say, my resolve faltering.

"I'm sure there is," he says, his words dripping with bitterness. "And I'm sure it serves His purposes nicely. But I wonder if it serves yours."

"Mine aren't important."

"That is where I disagree."

I'm silent. The chill left with the images of my bleeding father, and now I feel the burn of the sun on my face and neck. Sweat drips from my brow, and I hardly want to fight with the father of lies.

"Do you recognize this?" he asks.

Between us, on the salt platform, Canaan's halo appears. It sits there in its crown form, shining like always. Unchanged, untarnished. I could use its strength right now. Its fire. I reach out, but the Prince grabs it first.

"Do you know why Canaan was given this crown?" he asks.

"Because he refused to join your rebellion."

"I love that word: *rebellion*," he says, nostalgia brightening his face, "but that's not precisely what it was. *Rebellion* indicates that there was one person in charge, but that's not accurate. The Creator had divided His kingdom, had given responsibility to many of His angels. It was only when I excelled that things changed. He didn't like sharing His glory. He was the one who incited the rebellion, Elle. He demanded the angels choose. It was not my doing. When a third of them chose me, His anger was kindled. I was cast out, deprived of the only home I'd ever known."

"It's a sad story, but I don't believe it."

"Unlike the Creator, belief isn't something I require. Doubt is only natural. You've been subjected to a lot of information—propaganda, if you will—but there is something you *should* believe: I can ensure you and Jake a long life together."

His declaration takes me off guard. At first I feel relief—relief that Jake and I forever is still a possibility—and then my stomach heaves. I turn away from the Prince, vomiting over the side of the platform. It's the kind of offering that feels impossible to turn down. And yet our futures aren't the most important thing, are they? It's our souls. I remember thinking that just yesterday, just today even, and yet the memory of that feeling is locked away in a cage of ice too thick to break through. I can't feel it anymore—the sentiment behind the words—and I can't help thinking it's . . .

It's dishonest. The words slink into my mind and I sit up, swiping an arm across my mouth.

"What did you say?" I ask the Prince.

"I said I can ensure you and Jake a long life together."

"No, after that. You said . . ."

His smile is light, concerned even. "I didn't say a thing after that."

He's lying. At least I think he's lying. Still, I stare at the Prince and wonder: is it dishonest to speak truth even if I don't feel it?

"You can't promise me Jake for a lifetime," I say. "You don't have the final say."

He draws his knees up and wraps his arms around them, leans forward like he's telling me a secret. "I've been given power. More power than I think you're aware of. If that weren't the case, would you be here now?"

"But the Scriptures say—"

"Propaganda."

"Of course you'd say that."

"It doesn't change the fact: I can offer you a life with Jake."

I shouldn't consider it. I shouldn't ask the next question, but I'm stupid enough to keep talking. "What would I have to do?"

"Wear this," he says.

Where it comes from, I don't know, but there in his hands

is a halo. Not Canaan's. Canaan's hangs from the crook of his elbow now. But this one is similar in size and shape, a slick ring the width of my thumb. A crown. But where Canaan's is gold, the Prince's seems made out of the yellow salt that surrounds us. Darker than Canaan's, it matches the platform perfectly.

I lean closer, shielding the sun with my hands. I'm surprised by what I see: my own blue eyes staring back at me from the surface. A strand of blond hair is caught in my lashes; I brush it away and run my finger over the halo. It's not made of salt. It's crafted from some sort of mirrored surface. Dark when the light is closed out. Dull without the sun shining down on it. I suppose its beauty isn't inherent like Canaan's. I suppose it depends on what it's reflecting. The Prince's pale blue eyes come to mind. I sit up and find them now.

"What will I see?"

"The appeal isn't in what you'll see. It's in what you won't see." He moves closer. "You won't see fear. You won't see pain. You won't see the brokenness that surrounds you. And why should you? Why should you see the damage my war with the Creator has caused? It's our battle to fight. Our dispute to settle."

So many lies. They roll off his tongue like buttered candy, and yet there is truth in them. It tickles my ears, climbs inside my mind and nests. I think of all the glorious, wonderful things I've seen with Canaan's halo: the angels and the light. The color and the fire of the celestial world. But sitting here with the devil staring back at me, I can't think on any of that without remembering the fear and the darkness, the demons that slink so easily into our world, slide into our flesh and masquerade as mortals.

How many times will I have to see Helene's battered body? Or Canaan's wings stripped away? How much longer will I see the fear that grows in Jake's heart? That blossoms when the world tumbles out of control?

I feel thin, my bones brittle, the desert temptations threatening to break me. I can't see the light without the darkness. I can't see angels and not demons. I can't unknow all that I've learned, but maybe, just maybe I can unsee.

There's comfort in the idea. That I don't have to open my eyes to every fear that clings to others. It's an ignorance that sounds suspiciously like freedom. And yet . . .

"I won't deprive you of Canaan's halo," the Prince says, setting it down next to his. "It's yours to take as well. But take this one, wear it when seeing becomes too much. And I promise you: soon, it will be too much."

I feel the threat in his words, his hatred evident. He'll do anything to stop the Creator's plans for Stratus.

"That's all?" I ask. I don't believe him. I want to, but I don't. "You want me to accept your crown and you'll promise me Jake?"

"Forever," he says.

"You don't hold forever in your hands. I know that much."

"You know nothing."

"What if I die? What if Jake dies? You can't stop that."

"I just stopped it for your father."

It's true. He did.

I reach a hand out and run my finger along the rim of the dark halo once again. It's cool—a reprieve from the heat of the desert. The metaphors are endless. It's so easy. So tempting. I could have both.

"You've spoken with Jake?"

"I have."

"He wouldn't want me to take this from you."

"Stratus is under attack. The fighting is going to be severe. The Creator has unleashed His Sabres. They're going to tear through the veil, and I can't have that. You shouldn't want it either. If everyone can see the Celestial, what makes your gift special? What makes you *you*? War is unavoidable, but you need not be one of the casualties. You don't have to see the carnage. This will keep your eyes safe, your mind protected. It will keep your heart in one piece. Why wouldn't Jake want that?"

He lifts his crown from the salt platform. It reflects my shirt, my chin. He holds it in his ivory hands, and together we watch as it transforms into an arm cuff. So similar to Canaan's, and yet so very, very different.

"Jake loves you. He wants forever with you. War breaks people. And I'm certain he wants you to be complete, to be whole for the rest of your life."

Jake *would* want that. He's a fixer; he'd want me in one piece.

"Did you tell him you were going to offer me this?"

"I didn't. That'll be yours to share if you wish. Or not. You're the one with the gift of sight. Perhaps he need not ever know."

The Prince slides it on my wrist. My body floods with cool, fresh air. The blisters forming on my lips are soothed, the burn on my face calmed. It's appealing, this crown. And guilt inducing. I doubt I could keep it from Jake.

"Canaan would know," I say, picking up his halo. It hangs from my finger, the Prince staring back at me, his face framed by its gaping hole.

"Another painful truth I'm sure we can find a way around."

Canaan's halo transforms, molding itself into the cuff. "And I can have both? You won't take this from me?"

"Never," he says. "Freedom. Choice. That's what I offer you."

It's the most natural thing in the world to slide Canaan's halo onto the other wrist. Its warmth travels up my arm and across my body, colliding with the cold that has spread to my heart. I gasp at the violence of it, but a minute passes and the temperatures mingle, slowly arriving at something more moderate, more comfortable.

The Prince smiles at me and I smile back, but something in his eyes has changed. They look . . . victorious. The fear returns in gushes, but this time it feels healthy and strong. The kind of fear that keeps me from sticking my hand into a fire or walking off a cliff. I hook a finger inside the Prince's halo and start to tug it off, but he stops me with a firm hand.

"Try it and Jake is yours, with or without heaven's consent. You can expect me in Stratus before this war is over. You can tell me then how you like my gift."

And then he disappears, and I'm left alone in the cruelest place on earth with Canaan's halo on my right wrist and the Prince's on my left.

19

Brielle

A tiny girl appears in front of me. I recognize her, but only by the ferocity on her face, the graceful quickness of her moves. I've not seen her human form before.

"Pearla?" I ask.

"Yes," she says. "I'm Pearla." She's wearing a simple orange shift over her creamy black skin. Her hair is pulled into a knot atop her head. She looks like she's ten years old at the most, but I know she has thousands and thousands of years on me. "It seems you have a choice to make." Her eyes are on my wrists. On the mirrored halo and the golden one.

When I speak my voice is small; her child eyes embarrass me. "He said I can keep both."

"I think you'll find that impossible," she says. She points to my right wrist. "And I'd put that one on if I were you."

I yank Canaan's halo from my hand, and as soon as it's transformed I slip it onto my head. The Celestial explodes before me. Light and color everywhere. Wings, both black and white; swords, both straight and crooked; every blink brings a new sight. By the time I've got my bearings, Pearla is gone.

I see the Prince. Just as Canaan was recognizable in the Celestial, the Prince's form is still distinguishable from the other angels filling the skies. His celestial body is taller, broader. I wish he were hideous. I wish he looked like a twisted gargoyle, but he doesn't. He's glorious. His black-tipped wings set him apart from the angels of light, but from the ground that's nearly all that does.

Several charred, heavily armed demons hover at his back. Before him, three demons engage two enormous angelic Warriors. Warriors of light. It's hard to tell from here, but they look nearly as tall as the Sabres. Their chests are covered in armor, their swords drawn. One, a male with rust-colored hair and a bow slung over his shoulder, swings his sword valiantly, an arrow between his teeth. Next to him is a female. Her skin is dark and light all at the same time, and her raven hair is tangled in the feathers jutting from her back. A wild ferocity curls her lips as she darts back and forth. She's fast. And smart. She flattens her wings out and spins, her hair whipping one way, her sword the other. The demon before her takes a face full of hair before her sword slices from one of his hips to the other. He hisses and spits into nothingness.

The male bends his feathered wing, positioning it like a shield, his sword swinging at the two remaining demons. There's something very Peter Pan about him. He's enjoying this. With a flick of his wrist, a demon is disarmed, his sword falling away. The beast is stupid and glances after it. And that's when he's smacked in the face with that shrugged wing. The demon's head flies back, his helmet askew, leaving a sliver of his throat vulnerable. Pan's sword finds it, and with a burst of ash the demon vanishes.

But the final demon is closer now. His crooked sword slices through the Warrior's feathers, knocking away his sword of light. The demon squeals and taunts, swinging his blade eagerly. I look to the female. I don't think she's close enough to help, but she tries, pushing her wings hard. It seems Pan is just as quick as she is. With movements too fast and too precise for me to track, he slides his bow over his shoulder, nocks it, and looses an arrow into the demon's face.

I'm amazed. Stunned.

I glance to the Prince, to the demons at his back. I wonder if he'll send in more to take the place of those he's lost. Is that how this works?

Before I've received an answer, a massive white angel soars overhead, his sword drawn, a tiny black cherub at his back. This has to be Michael. I've only heard stories, but there's no mistaking him. As large as the Prince, armored, a golden helmet on his head, a spear at his back and a sword of light in his hand, he flies hard.

The Prince lurches around. His face hardens, and he raises his sword high. His mouth opens, and the most hideous sound I've ever heard pours from his lips. I throw my hands over my ears and slam my face to the platform. I feel the cut it makes, the salt that stings it, but the sound . . . the sound . . .

I've heard Damien do this once, cry for his brothers. But this is a hundred times worse. It's all my agony, all the fear I've ever felt, all the pain I've ever suffered in one constant note.

And it feels like it drones on forever.

When at last the Prince quiets, I tip my face to the sky, my hands still close to my ears. And I swear my heart stops.

The Guard around the Prince has doubled. With the Prince

at their head, they fly in formation toward Michael. Where Pearla's gone, I can't say, but Michael's two Warriors flank him, the male on one side and the female on the other. And then from the sky itself a warhorse emerges, a creature of cloud and light. Michael falls astride the animal and in the same moment hefts his massive spear toward the Prince. The Prince collapses his wings and drops, avoiding the spear. The Guard behind him scatters as the spear divides their forces. Before they can regroup, two more warhorses surface between them, one with a coat of cerulean blue, the other a mottled yellow and orange. They rear up on their hind legs, batting at the Guard, keeping them divided in half.

The female flies toward the group on the right, the male taking those on the left, their horses snorting and pawing, bucking and causing confusion among the Prince's Guard. The Prince flies hard at Michael, who drives his steed faster and faster, drawing his sword and swiping it at the Prince. Their swords connect, and Michael chops again and again, pushing the Prince back.

"You were created to sing, Dragon," Michael's mind calls. "Not to fight."

The Prince answers with a bitter reply. "Pity for you I've acquired a taste for the latter."

Michael cartwheels off his steed, which then disappears into the Celestial. He soars over the Prince's head, his sword continuing to swing, the Prince meeting his attack boldly.

I watch, mesmerized by the fighting horses, by the angelic Warriors, by the Fallen. I stare gape-mouthed at the skills exhibited by Michael and the Prince both. But after a time it's clear that the Prince is outmatched. Michael's the warrior, and on this kind of battlefield the Prince can't win. Even outnumbered, Michael's Warriors have all but devastated the Fallen that fight alongside the Prince.

The Prince knows it too. He kicks away from Michael, his wings tucking as he flips backward and toward the ground. Toward me. What's left of his Guard follows, two more eliminated before they get very far.

I curl into a ball on the salt platform, try to make myself as small as possible as the Prince approaches, diving toward me, four or five of his kind just behind. He doesn't slow as he approaches, his sword aimed at the ground, his pale blue eyes on me, my own terror reflected in them. I watch as he disappears into the desert floor just feet from where I lay huddled.

He's gone.

He's gone.

And then my eyes fall on the halo still fastened to my wrist. The dark halo. In its reflection I see Michael descending from above. I tip my face up to greet him, but around me the desert turns to ice and I hear the Prince's voice in my head.

"You have a choice, Elle. Don't be a casualty of this war."

20

Brielle

When I wake, I'm in Jake's arms. I think we're on a couch, but it's hard to tell. It's hot, so I start to panic, but then I realize I've somehow ended up in his sweatshirt again. Sand and salt chafe wherever my clothes touch my skin, but I don't care.

Jake's here. Wherever here is.

I tell my eyes to open but they refuse. Minutes pass before I'm finally able to force them into slits. Jake hangs over me, one hand on my forehead, the other wrapped around my waist. I hear the ticking of the clock, smell the coffee brewing, see enough of the couch to know I'm in the old Miller place.

My eyes fall shut again.

And the nightmares find me.

They're worse than they've ever been. I watch my mother disappear three, four, five times. Into the same flames that killed Olivia's mother; the same flames that melted the skin on Olivia's legs. On every wrist I see a mirrored halo. And echoing from every mouth, the Prince's words.

"Don't be a casualty of this war."

Sometime later I wake. My wrists are heavy with the weight of two halos. I have no idea how I got back to Stratus, no idea how the golden halo got moved from my head to my wrist. I have a small, silent panic attack when I realize Jake's probably seen the Prince's halo. I can't imagine what he thinks about it and I want to explain, but he's asleep now. His face is pressing into my shoulder, his legs curled around mine. It's hard to tell where he ends and I begin, and though I'm far from comfortable, I don't dare move. Because when he wakes and we're torn apart, he'll have questions, and I'm not sure I'll have answers. I tug both halos off my wrists and jam them into the large sweatshirt pocket.

I stare at the ceiling, wondering just how I got here. How I got landed with a choice I never wanted to make. And no matter how I turn it over in my mind, I can't shake the feeling that I've lost somehow.

And I don't know . . . I can't tell . . .

Was it the first lie I told the Prince or the first truth that undid me?

"She'll be okay," Jake says. He's carrying me now. The noise is different. Closing doors, footsteps, air-conditioning. Dad's here, leaning close.

I'm home.

And Dad's okay.

The scene the Prince showed me in the desert plays out quickly in my mind. I suffer through the emotions it evokes in fast-forward, and then just as I'm about to open my eyes, throw my arms around Dad, and tell him how glad I am that he's okay, his words surprise me, stop me.

"Thank You, God," he says. "Thank You, thank You."

It's a desperate, whispered sort of statement, but that he says the words at all is extraordinary.

Jake's feet are heavy on the linoleum floor. Through my lashes I catch sight of Mom's Bible on the island. It's open, a Hershey Bar wrapper acting as a bookmark. It's almost too much to take in right now—Dad actually opening a Bible. Marking his place with a chocolate wrapper.

Feigning more exhaustion than I feel, I close my eyes again.

"I'll get the door," Canaan says. I feel him brush past us, smell the Celestial on his skin, before a door opens with a quiet whine. A moment later Jake lowers me onto the familiar stitching of the quilt Grams made me.

Home, I think. The thing I said I most wanted. The first lie I told the Prince of Darkness. Angst nearly takes me, but I feel Dad's callous hand brush my forehead and I realize I haven't lost everything. Not yet. He pulls his fingers away, grit falling to my cheek.

"What's this?" he asks.

"Sand," Jake says. "Salt."

"So she *was* at the beach," Dad says.

No one answers. They don't say a thing.

Dad must have assumed silence was confirmation because he's already onto another subject. "So, you're back then?"

"Yeah," Jake answers, the rasp of his voice thick. "I'm back."

Everything's quiet for a long time. So long I consider the possibility that I've fallen asleep. But then Dad breaks the uncomfortable silence.

"For Elle's sake, I'm glad. She was . . . upset. Cried a lot. I don't like it when she's upset."

I can tell it cost Dad to say that, but I'm proud of him for making the sacrifice. Both Jake and I could use a vote of confidence from him right now.

"I don't either, sir. I'd do just about anything to avoid that."

Dad clears his throat again. He's nervous. He always sputters and coughs and makes weird throat noises when he's nervous.

"That demon took you, then? That's what Elle said. She said he took you." He shifts and then stands, sending me bouncing into the wall. A warm hand finds my leg, steadying me.

"He did," Jake says, his words clipped. The edges of my heart crumble a bit, like the salt platforms at Danakil. He doesn't want to talk about it. What Damien did to him at Bellwether. It sends my imagination into overdrive.

"And my girl found you? She helped?"

"She did," Jake says, his voice scratching in that sweet, soft way it does. "She was my hero."

Guilt spirals through me. He should have called me something else. Anything else.

"I don't really like her playing the hero," Dad says.

"It's who she is though." Canaan's voice is both soft and firm. The voice of reason. "It's who she was born to be."

I expect Dad to react to that, to demean Canaan for claiming to know me better than he does, but he doesn't. They're just quiet. The three best men in the whole world—well, two men and an angel—and they're standing at my bedside, worried about me.

About my safety.

And all I can think about is the fact that I've brought home the promise of Satan. A dark halo and a guarantee that the Prince himself will visit our tiny town. As starved as we are for entertainment here, that's not the kind of excitement I was hoping for.

"I'm going to go," Jake says. "I'll see you at home, all right, Canaan?"

"Of course. I'll be there shortly."

Jake's hand brushes my shin and then my shoe before Dad's voice stops him.

"Kid?"

"Yeah?" His fingers rest on the toe of my left Chuck, their warmth bleeding through.

"Thanks for what you did. You know, with my shoulder."

Jake squeezes my toe. "Anytime," he says. I try to read his voice, to summon his face. Is he smiling when he answers? I'd like to think so, but I just hear fatigue. And then I hear his feet press softly into the carpet, and like that, he's gone. I feel that panic thing start in my chest, and I have to talk myself out of believing it's permanent. Jake's not leaving me. He's just going home. Just going to bed.

"Your boy okay?" Dad asks.

"He's had a rough couple of days. They both have. She'll probably sleep for a while," Canaan says. "She fought hard."

"She fought?"

"Hard."

Suddenly Dad's defensive. "Look, man . . ."

"I'm not a man," Canaan says. Laying it down. Putting it out there. I've never heard his voice quite so assertive. It's . . . inspiring.

Dad grunts, and I can almost see him scratching at that ruddy beard of his.

"I know there are things going on around here. Strange

things. Churchy things. But God and I, we don't get on much. I'm not even sure I believe in all this . . ."

"Oh, I think you do," Canaan says. "You may not want to. You may be angry at God for taking your wife. You may think it hurts His feelings when you say you don't believe in His existence. That might give you some sense of retribution, but I think you absolutely believe in God, and right now it's more important than ever for you to stop pretending you don't."

"And why is that?" It's funny what I hear in Dad's question. He's not being sarcastic; it's like he really wants to know.

"Because there's a battle raging here in Stratus, and while it's bigger than all of us, one thing's become obvious."

"Well, something should be," Dad mutters under his breath.

"Your daughter's been chosen. For this time. For this moment. And the last thing she needs from her father is disbelief."

That starts Dad huffing. "But I don't even . . . I can't . . ."

"You can't what?"

Dad groans. "I can't hear the music anymore."

I'm so surprised, my eyes slip open. The Sabres were loud when I left for Bellwether. How long have I been gone? Through the tiniest of slits, I watch Dad. The exasperation on his face, the frustration. I swear he sounds disappointed.

"I haven't heard a thing today."

"They must've pushed the Palatine away from Stratus," Canaan says, his words slow, thoughtful.

"The what?"

"The Palatine," Canaan says, slapping Dad on the back. "I think it's time you and I had a little talk."

I pinch my eyes shut once again. That's a conversation I'd rather they have without me.

"Now?" Dad protests. "I've got to be at work in a couple hours."

"Come on. I'll make sure you're at work on time."

"I have lots of questions," Dad says, the tiniest strain of curiosity in his tone.

"That's okay. I have lots of answers."

"Well, all right then." A moment later I feel Dad's lips on my forehead. "Don't be a hero," he whispers. "Please, please don't be a hero."

And then the air shifts again and I hear the soft rustle of carpet, the click of the light switch, and my door squeaks shut.

I open my eyes, but the moon is dull tonight and after several lazy blinks, it's easier to just leave my eyes closed. I lie there for a long time, thinking about Dad, about Jake, about my conversation with the Prince.

I slip my hands into the oversized sweatshirt pocket and withdraw the golden halo. I watch as it grabs the starlight outside my window and sends it back to warm my face. And then it's transforming, slowly, deliberately. There's a twinge in my chest as I slide it beneath my pillow. I know I can count on Canaan's halo to ease my transition into the nightmares, but with the Prince clinging to every thought I have, I can't help thinking just how awful they're destined to be now.

In so many ways I was wrong about him. About the Prince. I know he's evil. I don't question that, but I wonder if I should feel sorry for him. If I should sympathize with the one creature brave enough to challenge the Creator of the universe. He certainly wants me to. I assumed he'd use brute force, that he'd do whatever it took to get me to work for him, like Damien tried at the warehouse.

I thought he'd take Jake from me. Thought he'd threaten to harm him.

Maybe he would have if he hadn't been interrupted? Maybe his boy-like persona would have worn thin? Who knows?

But Jake and I are both home. Safe. And instead of an ultimatum, the Prince gave me a crown. He offered me blindness.

And for a girl who sees too much, the temptation is clear.

My pillow is warm now and the colors dance on my eyelids, just like they always do when the halo's near my head. And then a strange thing happens. Inside the pocket of Jake's sweatshirt, the dark halo unravels. I don't move, even to withdraw it. I know what it wants. It wants me to slide it under my pillow, wants me to choose not to see tonight.

Wants me to choose oblivion instead of nightmares.

But I've promised Canaan that I'll search my dreams for answers. That I'll pay close attention to every detail so that I can understand what's going on in Stratus.

The last few days have been so chaotic, though, so violent, so exhausting, and I need a good night's sleep. Feeling the lash of guilt, but ignoring it altogether, I take the dark halo in my hands and slide it beneath my pillow, next to Canaan's.

"I'm experimenting," I tell myself. "That's all. I need to know. I need to sleep."

And when at last I drift away, the colors have disappeared, my bed is lukewarm, and I've crossed all my fingers hoping I've found a cure for the nightmares that plague me.

At least for tonight.

21

Jake

It's just past nine in the morning, but it's hot. Jake rubs at his chest, at the sweat that's started to bleed through his gray T-shirt. With his face pressed against Delia's front window, he sees Marco's bag propped against the couch. He knocks again on the blue door.

Hanging from the awning are hundreds of wind chimes. Today they're too still, too quiet. Dangling near his face is a model of the solar system. It's old, the metal rusted, the paint chipping. He flicks it. The rusted thing bumps and clanks, but the sound is grating, and he stills the planets with his fist. When he pulls his hand away, a red fleck sticks to his palm—the skin of Mars.

The chime is a pathetic replica of the created order, but the rusting, flaking planets remind him that it's all temporary. One day these worlds will fade away. A new heaven and a new earth will replace them, and everything he now sees will be gone. Even the morning sun beating down, burning his neck. It's nearly impossible to imagine life without it, but as bright, as powerful as it seems, the sun is nothing compared to the light of the Creator. It's a strange thought. But there's peace in it. That the fear and the pain, the angst and the warfare—all of it will disappear.

One day.

Behind him, a car crunches over dirt and dried grass. It's Kaylee, her brakes squealing as she pulls to a stop. But no, it's not the brakes squealing. It's Kaylee. The tightness in his muscles eases a bit as he watches her bounce in her seat.

"You're back, you're back, you're back!" She trips climbing out her door but recovers quickly. "I'm so glad you're back. And you're okay?"

"I am."

She releases the plastic grocery bag in her hand and lets it fall to the porch. Something glass shatters inside, but she ignores it and pulls Jake close, pinning his arms to his sides.

"You owe me a pair of slippers," she says.

"I do?"

"I wore mine to Bellwether, and now my right Tasmanian Devil is missing an eye."

He grabs her shoulders and pushes her to arm's length. He looks at her now, carefully. Sees the bruise on her face. It's a sickly green and purple. Her jaw and lip are swollen as well.

"You went to Bellwether?"

"Of course I went to Bellwether. What kind of loyal sidekick would I be if I didn't?"

"And your face . . ."

"Damien."

Jake stiffens. "That sick, twisted . . ." He squeezes her shoulders. "I'm sorry, Kay. Man, I'm sorry." He reaches out a hand, but thinks better of himself with the occasional car rumbling past. "Here, let's—Can we go inside?"

"Of course," she says, scooping her bag from the porch, something pink and gloppy dripping through a slice in the bottom.

"Here," Jake says. "Let me." He takes the bag from her hand, and as he follows her inside he does his best not to drop the strawberry-smelling gunk all over the carpet.

"Elle's back too, then? Please, please tell me she's okay. She hasn't been answering my texts."

"She's back. She's . . . she's good, I think."

"You think?"

"No, I know. I mean, she's good. There's nothing physically wrong with her. Nothing I can heal, anyway."

She grabs a plastic trash can just inside the kitchen and brings it over. He drops the entire grocery bag into it.

"Well, that was a waste," she says. "Delia's gonna be ticked."

"So, slippers then?"

"Slippers. And nothing boring, okay? They need to make noise or have an obnoxiously large cartoon character on the front."

"Obnoxiously large cartoon character," Jake says. "Not even sure I know where to look for those."

"I have complete and utter confidence in you," Kaylee says. She grabs a very green banana off the counter and starts to peel. "I won't ask about Danakil because you seem a little . . ." She twirls the banana in the air. "But where's Elle? I expected you two to be glued at the lips for days following that craziness."

He slides his hands in his pockets, pulls them back out. Picks at a loose thread on the bottom of his shirt. "She's sleeping. I'm sure she'll fill you in when she wakes up."

"I'm sure she will." She points the banana at him. "All right. Spill it. What will it take to make you less twitchy?"

"I'm sorry, Kay," he says, forcing a smile. "I just . . . I need to talk to Marco. Is he here?"

She throws her hip into the counter, takes a bite of the banana. "Is that all? Go on back. It's the room at the end of the hall. Not the one with the hole in the door. That's mine. His is the next one."

"There's a hole in your door?"

She opens the fridge and disappears behind a wall of souvenir magnets. "Long story."

The hall is short, pictures of Kaylee filling up every inch of the walls. Delia gives her niece a hard time, but she certainly loves her, may even be proud of her. Jake runs his finger over the star-shaped hole in Kaylee's door. Whatever caused it left behind lumps of purple glitter. He shakes his head and moves to the next room.

The door's halfway open. Tired of knocking, Jake pushes inside. Marco's there, lying on his bed, staring at a book draped across his pillow. At first Jake thinks it's Ali's journal, but this book's too big, too thick. Looks an awful lot like a Bible, actually.

"Hey," Jake says, not wanting to startle him.

Marco lurches anyway. "Jake? You're here." He swings his feet over the side of the bed and stands. "And Elle? You're both okay?"

"We are. We're both okay. What about you?"

"I'm . . . yeah, you know. My wrists are great, thank you, by the way. And Kaylee's been helping, answering questions." His face colors. "Anyway. Where's Damien? What happened in Danakil?"

Jake hasn't figured out how to answer these questions. The truth is, until Brielle wakes up, he won't really know what happened, and that embarrasses him. He still can't believe they left her behind. Can't believe God willed it.

"I'm still trying to sort it all out, to be honest."

But Marco's eyes are relentless—like Kaylee's—and Jake turns his face away. The room is small, and there's not much to look at. Wood paneling covers the walls. Overhead, a dirty skylight drops a circle of sunlight into the room, brightening it some. There's a bed and a doily-covered dresser. A high-back wicker chair sits in the corner. His eyes find Marco's again. Still staring. Still questioning.

"Actually, Marco, could we . . . I wanted to talk to you about something else."

"Sure." Marco turns his back on Jake and closes the Bible. "You, uh, you want to talk about when we were kids, don't you?"

The sweat on Jake's back and neck goes cold, his hands clammy. "How long have you known?"

Marco drops onto the bed, looking again at Jake. "Not until last night."

"What happened last night?"

Marco taps his temple.

"You had another dream," Jake says.

"It was a lot like the dream I had of the school fire, actually. The one where Liv's mom died."

"How so?"

"I've had other dreams since the halo. Images that are new. Events I've never seen, things that aren't at all familiar. But this one—I think the memories have always been there. You know, in my head. Just buried or . . . hiding, maybe."

Jake can't help but notice that Marco seems far less disturbed than he did at Bellwether. Like he's grown accustomed to the dreams. Like he's found some level of comfort with them.

Marco shrugs. "I don't know. This is all new to me, man. When did *you* figure it out?"

"Just a couple hours ago." Jake stands and pulls a small plastic action figure from his pocket. He passes it to Marco.

Marco smiles. "Professor X," he says. "Haven't seen this guy in forever. Have you had it all this time?"

"No," Jake says. "But it's hard to explain."

Marco purses his lips, nods. "Showed up in Canaan's chest, then."

"You know about the chest?"

"Kaylee attempted an explanation."

"That's a conversation I'd have loved to hear. Even I have trouble explaining it. You'll have to give her credit for trying."

"She deserves more credit than I could ever give her." Marco's voice is quiet, his eyes on Professor X. "He's still in really good shape."

"You gave him to me when I was a kid. Do you remember that?"

"I do now," Marco says, handing it back.

"What else do you remember?" Jake asks.

Marco takes the Bible in his hand, runs his fingers over the cover. "You want to know about my dream."

"Yeah," Jake says. "I do."

"Better sit then," Marco says, gesturing to the wicker chair.

Jake takes a seat, the chair bending under his weight. He waits, but Marco's quiet, his index finger tracing the golden letters engraved on the leather cover.

Holy Bible.

Jake leans forward, his elbows on his knees. "Look, Marco. If my childhood is involved, your dream couldn't have been pleasant. I don't remember a lot, but I remember enough to know that. I need to know what you saw though. It . . . matters."

It's another second, but Marco's face lifts and the actor in him pushes through. "Okay then. I saw your mom."

"My mom?" It's not entirely unexpected, but in this moment Jake envies Marco. There are days he can't quite remember her face.

"Her name was Jessie, right?"

"It was," Jake says. "I forgot people called her that."

"You lived across the hall, I think, and in my dream she was banging on the door. Our door. It was early in the morning—like still-dark-outside early. She was panicked, half dressed. Said your father'd been arrested." Marco stops. "Do you remember that? Your father being arrested?"

"I don't remember it, no. But it happened. I know it did."

Marco nods. "Your mom needed someone to watch you for a couple hours. Asked my mom if she could help."

Jake remembers Marco's mother, but just barely. He tries to picture her now, but the image is nothing but soft, round shadows.

"Mom babysat every kid in the neighborhood in those days. Told your mom to bring you right over, to take her time, do what she needed to do." Marco's words fall away, and they sit in silence for a moment. "And that . . . that's what she did. She brought you over."

He hasn't said everything. Jake can tell. "What else, Marco?"

"It wasn't a long dream."

"But there's more. What else?"

Marco's hands are still on the gold letters. "Just you. She

brought you over—your mom did—put you on the couch with an old blanket. You were all . . . you were messed up. Blood dried on your face, black eye."

"My dad," Jake says. "He drank. Had a temper. Bad combination."

"I'm sorry, man. It made for a pretty awful dream. I can't imagine living it. We were broke half the time, but no one ever hit me."

"It's okay," Jake says.

"It's *not* okay."

"What I mean is, I don't remember it. Not much, anyway." But he remembers the fear. He rubs his damp hands against the rough wicker chair. "Go on. What else?"

"That was it. It was a short dream. Repeated itself a couple times before . . ."

"Before what?"

Marco drops his gaze to the floor. "I've been having this other dream. A good dream. Better than the one about you, anyway." His fingers resume their circuit. *H O L Y.* "That dream cut in, pushed yours out. But you were with us most afternoons after that, weren't you? For a couple years. Until my mom had to get a real job."

"It sounds right, what you're saying, but I don't remember." He stands and reaches a hand out for the Bible. Marco hands it over. Jake talks while he flips through the tissue-thin pages. "I do remember the day you gave me Professor X. You said he could find anybody, anywhere. Do you remember that? You said if I ever needed him to, he could find you."

Marco laughs. "I've always been dramatic."

There's a ribbon sewn into the Bible. Jake slides it between two pages and continues flipping. "Do you remember why my dad was arrested?"

Marco exhales, leans back on his elbows. "I don't. I'm not sure I ever knew."

"He was arrested for arson," Jake says, looking up.

"For arson?"

Jake weighs his next sentence. Tries to decide how best to deliver it. But there's only the honest thing, the right thing. And there's no use dragging it out any further.

"My dad burned down Benson Elementary."

Marco shoots off the bed, his eyes on Jake. His hands hang out in front of him, awkward, curled like they're grasping for something. "Your dad started the fire that killed Liv's mom?"

"Yeah." Jake clears his throat. "He did."

Marco sits, the bed frame protesting. He twists his hands into the comforter. "Where is he now? Did he . . . Was he convicted?"

"He died in custody six weeks after he was arrested. Before the case went to trial."

"Dead." Slowly, Marco's body starts to unclench. His shoulders drop, his hands relax. "I had no idea the arsonist died. It's weird that I never knew, isn't it?"

"Not really," Jake says. "We were kids."

"But I was ten when that happened. And Liv was my friend."

"All the more reason for your parents to keep the gory details from you. It's easier to tell a kid it was all an accident. Easier for a kid to believe that."

"But how do you . . . how did you . . ."

Jake pulls a gum wrapper from his pocket, flattens it.

"I've been looking for a tie between the two of us for months."

That surprises Marco. "Between you and me? Why?"

"I recognized you. When you showed up last fall, I knew we'd met before, but I couldn't figure it out. I hadn't made any progress, not really, until the day you left Stratus with Liv. I went into the city that day, talked to a guy. A tattoo artist. He knew my father."

Jake's eyes trail to the carpet. Brian Hughes was his father's name. Before Professor X showed up in the chest that morning, Jake had been on the computer reading through every news article he could find on the fire at Benson Elementary.

"You okay, man?"

"Yeah, I just . . . Anyway, this tattoo artist told me my father set the fire. Once I'd made the connection, it was easy. Terrible, but easy. Professor X brought back my memories of you, and the Internet gave me everything else."

Jake slides the flattened gum wrapper into the Bible, marking a second passage.

"Have you told Liv?"

"I haven't even told Brielle. There's just . . . there's so much more."

Marco drags his hands through his hair. "Do I want to know?"

"*Want* has so little to do with any of this," Jake says, closing the Bible. "It was Brielle's mom you saw disappearing into the fire that day."

"What?"

"The woman you saw through the window. The woman you thought was Brielle. It wasn't. She was three years old at the time. It was her mom, Hannah. She dragged Liv out of the building that day. Saved her life."

"Wha—I don't . . ." Marco's face freezes, a computer given

too many commands. "There was only one body found in that building—I know that much—and it was Liv's mom."

Jake hands the Bible back to him. "What happened to Elle's mom is a bit of a mystery after that."

Marco's eyes go wide. "An angel mystery?"

"Most likely. Brielle's been trying to figure it out for a few weeks now."

"How?"

"You're not the only one having dreams, Marco."

Jake leans against the door frame. He can hear Kaylee from here. She's singing somewhere down the hall. It reminds him that he needs to see her one more time before he goes.

"What's this?" Marco asks, his fingers falling on the first bookmark.

"It's a story. Thought you'd like it. It's about a guy named Jacob."

"Jake, huh?" Marco says. "Cool name."

"Yeah, well, this guy didn't keep it long."

"No? Why?"

"It's all there." Jake nods at the book. "The second story—yeah, the one with the gum wrapper—that's an entire book dedicated to a man named Daniel."

"Another story I'll like? Why?"

"Because they were dreamers," Jake says. "Like you."

Marco lays his hand flat on the open Bible. "It's not new then? The weird dreams. Not unique to me."

"It's definitely not new. God's been using dreams to speak to people for ages. But unique? Gifts like this are always unique."

Marco drags both hands through his hair. "Last week you never would've convinced me these dreams were a gift."

"And now?"

Marco's eyes fall back to the page. "I'll let you know. Looks like I have some reading to do."

Jake turns to leave. "I'll let you get to it, then. I need to see Kaylee."

"Jake?"

He turns back. "Yeah?"

"Do me a favor, will you?"

"Sure."

"Fix her before you go. I wish I could, but . . . you saw her face. She says it's no big deal, but . . ."

"But it is," Jake says. "And Damien's going to pay for it. You know that, right? He's going to pay for a lot of things."

The sun has shifted some, and the light from above sits on Marco's face now, brightening his green eyes.

"Because of providence," he says. "You believe he'll pay for what he's done because God has willed it. That's a can of worms I'm not sure I'm ready to open."

"Sometimes I'm not sure I'm ready, and I've lived this stuff my whole life."

"But you still believe? Why?"

Jake smiles, glances at the book in Marco's hand.

"Because the Bible tells me so."

22

Brielle

When I wake, the venetian blinds that cover my windows are yellow with afternoon light. Sand and salt scratch the soft skin between my toes and scrape at my back. I desperately need a shower, but I flip onto my side, facing the *Les Misérables* poster over my desk. I stare into the eyes of Cosette, trying to understand why I feel so awake, so light. My arms and legs are exhausted, but I feel rested.

And then I realize: no nightmare.

Neither my burning mother nor the child Olivia visited me while I slept. For the first time in forever, I'm more concerned about myself and my own choices than about others and theirs. I find a sense of freedom in that.

Sulfur clings to my clothes, and a ratted lock of hair is pasted to my face in some sort of crusty concoction. I lift a hand to free my cheek of it and then reach beneath my pillow. Both halos are there. One still warm. The other cool.

I pull them both out and sit up. They've reformed into cuffs, and I place one on each knee. Within seconds my right leg is warmed through. And my left? Well, it's not cold. Not really. Not uncomfortable at least. And yet . . . images dance in the mirrored surface of the dark halo. My father's truck slipping, sliding down the grassy incline, the Prince's eyes sparkling as he offers help, my own hand trembling as I accept his crown.

No. Not accepted. I didn't choose his crown. I ended up with it.

He disappeared, and I ended up with it.

I scratch the hair from my face and sit up. I'm rested and completely unprepared to confront the big questions Danakil left me with. So I won't. Not yet. I grab both halos and set them side by side on top of Mom's Bible on my bedside table. Briefly I envision Mom's Bible singeing a hole through the dark halo, like the Ark of the Covenant burning through that Nazi crate in *Raiders of the Lost Ark*. But nothing so dramatic happens.

The gold halo winks at me, gathering the light from the room, shining like my favorite wishing star. I'm glad the Prince didn't take it from me. Next to it, the dark halo reflects its surroundings: the golden halo, Mom's Bible, the afternoon colors of my room. It's absolutely ordinary next to Canaan's.

Unable to stand the chafing a second longer, I kick out of my shorts and strip off my shirt. Sand and salt fall like rain, covering my sheets. I stand and ball all of it up—my sheets and blanket, my dirty clothes—before sliding into my zebra-print bathrobe and carrying my dirty things to the laundry room.

My bare feet are quiet on the carpet, the house silent. I stick my head into Dad's room but it's empty. I find a note from him on the kitchen counter.

Ran to the office. Dinner tonight. We need to talk.

He's a man of many words, my dad. I lean into the island fingering the note. I'm glad he's working. That's a good thing, but I think again about the image in the desert. I try to conjure the picture in my mind, the way Dad's truck was tangled in the foliage, the way his head gushed blood. Maybe the Prince did more than call for help. Maybe his minion sped Dad's healing?

But that question opens the door to a million more equally uncomfortable questions, and I don't want to feel any more indebted to the Prince than I already do. I shove away from both the counter and the questions, nearly sprinting to the bathroom across the hall. My little stereo is there on the counter and I crank it up, desperate to get lost in the noise, hoping it will drown the questions that feel like they weigh more than I do.

The water is hot, but not nearly hot enough to burn away the fear chewing at my stomach. With every drop of water I feel the questions I don't want to answer. I see Jake's face as he asks them, imagine Canaan's brows drawn together in consternation as I struggle to explain just why I have the Prince's halo.

And Dad obviously has his own questions. It's not unexpected. I mean, I did leave town without letting him know. I did drive Slugger to the coast when my little Bug isn't allowed out of Stratus.

But it's more than that. Canaan told Dad stuff. I just hope he answered all the hard questions, because I'm still learning. And if I'm honest, today I have more questions than I've had in a long time.

I scrub ferociously at my head, clawing at the grit that refuses to release my hair. I shampoo three, four, five times, but it's still not enough. I scrub my skin until it's raw and the poor loofah is left in tatters, but I still smell of rotten eggs. When I climb from the shower I've decided one thing: it's not possible to wash Danakil away.

And that's unsettling.

I wrap a towel around my body, the ease I woke with gone. It washed away much more quickly than the grime, and I can't help but wonder which halo would bring it back. The one that thaws me, eases my fear? Or the one that promises to hide it from my eyes?

And then I see my phone. It's on the counter just inside the kitchen door. I thought I left it in the car at Bellwether.

Geeze, Bellwether!

Marco!

Kaylee!

I snatch up my phone and unlock it. There, waiting for me, are seventeen missed calls, one voice mail, and one text message. Fifteen of the missed calls are from my dad. Two are from Miss Macy, missed this morning. The text is from Kaylee.

> Slugger's out front. Marco's with me. Your dad called my phone last night looking for you. I told him we drove to the beach, which is absolutely true so don't you dare let him call me a liar when you confess all. Call me when you can.

I dial my voice mail and hear the message from my very irate, very concerned father. I could kick myself for not leaving a note, not texting. I hate worrying him, and I have no idea how I'm going to answer the kinds of questions he's likely to have about where I've been and what I was doing. After his conversation with Canaan, there's no way Kaylee's beach story will be adequate.

I exit the message screen and see the date on my phone. It's Sunday. Almost two days have passed since Kaylee and I drove to Bellwether, but I'm unclear just how that breaks down. How long was I actually in Danakil? How long have I been sleeping? Things that are going to matter when my dad launches into his inquisition.

The clock says it's nearly four, which means I have at least an hour and a half before Dad walks through the door. I stare out the kitchen windows and watch the shadows shift on the gravel drive. It's been a long time since I've been nervous to see Jake.

Excited? Yes. Anxious? All the time. But nervous? Not since his first week in Stratus.

But I can't shake the feeling that I've broken something that can't be repaired. And yet . . . it's Jake. My Jake.

The Jake who promised me forever.

The same Jake the Prince promised me if only I'd take his crown. If I'd just try it. How much harm is there in trying, right?

My stomach rolls and I turn away from the shadows. Back in my room I realize just how badly I need to do laundry. The lid of my hamper will no longer close, but having a gazillion outfits from my modeling days pays off. Five minutes later I've slipped into a pair of yoga pants—from an overly ambitious online campaign for a dot-com store that has now gone belly-up. Mom's necklace rests against my chest, still damp from the shower. Over it, I throw a stretchy polo in pale green. I look like I've just come from the gym, but it could be worse. I'm too lazy to grab socks, so I just slide my feet into my sneakers. I grab the dark halo off my nightstand, and before I can fixate on the thing anymore, I grab a purse that's hung on the post of my bed for years—something very Rastafarian—unzip it, and drop the halo inside.

I even zip the purse. When I turn to grab Canaan's halo, I can't help but feel slightly victorious. I slide it on my wrist and that same familiar heat washes over me. It feels warmer than it's felt in some time, and suddenly the world doesn't seem so confusing.

I didn't accept the Prince's gift. I ended up with it. I'll just give it to Canaan and be done with the stupid thing. I don't know what that means for Jake and me—I have no idea—but the answer can't be anything I received in the desert.

The Prince can't make me promises. He doesn't have that right.

With the purse slung over my shoulder and the golden halo on my wrist, I walk out the door and across the grassy field that separates my house from Jake's. Halfway there it hits me. It really hits me.

Jake's home. He's home. And he's safe. The excitement returns and my pace quickens. But when I burst through the door of the old Miller place, I stop.

Jake's there on the couch, but he's not alone. A stranger companion I could not have imagined. Ali's mom is with him. Tears sparkle in her chocolate-brown eyes, the only feature she shared with Ali. And even that was coincidence, not genetics. Ali was adopted.

"Serena?"

"Elle!" She jumps off the couch and embraces me. Taller than my five foot six, she spent her twenties as a runway model. Her skin is several shades darker than her chocolate eyes, and her limbs are long and lean. Ali said she took up running after her modeling days, and it shows. More so now than when I saw her at the funeral. "You look lovely. It's been ages." Her British accent brings back a flood of memories. Ali tiptoeing on the planter boxes outside the school, mimicking her mother on the runway. Ali trying to convince her mother via e-mail that just because there are two *Ls* in the British form of the word *traveled*, that doesn't make it more correct than the American spelling, which is perfectly satisfied with just one.

Serena's embrace quivers and then it shakes with the sobs wracking her body. I wrap my arms around her and let her cry. I don't know what's wrong, but it could be anything really. She could have found something of Ali's, or lost something of Ali's. Today could have been the anniversary of some special or even arbitrary event that they celebrated as a family. Any of those things could send a grieving mother into tears, and understandably so. I still have my days where I miss Ali so much it makes me ill, and I didn't raise her.

It's only after she's cried herself out that I guide her back to the couch and sit down next to her. Jake's eyes follow me all the way, and as I meet his gaze I realize how much there is to say. Not just about Danakil, but about the missing engagement ring and Damien's dagger in the chest. And now that Serena's here, I think of Ali's journal and the quote she'd penned there: *Men loved darkness rather than light, because their deeds were evil.* And then I remember the picture of the tattoo and Jake's trip to the Evil Deeds Tattoo Parlor in Portland, and I realize I still don't know what he found there.

For now, the words will have to remain unsaid.

"What's happened, Serena?"

"Forgive me for popping in like this. I've actually been handling this all quite well, but seeing you . . ."

That's all she gets out before the tears start again. I grab a wad of tissues out of the box on the table and press them into her hand.

"Serena," Jake says, a hand to her shoulder, "would you like me to . . ."

"Yes, won't you? I can't say it again." She stands and stumbles past me, through the kitchen and down the hall. I call after her, but a second later I hear a door slam and the sound of water running.

"What happened?" I ask.

"Her husband passed away."

"Manny?" I ask, stunned. Emmanuel Beni is—or was—a family court judge in Portland. He was successfully working his way up the justice system last I heard, but admittedly that was some time ago. "How?"

"Heart attack," Jake says. "She came home and found him on the floor of his office. A couple weeks ago now, I guess."

"Wow."

"Did you know him?"

"No, not really. Spoke to him a couple times at the school and then at the funeral, of course. But Ali was an only child. Adopted, obviously. Losing both of them so close together has to be awful for Serena." I feel thin, stretched. With all the other emotions I carried over here, the weight of this news feels that much heavier. "How did she end up *here*?"

"She came to see you, but when no one answered your door, she tried here. She didn't want to leave these on your doorstep." Jake slides a stack of paper across the table. It's alligator-clipped together, colored Post-it notes jutting from the sides.

"What is it?" I ask, scanning the top page.

"Correspondence," Jake says, "between Serena and the law

firm that handled Ali's adoption." He's speaking slowly. It's weird.

"Why does she want me to have it?"

"I don't know, but read the second paragraph on that one," Jake says.

> Thank you for stopping by the office. I'm sorry I missed you. Your paperwork is in process as we speak, but I've come upon an extraordinary situation that could expedite your adoption. Clients of mine, a husband and wife, had hired a surrogate to carry their baby. This weekend they were killed in a car accident. Their will indicates that their only living relative should take custody of the child should anything befall them, but the relative patently refuses. What makes the situation more desperate is that the surrogate is to give birth any day. If you would like to pursue this adoption, I'm nearly certain we can make this happen.

I read it quickly, silently, and then I turn my eyes back to Jake. He takes the packet from me, removes the Post-it notes lining the top of the page, and slides it back across the table.

"Look at the stationery," he says.

The Law Firm of Madison and Kline. Below the block-style logo is a list of attorneys. The first name on the list is Henry J. Madison, Senior Partner.

Henry.

Again.

I haven't seen him since the warehouse, but he's everywhere. Why does that old man keep squirming into my life? Into the lives of everyone I love?

"We were entirely unaware that we were dealing with traffickers," Serena says, entering the room, rounding the couch, her steps steady now. "Not for some time. Madison and Kline, you see, was a firm my husband was familiar with in his proceedings. They came with the highest recommendations. We should have spotted it before, of course, but it wasn't until after Ali had been placed with us that we understood with whom we had become involved."

I sit up a little straighter. "I don't understand . . ."

"She was sick. Very, very sick. The birth mother was by no means a surrogate. She was penniless, an addict in a hopeless situation. She agreed to sell her baby for a thousand dollars."

"A thousand dollars?" I ask. I'm not even sure what mortifies me more. That someone thought Ali was worth so little or that she was purchased at all.

Serena's face is grim. "We paid Madison and Kline over $300,000 for the adoption. When Manny threatened to turn them over to the authorities, they produced more than enough documentation to cast a shadow on any ignorance we could have claimed." She nods at the paperwork. "That's what you have there."

"They blackmailed you," I say.

"They did. But we loved Ali, and there was every indication that we really were her best option. She came to us malnourished and underweight, but my brother agreed to come over from England to help us with her. He's a doctor. Thankfully, she sustained no permanent damage. Not that it did her much good in the long run."

She picks at a tissue in her hand as she speaks, cottony snow falling to the arm of the couch.

"The truth is we wanted to keep her. Horribly. It was devastating to learn we couldn't conceive, and adoption is such a sticky process, especially if you try to do it by the book. My immigration status here made things even more difficult. Everything was drawn out. Everything took years. At first Manny was unwilling to use his legal ties to move us up on lists—said it wasn't fair—but after a while he gave in. He felt responsible, you see. But even that wasn't enough. Red tape. Red tape everywhere. We fought and fought to make it happen. By the time we found out Madison was dirty, we'd fought ourselves out."

There are seven silver buttons lining the collar of Serena's expensive elbow-length blazer. I concentrate on the light bouncing off each of them, trying to make sense of the story she's telling. I thought we were free of trafficking—after the warehouse. But I should have known our one little foray didn't solve the problem everywhere. Of course it didn't. Maybe it didn't even solve all of *that* problem.

"So you stayed silent," Jake says. There's no condemnation in his voice, but I watch as fear sparks like a firecracker in Serena's chest. Black tar is splattered everywhere; I'm hit in the face with it and immediately feel its effect. Goose bumps pop up on my arms.

I turn to Jake, but his eyes are on Serena, his lips moving silently. He's praying. He reaches across the arm of the couch and takes my hand. I watch as the fear on my arm hisses and spits, smoking as it dissolves.

"We did," Serena says, gripping her hands tightly together. "I'm not proud of it, but we did. We didn't want to lose Ali, so we kept our mouths shut. Manny made it his life mission to get the firm shut down."

"Did he?" I ask.

"Yes. It was several years before he had enough on Madison to turn the tables and force the swine to walk away from family law."

"You blackmailed Henry?" Jake asks, his voice a mixture of awe and concern.

"My Manny did. He never would tell me what he held over the man, but whatever it was, Henry walked away from the law. His departure destroyed the firm. To the day he died, Manny considered the death of Madison and Kline to be his greatest accomplishment."

The fear in Serena's chest is no longer sparking, but a steady stream flows from her sternum to the floor. Jake's prayers seem to be keeping it from the two of us, but I stand and pull Serena closer, wedging her between Jake and me. The fear on her forearms hisses in anger.

"Why are you bringing this to me, Serena?" I ask gently, carefully.

"Because I have to know . . ." She curls into herself, misery and regret reverberating from her tears. I squeeze her against me. "Did my baby girl hate me?" Her tears soak through my shirt, but she doesn't sob this time, and it's not fear pouring from her chest any longer, it's sorrow. She leans forward and lifts the papers from the table. "I found these in a box of books the school had packed up after she was killed." Her eyes go all wonky and unfocused then, but it's only a second before she's recovered. "Anyway, there were several boxes like this—books and scripts, old homework assignments—things I just didn't have the heart to go through after she died. Going through her clothes was hard enough. You saw me, Elle, I was bonkers. But now that Manny's gone, I can't stay in that house any longer, and before I can move, the boxes must be sorted. It's a horrible kind of misery, going through both of their belongings. To know I have to be the one to do it because there's no one else left."

I squeeze her hand. Why hadn't I thought of her? Why hadn't I done more? Because she always looked so together. So polished. And she had Manny.

But clearly things have changed.

"Serena, I can help. I will help."

"I may take you up on that, love. Goodness, you're warm." She pats my hand, and I watch the goose bumps on hers vanish. She takes a breath that hitches once or twice, but when she exhales the sound is clean and smooth. "We haven't talked about her pregnancy, have we? Or her anemia. But after the truth came out about her death, they had her body exhumed and a proper autopsy performed."

I knew about the exhumation. I'd read about it, seen it on the news.

"So, I know. And I think it was her pregnancy that led her to search for this information about her birth parents."

"Why would you think that?" I ask.

"She called me once, from school, asking me about her medical history, if I knew how to contact her birth mother. She'd never asked before, said she was perfectly content not to know, but now she was asking, and I'll admit I was unprepared."

"Did she give you a reason?" I ask.

"Said she needed it for some kind of assignment. I told her I'd see what I could do, but didn't know how long it would take. I figured she'd just talk her way out of the assignment. She was always good with words." Her voice is bitter now. "It was daft of me, wasn't it? I should have known she'd go searching herself."

I pat her back, wishing I could ease her regret, but I'm sure Serena's right about Ali's intentions. It's so like her to want to have her ducks all in a row, to want to understand her own health history and what she could be passing on to her child. Especially with the unexpected complication the anemia must have caused.

"You were her best friend. Your opinion meant so much to her. You can be honest. Did she hate me?" Tears slip down Serena's smooth face once again. "For not being brave and noble and exposing Henry Madison for what he was? She spoke so little to me in the days leading up to her death, I think she must have." Her lip trembles, tears streaking down it, falling to the floor. "Did she despise me?"

I rub the long, thin muscles of her arms, hoping to spread some of the halo's warmth. It takes me a minute to find the right words. To frame them just so.

"The last time I remember her talking about you was a few days before she died. We were walking past Hatfield Hall, on Broadway. You know the theatre? Okay, well, one of the companies there was doing *West Side Story*, and when she saw the playbill Ali launched into this diatribe on why it's the worst show ever, but that she'd have to do it one of these days. I couldn't understand why she'd ever do a show she hated, especially when she could play anything, you know? So I asked her why. And you know what she said? She said, 'Because it's my mum's favorite.'"

Serena pushes at the skirt inching up from her knees. "I never did understand why she hated that show so much. She would have made a beautiful Maria."

"If she said a single hateful word about you or Manny, I wasn't there to hear it. She loved you both, wanted to make you proud." I'm very, very careful about what I say next. "I think that's why she didn't tell you about the pregnancy. She didn't want you to be disappointed in her. She didn't tell me either, Serena. I think disappointing all of us was her biggest fear."

We cry together now, the sorrow clear and bright as it flows from our hearts to the floor. Jake's whispered prayer is the only other sound in the room. He squeezes my hand, and I look to him. My celestial vision spreads, the room splashing with a waterfall of yellows.

Serena lays her head on my shoulder, but I keep my eyes on Jake. I watch as the white light of love's greatest expression cuts through the hazel of his eyes, and something sharp catches in my chest. I wouldn't see him this way if I wore the Prince's crown.

"Thank you," Serena says. "I needed this."

I squeeze her tight.

"Me too."

23

Brielle

Serena doesn't stay long. She wants to get back to Portland before it's too late, she says. But she looks embarrassed. I try to convince her to stay for dinner, but she's decided. I promise to visit soon, and like that, we're alone.

Jake and I.

Really alone for the first time since I called him a liar.

Without Serena between us, the old couch caves, and one shift of my hip throws us together. Not that we fight it. On the contrary, we elbow the bunching material out of the way and move closer. Should we talk about Henry? Should we talk about Jake's trip to the city and the picture of the tattoo the Throne Room sent us? Should we talk about the Prince? Maybe. 'Cause there's this knot of sickness in my stomach, and I'm so afraid I've messed up somehow. I want Jake to tell me I haven't. That there was nothing I could do. That leaving with the Prince's halo was inevitable.

But Jake's hands tangle in my hair and he pulls my face to his. Our eagerness makes us clumsy, and our teeth and noses are more weapons than anything else. But we're close. And he's here. And if I wanted, if I was willing to give everything else up, Jake could be mine. Forever.

I let myself get lost in that. In the possibility of it. Regardless of what it means, regardless of what it costs. *We* are a possibility. And it's wonderful. For approximately seventy-eight seconds. I wasn't counting; I was busy. But I'm a pretty good guesser these days. And seventy-eight seconds is not quite enough oblivion.

Jake pulls away, moving back toward the arm of the couch. His lips are plump, his face flushed. And then he's not sitting anymore. One bounce and he swings his feet over the back of the couch.

"Where are you going?" I ask, sprawled across the old sofa.

But Jake's down the hall already. "I'm checking the chest."

"Now?" I groan.

"If there was ever a time for an engagement ring to materialize, now's it, Elle. Right now."

I stand and follow, a silly grin pulling at my face, my lips feeling just as full and rosy as Jake's look. I move slowly, straightening my shirt and purse, braiding my hair. I let myself consider the happy possibility that it was that simple: a little chat with the Prince, his halo zipped away, and my engagement ring is suddenly and inexplicably returned.

Canaan's door stands open and I enter, but Jake's sliding the lid back in place. He drops to the chest, the grommets on his jean pockets scratching at the finish, his elbows on his knees.

I don't say anything. I don't have to. The disappointment is mutual and thick between us.

He drags his hands through his hair. "I'm not sure what we need to do, Elle. What we need to be. If I knew, you know? If *we* knew . . ."

"We'd do it. Whatever it is. Without hesitation." I kneel before him. "But we don't know."

I keep my eyes on his as he moves a hair out of my face. He just looks . . . lost. I search for words to make him better, but he's the fixer and it's only his words that come to mind. I regurgitate them now because they're all I have.

"You told me once that we're God's creation. Not the other way around. You said we can't make God into what we want Him to be. And I guess He wants us to wait. To trust."

With a warm hand he traces a line from my forehead down to my jaw. And then my lips. He traces them lightly and a huge, tragic-sounding sigh rattles him.

"I'm sorry," he says.

"Why are you sorry?" I ask.

"Because I couldn't keep the Prince away from you."

I narrow my eyes. "Did you just apologize for being human?"

A smile pulls his lips into the crescent moon I love so much. I lean in and kiss it.

"I think I apologized for not being *superhuman*," he says.

I feel my face stiffen at the memory of the Prince suddenly there before me. On that salt platform. Like he owned the place. Like he owned me. "I don't even think a superhuman could have kept the Prince away. He wanted to talk." I shrug. "I listened. We're done."

I want that to be true. I want to be done with him, with everything he has to offer, but something like a sick eel swims in my gut and I can't convince myself.

Beyond the window, the sun is wrapped in amber clouds, and the filtered light it dumps into the room gives Jake a gritty, almost commercial quality. Like all those filtered Instagram pictures. The green in his eyes is near impossible to see, the russet taking over. I search for the brightness of the jade, but in the amber light all I see is wood smoke and fire.

He sees through me. He must.

"You saw his halo," I say. "The mirrored cuff, you saw it?"

"I saw it."

"I didn't mean to take it, Jake."

He drags a hand over his chin, the scruff scratching. "I believe you."

"But I have it," I say, shrugging out of the purse slung around my body like a quiver of arrows. "I thought Canaan should have it."

Jake stares at the bag clutched in my hand like it's a grenade and I've just pulled the pin. "Why?"

"Because the temptation's too much," I say.

He's trying hard not to let his disappointment show, but I've memorized every line on his face, studied every curve. And right now the softness is gone, the lines are too many.

"What do you see?" he asks, the purse still hanging between us. "With his halo?"

I shake my head. "He said I won't see fear any longer. I won't see pain."

"It takes your celestial eyes from you, and you're *tempted*?"

"He promised me you," I say, standing. Needing more air. Moving away.

"He what?"

"If I took the halo with me, if I gave it a try, he said he'd guarantee us a lifetime together."

"Why not three or four lifetimes?" Jake says, standing, his voice scratching out sarcasm. "He doesn't hold forever in his hands, Elle. He can't promise that."

"I know. I do. I just . . . With my ring, with it . . ."

"Missing."

I close my eyes and try the sentence again. "With my ring missing, the idea of it—his promise caught my attention is all. I know he can't make good. I know that. I just . . . I hesitated a moment too long and then the Prince was gone. And I had this."

I hold the bag out to him again, but he still won't touch it. Won't really look at it. His eyes meet mine over the black zipper on top.

He blinks four times before he asks, "Have you put it on your head?"

I shake my head, debating whether or not to open my mouth, whether or not I should tell him everything. Tell him the whole truth. I nearly talk myself out of it. But he waits. And he waits. And even though Jake found a way to lie to me once, I don't think I have it in me to do the same.

I clench the bag to my chest, my arms tired of holding it out. Everything about me sags. "I slept with it under my pillow last night."

I resist the urge to let my eyes drop from his, to look away in shame. I need to know how badly I've messed up. But his face doesn't move. No twitching brows, no clenched lips.

"No nightmares?" he asks, his voice as unknowable as his face.

"No nightmares," I answer.

His head drops. "Okay, but is that a good thing?"

"I don't know," I say. "No, I don't think so. But it *felt* good. It felt nice to actually sleep through the night. Especially after Danakil. But Canaan told me to dream. So, take it. Please."

He steps closer, but his hands don't move. "So it's just duty, then, that has you turning this over?" His voice is soft, but the question feels spiked with judgment.

"It's not duty, Jake. I want to know what happened to my mom as much as anyone. More than anyone. You know that. But come on! Not seeing fear, not seeing misery and terror, getting to hold on to you. Can't you understand how amazing that sounded to me?"

"I'd never want to spend forever with me," Jake mumbles.

"Well, we can't agree on *everything*," I say.

After a moment he reaches out a hand and takes the purse. He lets himself look at it now, those dark brows of his drawing closer together. I wish I could decode his face. Wish I knew what it was telling me. Have I messed up that bad? Did I break us?

He unzips the purse and tips the halo out onto the floor.

"Did he touch you?" Jake asks, his voice soft.

"No," I say. "I don't think so. Would it have been bad if he did?"

"I don't know," Jake says. "I just can't stand the thought of that creature touching you. Hurting you."

"He doesn't have to touch me to hurt me, Jake."

"A truth I'd rather not think too hard about."

Truth. I don't know if I'll ever hear that word again without remembering my conversation with the Prince. Without remembering the truth he showed me about my father. The truth he fixed.

"Did you get a good look at his wings, Elle? At how white they are. At the char on the tips?"

"I did, but only from a distance," I say. "When we spoke, he'd taken a human form."

Jake rubs my arm. "Was it terrifying?"

I bite my lip. "Not exactly. He's . . ."

"What?"

"Well, I was going to say hot, but that's not exactly accurate."

"I thought that adjective was taken."

"It is. Very, very taken," I say, nodding like a fool. "He is stunning though."

Jake looks injured. "I was kind of hoping you'd find him vile and repellent."

"I do," I say. "It's not his face though. It's nothing I could see, actually. But I knew he was evil. I knew it here," I say, my hand on my chest. "And here." I move my hand to my temple.

"But stunning?"

I laugh. "In a charming, diplomatic kind of way."

"The Prince of Darkness is diplomatic?"

"Yeah. I don't know. It's just . . . as beautiful as he is, it's his power, his confidence that's the real attraction. He wears pride, you know? It's all over him. It's—"

"His calling card, Elle. His downfall." Jake drops to his knees and shoves the lid off the chest.

I don't move. I don't look for the missing engagement ring inside. And I consider myself quite mature for that restraint. Jake lifts the dark halo between his thumb and forefinger, holding it like it's a bloody rodent. He drops it into the chest, the reflective metal ringing against what I can only assume is Damien's dagger.

Jake slides the lid back in place and my heart flutters a bit, like the wings of a dying moth. I'm glad the dark halo's shut away. Glad it's there and not under my pillow. Not on my arm. But there's something of death in the experience.

I have no choice but to trust the Throne Room now. Jake

just shut away my only backup plan. I rub the bony spot over my heart, pushing away the anxiety. Jake leans back against the chest, his hair falling every which way, his T-shirt begging for an iron. Really, I just want to curl into his chest and forget everything for a while. I drop to the floor in front of him.

"It's a lie," Jake says. "You know that, right? Lucifer isn't confident. He's a wreck. And he's afraid. I saw his fear, Elle. Up close. It's the only thing he left heaven with—terror, deceit. It's all he has to offer."

I turn the words over and over in my mind and I think again of the Prince's story. Of his account of the Great Rebellion. Of how he was wronged. There's no denying the bewitching power of his words.

"You're tired," Jake says.

I shake my head. "Just thinking."

"He's a liar, Elle."

"No, I mean, I know. I do, Jake. I do."

He looks away then, to the carpet. His fingers picking away at the loose weave.

"What? Did I say something?"

"You said 'I do.' In fact, you keep saying it. Gah, I just wish . . ."

"I know," I say.

"No, you don't. Because, yes. I wish I could throw you over my shoulder and haul you away to the preacher. I wish I could marry you, but it's more than that. I wish I could offer you clarity. Understanding. I wish I could say 'Look, the Prince is the father of lies, the master of confusion. But God, well, He's neat and tidy. He always makes sense.'"

It's such a burden to him—my confusion. I inch closer.

"Jake, I don't hold you accountable for the complexity that is God. And I don't expect you to unravel the mysteries of the universe for me. I just . . . I need you to be honest with me. Always. Stop trying to protect me."

Jake makes a sound, deep and primal. "That's impossible."

I run a hand down his face. "At least tone it down a bit. I have Canaan and Helene for that. And you're in just as much danger as I am. You can't sweep me away. You can't hide me under your wings. So just be here, okay? With me. Help me figure out my nightmares. Help me figure out what to do with Dad. Help me fight. And just . . . leave the rest to the shiny winged ones, you know?"

"Yeah. I know. I do."

Now it's my turn to smile.

"What?" he asks.

"You said 'I do.'"

"I'm practicing," he says, closing the distance between us, sliding his bare feet on either side of my legs. My muscles relax at his touch. Really, everything relaxes. I twist my fingers into his wrinkled T-shirt and tug him even closer. I'm out of words, out of snarky comebacks. I just want to be close.

"I've been thinking," Jake says, his lips brushing mine. "What if you slept here?"

I feel my eyes widen, feel the ache of desire.

Jake kisses me. It's deep and crushing. His hands are on the back of my head, pulling me closer, and then he's not. It's dangerous for us to be this close. This alone.

"That's not what I meant," he says, a sleepy smile on his face.

"I know. But again, you can understand the temptation."

He clears his throat. "I mean, you sleep here so when the

nightmares come, you're not alone. Maybe I can even talk you through them."

It's a thought. Not nearly as sexy as the thought that preceded it, but appealing in a totally different way.

"I don't know if it'll work. I mean, when I'm inside one of these nightmares, it's like I'm there. I'm not even me most of the time. I'm inside whoever's memory it is."

"It might not work, you're right. But it might. And I want to help."

"Okay," I say. "We'll try."

There's a lightness that comes with those two words: *We'll try*. Because it's a plan. It's an effort. It means I'm dreaming for a reason, and that almost makes it palatable.

"But before I can bust out my jammies," I say, "I have dinner plans with Dad. He left a note."

"Yeah, he and Canaan had quite a talk."

That doesn't make me nervous. "What did they talk about?"

"Everything, I guess. Don't worry. Canaan said it was good."

"Good like brussels sprouts or good like chocolate? 'Cause, you know, those are two totally different kinds of good."

"I didn't get the specifics," Jake says, kissing my cheekbone. "Canaan had to duck out."

"Where?"

"He wouldn't say. Didn't want me to worry."

"Frustrating, isn't it?"

"Point taken," Jake says, laying his head back on the black chest. "You know, he's never been this secretive. I think it's because he knows I have the means to go after him now. I have a car, I have . . ."

"I think it's because he loves you. It's the same reason you kept things from me. The same reason I didn't want you to find the Prince's halo on my wrist. We're trying to protect each other from the things we can't control, but . . ."

"It just hurts," Jake says.

"You still haven't said it, you know?"

He sits straighter, his eyes even with mine. "Would you like me to say it now?"

I kinda would. But . . .

"No," I say. "Wait till you have the ring. If we don't find it . . ."

"The words wouldn't be any less true."

"I know," I say, standing, reaching down for his hand. "But I can wait."

24

Brielle

Dad's already home when I get there. His truck is parked out front and I walk around it, slowly. I look for signs of a collision, anything to tell me he rammed the side of Crooked Leg Bridge, but there's nothing. I have to stop on the porch to gather myself.

I was stupid in Danakil.

I fell for a sentimental lie. Because it's plausible, probable even. But a lie nonetheless. It makes me feel papery, transparent, easy to bend and fold. I could've kept my mouth shut. I *should've* kept my mouth shut. If I had held out against his lies a little longer, help would've arrived and maybe, just maybe, I wouldn't have ended up with the dark halo.

But beyond feeling like a failure, it doesn't matter, does it? We've shut it away. Jake's not angry—not really angry, at least. And we can move on. Move forward. We have a plan.

I just can't be that stupid ever again.

I still myself and push through the door and into the kitchen, as ready as I'm ever going to be for this conversation with Dad. He's here, working over the stove, cooking—er, burning—spaghetti.

I wave my hand at a plume of smoke that smacks me gob in the face.

"What happened here?" I ask, sputtering.

"User error," he says. "I got a phone call while the sauce was simmering. Walked away. Stuff burns. Who knew?"

Dad flips off the burner and dumps the pan in the sink. "You okay, kid? You're standing there like I stole your last Dr Pepper."

"You burned your famous spaghetti. It's so sad."

"Yeah, well. I'm easily distracted today." He looks good, a little depressed, maybe. But he's showered, his beard's trimmed. The wound on his head is still bandaged, but it's bright white. Just changed, it looks like. He's been home from work for at least an hour then. And not a sign of alcohol anywhere. "Pizza?" he asks, wandering toward the phone in the living room.

"Sure."

Dad pours a glass of milk to go with his pizza, and I do the same. Normally I'd reach for a Dr Pepper, but in the absence of fist pumps, I feel the need for solidarity. He grabs both our glasses and jerks his head toward the pizza box.

"Come on," he says. "Let's sit outside."

I grab the pizza and follow. Dad throws a blanket out in the back of his truck. It smells like wood chips and man, but it's not too bad. And to be honest, it might be just what I need. We used to camp out in the bed of Dad's truck a lot when I was little. He used to say, "Who needs a campsite when I can park this baby anywhere?"

We'd park out by the lake, pile the sleeping bags four or five high, and sleep under the star soup. I laugh into my pizza. It's funny remembering that now. It's what I called the night sky as a kid. Star soup. I run my hand over the sleeping bag beneath me, thinking about the time we woke to a truck bed full of rainwater. "I guess God let the soup bubble over," Dad had said. I was four or five, maybe, the first time I remember hearing the word *God*.

We chew in silence for a bit, and I grow nervous. I don't know where this conversation is headed, and I'd rather he steer. I take another swig of milk and flash my mustache at Dad. But he's grown serious.

"That Canaan fella is a trip," he says.

I mop up my milk mustache and look to the highway. It's empty, the dry field beyond it full of dirt clods and peeling evergreens.

"Yeah. You get used to him."

"Is he telling the truth?" he asks.

"I'm sure he is," I say, setting my pizza aside and looking back at Dad.

"You can see angels and . . ."

"Demons. Yeah. Dad, Canaan's not going to lie to you."

"Well, he ain't particularly forthcoming."

"I'm sure you can understand why."

He scratches at his beard. Not just a little scratch, but one of those manly, lumberjack, take-off-your-skin scratches. "Can you see them now?" he asks quietly.

I've been avoiding this, really. Looking at the sky, really looking. But Dad's asking. He wants to know, so I tilt my head up and focus. I remind myself that it's just a veil that hangs over us all, just a veil that separates us from the real, the true. And just when I think it's not going to happen, the dewy blue sky peels away and shows its bright orange underbelly.

The Celestial.

"Yes," I say. "I can."

I let my gaze fall, taking in Dad's pale face.

"What do you see?"

"Right now? Right now there's a legion of demons surrounding Stratus. They've been pushed back some, by the Sabres, I think. Though I can't see any of them now. That might be why you can't hear them, Dad. They might be too far away."

"You were eavesdropping last night," he says. "I knew you were awake."

"It was nice, you know? You three fawning over me. Talking in civil tones. I wasn't going to mess that up by opening my eyes." I look back to the sky. "Really, I just see a sea of black overhead. They're too far away for me to see anything else." I'm relieved that the Palatine are suffering setbacks, and I hope Dad hears hope in my voice because this might scare him a bit. "But I've seen them up close. I know they're heavily armed. They're damaged from the light. And they'll do anything to keep the citizens of Stratus from seeing them."

He folds a slice of pizza in half and shoves it into his mouth. I watch the sky as he chews. It's strange seeing the world like this, part Celestial, part Terrestrial. The sky is streaked with white clouds, a yellow sun hides behind the trees, but above it all, beyond it all, buried beneath it all, is the Celestial. Just as real, just as close.

"Why can I hear the Sabres, Elle?"

This is one of those questions. The kind I'm not sure I can answer. "What did Canaan say?"

"Said he doesn't exactly know why. Said most everyone has some kind of gift."

"I have a theory. It's a working theory, okay, so don't point out all the holes."

"Spill it, kid."

"I can't always hear celestial things. With the exception of the Sabres, I've never heard something I haven't seen. So I think maybe what we hear is connected to what we know. What we're willing to believe. Canaan's right. You've always believed, Dad. I think you hated that you believed, but you did."

"Other people believe much better than this old guy, Elle." He thumps his chest. "Why me?"

"I don't know if you're ready for this part, Dad."

"It's a theory, right? Shoot. I'm ready."

"I told you about my dreams, about the strange things I've been seeing and how they seem to be actual events from the past. I told you about . . . Virtue taking Mom to the school. Told you that Mom saved Olivia."

Dad averts his eyes.

"You told me."

"Okay, well. Before Virtue took Mom, I got to see her there in her hospital bed. I got to watch her hold me. I got to hear her sing. And Dad, her worship was just so . . ."

He looks at me, desperation on his face. "What?"

"Fragrant. And I remembered, Dad. I remembered what she smelled like. What her worship smelled like. It's probably the only real memory of her I have."

Dad swipes at his nose, his eyes.

"She asked Virtue something before they left the house." My eyes fill with tears at the memory. I swore I'd stop all this crying, but there's no controlling these tears, so I don't even try. It's too precious. "Mom told Virtue she wanted us to know the Father like she did. You and me. She asked that we be given ears to hear and eyes to see. Virtue told her that it wasn't within his power to grant that kind of request, but that she could be certain the Father hears and answers His children."

Dad stares at me with his mouth partly open, a pepperoni stuck to his beard. I grab the pepperoni and shove it into his mouth. He chews obediently.

I made Dad promise not to poke holes in my theory, but there are several of them, and I wonder if maybe there isn't a clear reason Dad can hear the Sabres. Any clearer than the idea that God allowed him to.

"I don't know," I say, backtracking a bit. "Kaylee heard the Sabres the other day too, so it can't just be Mom's prayer. But maybe . . . maybe it played a part. Who knows? It's just a theory."

Dad makes all sorts of throaty nervous sounds.

"It's a good theory," he says. "I like it. Like the idea that your mom had a hand in it. That she wanted me to hear." More throaty nervousness. "Makes it easier. Makes it better."

"I think so too." I reach out and take his hand. "Can I ask a question now?"

"I don't have a single theory if that's what you're getting at."

"No. Nothing like that. I just . . . How's the drinking, Dad? What are you . . . what are we doing there?"

"Oh. That. Well, as you can see, I've yet to replace the beer you so gracefully disposed of the other day."

"Does that mean you plan to?"

"Not if Delia can help it. She's dragging me down to the

community center tomorrow night. AA. It was a suggestion first made by Olivia, by the way."

"Ironic much?"

"She didn't have a thing to do with my drinking, kid."

I don't believe him. I think she nudged him along, but I also know she's damaged. Broken. Worse than most and somehow, some way, she got tangled up with Damien. "You've known her for longer than you let on. Since she was a kid. Why did you lie?"

"I didn't lie, Elle. I didn't know. Not until the Fourth." July Fourth. Independence Day. Our picnic at the lake.

"What happened on the Fourth?" I ask.

"Your boy Marco happened. When she saw him she got all . . . squeaky. And familiar. I had to know if she was the same Olivia we'd known as a child. And then I remembered your mom begging me to take pictures. Of her with her friends. With you. She knew her time was short and she wanted to leave us something, I think. So we kept the camera with us."

Even in her last days Mom was thinking of others, of what Dad and I would need when she was gone.

"Never had the courage to have the pictures developed before now, but the day after the picnic I scrounged up the old camera. Can you believe that roll of film was still in there? I'd forgotten. About Olivia. About her mom. That was a lot of years ago, baby. Too much has happened since then."

"She grew legs," I said.

"She certainly did."

"Eew, all right. I get it. You've got a thing for her."

"Nah. She's too young for me, kid. Too ambitious. Too attached to my memories of your mother, if I'm honest. Don't give another thought to Olivia."

"That's the thing, Dad."

"What's the thing?"

"I need your help."

He shifts forward, the truck lurching from side to side. "Whatever you need."

He says it like he means it, and while that's inspiring, it's also a bit daunting. I don't want to ask too much because he still seems emotionally thin, and I can't send him back to the bottle. I won't.

"All my dreams seem to be centering around Olivia," I say.

"Really?"

"Yeah. As a child. In the hospital with Mom. In a burning building." I don't divulge everything. I don't tell him about Henry or Javan. I don't tell about Olivia's upbringing. Dad doesn't need to know it all just yet.

"I know it sounds crazy, but the dreams are recurring, repetitive, and I think I'm supposed to be seeing something in them that will help us figure out how to fight from here. How to help the angels on this end."

Dad sits up straight, pizza crumbs falling from his chest. "I told you before, kid, I don't want you to be a hero. I've seen that Damien. I know what he can do."

I take Dad's hand and lean in. "Then you know there's no way to keep me safe. You can't protect me from him. We have to fight."

He grumbles, something incoherent and angry.

"Somehow what happened all those years ago is connected to what's going on now. And we need to figure out how. Mom would want us to."

"That's cheating," Dad says.

"I know, but you want to know what happened to her after

Virtue took her from the fire. I want to know. I need to know. And these dreams are going to help us. But I was only three when Mom disappeared, and I need you."

"To do what?"

"Help me fill in the blanks. I know Mom was being treated at a Portland hospital. Why not here? Why not in Bend?"

"Portland has better doctors, better treatment facilities. No mystery there."

"Okay." I figured it was something like that. "Then what about Olivia? I know they met in a waiting room . . ."

"How'd you know about the waiting room?"

"I dreamed it," I say, plowing ahead. "Mom was really sick, Olivia was drawing a unicorn, wearing a necklace . . ."

Beneath a fringe of fur, Dad's bottom lip trembles. I pause. It's too much, I think. Dad's not ready for this, but he wipes his chin with a callous hand and clears his throat. "I wish I'd saved the necklace. Your mom loved that thing."

"This necklace?" I ask, pulling the beaded rope from beneath my collar.

Dad's mouth gapes and he leans forward, taking the wooden flower in his fingers. "Where'd you get this?"

"Jake found it. At the graveside after . . . everything." Technically it was in a tree, but he doesn't need the details right now. "Why'd you bury it?"

He runs a thick finger over the fading paint of the plumeria. "I couldn't stand to see the thing. In those last days it was always around her neck, tangling in the cords and IVs. But she kept it on because the girl asked her to."

"Olivia?"

"Still seems strange that they're one and the same, but yeah.

Liv gave it to her. Told her to wear it for luck or some such non-sense. When your mom disappeared, she left it behind. Some luck, huh?"

I think about the memory Virtue gave me, the waking dream I had while standing in the orchard. I was wearing the necklace when Virtue took Mom. Me. Three-year-old me.

"Why'd they stay in contact?" I ask. "Mom and Olivia?"

"She was always there, at the hospital. Drawing or reading. Her mom worked there."

"With cancer patients?"

"Only on occasion. I think she was in the maternity ward or something. Pediatrics, maybe? Totally different floor. But that little girl wandered the hospital while her mom worked. Kind of sad, really, but safer than staying home alone, I guess. She and your mom built a friendship. There are letters around here somewhere. Found them when I was looking for the camera."

"Letters from whom?"

"From Liv to your mom. When your mom moved back home, they became pen pals of a sort. Liv kept writing, even after your mother was gone. I probably should have opened them, should have written back, but I didn't have it in me. If you think they'll help, I'm sure I can find them again. I was drunk the first time, though, so I might need to down a couple first. You know, retrace my footsteps."

"Not a chance."

"It was a joke, kid."

"A bad one."

"Yeah, well." He sighs. "You want the letters, you got them. What else can I do?"

"You can ease up on Jake," I say.

"Talk about cheating. That's worse than wishing for more wishes."

"I love him." I've said it to Jake, might as well tell Dad.

Dad laughs, really he chokes out this laugh-snort combo thing. "You think I don't know. I do. I remember what it's like. But you need to think this through. Really think, too, 'cause this world, this craziness that he's brought to Stratus, doesn't hang around every guy. And you'd have your pick, baby. Trust me. Finding another looker wouldn't be a problem. Especially if you took that scholarship, moved out East. All those college boys. I bet there are entire schools of them who don't think a thing about angels or demons. Thousands who'd cut off their left leg to be with you."

My face flushes—I feel it, the anger, the frustration. But I know Dad's just being Dad. Just being honest. Trying to help.

"Jake didn't cut off a leg, that's true. But he healed my ankle. He introduced me to the God who created everything, to the God Mom loved. He healed your shoulder, Dad, and if he and Canaan hadn't been here the other day, odds are fairly good you'd be dead."

Dad watches me for a bit, his brows casting his eyes in shadow. He takes a swig of milk, swishes it around his mouth and then swallows. He wipes his hands on his pants and pulls an ancient BlackBerry from his chest pocket. He should get an award for hanging on to that thing for so long.

"Who are you calling?" I ask, trying not to be offended that he's busted out a phone in the middle of our conversation.

"Not calling," he says. "It's vibrating."

"Who is it?"

"Hush, nosy."

"Oh, it's like that?" I slurp my milk loudly as Dad presses the phone to his ear.

"So grown up," he says to me. And then into the phone, "Hey, Mike, what's up?"

It's the sheriff. I should probably be a little more mature. But I just slurp louder.

Eventually Dad hefts himself out of the truck, throwing me a look. I deserve every bit of it, but it's not the look of annoyance I was expecting. It looks more like panic. I stop slurping and wipe my chin.

"All right," he says, his voice falling away as he tromps from the truck. "All right. Yeah. We'll be there. Give me a few minutes."

Where is he going?

His long strides are taking him across the field, toward Jake's. Toward his front door.

I watch as Dad pockets his cell phone and knocks on the front door of the old Miller place. Watch as it opens and Dad has something resembling a very short, very civilized conversation with Jake.

Then Dad turns and crosses back toward me, Jake just behind, his shoes in his hands. He pulls them on as he walks, takes a second to adjust his jeans, and then catches up with Dad, the sun bouncing off his white shirt. He's showered and changed in the hour since I left him.

Gosh, he's beautiful. I watch him approach. I could watch him all day, really. He looks nervous, apprehensive. Understandably so. I don't think my dad's ever knocked on his door, and it has me a little nervous too.

I'm still sitting in the truck, confused, waiting for someone to tell me what's going on, but Dad doesn't climb up next to me. He leans against the side of the truck, his eyes on mine. Jake rounds the truck on the other side, puts his hands on my shoulders. I feel surrounded. Very, very surrounded.

"Hey," he says.

"Hey. What's going on?"

Dad glances at Jake and then back at me. Weird, weird. It's like he was looking for strength, looking for it in Jake.

"You're killing me, Dad. What'd the sheriff say?"

And then he just says it. "Miss Macy was in a car accident."

25

Brielle

I feel like I've been hit with a baseball bat, run into an electric fence. Dad's words couldn't have caught me more off guard. "What? When?"

"Today," Dad says. "This afternoon sometime. Out at Crooked Leg Bridge."

A car accident at Crooked Leg Bridge? That can't be a coincidence.

"But it was supposed to be you," I say. "He said it was you."

"I'm sorry, baby. What?"

"Never . . . never mind." There's too much light and not enough air, but Jake squeezes my shoulders and I find center again.

"Elle, you okay?" Dad asks, climbing up next to me. "You need a drink or something?"

I shake my head. "I'm fine. I just . . . Tell me what happened?"

He leans back, the truck creaking under his weight. "She was driving that old minivan of hers, picking up girls for that whatchamacallit you ballerinas always insist on going to this time of year."

"Dance camp." I totally forgot that started today. Miss Macy's Dance Academy is one of the many sponsors. Every year she loads up as many little dancers as she can and carts them off to a ballerina boot camp in the city. "Was anybody hurt?"

"They all were, baby. Miss Macy came out of surgery about an hour ago, Mike said. They removed her spleen, but she's still unconscious. Hasn't been conscious since they wheeled her in. Whacked her head pretty bad, I guess. Won't know how bad it is until she wakes."

Dad's trying to be gentle. He is. But every word he says cuts. Deep. I can't lose Miss Macy. There's no way.

"What about the girls?" I ask, needing something positive to cling to. I wrack my brain, trying to remember who all had signed up to go. "She was taking Sharon Wilkie and the Sadler twins. And um . . . the new girl from the intermediate class, just moved here with her family. Tall, great feet . . ."

"Regina Glascoe," Dad says. "Her dad works at the mill."

"That's right," I say, remembering.

Dad glances at Jake and then back at me. "They don't think Regina's going to make it."

Fear bubbles from my nose. I swipe at it with my hands, try to pry it off my face, but it's thick. I watch as it presses through my fingers and slides down my arms.

"I called you for a reason, kid," Dad barks at Jake. "Hold her hand or something."

Jake takes my hand, and I hear him praying under his breath. The fear doesn't stop, but it slows a little.

"The older girl, Sharon, she's all right. Broke her collarbone, but they'll probably release her tomorrow."

"And the Sadler twins?" I ask.

"Doctors don't know," Dad says. "They're still running tests."

"Where are they?"

"Regina was life-flighted to Portland, but the others are at Stratus General."

"I have to get over there," I say, swinging my legs over the tailgate.

"Hop in the truck," Dad says. "I'll drive."

The ride to the hospital isn't a long one—Stratus General is just past the high school—but it seems to take forever. If it weren't for the Palatine here, the war raging overhead, if it weren't for all of that, maybe Canaan or Helene would have been able to stop the accident. Maybe they could have prevented this tragedy.

I'm crammed between Jake and my dad. The rattle of the truck is all the noise there is—that and the gurgling black tar that's everywhere. Jake strokes my hand, still praying. Always praying.

I wish I could stop seeing the fear. And it's not just mine anymore. It bleeds from all three of us, filling the floor of the truck, multiplying, leeching off our misery. Seeing how thick it is, how miserable we are, makes it all so much harder. Even the golden halo on my wrist isn't much help. I close my eyes and press my head against the seat back.

Regina's not going to make it. Twelve years old, and dead on her way to dance camp. What a waste. What a stupid, unnecessary waste. Did the Prince do this? Did he do it to force me into his halo?

Is Regina going to die because of me?

I make Dad pull over so I can vomit. I climb over Jake and into the overgrown grass on the side of the highway. There's a hill here. A few missteps and you could tumble a good hundred feet or more without finding a thing to slow your descent. It's tempting to try it. But Jake runs a warm hand up my back and hands me an old shirt that smells like the cab of Dad's truck. I wipe my face on it and fling it into the bed.

"You okay?" Jake asks.

"No," I say. Over his shoulder I see the fear spilling out the open door and onto the street. I see Dad's head pressed to the steering wheel. "It can't be a coincidence. A car accident on Crooked Leg Bridge the day I decided not to wear the Prince's halo? It's my fault the girls are in danger. My fault some of them may die."

"That's a stretch, Elle."

"No," I tell him, certain, adamant. "No, it's not. The Prince showed me this. In Danakil. He showed me a car accident on the bridge, but it wasn't Miss Macy. It was my dad. He was dying and there was no one here to save him. And that's . . . that's why I agreed to talk to the Prince. To answer his questions. Because he said he could fix it. He showed me, Jake."

Jake's eyes close. "It wasn't real, Elle."

"I know! But it was a threat. I see that now. It was a threat disguised as . . . as . . . something else. As help. He wanted me to feel indebted. And I did. I fell for it."

I want him to tell me it could very well be a coincidence, but Jake doesn't believe in coincidences, and he's not going to lie to me. Not again.

He grabs my shoulders now, his hazel eyes dazzling in the dying sunlight.

"It's still not your fault. We're each responsible for our actions. You for yours and the Prince for his. He's a created being just like you. Just like me. And he will answer for his sins."

He's fierce when he's like this, and I love him for it.

"We need to go," he says, taking my chin in his hand. "I'd like to see if I can help."

Of course! I can't believe I forgot about his gift. About his hands.

"Oh my gosh, yes. Let's go."

We wade through the long grass and back to the truck. And for the last four minutes of the drive, there's hope. That we could make a difference. That even if this is my fault, Jake could make it better. Could make them better.

Dad drops us at the sliding glass doors of the hospital and leaves to park the truck. I rush inside, Jake behind me. Pastor Noah and Becky meet us in the waiting room. They've been here for a while, I can tell. Sharon's little brother sits at a small table at Becky's side with a portable DVD player and earphones.

"His mother ran to the cafeteria," Becky explains.

"What about the other girls?" I ask.

"It's a waiting game with the twins," Pastor Noah says. "A couple broken bones and lacerations, but they haven't been able to wake them."

"And Miss Macy?"

"She's awake," says a voice behind me.

I startle and turn. I'm face-to-face with a doctor who looks remarkably like the giant orangutan at the Oregon Zoo. His arms are too long for his round body, his eyes are closely set, and his red beard is patchy. But he has a kind smile. "Brielle, I assume?"

"Yes," I say. "Can I see her?"

He nods. "She's asking for you. But just for a few minutes, all right? She needs to rest."

"Is she okay?"

"Seems to be. She can live without her spleen. We'll keep her for a while. Observation and recovery. She's got a drain in, so be careful with her."

"Of course."

Miss Macy looks very small and frail in her hospital bed. I enter, Jake by my side. The doctor almost didn't let him come with me, but I can be rather persuasive when I need to be.

"Elle, sweetness." Her voice is small and hoarse, but I burst into tears at the sound of it. "Now, stop that," she says, her words coming in short, raspy chunks. "I need you to tell me about the girls. That monkey man wasn't the least bit helpful. And this little gal here is under doctor's orders not to tell me a thing." She's talking about a candy striper stacking supplies in the cabinet beyond her bed.

"I'm a good soldier," the girl says with a little salute, "but if you'd like to update her, I won't say a thing to Dr. Olsen."

Jake gives me a look that doesn't take a genius to decode. He can't touch Miss Macy's stomach with the candy striper here. Can't even try.

"Come on, Elle," she says. "Spill it."

I tell her because I can't lie to her. Not well, anyway. But I wish I hadn't. I wish I'd lied or sent someone else in first, because the first thing that happens when I tell her about Regina is that fear gushes from her chest. Black and soupy. It runs down her stomach and onto the bed, pooling where the bed is folded and then dripping in rivulets to the floor. Her hands, jammed with IVs, tremble and her shoulders shake.

"We're going to do everything we can," Jake says. It's a weird thing to say. Especially to Miss Macy, who knows nothing about Jake's gift. But it doesn't faze her. She's always thought Jake had superpowers.

"You know what you can do? You can pray." She looks nearly as fierce as Jake did just minutes ago alongside the highway. "When we pray, things happen. Strange things. Miraculous things. You pray, young man. And you don't stop."

I hear her words but can't keep my eyes off the fear. Her fear. My fear. It's all mingling. Even the candy striper adds her own to the slick mess on the floor. Before I can gather myself enough to answer, we're interrupted by a nurse who shuffles in with a tray of needles.

"I'm going to need you two to head on out now. This wonderful lady here's got some recuperating to do."

I lean in to kiss Miss Macy on the cheek, everything about me slow and weighted down by fear.

Jake takes my hand and leads me out the door. "She'll be all right," he whispers. "If I was concerned at all I would have done it anyway."

"Okay." That's all I can manage right now.

"Let's see if we can get in to see the girls," he says.

But our efforts are blocked. We're allowed a glimpse of the twins through a pane of glass, but the doctors are running tests and everyone's been asked to wait outside. We stand with their parents for a while. Both of them are so bound by fear they can barely stand. Mrs. Sadler is hunched over, hugging her abdomen, the fear leaking through every meager gap. Her husband rubs her shoulders, his arms shaking, his shoulders trembling with the black weight pressing down on him.

He smiles at me though. When I talk. When I say hopeful things. And yet, the fear still runs. I wish again and again that I didn't have to see the fear. That I could let myself believe this man isn't entirely void of hope. But as I watch, as I listen to the tragic best-case scenario Dr. Olsen's painted for them, I can't help but succumb to the fear myself. It's not fair for these two little girls to lose their lives. Not fair to them and their futures, not fair to their parents.

When Mr. Sadler runs out of words, Jake and I stand by him and his wife in silence. We watch the little girls sleep, their chests moving up and down, helped by the machines on either side of them. Tia has one arm in a bright pink cast, and Pria's leg is in traction. But with their orange hair splayed across their white pillows, both remind me of Helene's celestial form. Small. Fragile. I pray they have some of her strength. Some of her fight.

Jake presses a hand against the window. I know he's praying, but fear marks every single one of his movements: a smear on the glass, a shoe print on the floor. He wants to fix them so badly. I know he does.

Eventually we're shooed away from the viewing area as well. "Family only," the doctor says. I squeeze Mrs. Sadler's shoulder and we go, Jake's hand burning hot in mine. There's nothing more we can do here. Nothing more to say.

Before we leave, and even though visiting hours are over, we slip into Sharon's room. She's alone, her neck in a brace, her arm in a sling, staring at a muted television.

"Hey, Sharon," I say, trying to remember if she's just turned thirteen or fourteen.

"Miss Brielle? What are you doing here?"

"Checking on you, of course." I try to smile. Try to inflect something other than sadness. Where the other rooms were full of fear, this one is drenched in the waters of misery. It runs down her face like tears, soaking her sheets, splashing to the floor.

"I'm okay. Better than Regina, at least. If I hadn't called

shotgun," she says, her voice warbling, "if I hadn't taken the front seat, maybe she'd be okay."

I want to hug her, but my hands are thick with fear. I'm afraid to touch her, afraid to pass it along, so I wrap my arms around myself and try to pray. But it's so hard.

Jake reaches out, takes her hand. "Don't give up on her," he says.

A sob shakes her, but the brace and the sling keep her from bending to it. "It was awful, Elle. It's . . . I don't understand what happened."

"The sheriff told my dad they're not sure," I tell her. "He said Miss Macy must've lost control of the van."

She takes a labored breath. "She ran into something, I think. We just stopped. The hood was all crunched up. And then the van flew sideways, right off the bridge."

"Through the guardrail?" Jake asks.

"Over it. And then I wake up here and my mom tells me Regina might not make it." The misery runs faster now, and I close my eyes just to escape for a second. The room grows very, very quiet.

When I open my eyes, Jake is functioning the way he was meant to function. Entirely in his element. His hand is on Sharon's shoulder, and she's fast asleep.

"Almost done," he says. Every bit of the fear on him has gone. Having the ability to act, to do, to fix, frees him from it. I wish I could figure out how to escape the fear that comes with my gift. Seeing only multiplies it, makes it harder to evade.

"Try it," the Prince had said. "That's all I ask."

Even if I didn't use the dark halo at night, if I let myself dream, it could still be helpful here, couldn't it? Where fear and misery are everywhere. Where it renders me useless. I'd be so much more valuable if I could do something other than shake at the sight of it.

"Okay," Jake says. "You ready to go?"

Sharon looks peaceful now, her head nestled into her pillow, her lips softly opened. It's tempting to take off the brace, let her be truly comfortable. She doesn't need it now, but it's best to let the medical professionals decide these things.

"Yeah," I say. "Let's."

Dad's in the waiting room talking to Pastor Noah. Well, kind of talking. He's got a magazine open, covering half his face, but he nods every now and then at the pastor's remarks. It's absolutely rude, but it's progress. When he sees me, he tosses me the keys to his truck. They smack me in the gut and fall to the floor.

"Sorry, baby," he says. "Thought you were paying attention."

"I was. I just didn't expect to be attacked by jagged metal."

Jake scoops the keys off the floor.

"I'm going to stay here tonight," Dad says. "We're going to take turns sitting with Miss Macy—Noah and I."

"And I'm going to keep this little guy," Becky says, ruffling the boy's hair. "I'll be back in the morning so the guys can go to work."

The gesture is overwhelming. "I could stay with you, Dad."

"Not a chance," he says. "I owe her. She sat lots of hours in hospitals for me. It's the least I can do."

"Still . . ."

"And," Dad says, standing, moving closer, "from what Canaan says, you've got some dreaming to do." His voice is quiet, his look far too knowing. It's weird having Dad in on everything. And kind of nice. "Get her home, kid. Truck's 'round back."

Dad punches Jake in the shoulder as we pass. I think it's supposed to be an attempt at camaraderie, but Jake rolls his shoulder as we walk out the door. I'm a good girlfriend, so I pretend not to notice.

Plus, I just need to get out of here. The waiting room, the hallway, the space between the two sliding doors—it's all coated with fear. I pinch my eyes shut and slide my hand into Jake's. I can let him lead me to the truck, but it doesn't really matter, the fear's still here. It wraps around my feet and I stumble.

Jake slips his arm around my waist and pulls me through a flowered archway that leads to the hospital's garden walk. Through a pair of cypress trees, the sun is nothing but a blood-red blot on the horizon, the misty blue of night rising above it. It's almost eight o'clock.

"You ready to dream?" Jake asks. His voice is quiet. I don't think he expects me to say yes. Which is good, because I'm not sure I can do this. I've had just about as much tragedy as I can stand.

"No," I say. "I'm not ready."

Square paving stones cut a serpentine path through blossoms of yellow and pink flowers. There's a man-made pond here, off the cancer ward. A place of solitude where the patients can come for peace and calm. Something other than beeping machines and worried relatives. There are benches, too, around the pond. Each of them placed in memory of a lost loved one.

I don't sit. Instead, I grip the back of an intricately carved wooden bench and will my hands to stop shaking.

"It's early, Elle," Jake says. "We have time."

"Maybe we don't."

"We have time," Jake says, moving behind me. He presses

against me, his hands covering mine on the bench, and I'm swallowed by warmth. I stare out at the pond, at the reflection of courting birds dancing overhead.

I want *this*. I want peace and calm. At least for a while. The fear is just so much. It's all the time, everywhere.

"I don't know if I'll ever be ready," I say.

Jake turns me toward him. His eyes leave me feeling naked, exposed. I feel like a coward. He takes my face in his hands, his thumbs resting on my lower lip.

"If I could crawl inside your head and slay every dragon, I would." He's shaking with intensity. "But these nightmares were given to you, and I can't dream them. I can hold your hand though. Will you let me do that? Will you let me help?"

I'm so tired of crying, so sick of being afraid, but I'm powerless against all of it.

"Do you think the Throne Room took my engagement ring because I'm going to choose the dark halo? Did they take it because they knew I'd choose blindness?"

"Elle . . ."

"*From hands that heal to eyes that see.* That's the inscription on the ring, Jake. What happens if I choose not to see?"

Pain flashes across his face, settles in his eyes, and for a moment I think his hands are going to fall from my face. But he pulls me closer, his lips on mine as he speaks.

"You won't."

26

Brielle

I haven't seen Canaan since we returned from Danakil, haven't heard his voice since he ushered my dad away for a talk, but Jake assures me he's around. The warmth of the old Miller place confirms it.

I stand in the doorway to Canaan's room wearing a pair of sweats, cut off just above the knee, and a tank top that says *Keep Portland Weird*. The golden halo's on my wrist, stilling the spasms in my gut, its heat spreading through my body, making me feel almost normal. There's a light switch just inside the door. I curl my index finger around it and tug the room into darkness. The dove over Canaan's bed seems to glow, the ghostly white of its wings contrasting like a great white moon against an inky sky. The window looks like the cover of a space opera, stars smeared across the horizon, caught in the trees, hanging from the rain gutter.

Star soup.

I'm going to intentionally close my eyes in a minute. In fact, I'm near-asking for a nightmare, but if it weren't for that—if it weren't for the angelic battle raging overhead—if it weren't for the girls fighting for their lives at the hospital just across town, tonight could have been spectacular. A blanket spread across the grass, a midnight picnic, dancing with Jake and his two left feet under an overfed moon . . .

Before I know it I've crossed to the window, my fingers resting lightly on the sill. I'm wishing for that. For a little bit of the sublimely normal.

"I'm here. Let the dreams begin." It's Kay. I catch her reflection in the window and turn. She's standing in the doorway, a polka-dotted pillow clenched to her chest.

I cross the room and pull her into a hug. "You got away, Kay. You called for help."

"I slapped Damien too."

We laugh.

"Thank you for coming, Kay. My dad would freak if he heard I spent the night alone with Jake."

She kicks off her shoes and climbs up on the bed. "I like helping. Anything I can do, you know? Did you see my face? Jake vanished my bruises, and he didn't even need a wand."

"Kind of amazing, isn't he?"

Jake's there then, standing next to me and pushing a warm cup into my hand. Everything's warm here, so unlike the hospital, where fear breeds in the hallways. I raise the cup to my lips, but the robust smell I was expecting is replaced by something flowery. I think immediately of Miss Macy. I feel guilty for being here, in the peace and warmth, when she and the girls are surrounded by so much pain.

"Tea," Jake says.

"Rebelling against tradition?"

"Only thing here that's decaffeinated."

I take a sip, but mostly to show him I'm thankful. The truth is I *am* ready now. Not to be terrified. But to get this over with. To find out what happened to Mom, to understand why her disappearance matters now. To do anything that feels like fighting. Because I am so tired of being helpless.

The change in my demeanor isn't lost on me. I'm greatly affected by the lack of fear here, by the peace, by the hope. I set the mug on Canaan's side table and climb up next to Kay. Jake grabs a fleece blanket from the dresser and lays it gently on my legs, unfolding it until I'm all but covered. The halo seems heavier all of a sudden, pressing against my wrist.

"Would you like to do the honors?" I ask, tugging my arm free of the fleece. Jake pulls the halo off and sets it on my stomach as it unravels. The pressure against my gut reminds me of my conversation with Marco, of the halo unraveling against my body while we spoke, of my inability to hide it from him.

It wanted to be found, I think. Wanted Marco to see it, to understand. And as Jake lifts the halo from my stomach and slides it beneath Canaan's pillow, I remember the way the halo flamed against my wrist at Olivia's touch. I remember her eyes wide with surprise and something else: need. And as my eyes close, I wonder why the halo never warned me about Damien. Why didn't it flash red-hot when he was near?

"Sleep tight," Kaylee whispers.

Colors swirl on my eyelids now. Stains of blue and purple seep into my consciousness, orange and red chasing after them. Gray and black fall like hail through the colors, shredding them, stripping them away, only to be replaced by the green of dew-kissed grass. And then a flash of white, like crisp linen sheets. It ripples and snaps taut before the blue and purple rise again through the cotton.

I want nothing more than to be lost in them. To wade into this ocean of heavenly lights and tones. But as expected, Olivia swims into my thoughts. Just before the colors swallow me whole, I have a tiny, fleeting notion.

Maybe the halo wasn't warning me about Olivia. Maybe the halo wanted something else. Maybe it wanted to be found.

But I'm drowning in the beauty of color now. Olivia grows smaller and smaller, drifting away on rainbow waves. And then, abruptly, the colors are pushed to the corner of my mind and Olivia's desperate eyes stare back into mine.

Only I'm not me.

I'm too small to be me. Too petite. Too bruised.

In my hand is a pencil, tapping the open journal resting on a knee that's been crossed over the other. From beneath my striped sweater a bruise the color of eggplant sneaks, covering the inside of my wrist and the pad beneath my thumb.

I'm Ali.

We sit perfectly still, Ali and I, her pencil tapping out a steady rhythm. Back at the Miller place, lying in Canaan's bed, I feel my breath hitch.

I don't think I can do this. I want to wake up. To wake up!

But a hand wraps mine. Strong and warm. "I'm here, Elle. Breathe."

And then another hand rests softly on my forehead. Cooler. Smaller.

I'm not alone.

Jake presses his lips to my cheek, to the soft spot beneath my ear.

"Good," he says. "Better. You can do this. It's just a dream."

It's a weird thing being entirely aware of two places, but it's better. It's easier with them here. I force myself to take another huge breath.

"What do you see?" Jake says.

"Olivia," I breathe. Her name sounds so eloquent in my head, so easy to say, but it comes out garbled and odd. Jake doesn't seem to notice.

"Okay, how old is she?" He's asking because my dreams seem to come out of sequence. Her age helps us place them, helps us piece the story together. But I've not had this dream before.

Through Ali's eyes I stare into Olivia's face. She looks at Ali a moment longer and then turns toward the window on her right. It spans the whole wall, as does the window behind her desk. Olivia seems to be contemplating something, her red lips recently glossed, her hair parted to the side and pulled into a low, sleek bun. Rain run downs the glass, blurring the skyline beyond, but I recognize it: the pink US Bancorp Tower, the Koin Center with its orange brick and blue crown, the cables of the aerial tram running through it all.

Ali's at Olivia's office in downtown Portland. She must be. She continues to study the woman before her. The expensive blouse, the carefully rolled sleeves, and three silver scars marking Olivia's forearm.

Jake's voice invades the dream once again. "Elle, how old is Olivia?"

I want to answer him, but I'm overwhelmed by the nerves running through Ali. She's obviously waiting for Olivia to speak, to answer some question I've missed. She lifts her journal and pencil, switches her legs, slides her pencil behind her ear, and all the while she's quoting Hamlet under her breath.

"Where's your father?"

"At home, my lord."

"Let the doors be shut upon him, that he may play the fool nowhere but in's own house."

The dialogue brings with it a bittersweet kind of wistfulness. It's Hamlet and Ophelia. When Marco performed Hamlet, she ran these lines with him over and over. Before tech week even hit, she could quote the iconic play from the guard's entrance to Fortinbras' exit. But she could never keep a straight face when Marco exclaimed, "Get thee to a nunnery." It sent her into hysterics. And even now, with all the anxiety running through her tiny body, her left cheek lifts as she whispers the line.

"She's smiling," Kay says. I hear Kay. She's there. Here. Somewhere in the back of my mind. "At least you're smiling."

I try to squeeze their hands, grateful that I'm not alone, but I can't tell if I've succeeded. Olivia turns back to Ali, her gaze vacant. Jake and Kaylee slip away.

"I wish I could help you. I really do. But Henry Madison is no longer involved with the Ingenui Foundation."

"I'm not interested in Ingenui, Ms. Holt. Not in the slightest. But it took quite a bit of research for me to connect the Henry Madison of Madison and Kline to the H. D. Madison who founded Ingenui. Can you put me in contact with him? If not, I'd be glad to speak to anyone who worked at Madison and Kline."

Olivia's face is all business, and I can tell by the set of her jaw that she's already decided. She's not going to help. "I'm sorry, dear . . ."

"He handled my adoption," Ali says, her voice desperate, "and I know he didn't use the proper channels. It wasn't legal, Ms. Holt."

Olivia stands and runs crimson-tipped fingers over her

designer skirt. "I'd be happy to take your information, and if anything—"

Ali stands too, the journal falling to the ground, her petite frame determined. She grabs something from her back pocket and drops it on the desk. It's a stack of paper, rolled and held together by a green alligator clip. The stationery on the top sheet is identical to the correspondence Serena handed me this morning. There are no Post-it notes on this stack, but at first glance that seems to be the only difference.

"What is this?" Olivia asks, her voice edged with razors.

"Research," Ali says, watching as Olivia flips through the stack slowly. "Look, I don't care about the shady stuff. I love my parents, and from what I've read"—Ali nods at the rumpled stack—"I grew up in a much better home than my birth mom could have given me. But I need to know my medical history. It's important, Ms. Holt. You can burn the rest of the information for all I care, but I'm pregnant."

The room tilts and I can feel Ali's stomach turn. She sits, the chair not nearly as soft as it was a moment before.

"Elle, you there? Talk to me." It's Jake. He strokes my face and my neck, his presence comforting, but I'm stuck in Olivia's office, stuck in Ali's head, and my stomach is threatening to empty.

"Miss Beni?" Olivia says, rounding the desk. I can't tell if she's genuinely concerned for Ali or repulsed by the possibility of her vomiting on the expensive rug covering the office floor.

"I'm fine," Ali says, clenching the arm of the chair. "I've just . . . That's the first time I've said it out loud. I haven't even told the father yet." Ali stares into Olivia's caramel eyes, and I swear I see something break.

"Congratulations," she says, her voice soft. Softer than I've ever heard it. It's weird, but I think she means it.

Ali's not convinced. "Whatever. I know what I look like to you. Some stupid knocked-up kid." She shoves her sleeves above her elbows, showing Olivia the bruises marking her arms.

Olivia frowns. "What happened?" she asks, running a cold finger over Ali's arm. I feel the cold deep in my bones and I shiver. "Who did this?"

"No one did this," Ali says. "I'm sick, and anything you can find on my medical history would really help. I'm not going to press charges. I don't plan to expose anything, but if I'm carrying anything other than anemia, I need to know. The doctors need to know."

Olivia's battling something. I can see it in the way her eyes flit over Ali, in the way her finger lingers over the purple bruises. She tries to stand but her heel catches the corner of Ali's journal. She picks it up and tilts her head at the open page. I can feel the words tumbling around in Ali's head. Apologies, explanations. Blood rushes to her face, and suddenly I'm light-headed—Ali's light-headed.

After another moment Olivia hands the journal back to Ali.

"You're good." She straightens up, a fake smile painted on her face.

I'm dying for Ali to look down at the journal, to give me a glimpse of what seems to have both of these very strong, very brave women shaken. But Ali's fidgety, and when she finally does drop her eyes, it's only for the briefest moment. Still, it's enough. I've seen this page before. It's the sketch of Olivia's arm. Manicured fingers loosely curled, the lines Javan cut into her forearm visible.

"I'm sorry," Ali says, folding the journal closed. "I sketch when I'm nervous."

"You're very talented," Olivia says, but as she moves back around her desk, she unbuttons the sleeve that's been rolled to her elbow and shakes it out. She stands with her back to Ali now, her curvy figure silhouetted by the gray horizon.

Embarrassed, Ali leans forward over the closed journal. "I really am sorry. I didn't mean to invade a private thing. I've just never seen scars like that before."

"I don't imagine you have," Olivia says, unbuttoning the other sleeve, shaking it out. The chinks in her armor hidden, she turns, her face stern. "Be grateful."

Her tone is sharp, final. But Ali needs this information. I can feel it in the stiffness of her neck, in the taut muscles of her legs. She's desperate. "Ms. Holt . . ."

"I'll see what I can find, Miss Beni, but there may not be anything left to pilfer through. The files from Madison and Kline were destroyed years ago."

"Destroyed?"

"Water damage. You can thank whatever deity you believe in for that. But if there's anything to be found"—she pauses here, squares her shoulders—"I'll find it. I'll promise you that much. Leave your number with my assistant."

She's been dismissed, but it's not like Ali to bend to that sort of thing, so I'm not surprised when she speaks again.

"I've read up on you, you know. You've done some impressive things with Ingenui. Noble things."

"Hard work pays the bills," Olivia says, crossing her arms.

Ali stands and tucks her journal under her arm. "I don't fault you for Henry's errors," she says. "I don't think anyone else would either, even if you are his granddaughter."

Olivia hardens, her red nails digging into her biceps. "Most people aren't aware of that small detail, Miss Beni."

"I assumed," Ali says, the bite in her tone surprising me. "It wasn't easy to track your lineage; some of the records are missing."

It's weird what happens then. The playing field seems to level. A begrudging respect slightly visible in the lift of Olivia's brows. "State employees." She shrugs. "What do you expect?"

Ali nods. "Right. But your father was Henry's son."

"Illegitimate son."

Anger runs through Ali's body. I feel every shiver of it. "I hate that word," she says, running a hand across her stomach. "Sounds . . ."

"Unplanned?" Something like annoyed amusement spreads across Olivia's face.

Ali's indignant now, her spine straightening. "We may not have planned for this baby, Ms. Holt, but someone did."

Olivia smiles at that. "I can appreciate your . . . conviction, but take my advice: get money out of the father if you can. Sentimentality won't pay the bills, and I don't imagine a young actress like yourself will have very many job opportunities in another trimester or two."

It surprises Ali that Olivia knows anything about her. "You've done your homework as well."

"Not in the least. I saw you in something at the Keller Auditorium last fall."

"*Our Town*," Ali says.

"Delightful show, if a little melancholy. I've said it once and I'll say it again, you're very talented. But that was long before this *unplanned* pregnancy of yours."

"We're getting married, Ms. Holt." Ali sounds every minute of her eighteen years.

"My advice remains the same. Make sure you're provided for. I don't envy you the road ahead, but you're strong—I saw that in your performance—and you won't be the first single mom to raise a child in this city."

"If either one of us is going to survive this pregnancy, I'm going to need those medical records," Ali says, her voice as steady as I've ever heard it.

Her statement seems to unsettle Olivia. She turns away, her long legs taking her back to the far window. The scars that should be marking her calves, the ones that were seared onto them the day her mother died, are gone. Piecing together her life is a complicated thing.

"No promises," she says.

Ali glances once more at the desk and then reaches for the door handle. Something's bothering her, beyond the obvious. Something I can feel in the constriction of her chest, in the focus of her thoughts.

And then she says it.

"You can keep the papers, Ms. Holt. My research. I have another copy."

The threat is a quiet one, but it's there. And before Jake's shaken me awake, I know why Ali met Olivia at Bellwether.

27

Marco

Everything's purple. The sky, the grass, his fingers. Marco sits in the field behind Delia's, his face turned to the train trundling through her backyard. Beyond it, the sun rises in ominous shades of violet.

He's been out here for hours. Initially he came outside for the cool air, needing to stay awake, needing to do anything but fall back into his most recent dream. He hoped Kaylee would come home, even Delia—he hoped for Delia—anyone to talk to. But no one came, and now his face is cold, his fingers numb, and his eyes droop against the light of morning.

He can't stay awake much longer.

If he had a car he'd leave. If he had a phone he'd call someone. He'd call Liv. But Delia doesn't have a home phone, just a cell. So he lies back, the dry grass rustling in his ears, the rocks beneath his head reminding him of the story Jake marked for him—the one about Jacob, a man who laid his own head on a stone. The man who dreamed of a ladder extending into heaven, angels climbing up and down.

He blinks against the exhaustion.

It wasn't a ladder he saw when he closed his eyes last night. It was Henry. In a wheelchair. The old man was pale, his breathing ragged, his eyes vacant. If it weren't for the rise and fall of his chest, Marco would have thought he was looking at a dead man.

But if he isn't dead yet, if Marco's dreams hold any truth, Henry doesn't have long to live. Because there, standing over the old man, was Damien, a blood-crusted dagger in his fist. Marco expected to feel elation at Henry's impending doom, but he didn't. Marco was afraid for him, a scream of warning, a cry of fear, clawing at his lungs.

But before Marco could release it, he woke. This dream didn't cycle like the others. It didn't drown him in slumber, force him to stay under. It didn't haunt his waking eyes either, but he knew it'd be there when he closed them again.

Why couldn't he dream of ladders like Jacob? Or winged beasts like Daniel?

He's seen enough of death. It's a thought that brings images of Ali. Of her blood on his hands. Of the life his ambition took. The family he robbed himself of.

Tears slip down his cheeks, wetting his ears, and suddenly the nightmare seems less ominous. Henry's looming death is far less painful than memories of Ali. He stops fighting the sleep that waits patiently nearby. The new sun warms his face, and his eyes fall closed.

And just as he knew it would, the dream visits.

But this time Henry's not alone.

This time Damien has another victim.

28

Brielle

"Olivia must've found Ali's medical history. Or at least told her she had."

I'm sitting cross-legged on a bench outside of Jelly's. Kaylee's here, sitting on the curb in front of me while I braid her hair.

"And you think Ali drove out to Bellwether to meet Liv?" she asks.

"Yeah. Or intended to. I don't have proof they actually met."

There's a demon skittering back and forth down Main Street. He's blind and snuffling, his nose pressed to the street. This morning there were two on my front porch lapping at the fear that had gathered there. A half hour ago I saw a gaggle of them in the alley between the community center and the stores fronting Main.

I'm just glad Kaylee can't see them. I refuse to shatter the illusion for her. I can't believe how well she's handling everything, but she's been forced into seeing too much, and I haven't the heart to tell her just how common the demonic seems to be around town today.

I turn my attention back to her, intent on ignoring the

scavenger. We've been talking about last night's dream, about the pieces we now have to assimilate into the puzzle. Jake had to work today. He offered to call in, but his boss's wife's sister is Mrs. Sadler, the twins' mom. The family is rallying around the girls, as they should be, and it didn't seem right for Jake to beg off when Phil was needed elsewhere. The downside of living in a small town is that eventually everything affects everybody.

I spent the morning calling the parents of all our students at Miss Macy's. She sent word through Dad that she wanted classes canceled for the week. I tried to argue that I could handle it, but with Dad as her emissary I was shot down. So I sat through each phone call, fear leaking through the phone, soaking my clothes, and I updated every single family. Told them we'd try to resume classes next week, and then I gave them the most recent news on each of the girls, which aside from Sharon's release hasn't really changed since yesterday.

It was a long morning.

And now I find myself here, with Kay, trying to remember what it felt like to not know, to not see. It's early afternoon and the sun shines bright. I'm wearing the halo on my wrist, but I can't seem to shake the chills that crawl up my arms and down my back. I braid faster—anything to keep moving.

"Ow!" Kaylee rubs at a spot behind her ear. "That one's attached, Matthews."

"Sorry," I say, swatting her hand away. "I'll be careful. How's Marco doing?"

"I don't know. Sometimes he's okay. He smiles every now and then, but he's always thinking. Delia has him ensconced in the spare bedroom. The one with all the doilies, you know? He's been in there for the last couple of days."

I haven't seen Marco since Bellwether. Haven't talked to him since he grabbed Jake's bag and left Stratus with Olivia. "Is he . . . Has he asked a lot of questions?"

"About the demon that dragged you and Jake away? Yeah," she says. "And I kinda let stuff about Canaan's chest slip, so I had to explain that, but mostly he's just quiet. Even quieter after Jake stopped by."

"Jake stopped by?"

"You were sleeping off Danakil."

"Huh." I finish the braid, pull the hair tie off my wrist and secure it. Fiddling with the tail, Kaylee climbs up on the bench next to me.

"I need to tell you something," she says, folding her legs and then changing her mind and tucking them beneath her.

I don't answer. She looks all squirmy, and I feel my emotions start to shut down. It's like they refuse to get involved in whatever Kay's about to divulge. I just don't know how much more I can take.

"When we left Bellwether the other night, Marco asked to make a stop. A detour, he said."

I think about Marco's frame of mind, about his anger. Jake didn't tell me much about Bellwether, but he did tell me Marco seems to be struggling with dreams and visions of some sort. That the halo seemed to magnify them.

"And you let him?"

She nods. "Before I agreed, I did make him promise not to kill Henry. Thought you'd appreciate that."

"I do. Thank you." I sit a little taller, cross my arms. "Where'd you go, Kay?"

"Fred Meyer," she says.

Well, that was anticlimactic. "The grocery store?"

"Yeah."

My arms loosen. "And this is scary because . . ."

"I don't know!" She's so dramatic all of a sudden, so flustered. "It's just . . . He bought a Bible, Elle."

I'm clearly missing something. "And you're disappointed?"

"Maybe. No, not disappointed. I just don't know what to make of it all."

"Because of a Bible? You're not at all weirded out by my Bible, and you actually made s'mores while I sat in the other room praying the other day."

"That's different."

"I love you, Kay, I do. And you've been amazing through all this craziness. I'm just not seeing how Marco with a Bible is any different from me with a Bible. Or Jake, for that matter."

"You guys are sane," she says. "Are we totally, 100 percent sure Marco's okay?"

"Kay . . ."

"Look, he just spent months locked away in a psych hospital, right? He totally freaked out about the whole halo thing. And now he's holed up in the doily room with a Bible and Ali's journal."

"You said he smiles every now and then," I remind her.

"Yeah, he does. But I wonder if these demons have really messed with his head. He only comes out of that room to pee and eat, Elle. Or to ask me questions I have to make up answers to. It's weird hiding away from people like that. It's very Branch Davidian, you know? Very David Koresh."

I laugh. "If there's anyone Marco isn't, it's David Koresh. Not everyone is as social as you. Some of us need solitude to process."

"Well, that's just sad," she says. "I worry about him. He

and Liv had a tragic sort of moment at Bellwether. A moment wherein—"

My lips twist. "You just said 'wherein.'"

"And you just used air quotes. Stop interrupting. It was a moment *wherein* Olivia claimed she'd never met Ali. And given the dream you just had, I worry that Marco knows she's lying to him. Being sad is okay. Depressed, I can deal with. But locking yourself away? That's too scary for me. I like him, you know. He's a nice guy. A good guy. He should be performing onstage, or writing uber self-aware screenplays. Not shut up with the doilies."

Kaylee's concerns, while extreme, aren't entirely unwarranted. Marco does have a thing for revenge.

"Jake gets off at eight. We'll stop by after that and check on him, okay?"

"Thank you," Kay says, unwinding a bit. "Maybe Jake can do his Miyagi hand thing or something."

"Miyagi hand thing?"

"You know, *The Karate Kid*. The original. Mr. Miyagi slams his hands together, rubs real fast, makes them all warm and stuff."

This is why I love Kay. The laughter she rouses just by existing.

"You know that's not how his gift works, right? He can't fix whatever's broken in Marco's head."

"He could try," she mumbles.

"And his hands are always warm. He doesn't need to Miyagi them."

She taps her cheek. "I remember. But, yeah, you should stop by."

"You working this afternoon?" I ask.

"Yeah, but it's been pretty dead around here." She swivels on the bench, peers through the diner windows behind us. "I could use a sick day if you want."

"You can use a sick day when you live with your boss?"

"Me not destroying the diner isn't that big a loss to Delia. She encourages my use of sick days."

It feels almost normal sitting here with Kay. If I could only get rid of the chill. And then, of course, there are the demons. The Vulture has been joined by two others now, all of them snorting and gurgling, bumping their way back and forth down the street. But other than that . . .

"Nah. That's okay," I say. "You're saving for the Peace Corps."

"If they ever get back to me," she says. "Here, you sit. I'll braid yours now."

I scoot off the bench and onto the pavement. I like it when Kay braids my hair. She's much more creative than I am.

"Have you decided what you'll be doing come fall?" She doesn't mention school or the scholarship Dad wants me to take. But I know she's thinking about it.

"I don't know," I say, enjoying the scalp massage Kay's thrown in. "Dad made me send off all the paperwork, so if I want to go, I can go. I have my dorm assignment and everything, but I haven't decided."

"You've had a lot going on, Elle. And Jake's here. I can understand not wanting to leave."

"It's not that," I say. "I mean, maybe that's part of it, but every time I think about going away, I feel . . . it feels wrong. It's like there's something else I should be doing. I just have no idea what that thing is."

"Then give yourself some time to figure it out," she says, releasing my head, digging through her bag. "No one would fault you for taking a semester off."

"Except maybe Dad."

"Dad shmad. He'll come around." She drags a brush through my hair. I close my eyes. Let myself enjoy it.

"It's just, if I go—okay, if I go, if I take this dance scholarship, dance is the only thing I'll have time for." I have no idea what she's doing now, dividing my hair, wrapping tiny bands in place.

"Isn't that what you wanted?" she asks. "To be onstage, dancing in front of thousands."

"It was. For a long time, it was."

"But?" She's tugging on my hair now, braiding maybe, looping. Whatever it is, it feels nice.

"But I see what you've done at the community center, how you've pulled so many people together. You've made a difference around here, Kay."

"But art's important too. Dance is important. It's like . . . telling a story. And Elle, you're so good at it. I wish you could see yourself."

"And I love it. I really do, but do I want it to be my life? My whole life? I don't know anymore. I think of Jake. I think of Canaan. Everything he does is to help others."

"That's kind of his job, Elle."

"But what if it could be my job too? Obviously it would be different."

"You don't have wings."

"True. But I could teach. I love teaching dance, and I could use the rest of my time to"—and then I speak the possibility that was planted in my gut last December—"maybe I could do something about people like Henry. Maybe I could make a difference, you know?"

Her hands pause in my hair. "You want to use your eyes to help."

The thought makes me shudder. "I don't know. Maybe.

Honestly, Kay, seeing is hard. When I'm with Canaan, it's okay, or with Helene. When I'm tucked in their wings, I'm safe—or mostly safe. But, without that . . . I wish I could turn it off. Most of the time I wish I could turn it off." It's an embarrassing thing to say. Because seeing is a gift, I know it is. And you don't return celestial sight like some decorative plate from T.J.Maxx.

"You mean use the Prince's halo?"

I had told her about Danakil, about the Prince's offer.

"No," I say. "I wouldn't."

"But it's tempting?" She flips my hair up from the bottom with one hand, rummaging through her bag with the other.

"Yeah," I say. "It's tempting."

She's jabbing bobby pins at me now. Bobby pins are her favorite. I'm always impressed that I survive this part.

"There," she says. "All done."

I pat my head. Feels like a gazillion braids tied into a bun of sorts. Cool. Much cooler than the simple fishtail I did for her.

"What's Jake going to do?" she asks.

I climb onto the bench again, watching as Kaylee crams a lapful of supplies into her bottomless bag.

"He doesn't know," I say. "I think he's been waiting for me to decide."

"You mean waiting for the engagement ring to rematerialize?"

"Maybe."

We're quiet for a bit. I stare at the flock of Vultures in the street. Yeah, it's a flock now. Eight or nine of them meandering, tripping over one another.

"So let me ask you this, Elle. If that ring were to show up in the chest right now, if Jake were to propose to you tonight, what would you do?"

Stupid question. "I'd say yes."

"Would you? You want to be married at nineteen?"

"We wouldn't have to be married right away," I say. "I don't know. I guess I haven't really thought that part through. I've been so worried about where the ring went and what we have to do to get it back that I haven't thought about what happens next."

She hands me a stick of Big Red. "Well, I definitely think you should."

I peel the foil off the gum. Slowly. Thinking.

"Don't misunderstand me, okay? I love Jake. I hope you do marry him. I hope you have ten beautiful children and I hope you make every single one of them call me Auntie Kay. But your future's really iffy right now, and unless you two are planning to shack up with Canaan for the rest of your lives . . ."

"No," I say, folding the stick of gum. "Canaan could be reassigned at any time. We need our own place. Our own life."

"Then maybe the missing ring isn't the tragedy you think it is, Elle. Maybe it's an opportunity."

I cram the gum into my mouth, feel the burn on my tongue, taste the sweetness. My fingers find the wooden flower hanging around my neck. I like wearing it. It reminds me of Mom. I turn it in my hands now, a new possibility clamoring for attention. Even with celestial eyes, it's possible I've been seeing things all wrong.

"Maybe you're right, Kay."

"Of course I am!"

I let the necklace settle against my chest.

"Maybe."

29

Brielle

I spend the rest of the afternoon at the hospital. When I arrive, Becky's there. She's tucked in the corner of the room reading while Miss Macy snores softly. I squeeze her hand and walk to the viewing area where Mr. and Mrs. Sadler hold vigil.

It's still black, still smeared with fear. Mr. Sadler's doing his best to sleep on a cot that's been rolled into the corner, but he's fitful. Twisting and turning, shaking. And it's no wonder; the fear is so thick here I can hardly move through it.

Mrs. Sadler tells me there's been no change. The large chair swallows her, and I can see she's been trying to knit, but her hands are mostly tangled in the yarn. I offer to bring her lunch; she refuses, and when I step into the hall I feel more miserable than I've felt in a long time.

It's different from the fear of Danakil. Different from my hatred of the demonic.

This is a desperate kind of misery.

I make my way back to Miss Macy's room. It's brighter here, warmer. There are splotches of fear here and there, but most of it's gone. Becky and Miss Macy speak in soft, docile tones. I pull up a chair next to them and sit, let them hold my hand. We pray together, and I realize that though I might be gifted, though I might see the spiritual world in a way they may never see it, there is so much I can learn from them.

"We're not giving up on the girls," Miss Macy tells me. "We aren't, are we, Becks?"

"Not at all," she says. "We've learned from our mistakes."

"We're going to keep fighting," Miss Macy says. "And we're not going to stop. I expect you to do the same, sweetness."

When I leave the hospital, I don't go home. Instead, I park Slugger in front of Miss Macy's studio and let myself in. I don't bother flipping the lights on. Sunlight is scarce beneath the awnings, but enough of it makes its way through the large front windows to light the studio.

It's just me.

And I'm not here to perform.

But I'm out of words to pray, so I'll let my body worship for a while. I'll fight, just like I promised Miss Macy. Like I promised Canaan.

I text Jake and ask him to meet me here after work, and then I drop my phone into my dance bag and pull out a case of CDs I carry with me. The first is a compilation Jake made awhile back. It has a bunch of his favorite bands on it. I drop it into the CD player and make my way to the floor. The vocalist is female; I always forget her name, but her voice moves me.

I listen to the music, to the words. I let them fill me up before I move a step.

"You hold my every moment. You calm my raging seas."

When I do move, I keep my mind on the words, not my feet. I let the song tell me what to dance. I think about the things I've learned about God over the past seven months, and I let the truth lead me into worship. An hour passes before I slide to the floor against the mirror. The room is full of color now—ribbons in a hundred different shades of yellow. I watch them curl around the room, up and through the ceiling. There is so much darkness to see, so much fear. It's easy to forget the beauty. But it's here. Always close.

I'm tired, but I have words now. So I pray them. It's awkward and stilting, but there's no one here to overhear. Even the old men who hold court at The Donut Factory across the street have called it a day. I pray until Jake walks through the doorway.

"You're the most beautiful thing I've ever seen," he says.

I grab a towel from the barre and wipe the tears from my face. "You here for a dance lesson?"

"I wish. You get Kaylee's message?"

"No, I've been—"

"Marco's headed to the city," he says. "We need to go."

When we get to Kaylee's, she's sitting on the front porch, wind chimes tinkling around her.

"Is he gone?" I ask, climbing out of Slugger.

A gust of wind hits me. Cold. Really cold. The Northwest is like this. The cold creeping up, elbowing its way into summer, but this feels different. Turbulent. The wind chimes on the porch go manic, and I crane my face to the sky. What is going on up there?

"Not yet," she says. "He's waiting on a cab."

"It could be awhile then," I say, but Jake's already up the stairs and in the house.

I stop in front of Kaylee. "What happened?"

"Said he had a dream. That Liv was in danger. Insisted on going into the city."

"But you don't think he's telling the truth?"

"What do I know?" she asks. "But it sounds an awful lot like he's using Liv as an excuse to go after Henry."

"I don't think he knows where to find Henry," I say.

"Like I said, what do I know? But he doesn't look normal, Elle."

"How does he look?"

"See for yourself."

I start up the stairs, but Marco flies past me. He's got a backpack on his shoulders, Ali's journal in his back pocket, and a Bible in his hand.

"I'm going," he says. "I have to. Damien's there. At her place."

"And you saw this in a dream?" Jake asks, stepping out the door.

"Yes, I told you."

I'm not sure what to do, what to believe. I've never dreamed of the future before, just the past, but who am I to say it isn't possible?

"What exactly did you see?" I ask.

He pinches his eyes shut. "Fire. There was a fire."

"Like at the school?" Jake asks.

"No," Marco says, frustrated. "Smaller. But Henry was there, in a wheelchair. Damien stood over him with a scabby-looking knife. And Liv was there, you guys! She was screaming."

He gave us the whole dream, but I heard only three words: scabby-looking knife.

"Kay, did you tell Marco about the dagger in Canaan's chest?" Despite the gravity of the moment, the tiniest laugh lodges in my throat. "There really is no good way to say that, is there?"

"No, there isn't," she says. "And no, I didn't. I swear I didn't."

Marco steps between Kaylee and me, demanding my attention. "What are you two talking about? What dagger?"

I turn to Jake, all kinds of questions begging to be asked. He looks down at me, answers every single one of them with his eyes.

"Get in the car, Marco," I say.

"You'll let me take Slugger?" he asks, his eyes wide, his hands in his hair.

"Not a chance. I'm driving. And we need to swing by Jake's first."

His hands fall to his sides. "Elle, I don't want to put anyone in danger."

"Join the club," I say. "Climb in. You coming, Kay?"

She stands and shakes her head, her face drained of color. She really, really hates this idea. "I would. I really would. Slapping demons is cool and all, but I'm pretty sure Liv won't want to see me right now. Not after Bellwether. Not after I told her she wasn't welcome in Stratus."

I climb the stairs and pull her into my arms.

"Pray for us, Kay. Pray for Olivia."

And then I'm in the driver's seat and we're flying down Main. If Damien's dagger isn't in the chest, if he's been here, if he's taken his weapon back, he had to waltz through twelve Sabres to get it. He's either determined to have the thing or determined to have something else that resides in Stratus.

It's that thought that has me slamming Slugger to a stop in

Jake's driveway. Has my feet pounding up the stairs and into the house. The threat of Damien is what has me stumbling into Canaan's room determined to rip the lid off the chest so I can see. So I can know.

But I don't need to remove the lid.

It's on the floor. Tipped there haphazardly, it seems.

I step closer, blood beating against my eardrums, fear shaking my hands. The Prince's halo lies inside the chest, but Damien's dagger is gone.

He's been here.

And if Marco's dream is accurate, Olivia really is in danger.

30

Brielle

Three and a half hours later I'm pressed between a wooden file cabinet and the wall. Welts are forming on each hip—I feel them, but I don't move. Across from me, on the other side of the room, Jake is hidden away in a closet with plantation-style louver doors. Maybe it's just because I know he's there, but I swear I see the tips of his fingers resting on the slats.

Marco's closer. He's wedged behind an antique wingback chair and the wall, a planted ficus doing a pitiful job camouflaging his long legs.

It's a small miracle we haven't been seen. Marco knew exactly how to get to Olivia's house, and even through a summer storm, we made excellent time. But when he knocked on the door, and when she didn't answer, Marco had a mini panic attack right there on the stoop.

"I don't think she's here," Jake said.

But Marco argued, "She's here. She has to be."

Dodging overgrown hedges, he led us through the side yard around back to a gorgeous Mediterranean-style veranda that overlooked the city. I stepped under the overhang to avoid the raindrops splashing down. A large door made up of square panes led from the veranda into the house. Marco unzipped his bag, grabbed a shirt, and wrapped it around his fist.

"I don't think this is a good idea," I said, but he'd already slammed his fist through one of the panes.

I stood there frozen, Jake's hand on my waist. If there was an alarm, it must've been silent, because we heard nothing. Nothing but Marco opening the door and stepping inside. Against all kinds of better judgment, we followed. Maybe because we really were afraid for Olivia. Maybe because fear is easier to believe.

She showed up ten minutes later. The three of us were standing in a hallway when we heard the key in the door, when we heard her voice.

"Hide, hide!" Marco yelled.

So we did. Because we're stupid. We dived into the first door we could find. I didn't realize we were in an office until Olivia stepped into the room and turned on the light. She was pushing a wheelchair.

Henry's wheelchair.

Marco was right!

But if Henry's here, if Olivia's here, where is Damien? I focus hard on the room. As hard as I possibly can. And then the room blushes and I see it all with celestial eyes. But Damien's nowhere to be found.

I glance back at Marco, terrified at what he'll do now that Henry's in the room. But he's gone still. Fear wraps him like a straitjacket, pinning him to the wall. It's ugly, what the fear has done, and I feel for him, but I'm kind of okay with him being scared right now. Until I figure out what's going on, I need him to stay put. Out of sight.

I turn my eyes to the far corner of the room, where Liv has parked the wheelchair. My vision is clear, complete, and I see the old man as he is. Strapped in place, his eyes putrid and vacant, his body a gray mass staining the Celestial.

He's a bug smashed against a windshield, the flaw in a diamond, a wolf among sheep.

I hate him. I do. More than I've ever hated any one person. I can't imagine why Olivia brought him here.

With the flick of a switch, she has a fire blazing in the hearth. She sits before it, a glass of red wine in her right hand, a stack of papers in her left. Several sheets of it, all folded in thirds. Correspondence of some sort. The old-school kind. The snail mail kind.

I twist the halo on my wrist. It's uncomfortably hot and has been since Olivia walked through the door.

She's talking now, to Henry. Her back is to me, and I catch only a word here and there. "If I had known Javan's disappearance would . . . diminish you, I would have tried to get rid of him earlier."

Her body is such a strange, dark distraction I can hardly concentrate on her words. I've never seen someone so clothed in fear. It's like a cat suit, fitted, cut to her size, made just for her. She looks almost comfortable in it.

"That nurse of yours offered me a little cocktail, Henry. Did you hear? Something that will ease your passing, she said. Something to make all your pain go away. I didn't get the specifics—a pill, a shot, an IV, I don't know—but it's something that would suck your life away and let you forget. I'm sure you'd like that. But I told her no. *Thank you, but no.* And do you know why?" Olivia spins, points her goblet at the wheelchair. "Take a guess, old man.

Oh. That's right. You can't. Nothing works. Not your wandering hands. Not your twisted legs. Not your filthy mouth. You're all but paralyzed. Just a body. Maybe a brain." She sets the letters aside, pushes to her feet, and walks toward him. "And that's why I refused your nurse. Because there's a chance—a feeble, thin, speck of a chance—that your twisted mind's still ticking away in there. And if anyone deserves to be trapped inside his own broken body, inside an asylum of sick memories, it's you."

She leans into his face, her voice low, throaty. "They say you're dying. That you have days left. Maybe hours. I hope every second of them is full of regret for what you did to all those girls. For what you did to my mom. Yes, I know about Mom. Did you order that greedy little pauper of yours to set the school on fire, or was he just as inept as you hoped he'd be? Speak!" she cries, throwing the wine in his face.

He doesn't sputter. Doesn't blink as the wine rolls down his forehead, down his nose and chin. He's beyond response, so close to gone.

She throws the wine glass into the corner. It shatters, celestial light bouncing from each sliver. She walks back to her place by the fire and picks up the letter on top of the stack.

"I told someone about you, you know? A long time ago. Told her about Javan. But she never got the letters. Not the ones about you two, anyway. It's strange to read my thoughts from all those years ago. Strange because my pen has steadied, my writing is clearer, but the terror I see here on this page, it's the same as it always was. Here. Listen to this one.

"Dear Hannah,

"My mom is dead. But I think you know that. I think you

were there. Did you follow me to the school? No one believes me that you were there. That you shoved me out the door. Tell them it's true, okay? I don't like talking to Grandfather's psychiatrist.

"Oh yeah, I'm living with my grandfather now. Mama always hated him, said he hurt kids. But there's a man here, Javan. He promised to protect me. He's handsome but scary. He might be scarier than Grandfather, but he taught me how to pick locks today. It was kind of fun. We practiced on Grandfather's office. But I wish we hadn't. I wish we'd used a different room, because Grandfather still hasn't thrown out last week's newspaper. The one about the fire that killed Mama. It was on his desk. They say a man named Brian Hughes did it, but he's so handsome in his picture it's hard to believe. Men who do bad things should be ugly. That's what I think anyway.

"Can I come live with you? I can share Gabby's room and babysit when you get sick. I'll come as soon as you say. You don't even have to write a whole letter. Just check yes or no and send this one back. You'll have to send it to Grandfather's though. They won't let me go home.

"Your friend, Olivia."

The letters she wrote to Mom. She must've taken them from our house sometime after July Fourth. Sometime when she was with Dad. I'm so distracted by the thought I don't notice that Jake's left his hiding place until the toes of his Chucks are on the massive rug that covers the center of the room.

"Olivia?" he says.

She looks up from her position on the floor, her hair covering half her face. "Are you kidding me? How did you get in?"

"Marco. He thought you were in danger. We broke a pane on your back door. I'll pay for it. I just . . . Can you tell me about Brian Hughes?"

Her phone's on the mantle. I'm terrified she'll reach for it, that she'll call the police and report a break-in. But she just laughs. And cries.

"Why are you crying?" Jake asks, kneeling before her.

"Because I'm drunk. I always cry when I'm drunk."

The fire crackles, a log shifting, sending up sparks.

"I didn't know, Jake. I didn't know about the babies. Not until Ali came to Ingenui last fall." She drops her head, hiding behind a veil of hair. "And I didn't know she was Marco's girlfriend. I didn't know he was the father."

She reaches for the wine bottle propped against the hearth, but Jake gets there first. He moves it to the mantle, his motions slow, deliberate. She turns her back on the room, watching him.

"I believe you," he says, dropping to the hearth. "And I know Marco will believe you."

I can't see her face, but she seems to shrink at his words, her shoulders hunched, her back shaking.

"In your letter you mentioned Brian Hughes. Do you know anything else about him?"

I'm not entirely sure where Jake is going with this. The name sounds vaguely familiar, but I don't think I know who Brian Hughes is.

"Brian worked for Henry," Olivia says. "Not at the foundation. Before."

"At the law firm?"

"He was employed by Henry, not by Madison and Kline." She shudders when she breathes, two, three times, and then the words come fast. "Last year Alison Beni came to me. Marco's Ali. Isn't that ironic?"

"It's a small world," Jake says.

"Too small. She was looking for information on her birth parents. Said Henry handled her adoption and that it wasn't legal. It was the first I'd heard of the babies. Of Henry selling children. I knew he bought girls. Paid money for his own pleasure and then threw them away, but before then I never thought to look into his past dealings as a lawyer. I didn't know he trafficked infants."

Jake leans forward and places a hand on her shoulder. "But you know now."

She stills, and I watch as the heat travels down her back, cutting a hole in the thick armor she wears so well. "Olivia, I need to know. How was Brian Hughes involved?"

"I told you, he worked for Henry." Her voice is quiet, but it's steady now.

"What did he do for Henry?"

She licks her lips, her eyes blinking slowly. "He couriered children."

Jake's hand falls away, the colors on his skin moving faster as she continues.

"I'm sorry, Jake. But it's true. Lackeys like Brian singled out women from the clinics and maternity wards across the Portland area. Poor girls, addicts usually, were offered money for their unborn children. Henry used his firm, his connections, to generate the documentation and push it through. Then he pocketed the cash. Used it to pay for his own addictions."

My stomach clenches at the thought. Olivia's said so much. She knew so much. And she never did anything about it?

"And my father. When did he work for Henry?"

Jake's father?

"Late eighties, early nineties, I think. There's a file." She stands, moves toward the desk, and unlocks the safe she has stored beneath it.

"Henry kept incriminating files?"

She returns to Jake with a single manila folder, hands it to him. "The old man kept files on everybody. Something else I didn't know until Ali's visit. He found dirt on every single person he worked with. And he had Javan. Incriminating or not, no one was prosecuting Henry while Javan was around."

It's quiet for a long time, Jake reading the file, Olivia watching him. I listen to the fire snap and pop as my mind whirs. Ali's visit was the start of something for Olivia. Her undoing, maybe.

"Your father was a monster, Jake. But you look like him, you know that? Handsome, trustworthy. You're the reason I came to Stratus. You and Brielle."

He looks up. "I thought you came to Stratus for the halo?"

"I was already in Stratus when Damien found me. I'd been back and forth a few times by then, but I came because of your face. I saw it on the news after the trafficking ring at the warehouse was exposed. I saw you and then I saw Elle. You looked so much like your father, and Brielle is her mom entirely. Two ghosts from my past. An angel and a demon side by side, and I had to know."

I shove the halo higher on my arm, giving my wrist a break from the heat.

"Did you ever meet my father?"

"No," she says, scratching her hand, picking at the fear

clinging there. "He was arrested the day I came to live with Henry."

"He was arrested for starting the fire. At the school. The one that killed your mother."

What? WHAT? I'm dizzy. My vision breaking apart, the colors swirling. Brian Hughes is Jake's dad? He's responsible for the fire? The fire that burned Olivia's legs. The fire that killed her mom. The fire that was quite possibly the last thing my own mother ever saw. I rub my temples and command my eyes to steady.

But this news doesn't seem to surprise Olivia. "I don't blame you, Jake. I want to. I like blaming. But all my hate, all the guilt belongs with Henry. I can't prove it, but I think he had your dad kill my mom. I think she found out about the trafficking. She worked in obstetrics. I told you that. She always hated Henry, and I think she figured it out."

"So you did know Ali?" It's Marco. He's standing now, moving toward her, his voice steady, the fear weaker with every step.

She starts at his sudden appearance, but she doesn't answer. She really doesn't have to. But there are questions that do need answering.

"Did you meet her?" I ask, standing, forcing strength into my legs. "She wanted information about her medical history. Did you give it to her?"

"Oh good," Olivia says, her right eyebrow raised. "You're here too."

The closer I get to Olivia, the hotter the halo gets. I wince and shake it back to my wrist.

"Did you meet her, Liv?" Marco asks.

"I did," she says, turning away, her eyes on the fire. "At Bellwether."

"What did . . . How was she? Did she . . ." Marco releases a half gasp, half sob that nearly knocks him to the floor. I grab his arm.

"She was grateful," Olivia says, her voice quiet. She glances at Jake while she talks. Jake, whose face is buried once again in the file before him. "Her parents were addicts, but beyond that their health was okay. Okay enough, at least."

Marco sobs. It's a lot. Too much, even.

"Is this true?" Jake asks, holding the file out to Olivia, pointing. His celestial form leaks sadness and fear in equal amounts now. I've seen fear on Jake plenty. But sadness isn't something he normally wears. I let go of Marco and lean into him, my eyes scanning the open file. There's a picture in the left-hand corner. Olivia's right, Jake bears a striking resemblance to Brian Hughes. On the right side of the file, several pages are held in place with prongs. The top page is split into categories: *Appearance*, *Income*, *Background*, *Associations* . . . The list goes on. But when I get to *Family*, I stop.

> Girlfriend Jessica Rose gave birth to twins. Male and female. Female was adopted by Judge Emmanuel and Serena Beni. Jessica and Brian were compensated.

"Ali was your sister," I say, my words a rush of air.

"How is that possible?" Jake asks.

"It can't be," I say.

"I assure you it is possible," Olivia says, her voice measured. "Ali was Jake's twin."

"But Ali's birthday was in October. Jake's is in January." I'm running my finger over the page now, blood rushing through my veins at the revelation, pounding, shaking my arms and legs.

Jake wraps an arm around my waist, steadying me, but there's a tremor in his grip. "Canaan chose my birth date, Elle. I couldn't remember."

I need to keep it together. This is about him. I need to be strong for him.

"What else, Olivia?" Jake asks. "What isn't here?"

"Your parents needed cash, Jake, and they couldn't afford two babies. Lucky for them, Brian worked for someone who could help." Where are the air quotes when you need them! "They traded Ali for a thousand dollars."

She doesn't slur. Her tone is staid, the truth sharp.

Jake's chest rumbles. But Marco goes rigid. The knife entering his heart was so quick, he hasn't had time to feel the pain. And then it comes, the sadness, the words, all in one frigid breath.

"Ali was a paycheck?" Marco's agony mirrors mine. I can't imagine trading in children, bartering with babies.

Olivia's forehead puckers. "I'm sorry . . . I'm usually more diplomatic than that."

"We don't have time for diplomacy," Jake says, dropping to the couch, his eyes ravaging the file. Marco follows, leaving Olivia and me before the fire.

I'm still reeling, still trying to make sense of it all, but Olivia's staring at me, so I stand up straight. I pretend to be strong.

"You don't like me," I say.

"The feeling is mutual, I'd guess."

I shrug. "You aren't good for my dad."

"I wanted the halo, Brielle. Not your father."

My eyes slide to the stack of paper on the hearth. "And the letters?"

"I wanted those too."

I let it be. They're her words, written to my mom. They have nothing to do with me. Except . . .

"Did she always call me Gabby?"

"She did. I was surprised to hear your dad call you Brielle. I slipped once or twice, and he corrected me."

"I have pictures," I say. "Of you and my mom. I didn't know if you remembered her. Tragedy can make us forget."

"I'll never forget. Hannah pushed me out of the classroom that day. It was a long time before I knew she died. I kept sending letters. I would have given anything for her to rescue me from that inferno as well. But she never wrote back. Eventually I figured it out."

"You remember more about her than I do," I say, hating that the words are true, but knowing that somehow they might help Olivia. "She's the reason you didn't die there. She gave you a chance to end what Henry started."

"Henry's death will end what he started." She glances toward the old man, his rotten yellow eyes staring, wine drying on his face. "As much as I'd like to prolong his misery, he doesn't have much time left."

"But you can make things right," I say. "There are kids, grown now, and they have no idea who their parents are. Like Ali. What are you going to do with the files?"

"Destroy them."

"What?" It's Jake. "Why?"

"I have to destroy everything that links Ingenui to Henry's corruption. If I don't . . ."

"You can't destroy it," Jake says. "People need to know."

"I'm sorry, Jake, but that's not going to happen. Read that one, and then it gets destroyed like the rest."

"What good is destroying them?" I ask. "There has to be a paper trail somewhere, computer records."

Her gaze wanders to the fire. "The hard drives were destroyed a long time ago. And Henry was very careful when it came to the contacts he used. I doubt any paper trail would lead back to him. Some poor desk jockey at the state, sure. But not Henry."

"Then you have the only proof that these children were stolen," I say.

"Not stolen. Purchased."

"And that's supposed to make it right?" I argue.

"No, not right. Henry never did anything right. But it does make it different. Who's to say the truth will actually help them? It could do more damage than good."

"That's not the point," Jake says. "Telling them is the right thing to do."

She loses it then. "It would kill Ingenui. The only things I've ever done that were worth anything, I did in the name of this foundation. I'm not a good person, I know that, but Ingenui has helped a lot of people. Everything could crumble if I tell the truth. What would I have then?"

"I'll help you," Marco says. He stands very still, very straight. His eyes never leave her face. Which is kind of a big deal since the man he's wanted to kill for months sits just beyond her, his crimes against Ali continuing to grow. "I'll go with you to turn these files over. And I'll be here, we'll all be here . . ."

"Well, I won't," she barks. "The minute I expose Henry, I'll be arrested for obstruction of justice. I've known about this fiasco since your girlfriend came to visit. And I've done nothing. I've sat on it."

"You'll be exposing something huge," I say. "Something important. They're not going to arrest you."

"And if they do?" Olivia snaps.

The halo flames hot, burning my arm. I yelp and yank it from my wrist. It tumbles to the floor, and then it's moving and shifting, remolding into the crown.

"I thought Damien took that," Olivia says.

"I brought a lot of things back from Danakil."

We all watch the halo, like we expect it to do tricks, entertain us.

"I don't understand," she says.

I scoop it from the ground, glad it's cooled a bit. "I think I'm starting to. Take it."

"Not on your life," she says.

"I'm serious. Take it. It burns the heck out of me whenever you're near."

She frowns. "You're an awful salesman."

"At first I thought it was warning me about you—you know, with my dad and all—but I think . . . I think it's time for me to pass it on."

She narrows her eyes. "And you chose me?"

"No, I didn't." I look to Jake. His face is bright, the sadness slowing to a trickle, his smile encouraging. And those eyes . . . "If it were my call, I probably wouldn't choose you, but you're supposed to have it. I'm sure."

I hold it out to her with both hands, like a present. Like an offering.

"It won't hurt me?"

"There was a time when I would have said no, but the thing just blistered my arm, so who knows what it'll do?"

"And you don't need it?"

I shrug. "I don't think I do."

She's still not convinced, but as we watch, the halo starts to shift against my hands, and in seconds it's nothing more than a beautiful bracelet.

Well played, halo. You look much less intimidating this way.

"You wanted one of these, right? That's what you told me."

"I lied." But she's considering it, her eyes bouncing from the halo to Marco and then back to me.

And then a knock at the door.

I drop my hands, keeping the halo by my side, out of sight.

"Has to be Henry's nurse," Olivia says, stepping past us, walking to the door. "No one else has a key." She grabs the handle and pulls. "What is it, Melva?"

But it's not Melva. It's Canaan.

"You knocked?" Jake asks.

"Helene said Olivia prefers us to use the door." Canaan gives a little bow. "Excuse the intrusion, Ms. Holt, but I need to steal Jake and Brielle away. We have a situation."

"By all means," she says.

I don't like the way he's just said *situation*. And I don't like the creases marking his face, or that his suit shirt is rumpled. But I slip my car keys into Marco's hands. "You better take these."

He squeezes my fingers. "Be careful, okay?"

"Of course."

Jake grabs my hand and we head to the door.

"Canaan," I say, stopping before the threshold, "I was going to give the halo to Olivia. If that's okay with you."

He smiles that perfect thousand-watt smile. "It's yours, Brielle. I trust you'll do with it whatever the Father asks."

I turn to Olivia, but she still seems reluctant. "There," I say, placing it on the bookshelf just inside the door. "It's yours. Wear it or don't. Your call."

She frowns at it. Not the response I was hoping for, but I'm confident I did what I was supposed to do.

"And for this," Jake says, holding the folder out to her, "thank you. It's more information than I've ever had about my parents. And I wouldn't know the truth about Ali if it weren't for you. I'm grateful."

Ali was Jake's twin. It's something I can't process.

Olivia takes the folder, pressing it against her chest. I watch as the fear swallows it.

"I wish I could do more," she says.

He smiles. It's small but genuine. "Maybe you will."

31

Liv leaves the door open and walks back to the seating area. The air moves when she steps in front of Marco. She smells of fall. Of cinnamon apples and spice. He lets her pass, Brielle's keys flipping on his finger.

"You going to put it on?" he asks.

"Is it going to make me change my mind about the files?" She drops back to the hearth. "Is that why she gave it to me?"

"She doesn't have an ulterior motive, Liv."

"Everyone has an ulterior motive."

Marco slides the letters aside and sits next to her. "I don't. If you want me to help you destroy the files, I will. Just like that."

"There are only eighteen files, Marco, and I have a fire. I don't need help."

"Then why haven't you done it?"

"I don't know," she says, looking around. "Where did the wine go?"

"You always know. Why are they in your safe when you could have burned them next to those hard drives?"

"Because I'm not sold on destroying them, okay? I just . . . Ah! I hate having that little know-it-all dictate to me."

Marco stands and retrieves the bottle from the mantle. "You have a warped view of Brielle, you know that?"

"Do I? You don't think she's pulling strings? Trying to get everyone to do things her way?"

"Sure she is," Marco says, handing her the bottle. "But aren't we all? Aren't you?"

"Always." Her eyes drift to the bookcase by the door. To the halo sitting there, shining, beckoning.

Marco watches her. "Liv, when was the last time you felt hope?"

The creamy skin of her brow gathers, and she blinks her focus away. "When was the last time the Seahawks had a shot at the Super Bowl? 2006?"

"You don't even watch football."

"I do when we have a decent team," she says.

"Liv."

"Look, Marco. I've survived. Survived Javan and Henry. Survived Damien. That has to count for something. And what's up with you, anyway? You were jonesing to kill Henry, what, two days ago? What kind of hope is there in that?"

He turns, stares at the old man.

"I don't know what's happened to me, Liv. Honestly, I have no idea, but it's better. Whatever's happening in my head isn't as miserable . . . I haven't felt hope since Ali. And even then, it was just hope for *us*, hope for our future and our little family. But that halo . . ."

She stands, moves away.

"Listen to me, Liv," he says, standing. Following her. "I have hope now. Beyond just me. I have hope for you and for your future. For Jake and Brielle. For all those children you want to help in Beacon City. I even—gah, Liv, I even have hope for Henry."

"Don't you dare," she says, spinning, jabbing a finger in his chest. "Don't you dare. He doesn't deserve hope."

He grabs her wrist, refusing to let her walk away from the conversation. Needing her to understand.

"And I do? The warehouse Ali died in, I sold it to Damien. I knew he was up to something, but I didn't care. I was selfish and I got my girlfriend killed, my unborn child murdered. I don't deserve hope."

"Marco . . ."

"Hoping good things for you is easy," he says. "For Jake and Brielle it's cake. But I've seen what Henry could have been. In my dreams I've seen what he could have done in this life if it weren't for the disease, for all his diseases. And for the first time in months I know that darkness isn't all there is."

She tugs her arm free. "It's all I've ever seen."

He stands eye-to-eye with his childhood friend. "Then put it on."

Her eyes flit to the halo once more, and Marco thinks, *Maybe, maybe*. But a cool breeze appears out of nowhere, and her hair lifts. The room goes cold and the air whistles as something slices through it. And then in the corner of the room, Henry sputters. Marco turns toward him. Wine dribbles from his lips, down his chin.

But wait, it's not wine, it's blood.

"He's been stabbed." Marco hurdles the coffee table and stumbles over the corner of the rug in his attempt to get to the old man.

"That's impossible," Liv says, her voice trembling. "It's just us."

And then it isn't.

Damien stands between Henry and Marco. He has some sort of army knife in his hands, Henry's blood dripping from the blade to the floor. Marco tries to back away, stumbling over the rug he just upturned.

"Why?" Marco asks. "He's all but gone."

Damien wipes the blade on his pants and slides it into the sheath strapped to his thigh.

"Oh, I'm just finishing him off. I cut his soul down days ago, while you were in Stratus securing me the halo." His eyes are on Liv now. "Without Javan, he was showing signs of remorse, and I promised my old friend I wouldn't let his pet project switch sides. I gave you a few days, though, doll. Thought you'd like to watch him waste away." He grins. "You're welcome."

"Don't talk to her," Marco says.

Damien shoves him aside. "She's mine. I'll do what I want with her." He strides across the room, leaving Henry slumped in his chair. Marco stares at the old man, everything in him screaming out, wanting justice and wondering if justice was just served.

Liv backs away as Damien approaches, her calves striking the coffee table behind her. But Damien turns, cutting between the couch and the desk. He's heading for the door.

"Why are you here?" Marco asks.

"I came for her," Damien says, his back to them. "But there was a Shield nearby."

"Canaan," Liv whispers.

"So I waited."

"Chicken," Marco says.

"Oh, Canaan will get his. Don't you worry about that. But speaking of cowardice, I find it ironic that this thing"—he turns around, the halo clenched in his fist—"frightens you, Olivia."

"It speaks to me," she says, pressing a hand to the soft spot between her ribs. "I . . . I feel the words. Here."

A low growl rumbles from Damien's chest. "And what does it say to you?"

"Liv," Marco says, "you don't have to talk to him."

Damien disappears from his spot by the door and reappears in front of Marco. He grabs Marco's shirt and lifts him off the ground. He doesn't even have time to flail. Two steps and Damien's pressing him against the mantle, a knife pressed to his throat.

"I have no use for you," Damien rumbles.

Marco tries to find the ground with his toes. "But you won't kill me," he says. "You can't."

"And what makes you think that?"

The air is thin, his windpipe collapsing with Damien's weight. "He showed me."

Damien shoves him higher, the knife scratching, drawing blood. "Who showed you?"

"God," Marco gasps. "He showed me."

Damien pulls the knife back, its blade aimed at Marco's heart. "Showed you what?"

But Marco can't breathe, much less speak.

"He showed you what?" Damien yells, spit flying.

"The future. And I'm there. I have one. So you can't"—Marco gasps and gasps—"I know you can't."

Damien falters, his knife hand dropping maybe a millimeter. Marco's vision is sketchy, spots starting to form, but out of the corner of his eye he sees Liv grab the poker off the fireplace and swing it at Damien. It hits the demon's abdomen, but all it seems to do is shake him from his lapse. He raises the knife as Liv swings again. She's aiming for his knee this time, but Damien's fast, and the makeshift weapon is kicked away before it does any damage.

Damien howls. The knife drops from his hand, disappearing before it hits the ground.

Damien releases Marco and spins around.

Helene is there, holding his knife. She's not smiling, not really.

"It's always the little ones," Damien growls.

"New knife?" she asks him, turning the weapon in her hand.

"Same knife, new victim," he answers.

"You entered Stratus?" she says, incredulous. "With the Sabres there? With Michael's forces engaged?"

He taps his temple. "New eyes, remember."

"It seems they've made you stupid."

"I prefer *fearless.*"

"I'm sure you do."

He swings at her, but she steps to the side and jabs at him with the knife, nicking his knuckles.

"I'm faster than you in this realm as well," she says.

"You weren't faster than me last time."

"I made a mistake last time," she says. "Today I have reinforcements. See for yourself."

He looks doubtful but vanishes.

Liv crawls to Marco's side. She tips his chin and presses a silk handkerchief to the slice across his neck.

And then Damien's back. "Why bring reinforcements if they're going to remain at a distance?"

"Because you won't be destroyed by a blade of light. Not tonight."

He steps closer. "And why is that?"

"Because you're going to leave. You did what you came to do. You finished off Henry. Now go."

"You let me kill him?"

"My hand was stayed." There's sadness in her tone, but no regret. "Now go."

Marco watches as Damien slides the halo into his pocket. Liv's halo. It's hers now. And Damien doesn't get to take anything else from her. He lurches forward in protest, his voice box bruised, refusing to cooperate. Liv grabs his arm and pulls him back.

"Let him," she says. "It doesn't matter."

"Yes," Damien growls. "Let me." He rounds on Marco, but Helene's fast, moving in a blur, cutting him off.

And then the room explodes in light and color. And heat. Marco blinks and blinks, but the colors won't stop moving. He gasps, chokes, inhaling air and fire. Somehow he is yanked to his feet. He can't move, he can't breathe, his eyes stream tears, and Liv is pressed next to him, her screams deafening.

"Peace, peace." It's Helene. He can hear her, but he can't see her. And he can't move.

"Where are you?" he cries.

"Closer than you can imagine."

"And Damien?"

"You're safe. We have him surrounded."

But the room is empty. And so, so bright.

"Where?" Marco asks.

"I'll show you," she says. Is her voice in his head? And then air presses against them and his feet lift off the ground. His peripheral vision catches white flashes against a red sky and he turns his head, first left and then right.

Wings. Moving up and down, lifting them off the ground.

They're flying!

"You're carrying us." He turns to Liv, sees her golden face, her glowing eyes. "She's carrying us," he says.

Liv is quiet now, small black beads breaking out across her forehead. He watches as they dissolve in the heat. "There," she says, tilting her head to the sky. "Look."

Marco obeys and catches his first glimpse of Helene's angelic face. So bright, so beautiful. She's looking upward as well. Past her chin, he sees what Liv's pointing at.

It has to be Damien, but he's never seen anything so ugly, so vicious.

"He really is a demon," Marco says.

"Did you doubt it?" Liv asks.

"No, but seeing makes it hard to deny."

Helene rights them, the demon twenty, thirty feet away. And she's right. They have him surrounded. Gigantic armed angels encircle him. They're easily one and half times his size, but they keep their distance. Helene takes her place among them.

Damien flies in a circle now, snarls vibrating from his lips.

"You can't touch me tonight," he says. By the look on the faces of the angels gathered, Marco's not the only one hearing Damien's voice in his head. He watches as Damien draws a sword from the sheath at his waist, something like dry ice spilling from the blade. He shakes it at the angels positioned around him. "The little one told me. You've not been granted my destruction."

His lips spread wide, and a celebratory kind of cry escapes. The angels remain where they are, their massive wings holding their circle in place. He flies higher, but the angels rise with him, keeping Damien at their center. A raging cry rips from his chest and he lashes out, flying toward an angel on Marco's right. He swings his weapon, the white angel drawing his. Sparks fly, smoke hissing as the swords collide. Damien swings again and again, trying to wound, trying to maim, but the angel only blocks his blows.

Damien moves to the next angel, striking, striking, absorbing the vibrations of the Warrior's sword, but doing no damage.

"Why aren't they fighting?" Liv says.

"Because they don't have to." Helene's voice is steady, certain.

"But they're stronger than he is." Liv's words tremble. "They could destroy him."

"Watch."

When Damien gets to Helene, she draws her sword, but the angels on either side of her close in, drawing theirs, blocking Damien's access to her. To Liv and him.

"Is that all I had to do to get your attention? Approach the humans?"

Marco watches between the heaving wings of the angels before him.

"I said, is that all I had to do?"

But they remain silent, something that seems to enrage Damien. He shakes, spit and fog spewing from his mouth. He's close now, a slick, black tar slipping and sliding over his warped, muscled body. The thick talons of one hand wrap around his sword, the halo clenched in his other fist.

And then next to Marco, Liv speaks. "Are you scared, Damien?"

Her question takes Marco off guard. But it's not just the question itself, it's the tone. Damien seems surprised that she's addressed him as well. But he answers, swinging his sword wide.

"Of these? Never."

"Of the halo," she says.

Damien smirks, holds it out. "Am I scared of this? This trinket that gave one healing powers, another sight, and your boyfriend here nightmares? No, doll. I am not scared of something that can only give what I already have."

"I think you are," she says, holding his gaze. "I would be."

He leans as close as the angelic guardians will allow. "You're human."

Her hand finds her chest. "I can hear it, Damien, and it's talking to you."

He scoffs. "It's not—" But he stops midsentence.

"You can't feel regret, can you?" she asks. "You can't feel what you've done to me, to any of us. I feel every mistake I've ever made. But not you. You feel nothing but rage."

"Stop talking," Damien says, but his eyes jump from the halo to Liv and back again, and Marco's not convinced he's speaking to her.

Liv's eyes are glued to the halo, as though she can see the words it whispers. "He offered you forgiveness, but you walked away from it. And He still shows you mercy." She pauses, confusion in the swirling colors of her face. "Without hope of forgiveness, remorse is the worst kind of torture. It's a kindness that you can't feel it."

He lurches then, like he's been shot through the heart. His wings are flung forward, his chest caves inward, and he moans. The blackness smeared all over his body triples, dripping down his legs, down his arms, falling like hell's rain through the air.

His voice comes in halting yaps. "I can feel it." In Damien's massive hand the halo twists and turns, shifting, reshaping into the crown.

"I think it wants you to put it on," Liv says.

"I won't." He tries to fling the halo away, tries to release it, but it's stuck. He shakes his arm, pries at it with the talons on his other hand, but it won't be removed.

"I thought you were fearless," Liv says, disgust finding its way into her words. She's shaking now, but she's not scared. Marco's seen her scared, and this is something else. This is anger.

Damien's body twists again, and then he straightens. His eyes find Helene's sword and he offers his arm. "Make it stop. Please. I didn't know."

"Put it on!" Liv screams. She presses her face to the thin barrier separating them from the night sky. "*Feel* what you did to me. Feel it!"

But Damien doesn't spare her a glance. His pain-filled eyes are locked on Helene's.

"I'm asking. I'm begging."

But Helene sheathes her sword. "It is not by a sword of light that you will be destroyed this night."

Damien does it then. He draws his own weapon and—with his body twisting and blackness pouring from him in sheets—he shoves the hilt at Helene.

"Do it," his mind says. "The fiery chasm is nothing to regret."

It's a moment before she moves. Marco hears a song building in her chest, a prayer skating across her mind, open for all to hear. She's waiting for something. Waiting, waiting. And then her eyes widen, and she takes Damien's crooked sword in her tiny hands.

She hefts it once, twice.

And then she swings.

Damien's arm is severed at the elbow, ash spewing everywhere. Marco gags at the smell, but his eyes are on the halo tumbling through the sky, Damien's arm turning to dust as it falls.

The mouths of the angels around him open as Helene swings again. It's fast, so fast. But just before she connects with Damien's chest, Marco swears he sees relief on the demon's face.

Respite.

Damien's nothing but smoke and stench, and the skies fill with song.

32

Brielle

The flight from Olivia's place is short. So much shorter than I anticipated. When Canaan starts his descent, I haven't had near enough time to sort out everything we just learned. So many new puzzle pieces and not nearly enough time to put them together. I turn to Jake now, but his eyes are on the building below.

"Where are we, Canaan?" I ask.

"Good Samaritan Hospital," he says, his voice quiet in my head.

My heart bounces in my chest. "Regina?" I ask.

"I'm sorry, Brielle. She didn't make it."

I'm aware of a lot of things after that—Jake taking my hand, whispering prayers in my ears; the raindrops sparkling like psychedelic art as they fall to the ground; Canaan's wings slowing as we dip through the roof of the hospital—but I think I stop feeling altogether. There's just too much to think. Too much to understand. Too many questions that will never have answers. I'm a sponge that's reached capacity, and I sink into the absolute numbness of the moment.

And then Canaan sets us down in an empty elevator and releases us from his wings. He pushes the number three, and the elevator jolts into motion.

"Have you . . . ," I start. "Did you try . . ."

"I tried," Canaan says. "But my hand was stayed."

"What about Jake? Can Jake . . ."

"That's why we're here," Canaan says, his voice gentle.

The elevator doors open onto a hallway that may have once been beige but is now black and morbid. Fear crawls like a thousand fingers down the walls and across the ceiling. It drips to the floor and oozes toward us. Still, we step out. We walk toward it. Canaan goes before us, Jake's hand in mine. The fear parts for Canaan, and we stay close. He rounds one corner and then another before turning back to us.

"Her room's just ahead. Across from the nurses' station. I'll be right here."

And then his celestial form replaces his human one, and I realize he's transferred. I'm the only one who can see him now. Silently, we walk forward. Canaan stays ahead of us, his wings brushing the walls, the fear dissolving on contact. I'm grateful, so grateful he's here.

I can see the room now, the family gathered around, spilling out into the hall. When we reach the nurses' station, Regina's mother sees us. I release Jake's hand and let her envelop me. I squeeze back, so lost, so empty.

"Thank you for coming," she says.

Jake places his hand on my back, and I remember why we're here.

"Mrs. Glascoe, may I see Regina?" I ask. "Would that be okay?"

She mops at her face with a tattered Kleenex. "Of course," she says. "Of course."

The family parts for us, a lot like the fear did for Canaan. I keep close to Jake, close to his warmth. I don't seem to have any of my own left.

And there she is.

Regina.

The sheet's been tucked around her small body, but her face is clear, her eyes shut, her hands crossed gently on her stomach. There are still bandages on her head, her jet-black hair spilling over them, over the crisp, white pillow.

We step to her side and I pray. As hard as I can.

There's a chair next to her hospital bed, and Jake sits. He's trying to get closer, trying to figure out how to lay a hand on her without it being weird. Sitting on his knee, I take his hand. After a moment, I lean forward and lay our knotted fingers on Regina's open palm.

But there's just nothing. I shift, letting Jake's palm touch hers, but I know the minute it does that she's gone. Jake's hand is as warm as ever, but I know what it feels like when his gift is flowing, and this isn't it. Jake's body shakes with understanding.

I hear the rustle of Canaan's wings, and I look up. He hovers over us, over Regina.

"It was time, then," he says.

How can it be her time? I think. *How? She was a child!*

After another quiet moment Jake and I stand, our faces wet, our hands still clenched, and we walk back through the gathered family. Mrs. Glascoe is weeping when we leave, her arms wrapped around Regina's older sister.

"Thank you for giving me a minute," I say. I touch her

shoulder as we pass, her elbow, her hand. We follow Canaan past the rest of the family, past the nurses' station, down the crooked hallway, and together we step into the elevator. The doors close, and though I can't see it happen, I know we disappear.

33

Marco

Marco wanted to go in with her, but the detective shook his head, told him to make himself comfortable in the waiting room. With a cold cup of coffee, he watched as Liv followed the man back, her arms laden with files, the halo bright on her wrist.

Beyond the duty officer, a series of bulletproof windows gives him a glimpse of officers milling around, paperwork changing hands, coffee cups being filled, but for a police station it's quieter than he expected.

Emptier.

It's early. The clock in the waiting room says it's almost four a.m.

Last night, after Damien, Liv called the police. She couldn't leave Henry there, dead in the corner of her office. It was late when the officers showed up, late when they sat down and gave their statements. Even later when the coroner took Henry's body away.

The more Marco thinks about it, the more he realizes what a disaster that investigation's going to be. He and Liv were the only ones in the room with Henry, and they both had plenty of motive. But once the body was gone, Liv was determined to get the rest of it done. To turn Henry's files over.

She always meant to do it, he thinks. But she needed something, a push, the courage. Maybe it was the halo, maybe it was Elle. Whatever it was, she's here.

Helene's here too, said she'd stay with them. He can't see her, but she's probably in with Liv. Marco settles back in the plastic chair, takes a sip of the syrup masquerading as coffee, and closes his eyes.

He's not scared anymore.

Not afraid to dream.

34

Brielle

Entering Stratus is no easy thing. The sight that meets us is staggering. The orange sky seems almost blotted out as we approach, filled instead with the sights and sounds of heavenly warfare.

The colors of worship are everywhere, ribbons and tendrils curling high. From the angels of light, no doubt, but also from the ground. I watch them rise from beneath us, and I know there are people praying, worshiping—there are people fighting below. I wonder who they are. Miss Macy, maybe. Becky, Pastor Noah. Others from church. But the worship is . . . it's almost lavish. There's just so much of it. I didn't realize there were so many worshipers here.

Canaan draws his sword, dipping, his wings pulling inward.

Masses of dark, writhing bodies collide with those of color and light. I'm sure there's organization in the chaos, but it's too much to take in. I close my eyes and try not to think about Regina or the battle raging around me. I try not to think about the dark halo sitting in the chest at the old Miller place, but when at last we hit the ground, it's all that consumes me.

I don't have to see all of this.

I don't have to be a casualty.

I have a choice.

"I'll be back soon," Canaan says. "The Commander called to me on approach. I need to go."

And then he's gone, and it's just Jake and me. We stand on the porch of the old Miller place. A place that should be fairly safe. A house that's always offered strength, but what I see has me wishing for the safety of my last nightmare. Because what's going on out here is truly terrifying.

Only Jake can't see it.

I step down onto the second stair, trembling but unable to look away.

"What's wrong?" Jake says, walking up behind me. "What do you see?"

I'm sure he sees a gorgeous moon, a starry expanse, trees clinging to their nighttime moisture. But me? I'm frozen to these wooden stairs, fear pooling at my feet, heavenly carnage demanding my attention in the empty field across the highway.

"Are you seeing the Celestial?"

My nod is stiff but it's all I can manage. "There are f-f-feathers everywhere," I say. "White feathers."

Jake turns toward the highway, and while I can't be sure of what he sees, feathers—glossy, shimmering feathers—rain down like snow. Vibrant, glowing bodies—six or seven of them—lie curled in the dirt. I can't see the celestial sky, just the injured angels, just the remnants of glorious wings.

And the smell of sulfur. The putrid stench of demonic destruction. It stings my nostrils and burns my lungs, but I don't care. It tells me the Palatine are losing soldiers too. I look again at our injured—at the broken angels. They're here, injured but healing, while the demons that have been destroyed fester in the fiery chasm.

And then I hear the clanging of swords and the grunt of battle. I stumble down the remaining stairs, Jake next to me, keeping me upright.

His white eyes are wide. "Tell me," he says.

I crane my neck to the night sky. "My vision is coming in part right now, and they're hard to see in the darkness," I say. "But they're close. The Palatine."

"And the Sabres?"

"I don't see . . ." I shake my head. "Wait." A song mingles in the cold night breeze. Quiet, haunting. "I hear them."

I grab Jake's hand and pull him with me around the house and through the field separating the old Miller place from mine. The needles of a pine tree scratch at my face and neck, but I press through them anyway. I clear its branches and trip to a clumsy stop.

"What is it?" Jake asks, his eyes on me.

"The veil," I say, looking at the orchard, still red, still fiery. "Look."

It's nearly torn through. Or worn through, maybe. That seems to be a more appropriate way to describe what I see. The cosmic material of the veil is all but transparent, rubbed thin by the violence of the Sabres' song. Mere inches off the ground, it flutters; yanked, it seems, from the threads that hold it firmly in place.

And then before me, an angel falls. Enormous and silver. I scream and move backward, stumbling over my own feet, over Jake. Finally falling to the ground.

"It's okay, it's okay," Jake says, crouching next to me. "What do you see?"

"It's a Sabre," I say. "He's been cut down."

I tell myself to breathe, to calm down, but I can't. I can't.

"I'm sorry you have to see it, Elle. So sorry." Jake reaches down for my hand. His voice is steady, but he's bleeding fear. His shirt, his hands, they're covered in it. "He'll heal. He just needs time."

But I have to know. There are only twelve, and I have to know. I crawl forward on all fours, circling around the dagger-like wings. But it's him. It is, and I know it before I reach his head. I smell the incense of his worship rising off his body, so distinctive. I see the lingering wisps of praise lifting into the sky. All so familiar. All so Virtue. And then I see his face, his beautiful face, and I can't take another eyeful of tragedy. I won't.

I jump to my feet, run back around the house and through the door to the old Miller place. Every part of me is shaking. Every part of me is terrified. I don't want to see anymore. Not the pain and sadness that surround a dead child. Not the demonic forces hemming in our town. Not the fear that Jake pretends not to feel.

I hear him behind me, but I don't stop. And then I'm in Canaan's room and I'm kicking the lid off the chest. I stare down at the dark halo for only a moment before digging it out, before sliding it onto my wrist. And then, like an addict, I close my eyes and wait for the drug of blindness to seep into my system.

It moves slowly this time, slower than it did at Danakil. Up my arm and across my chest, dulling my anxiety, slowing my heart. After a minute the chill is gone, but so is the heat. I open my eyes, expecting normality. Expecting all the peace that not knowing should bring.

But instead I see Jake.

Standing in the doorway of Canaan's room.

Heartbroken.

"It's a lie, Elle. You can't escape this. You will always see."

But I don't want to talk about any of it. I want blindness. Just for tonight. Just for now. I push past him and into the hall, through the living room and out the door. I watch my feet on the stairs, careful not to stumble, careful not to fall, but with my eyes on the ground I run into something.

Into someone.

My hands fly up to protect my face, but the collision is a soft one.

"Dad? What are you doing here?"

"Checking on you. You haven't been answering your cell."

"I'm sorry," I say. "I don't even know where it is."

"Where have you been? Where's your car? And what's this?" He grabs my wrist, flips it over, and then hollers a question over my head, up the stairs. "Heck, kid, ain't one fancy angel bracelet enough?"

He's talking to Jake. He must be. But I don't turn and Jake doesn't answer.

But Dad tries again, addressing Jake more quietly this time. "You all right, kid? I asked you a question. Isn't one halo enough?"

"I thought so," Jake says, disappointment marking every word.

I tear my arm away from Dad, and I run through the field that separates my house from Jake's, and I just keep running. This forest area runs parallel to the highway, so in another mile or two I'll spill out into downtown Stratus.

I hear shouts behind me, but I don't stop. I've disappointed everyone, I know. But it's just another thing I don't want to see.

The trees thicken, and I have to slow as I dodge through them. My stomach aches, but I inhale the night and push on. I try not to think about the halo on my wrist. I tell myself it's just for now. Just for tonight. Just until the destruction stops. But as I run I breathe in the lush green forest, I breathe in the darkness that surrounds me, and I don't know if I have the willpower to take it off.

Eventually my feet find the pavement again, and I slow to a walk as Jelly's comes into view. The neon jelly jar's painted Main Street purple. I step up onto the sidewalk and through the front door, a bell jingling as I walk inside. It's bright in here, and warm. The blue-and-white striped booths are all but empty.

"What are you doing here, Brielle-y girl? It's early." Delia's at the counter, a plaid apron accentuating her ample hips. Behind her a clock ticks away, and she's not kidding. It is early.

Like just after four a.m. early.

"I, um . . . I wanted to see Miss Macy," I say. "Could you give me a ride to the hospital?"

"Now?" she says, rounding the counter. "They're not going to let you in, I'm afraid."

"I'm on her family list," I say. "I just . . . I'd really like to see her."

She eyes me for a minute. "Does your daddy know you're here?"

"No, but you can call him if you'd like. He won't mind me seeing Miss Macy."

She reaches for the phone by the register.

"Can you take me first and then call?" I ask. "I'd appreciate it."

She eyes me again, but replaces the receiver. "Hey!" she calls over her shoulder. "Good-for-nothing."

A short, square guy wearing a lopsided chef's hat sticks his head out of the kitchen. "Yeah, boss. What's up?"

"You're in charge for a few. I'm taking this lady for a ride."

Delia drops me at the hospital entrance and waits until I walk through the sliding glass doors before she pulls away. I twist the dark halo on my wrist as I enter. It feels tighter than it did before. Tighter than Canaan's halo, anyway.

The waiting room is dim, most of the lights shut off. I stand in the center of it and look around. I'm not sure why I'm here. Not sure why I came. You'd think I'd steer clear of hospitals after seeing Regina tonight.

"You here to sit with Miss Macy?"

I turn my head toward the reception desk, and there sits the candy striper I saw in Miss Macy's room the other day. "Um, yes. If that's okay."

"Sure," she says. "You know your way back, right?"

I bob my head and make my way down the hall. Miss Macy's asleep when I enter, as is Pastor Noah. He's curled onto a cot they've pushed into the corner. The chair next to her bed is empty. I take it.

I half expect emotion to overtake me as I sit here. Half expect fear and sadness to attack, but mostly I just feel empty. And tired. But I don't see a drop of fear in the room, and for now that's enough.

I lean forward and cross my arms next to Miss Macy. I lay my head on top of my hands and close my eyes.

I don't dream.

35

Jake

Jake slams his way down the hall, past the study, past Canaan's room. His door is stuck on something and won't open, so he kicks his way in. The door splinters and gives, but Jake still has to climb over several mountains of laundry to get to his bed.

He tries to bury himself under the sheets there, tries not to think, tries not to want. He can't believe she put the Prince's halo on. Can't believe she gave in. There aren't words, just hurt. Just betrayal.

The thoughts are unfair, he knows that, but he's lost. Everything he thought he knew, gone.

Outside, the light of the orchard has grown. It's bright, lighting up his room. He slides his arms under his pillow, buries his face, but something slices his finger, something caught in his sheet. He sits up and pushes the pillow to the floor. It's the picture, the one he meant to give Brielle as a surprise. But he's broken it now, glass splinters poking through the wrapping. Carefully, he strips the paper away.

He sees Elle.

And Ali.

There's a crack in the glass just over her face. He lifts the shard and then another, setting them on the windowsill next to him. He sees her more clearly now. His sister. His twin. She's so alive in this picture. Mischievous brown eyes, a crooked smile. If he sees himself anywhere in her features, it's there. In her smile.

He's always been one to smile easily. He wonders if she was like that.

He shakes the rest of the shards onto the wrapping paper and moves them all to his windowsill. He flips onto his back and holds the picture to his chest.

He shoves away thoughts of Brielle, forces himself to think about his childhood. To think about everything he learned at Olivia's. So many revelations, so many shocks, but what he can't seem to shake is something that took place long after Ali was traded away.

When Canaan found him, abandoned in that ratty apartment, Jake had been recently abused. His wrist was broken, his collarbone shattered. It was the first time Canaan healed him, the first time he saw the Celestial. But Jake's father died in jail; he'd been dead for two or three years when that happened.

Jake doesn't remember his mother hurting him, doesn't remember much of her at all. But she must have been just as violent as his father.

Ali was better off, he thinks. Safer with the judge and Serena. They loved her. Something his own parents seemed incapable of doing.

And then Canaan is there, in his room. Jake doesn't even flinch when he appears at the foot of the bed.

"She put it on," Canaan says.

"You saw?"

"I did."

"Do you know where she is now?" Jake asks.

"At the hospital. With Miss Macy."

Jake closes his eyes, squeezes the picture tighter. "She was always so afraid that she'd do something, you know? That she'd be the reason we couldn't be together."

"Jake . . ."

"And then she did it," he says, angry tears leaking down the sides of his face. "The one thing that just might . . ."

Canaan steps around the foot of the bed. "This isn't over, Jake."

He opens his eyes. "What isn't over?"

"This battle, this war. You cannot stop fighting."

Jake sits up then, the idea sickening. "I'm not giving up. You think I'm giving up? I just . . . I don't know what to do. What do I do?"

Canaan stands tall, slides his hands into his pockets. "I raised you well, son. You know exactly what to do."

36

Brielle

I wake to the sound of a ringing phone. But I'm groggy and slow, my eyes swollen from last night's tears. I pat myself down looking for my cell, but it's not here. It's not my cell ringing anyway. It's the phone next to Miss Macy's bed.

I'm at the hospital.

In a chair.

And I'm wearing the Prince's halo.

By the time these things occur to me, I've missed the call. The room is full of soft yellow light, day pressing its face to the window. Next to me, Miss Macy's monitor makes easy whirring noises. Her eyes are still closed, her chest rising and dropping slowly.

"Good girl," she says. "Don't ever answer the phone before nine a.m. It encourages bad manners in the other party."

Despite my tear-stiffened face, I smile. "Morning, Miss Macy."

"Good morning, sweetness." She opens her eyes then, glancing over my shoulder. Pastor Noah is still there, on his cot, snoring away. "To what do I owe this pleasure? You *and* the pastor? Did I sleep through a slumber party?"

"I just wanted to see you," I say.

Her soft face wrinkles, a world of sadness in each new line. "They told you about Regina then."

I smooth the sheet with my hand. Fiddle with the necklace at my throat. Blink back the tears that seem inevitable.

"I don't know how to deal with all this," I say.

Her fingers find mine as the morning sounds of a hospital drift through the open door. Staffers shuffling breakfast carts down the hall; doctors knocking on doors, checking on patients; the first visitors of the day signing in.

Her head rolls toward me. "I had a strange dream last night."

"Did you?" I ask, dropping my haloed hand to my lap. I don't really want to talk about dreams.

"I did," she says, life rushing to her face, turning her cheeks pink. "Help me sit up, will you? There's a button just there."

It takes us a bit to get her upright. Her abdomen is healing but still tender. We have to adjust the bed to the right angle, shift her cords and blankets several times before she's comfortable. It's while I'm attempting to straighten the collar of her gown that she notices the mirrored halo on my wrist.

"How long have you had that?" she says.

I've been trying not to think about it, trying to ignore everything that happened last night. Especially my selfish tirade.

Miss Macy situated, I sit back in my chair. "Since the day before your accident, I think."

"Where's your other one?" she asks. "The one Jake gave you?" She looks a little disoriented now, like the move from horizontal to vertical was a really bad idea. I don't want to talk about the halo—either one, actually—but I don't really think Miss Macy does either. Her eyes are moving slowly over my face, searching for something.

"Are you all right?" I ask. "Can I get you anything? A drink, maybe? Breakfast?"

"I want to tell you about my dream," she says.

"Okay." She's so insistent, I'm curious despite my reservations.

"There was a mirror," she says, glancing at my wrist. "A very big, very long mirror. It hung over Stratus like a dome. Like a gigantic canopy."

I run a finger over the halo, my throat tight.

"Mostly we just ignored the mirror. We went about our business. The things we do every day. Work and play, family, church." Her eyes drift from mine to the window and then back to mine again, her hands twisting in her sheets. "But then a day came when a great black river broke through the streets. Up through Main, bursting through, flooding the town. Roofs were lifted off buildings, homes were destroyed. Lives were lost."

She clears her throat and reaches for the glass of water at her bedside. I hand it to her, and she sips through the straw. "It was in our desperation that we realized we needed help. That there was no one in town who could save us. Help had to come from outside, it had to come from . . ."

"The heavens," I whisper.

"Yes, from the heavens. But when we looked skyward, all we saw was a great reflection of ourselves. Our own misery, our own failures. Our weaknesses. Our own blackness. We couldn't see past it. So we wallowed. We waded through it. We succumbed to the misery of our circumstances."

I see the regret on her face, the loss. "What happened then, Miss Macy?"

"Fire," she says, "a rain of fire fell from above. From above the mirror even, and at first we couldn't see it, we could only hear the hammering of the fire against the back of the mirror. We didn't know what was happening. It was just noise, just hellish, terrifying noise, and we thought the worst had come. We ran."

Her breathing is suddenly labored, and I can't tell if it's fear that's making it hard for her to breathe or if it's sadness. Or maybe something else. Maybe it's something to do with her recovery. I try to hook my finger into the dark halo, try to tug it free so I can call on my celestial eyes, but it's too tight and my finger won't fit.

"But then a crack."

"In the mirror?"

"And then another and another. And soon the whole thing, this massive looking glass, was splintered. And then the first shard fell." She turns her face to mine now. "You can imagine how that panicked us. *The sky is falling, the sky is falling.* But as the mirror fell away, the storm broke through. Fire fell from the sky. It scorched the blackness, burned it all away."

And now it's my breathing that's labored. My heart that's trying to climb out of my chest.

"But the people?" I say. "What happened to the people?"

"They burned too. The blackness coating our skin was scorched away. We lost our homes to the fire, our land, everything we'd built for ourselves."

It's my greatest fear, I think. Beyond losing Jake. Beyond understanding what happened to my mom. I fear the loss that comes with salvation. The cost that living—really living—demands of us. But Miss Macy isn't finished.

"And then the rain fell. The flames that ravaged everything turned to vapor. And before we could be utterly destroyed, sheets and sheets of fresh rainfall drenched the city. It healed the people. Healed the land. And it washed the blackness away."

In the corner of the room, the pastor snuffles and flips onto his side.

"I'd like to see that, Elle," Miss Macy says. "I'd like to see the blackness of Stratus washed away."

I feel like Miss Macy's peeled my flesh back, exposed everything inside of me. There is so much there that I hate. But she's watching me, waiting for me to respond.

"Me too," I say, tears slipping over my lips, tasting of the ocean.

The phone rings again, and Pastor Noah shoots upright, his cot tottering. I reach the phone this time. It's Dad. He's more concerned than angry, but Delia called him, told him where she took me. He asks all kinds of questions and offers to come pick me up. But I decline. I need to think, so I tell him I'm okay, promise to be home soon.

When I hang up, Miss Macy's breakfast tray has arrived. Pastor Noah sits next to her now, another chair materializing from somewhere. He pours her a cup of coffee while she nibbles a slice of toast. Behind me something plunks into the window and I turn. Outside the sky has turned dark, a wind pushing at the trees. Their branches wave, tapping the windows, begging to be let indoors.

"I'm going to go," I tell Miss Macy. "Do you have someone coming to relieve you, Pastor Noah?"

"I do, dear. Becky will be here soon. Here," he adds, sliding a sweater around my shoulders. It's Becky's; the sleeves are too long, but it smells nice. "Take this. Those clouds look ominous."

"Thank you, Pastor. Tell Becky I'll get it back to her." I lean down and kiss Miss Macy's head. "Thank you for letting me sit with you. Thank you for telling me about your dream."

"I love you, sweetness. I hope you"—her brow scrunches—"I hope you keep dreaming. I know it's all been heavy. But maybe . . ."

"Maybe the rain is on its way?"

"Maybe it is," she says.

37

Brielle

I've just sat down on the curb in front of Fancy Hill's Barbershop when Jake steps out of Photo Depot and onto Main. All sorts of angsty feelings war in my gut, but there's no condemnation in his eyes when he sits next to me. I want to curl into his chest. I want to apologize. I want to hear him say he loves me.

But it's possible I've lost the right to all those things.

The wind is warm as it blows through, ruffling our hair, our clothes. Jake tips his face to the sky, and I do the same. It's grown even darker since I left the hospital. Smoky black clouds swirl overhead, turning the morning strange and shadowed.

I set my arm on Jake's knee. The sleeve of my sweater shifts, the dark halo reflecting the clouds above. It's impossible not to think of Miss Macy's dream.

"I can't get it off," I say.

He lifts my sleeve and looks at the halo, tries to slide it free. "What do you mean, you can't get it off?"

I pull my arm away. "It hurts."

"I'll be careful," he says, taking my arm again, gently this time. I feel the warmth of his hands and wonder if maybe, just maybe they could fix me. But their heat doesn't penetrate the Prince's halo, and I start to understand just how big a mistake I've made.

"It wasn't this tight before," he says. "It's not squeezing . . ."

"No, it's not squeezing. But I think it's attached itself to my skin. I can feel it pull when I move."

Jake's golden face drains of color. "We have to get it off."

My hands shake, my legs too. I can't see the fear, but I know it's there. And invisible, it's just as bad.

"I don't know how," I say.

And then the warm breeze turns hot. Violently hot. It rips down Main Street, knocking over trash cans, forcing pedestrians indoors. It presses and pulls, threatens to tip us over. Jake wraps his arms around my shoulders, and we huddle together against it.

"Do you think it's the veil?" I ask.

"I don't know," he says.

"We need to get home. To where the veil was thinnest." I look left and right down Main, my eyes drying in the heat. "Where's your car?"

"Canaan dropped me off," he yells, pulling me to my feet.

Of course he did.

Jake takes my hand and we run. The dark halo pulls at my wrist, but it refuses to fall off. I will it to. Pray it will.

The wind catches my hair and yanks it backward.

On we run.

Down Main. We pass Photo Depot and The Donut Factory. And then the theatre flies by on our left, Jelly's on our right. We slip and slide to a stop as we leave the main stretch. There's only highway between here and home. Between here and the tear in the veil.

I shield my hand with my eyes, looking in the direction of home. I can't see my house from here, but aside from the fiery wind, there's no sign anything's changed.

Jake jumps off the embankment and into the wooded area I ran through last night. It stretches all the way to our houses, past them, really, extending into the next town over. He reaches his hands up for my waist. I crouch and let him lift me down.

The wind is relentless. It pummels and pushes. It screams, a fiery siren kind of scream. We have to run. We have to get there, but I'm scared of what will happen when we do. What will the tear in the veil do to Stratus? How much will it burn?

I think of Miss Macy's dream. I think of the rain.

"You ready?" Jake asks.

I nod, the knot in my throat too tight for anything else. He takes my left hand again. My skin pulls against the cuff that's melded to my wrist, but I bite back the cry building in my chest. He presses my third finger to his lips.

"There's a ring made for this finger. A diamond set by the Creator Himself, made of gold fired in heavenly places. I will find it, Elle."

"But . . ."

"And we'll get this thing off you." He glares at the cuff on my wrist. At the mirrored shine. He hates it as much as I do.

He twists his fingers into mine and we run. Through overgrown summer grasses and trees that are smeared in shadow. My arm aches with the heaviness of the Prince's halo. I'm so tired of the thing that I don't even spare it a glance, but the wind slices through my sweater, stinging my arm, and I can tell it's cut into me.

I can't believe I thought it would help. That not seeing would help.

It's a shackle. A mirrored chain that keeps me prisoner.

We adjust our angle a bit, veering around a thick patch of trees. We clear them, and the houses come into view. Mine first and then Jake's, a hundred yards away. And that's when I see the tear, a gigantic isosceles triangle towering over the two houses. The orange celestial sky is visible beyond it, its edges rippling against the black clouds. This wind—this firestorm—is coming from beyond the veil.

"The Sabres have torn through," Jake says.

"Now everyone can see."

But it's not just the wind. It's like the northern lights are shining here in Stratus. The familiar, the ordinary, the very ugly town I've always wanted to escape is draped in heaven's colors. Tendrils of worship—green and blue, violet and red—curl around the two houses, around the trees, lifting into the sky. Those that curl beyond the edges of the tear are invisible to me.

And I'm reminded again of the wretched halo on my wrist.

Jake pulls us to a stop. "Are you okay?"

I'm sobbing. It's ridiculous, but I can't believe I sacrificed seeing this. I can't believe I entertained ignorance.

"We'll get it off, Elle," he says, mopping my face with his warm hands. But I'm a lost cause, my face a mess, my hair whipping about, stuck to my tears. Finally he gives up. "Come on."

My legs ache, but we run. I let myself cry. There's no reason not to. It's my fear I'm ashamed of, not my tears.

As we close in, I realize how loud the Sabres are, louder than I've ever heard them. Their song has changed again. It's not the same melancholy strain they've been playing over the past few days. This is different. It sounds like a victory march.

We run faster, my heart swelling with hope.

I lift my arm and cradle it against my chest, taking the weight off my wrist. I count our footfalls to keep my mind off the pain, but it's another eighty-seven of them before we're close enough to slow.

Dad's truck is parked in the drive, but Slugger's still gone, which means Marco's not back yet. We run past the house and into the field, the old Miller place just ahead.

From here, the fact that it's a veil is more obvious. It hangs open, the edges of the tear more defined. Beyond it I see several Sabres, their wings whirling, their mouths open. The Palatine are there too. Trying to intercede. Trying to fight. But the Sabres' wings are too fast, too sharp, and anything that approaches them is shredded. We watch as the sword of a Palatine warrior is batted from his hand by the wings of a Sabre. The fallen one tries to pull back, but the blades suck him closer, and like that he's a burst of sulfuric ash.

We don't watch alone. Dad's here. And Kaylee. She has a phone pressed to her ear, my phone, and she's yelling into the speaker. When she sees us, she ends the call and stumbles closer, leaving Dad staring into the light alone.

"That was Becky," she says. "The Sadler twins are awake. Both of them."

"They're okay?" I cry.

"Running tests now," she says. "But yeah. Looks like they're going to be all right."

Jake squeezes my hand, and I try to wrap my injured arm around Kaylee, but the movement tears my skin and I scream.

"What's wrong with your arm?"

"Nothing," I say. "I'm okay."

She grabs it and shoves my sleeve away. The skin around the dark halo is feverish and bleeding.

"You put it on," she says. "I didn't think you'd—" She shakes her head. "Elle, it's cutting you. Jake, have you seen this?"

I pull my arm away, ashamed. But Jake steps closer, the three of us forming our own sad little triangle.

"Take it off," she tells me.

"I can't." Tears fall down my face, but the celestial wind is so hot they're dry before they reach my chin.

"What do you mean, you can't?"

"I mean I can't. I've tried. Jake's tried. We can't get it off."

Jake places a gentle hand under my forearm. "Why didn't you tell me you were bleeding?" he says. "I might not be able to get it off, but my hands are good for something."

With both of his hands, he wraps my arm. The blazing wind and the long run have me sweltering. But when Jake's hands start doing their thing, the heat makes me weak. I close my eyes and lay my head on Kaylee's shoulder. Slowly we sit, the three of us at once.

When Jake takes his hands away, the cuts have healed. It's far from comfortable, but it's not bleeding.

"Thank you," I tell Jake.

"It's torturing her," Kaylee says. She's angry, her voice uneven. "We have to get it off."

"We will," Jake says.

I yank my sleeve down over the offensive thing. "Stop making promises."

"I said we'll get it off. Come on."

He stands and reaches a hand down for me. I slide my right hand into his and stand, cradling my left to my chest. We watch as the tear rips further, stretching higher and higher. Where the top is, I can't say. It extends into the black clouds above, a strange triangular window into the heavens. I wonder if the tear's visible from town now. Wonder what it looks like to everyone else.

Jake leads us toward Dad, the wind loud in my ears. I have to grab Dad's hand to get his attention.

"You okay?" I ask.

"Their wings. That's where the music's coming from."

Carefully, I wrap my arms around his waist. But it doesn't matter how careful I am; I feel the skin of my arm tear again, and my anger flares.

The Prince has taken everything from me.

I can't move without thinking about him.

Without knowing what he's stolen.

I can't move without remembering I traded my sight away.

"That's right," I say, struggling to keep my voice even through the pain. "It's their wings."

"Sabres," Dad says, his eyes moving from one to the other. "These are the ones who took your mother."

I don't answer, but I don't have to. Dad's made peace with the fact that Canaan's beyond lying. The wind rages, and Dad has to yell to be heard over it.

"Which one was it? Which one is Virtue?"

I squint into the wind, scrutinizing the angels before me. The Palatine have backed away for now, leaving all twelve of the Sabres alone in their worship. Unmuted by demonic forces, a pure, almost blinding silver light mingles with the red and orange of the Celestial. I have to believe he's healed by now. It's been long enough, hasn't it? But it's hard to see the Sabres' faces; they're all so bright, and their blades obscure everything.

"He's there," I say, pointing to a kneeling Sabre. I see only his profile, but it's enough. On his hands and knees, he faces the tallest tree in the orchard, old and gnarled. His perfect silver form presents a haunting, almost gothic beauty contrasted against it.

Dad pulls away, moving toward the trees. He's not rough, but it's too much for my arm. I fall to the ground, cradling it against my chest. I call after Dad, but he can't hear me. Not over the wind.

And now Jake's at my side. He slides his hand up my sleeve. When he withdraws his fingers, they're wet with blood.

"We need help," Jake yells, wrapping his hands once again around my arm. "I can stop the bleeding, but that's not—"

"Healing," I say.

"Look!" Kaylee screams. We turn to the orchard where my dad stands, staring up at the sky. The Sabres are now high above, a new wave of attack coming from the horizon. They continue to sing as the dark warriors approach.

It's not the Palatine. It's the Prince's Guard. I can tell by their armor, by their size. I count them quickly, twenty-four. Their number is twice that of the Sabres.

The Guard divides in two, and the Prince soars to the front.

My hands shake at the sight of him. I know it's fear, but there's anger mixed with it too. He's the reason I'm blind. The reason I hurt.

I stand, Jake helping me, keeping a hand wrapped around the dark halo.

"That's him, isn't it?" Kaylee asks. "That's the Prince."

"Why is he here?" Jake asks. "He has the Palatine. The Guard. There's no reason for him to risk—"

"He said he'd come," I say.

Jake's eyes meet mine, incredulous. "What?"

"I should have told you," I say. "I didn't think. I'm so sorry. It's my fault."

Jake cries out. Something angry. Indistinguishable. "No. He did this. It's his fault."

"It doesn't matter! He's here because of me! How do I take that back?"

Jake stares at me. "I don't know."

I'm stupid and foolish and most certainly brash. But if any created being knows how to get the dark halo off my arm, it's the Prince.

"Hey!" I yell, waving my uninjured arm.

"Elle," Kaylee hisses. "What are you doing?"

I grab her elbow and walk her back toward house. "Go inside, okay? I'll be there in just a sec."

"What are you going to do?" she asks.

"I just . . . I'm going to go talk to Satan." There's a tenacity in her eyes now, and I have to beg. "Please. Go inside. It's too hard with you here."

She stares at me for a long time before I can see she'll honor my request. "What about your dad?" she asks.

I turn toward him. He's still there, beyond the veil, staring up at the sky. The Sabres are keeping their distance from the Prince and his Guard, but their wings send off shards of lightning that the Guard has to block. Two demonic warriors are destroyed as I watch, their movements too slow for the Sabres' worship.

"I don't know," I say. "But he can't stay here."

"I'll get him," she says.

"Wait! No!" I reach for her, but my arm is useless and she slips away. The wind blows against her as she approaches the tear, but she ducks her head against it and pushes on. She slows further as she steps through the tear, her head turning right and left, taking it all in. She turns back to me, her face and clothes swirling with color.

And then I see it. The worship curling around her, lifting from her chest and lips. Tendrils of deep green fill the sky around her. I wonder what she's saying, how she's worshiping. But there's no doubt that she is. She grabs Dad's arm and pulls him toward us. They step from the orchard and back through the tear.

Dad's in shock apparently. His eyes are wide, his mouth agape. I pat his arm as they brush by. And then Kaylee shuffles Dad back to our place, and I'm glad. Not because they'll be any safer inside, but seeing how much I have to lose makes this all so much harder.

All the while, the Prince draws closer. He's so close I can almost see the pale blue of his eyes.

"Elle," Jake says, "I don't want you to do this. Not without a Shield of some kind. Not without Canaan."

"If God wanted Canaan here, he'd be here," I say.

I realize now how deeply I believe that statement. How desperately that dims everything I'm afraid of.

"His will's going to be done, right? Whether Canaan's here or not. If I believe in providence, then I have to believe that. And I do, Jake. I know I'm not in control. Canaan's not in control. And I know something else."

Jake's proud of me. I don't even need celestial eyes to see it.

"What else do you know?" he says.

"I know *he's* not in control either," I say, spinning, pointing with my good arm at the Prince of Darkness. "He's going to lie to me. I know that. But he's here. And I'm going to tell him just how much I despise this *gift* he gave me. I'm going to tell him that he can hurt me every day for the rest of my life, but I'll never, ever choose his crown. Not again. He can"—I sob, but I keep going—"take my celestial eyes, he can take Dad, he can even take you from me. I'm sorry, Jake, but he can. He can take you and our happily-ever-after, but he can't touch providence. He can't touch God's will, and even when it sucks, I have to cling to that. Good wins. God wins."

Jake's so close. The heat of the Celestial warms his skin, and I breathe him in. One of my favorite things to do. To be close and to breathe the air that smells like the man I love. The coffee and the chocolate, the sugar on his lips, the salt of his tears, the sweat on his brow. I know now that I don't need Jake to survive. But I want him. I want him more than I've ever wanted him before.

"Regardless of what the Prince says, regardless of what he threatens, *we get forever.* Maybe not here. Maybe not as husband and wife. But it's ours, and he can't take that away."

Jake's eyes widen. I've never seen them so large.

"He's behind you," he says.

"Don't leave me," I say. "I'm braver when you're here."

I turn quickly, wanting to get this over with. Wanting the Prince out of Stratus.

And there he is. Standing at the edge of the orchard.

He steps through the tear, and his celestial appearance melts away. I see the boy I met in the desert. Black curls, pale blue eyes, faded jeans, and a white pocket T. He's playing to my humanity. I steel myself, because I've always been a sucker for a guy in a white T.

Jake's hand finds my waist, and my heart triples in speed. He's still here. I'm not alone. I've never been alone.

"I told you the war would be too much. I warned you, didn't I? And now it seems Michael and his army have left the Sabres to fight alone. Seems unwise. But what does it matter to you?" the Prince says, his tone patronizing, his lips pursed. "Look at you. Two beautiful people. And gifted. I couldn't be happier with our arrangement, Elle."

I stiffen, but find it hard to form the words. All my eloquence, all my resolve feels frail with the Prince so close.

"May I?" With a cold hand, he pulls my left arm away from my body.

Jake's fingers tighten on my hip, but he doesn't try to stop the Prince when he lifts the sleeve of my shirt. We just watch as slowly he rolls the cuff.

"Take it," I say.

He continues to fold. "You don't like my halo?"

"I hate it. I never wanted it."

His fingers go still on my arm. "I thought we agreed to stop lying, Elle."

"Don't call me that," I say through clenched teeth.

"If I take the halo back," he says, "our deal is off."

Behind me, Jake shifts. "It wasn't your deal to make," he says. "It was never within your power to promise."

"Oh, look at that," the Prince says, ignoring Jake, tucking my sleeve into the crease at my elbow. "This is out of my hands now. It's already become a part of you." He turns those pale eyes on me. "*I've* become a part of you."

"What?" I look down at my arm. Jake leans over my shoulder to do the same.

"The halo's grafted to your arm," he says. He turns his attention to Jake. "But you? You tried to heal her, didn't you? Here's a lesson I bet your Shield never taught you. Some things can't be healed. Some things must be cut away."

"You can remove it," Jake says.

"I can't." The Prince raises his hands. "I'm very good at getting into things, latching on. But the getting out, that's never really been my thing."

"So what do I do?" I don't know why I'm asking him. He'll only lie.

"Live with it," the Prince says, his eyes like ice. "Appreciate that you don't have to see pain and fear. That once I get this veil stitched up, you won't have to see angels and demons either. You won't have to see me."

I can't think of anything else to say. I have arguments, good arguments. That spiritual blindness solves nothing. But they'd be wasted words here. He knows that. He tricked me into this thing, and he's not going to offer me a way out. But that doesn't mean he's telling the truth. That doesn't mean hope is gone.

"Come on," Jake says. "Let's go. We'll find another way."

We start to back away, but the Prince's words stop us. "Where's the other halo?"

"Why?"

"Because you have no use for it. Blindness is your gift now."

The truth of his words hurt; the cut they make on my heart is deeper than the one on my arm. But it doesn't matter. I gave the golden halo away. It's not mine anymore.

I turn my back on the Prince, on the celestial porthole behind him. And that's when I see them. The Army of Light.

Despite the dark halo on my arm, I see them. With celestial eyes.

I don't understand how, but I do.

They're everywhere. They line the field between the old Miller place and my house, filling every inch of it. Warriors hover above those on the ground, bows drawn. I recognize the Peter Pan Warrior I saw at Danakil. He's positioned near the middle, an arrow nocked, another between his teeth. Below him stands Michael, Commander of the Army of Light. On his left is the female Warrior from the desert, looking as wild and fierce as she did some days ago. On his right stands Canaan, and next to Canaan is Helene.

Strapped to her chest are Marco and Olivia. She's loosened her inner wings so that her charges can stand on the grass, but she keeps them covered. Both Marco and Olivia are taller than she is, but between their shoulders, I see her lift a finger to her lips, and I hear Canaan's voice in my head.

"He can't see us, Elle. Not in his terrestrial form. Not from this side of the tear."

Jake squeezes my hand. Heat, blessed heat pushes up my injured arm, soothing it.

He hears Canaan too.

I keep walking, afraid of giving away their position, afraid of sounding the alarm. I stop just in front of Canaan.

"Give it to him," Canaan says. The golden halo's suddenly in his hands. I look to Olivia, my eyes questioning.

But she nods, and I can't help myself; I glance at her arm. She turns it, shows me that the silver scars are gone. I smile at her and she smiles back. I let Canaan slide the halo onto my right wrist.

And then there's another voice in my head. "You must hurry," it says. I recognize it. From Danakil. My eyes find Michael's. "The Palatine are mounting another attack. I don't know how much longer we can keep the veil open."

This exchange hasn't taken longer than a few seconds, but

I'm suddenly anxious that the Prince will step back through the tear, or that he'll transfer. I turn back, Jake behind me.

The Prince is just starting to back toward the tear when I yank the golden halo off my wrist.

"Take it," I say, throwing the halo at his feet. "You've taken everything else." I make sure to throw like a girl, the halo falling just short enough that he has to step toward me to scoop it up. Over his head, I see the Sabres. Their wings spin slowly, still worshiping, the air around them thick with demonic ash and smoke. The remaining members of the Guard are gone. Destroyed.

The Prince lifts the halo from the ground. He spins it in his hands, his response so similar to mine when I first saw it.

"I can hardly see my reflection in this one," he says. "I think I prefer mine."

He's lying. He wants to put it on. I know he does.

"I told you she'd give it to me," the Prince says, his eyes on Jake.

Jake tenses, and for a moment I think he's going to lunge at the Prince. I twist my fingers into his. And then behind me I hear an entire legion of angels inhale sharply as the Prince lifts the halo above his head, and with all the arrogance that made him what he is, he crowns himself.

I swear I don't breathe.

I watch and pray. And then he shakes his head and swipes at his ears. For the tiniest of moments his gaze finds mine, but I can see he's far away. He's seeing a time and place that is not now. That is not here. And then his eyes glaze over and he buckles, his hands on his knees, his breathing ragged. And then he's weeping. Tears run down the Prince's human face.

I turn to Jake. The wind is a torrent now, and we're back to yelling.

"What's going on?" I ask.

But Jake just shakes his head, his confusion echoing mine.

The Prince stumbles backward, and I know a second before it happens that he's going to tumble through the tear in the veil. I expect the halo to fall from his brow, but it doesn't. It's stuck there, his celestial form coming into view as he backs into the orchard. He's immediately taller, broader, his wings spectacular. They lift him into the sky.

If he sees the Army of Light before him, he doesn't acknowledge them in any way. With lily-white hands he claws at the halo, but it will not move. And that's strange, because I've never had a problem removing it. If anything, it fell off my head more often than I liked. But Canaan's halo seems glued to the Prince's head.

Not glued.

Grafted.

Like the dark halo on my arm.

And whatever the halo is showing the Prince has him writhing in the sky. He arches and cries out—wailing. Not the same terrifying cry I heard in the desert. This is not a call for his kin. This is agony.

But his kin arrive nonetheless. Black shapes fill the sky. Wings and swords, armor. I don't even have time to tremble before the army behind me soars overhead, Michael at their helm. The sound is so loud, so fierce, I fall to the ground, Jake huddled by my side.

We stay there, on our knees, and we don't stop praying until the sky falls silent.

38

Brielle

The Prince is burning now. Returned to the pit. Michael's sword cut him down at the height of his misery as he twisted and cried. As he begged for forgiveness.

Forgiveness might be out of his reach, but it was a kindness that Michael sent him into the fire. I heard the Prince's wailings, his mind wide open as he faced the one thing he thought he'd escaped: remorse.

He felt his rebellion for the first time. Regretted it. Yes, it was mercy that cut him down.

I know he won't remain in the pit for long. I know that his final judgment hasn't come, but Canaan assures me it will be some time before he claws his way out.

The golden halo survived the Prince's demise, but I returned it to Liv. I don't think it's done with her yet.

Far above, the battle still rages, but Michael's army has pushed the Palatine back and the veil remains open. Stratus has gone quiet.

Jake sits next to me on the orchard floor. We're inside the tear, and everything we see is colored with the Celestial. I know

now just how precious a gift it is. Because soon the fighting will end, the Palatine will stitch up the veil here, and there's no guarantee I'll ever have angel eyes again.

Virtue crouches before us, his wings still.

"You took my mom," I say. I don't know when I'll get another chance to talk to him, and I need to know.

"I did."

"Where?"

The question seems to confuse him. "She's gone. I thought I showed you that."

I choke. Not because I didn't know she was dead, but because I had hoped she wasn't.

"But where is her body?"

"Is that important?"

Everything's tight now: my throat, my chest, my gut.

"Yes," Jake answers, squeezing my hand. "It's important."

"She's here," Virtue says.

"What do you mean 'here'?" I ask. "Here in Stratus?"

"Here in the orchard." He offers me his hand and I take it, Jake standing with me. We follow Virtue through the trees, through the light, to the middle of the orchard. "Hannah used to walk here. Every morning she'd bring her Bible, she'd walk the rows of trees, and she'd sing. It wasn't so neglected a place as it is now."

"So you buried her here?"

"I did. She wanted to be useful in her final moments. She wanted to be the Father's hands and feet one last time. But she wasn't ready to leave you. She wasn't ready to leave *your* father, so although life wasn't mine to give, when it was time for her body to rest, I brought her home. She's buried beneath this tree."

I stare at the tree. It's beautiful in the light of the Celestial. All bright browns and greens. Lush. Vibrant. But I know when the veil is sewn shut, it'll be hard to identify among all the others. I tug the flowered necklace from beneath my shirt and gently, so as not to tear my arm again, I lift it over my head.

Jake found it in a tree above Mom's pretend grave. I hang it now in the tree above the place she was buried. And I cry. Because that's what I do. I'm a crier.

And maybe I'm okay with that.

Jake pulls me into his side, and we mourn together. We grieve the loss of my mother, a woman who changed Stratus with her prayers and is now memorialized here within the tear of the terrestrial veil. I give myself permission to cry for another minute, and then I pull away from Jake and turn to Virtue.

"Thank you for taking care of my mother," I say. "I want you to know how grateful I am."

"It was the highest of honors to watch her greet the Father, Brielle. But you are welcome."

Carefully, very carefully, I hold out my arm, showing him the dark halo.

"Can you cut it away?" I ask.

"I can," he says. "But it won't be easy, and it will hurt."

I take Jake's other hand in mine. "That's okay," I say. "I'm done with easy."

"Come, then, and let's be done with it."

Virtue was right. It wasn't easy. He did what he could to make the process swift, but I bled, a lot. It's not possible to cut something like that away without killing the flesh. So I screamed. I cried and I begged him to stop. But he didn't. Because he knew I wanted it gone. And when at last the Prince's halo was cut away, I lay there in the orchard with Jake's hands wrapped around my arm. And I let healing come.

39

Brielle

Two weeks have passed and still the veil hangs open. I'll be honest, it was easier when I was the only one who could see the battle raging. But if I've learned anything this past year, it's that *easy* has never been heaven's goal. I just didn't realize how crazy the world would become when the invisible is seen.

Stratus has become a magnet for all sorts of scientists and news reporters. They stand in the field between Jake's house and mine, and they watch. They try to film what they see, but for some reason the Celestial doesn't translate that way. So they do what they can to explain the phenomenon to their audiences, but they're learning what I've known for a while: putting heaven into words is hard. There are some things you have to see for yourself.

The Sadler twins were just the start of the miraculous stuff. They woke up that day, the day the veil tore. But they weren't alone. I have a thing for numbers, so how's this for counting?

In the past two weeks one brain-injured toddler regained cognitive function, four terminal patients have been declared cancer-free, a man warped by rheumatoid arthritis told Pastor

Noah he was completely healed, and Dad hasn't had a drop of alcohol.

There are other things happening too. Hard things. Angry people. People who still refuse to believe. Who mock those who do. It's like my arm. Blindness is being cut away, but there's pain and loss to contend with.

We're contending as best we can.

I have no idea how long the veil will remain open, but it's changed Stratus. It's changed our little church, and come fall I'm not going anywhere. I've decided to stay, to teach. I'll be taking online classes for a while, and I'm keeping my eyes open for opportunities to help.

"What do you think, Elle?" Jake says. "This one?"

We're in Canaan's room, and Jake's trying to select a tie. I jab a finger at the one on the left, but it doesn't really matter. He'll look gorgeous in whatever, and today's not about us. It's about Regina.

She was buried last week in a family plot near the coast, but Pastor Noah wanted to honor her life with a memorial service here in Stratus. Jake slips the tie over his head, and I step forward to tie it. He can do it, of course. Probably better than I can. But I like to do it. And he likes to let me.

When I'm done, he pulls me close and kisses me. He's going away in another month, so I take advantage of every moment I can like this. Yesterday an acceptance letter appeared in the chest. Jake's heading off to Portland State. They have a great photography program there, and really, it's the first step in preparing for the future.

"Do you think the Throne Room will ever replace the ring?" I ask.

"I hope so," he says. "They're setting the bar pretty high."

"I'd marry you if you put a zip tie on my finger."

"You still want me to wait to say it?"

"You are saying it," I say, watching the white fire in his eyes.

My celestial vision returned the moment the dark halo was cut away, and now I rarely see anything without it. My world, so dark just days ago, is now bright with color and light. With truth. And yes, there's fear, but I'm learning to fight it again. Not for my sake, but for those who suffer. For those who don't know they're bound.

"You always say it. Even when I gave up, when I lost hope, your eyes never stopped telling me."

Jake crushes me to his chest. "But maybe my lips want to say it," he says.

His lips find mine, so soft, so warm, and he speaks the three words he's never been able to hide.

Afterword

Jake

Four years and two months later

His fingers are blistered, but Jake could play here for hours. The smell of cinnamon and sugar on the air, the ocean crashing against the cliffs outside. From a barstool in the corner, he sings and watches the crowd. Tourists and locals alike have made themselves at home here, talking and laughing while teens from Beacon City's group home program serve them coffee and pastries. Looking at the place now, it's hard to imagine he spent hours strapped to a chair in the basement below.

Liv's turned the Bellwether into a tower of refuge for these kids.

His set finished, Jake lifts the guitar over his head and props it against the wall. A sugared doughnut sits on the corner of his music stand. He lifts it and takes a bite. Shrieks split the hum of conversation, and his gaze falls on the table by the window.

"We're going! They said yes!" Brielle runs toward him,

cutting through a jumble of flowered chairs and tables. When she reaches him, she's out of breath and her face is beautifully flushed. "The board said *yes*. We leave tomorrow."

"I know," Jake says, popping the rest of the doughnut into his mouth.

"How could you know? Liv just got the call. I was sitting next to her when her phone rang."

He licks the sugar from his lips. "I had a letter from Canaan this morning."

"A letter? Like in the mail?"

The Throne Room's moved Canaan around several times in the last few years. He checks in every couple of weeks, calls mostly.

"It was more of a note than a letter," Jake says.

"Well, give it."

He pulls the note card from his pocket and hands it to her.

"'This arrived yesterday,'" she reads. "'See you in Thailand.'" She flips the card over. "What arrived yesterday? Canaan's in Thailand?"

Jake starts to answer, but then Liv's there and Kaylee.

"Marco's going too," Kay tells them.

"Of course he's going," Liv adds. "We couldn't do this without our videographer."

"So the board said yes," Jake says, clapping Marco on the back. "And we're cleared to film?"

"We are, but this is new territory for Ingenui, and the board is keeping us on a tight leash."

He can see it pains Olivia to say that. One of the stipulations the board had for reinstating her at the foundation was board approval on all her business transactions moving forward. She wasn't prosecuted for withholding information from the authorities, but Ingenui spent a year in the headlines after she turned over Henry's files. She's done her best to toe the line, something Jake doesn't imagine she's quite used to.

Earlier this year she got approval to put together a team to actively join the fight against human trafficking. With Liv at the helm and Kaylee handling the details, Henry's money is being used to fight the evil he once helped spread.

The goal is to push the issue out of the shadows. To start, the team will fly to Thailand to meet with a family providing aftercare to those who have been exploited. The plan is to shoot several short films, not only to highlight the tragedies of trafficking, but to show that there is hope. There are individuals and organizations rising up to take a stand, and their stories need to be told.

Liv has put together a top-notch team, and she's asked Brielle to be the face of the campaign. She'll conduct the interviews, sit face-to-face with the victims. At first, Jake wasn't sure she'd agree—that's a lot of fear to be seeing up close—but Brielle signed on without hesitation.

A couple months ago, after Jake graduated from Portland State, he was hired as the team's lead photographer, and he all but insisted they hire Marco to handle direction and filming. Liv didn't argue.

"We'll be all right," Marco says, sliding his arm around Kaylee's shoulders. "I know who to contact when we get down there."

The team's not authorized to get involved, not by Ingenui, at least. They're being sent to film, to inform, but with Jake and Brielle on the team, with Marco dreaming of stories they've yet to shoot, they're prepared to do whatever they can to help. There are things they can do that other people can't. Things the board doesn't need to know about.

"Kay," Liv says, sliding the halo off her wrist. "I want you to take this."

"What? Why?"

Liv pushes the halo onto Kaylee's arm. "I'm going to need you guys to do me proud out there."

"You're not going? You said you were going. Holy moly, this thing is hot."

"I thought we'd get the nod earlier." Liv runs a hand over her round stomach. "The doctor says I'm too far along to fly and the husband says I'm far too used to Western amenities. No one wants to see me go into labor in the middle of a red light district."

"Totally sucks," Kaylee says, but her eyes are on the halo.

Brielle pulls Liv in for a hug. "You made this all possible. You know that, right?" They're both crying now. "Send us pictures of the baby, okay?"

Liv wipes her eyes. "I will." She and Kaylee head back to their table, the clipboard moving back and forth between them. Brielle's still holding the note card.

Marco eyes it and nods. "You show her?"

"Show me what?"

"Not yet," Jake says.

Marco flashes him a grin. "I'll go get the video equipment together. Give you two a minute."

"Show me what?" Brielle asks again, bouncing on the balls of her feet.

"Come on," Jake says, taking her hand. He leads her out

the door of the keeper's house and onto the white wraparound porch. It's fall now, officially. Red and yellow leaves jut here and there among the evergreens. The ocean is calm today, gulls screaming.

Brielle leans against the railing, her arms crossed. "You have something to show me apparently."

"I do," Jake says, pulling a slip of yellow paper from his shirt pocket. "Canaan sent me this with his note."

She takes it from him, unfolding the small square sheet.

"It's a carbon copy," she says, tilting her head, trying to read the writing. "A claim check from . . . Siam Jewelers." She looks up at him, her blue eyes wide. "I can't read the rest. It's in Thai."

He steps closer, takes the claim check from her hand and slides it back into the pocket just over his heart. He's waited a long time for this.

"Jake, is that . . . is it . . ."

"According to Google Translate, it's a claim check for a custom-engraved diamond engagement ring."

Her mouth opens and closes. "Custom-engraved?"

"I called the jeweler this morning," he says.

"You called?"

"They said it's ready. We can pick it up whenever."

She looks down at her hand. Her left hand. "Are you sure it's mine?"

He shrugs, but he can't stop the half smile that creeps up his face. "You want to go find out?" he asks.

For a moment she's frozen, an ice sculpture, a stone angel. And then she pushes off the railing and her lips find his.

"Yes," she says. "I do. I absolutely do."

Reading Group Guide

Spoiler alert!

Don't read before completing the novel.

1. When this story opens, Brielle is feeling Jake's absence intensely. Have you lost someone you care about? How did you cope?
2. Brielle's dad is learning to believe in the invisible. The Bible says, "Faith is the substance of things hoped for, the evidence of things not seen." (Hebrews 11:1) Does faith come easy for you?
3. Canaan gives Brielle a task; he asks her to wait by the chest for instructions. Brielle would rather do something to help. She'd rather fight. Do you have a hard time waiting on God when hard things happen?
4. Marco sees revenge as the only way to make amends for his part in Ali's death. What are your thoughts on vengeance?
5. Olivia's life is a tragic one and she's involved in some horrible crimes, but in the end we see her redeemed. What does redemption mean and what does it look like to you?
6. In Danakil, the Prince lays out a compelling case for Brielle. He wraps his lies in truth. Have you ever had trouble deciphering good from evil?

7. The dark halo is appealing to Brielle because she thinks it will make life easier on her. Do you think life is supposed to be easy? When things get hard, what do you do?
8. With the engagement ring gone, Brielle feels like she and Jake have lost "heaven's blessing" on their relationship. Have you ever felt that way?
9. Brielle and Kaylee have a heart-to-heart on Main Street about love and marriage. Do you have a friend you can talk to about these things? Are you a good listener when others need to talk?
10. Olivia tells Jake she likes "blaming" other people. Are you like Olivia? Do you feel the need to assign blame for wrongs done?
11. Brielle is easily rattled by the fear she sees around her. With the constant onslaught of tragedy and evil we see reported daily, it's no wonder many of us can relate. How do the things you see and hear throughout the day affect you?
12. Human trafficking is a term that includes a number of crimes. These crimes happen close to home and across the planet, but a lot of good things are happening in the fight against trafficking. How can you get involved?

Acknowledgments

My name is on the front of this book, but the truth is I couldn't have written it without the help of so many others.

To my husband, Matt, for daily inspiration and strength, for letting me be one of those crazy author people, and for working hard every single day so I can stay home with our kids and write. You are the reason these books are possible. Thank you for sharing me.

To Justus and Jazlyn. One more adventure down and a million to go! Thank you for traveling this road with me. I want to be just like you when I grow up.

To my friends at Nelson Fiction, to the editorial team, to marketing and publicity, to the sales teams, and to everyone who works behind the scenes, thank you. These stories are yours as much as they're mine and I'm so glad we're in this together.

To my editors, Becky Monds and LB Norton, your fingerprints are all over these pages and this trilogy is better for it. You challenge me and you make me better. Thank you.

To my agent, Holly Root, who just might be the author whisperer. I'm forever grateful for the time and commitment you've given my stories. I am blessed to be on your team and to have you on mine.

To Mom and Dad, Stephanie and Sharon, Scott, Sayth, and

Londyn. To Nana and Papa and Grandma and Grandpa. You've spread the word about my books far and wide. Thank you for being proud of me, for telling me so, and for supporting everything I try. I have the best family in the world.

To my families at Inspire and Living Way, to the bloggers and the readers who have rallied behind Brielle, thank you.

To my childhood friend, Phillip O'Brien, who taught me how to tie up a prisoner. I can't thank you enough. For your help and for your service to our country.

To my Soul Sisters (notice I didn't call you my Gangstas), you pour into me weekly and I thank God for each and every one of you.

And to Jenny Lundquist (my BWFF!), who triple dog dared me when I needed it most. You're the reason this thing has an ending.

Dear Readers,

We hope you've enjoyed reading the thrilling conclusion to the Angel Eyes series, *Dark Halo*. One of the joys of our role in publishing is connecting talented authors with one another. Shannon Dittemore and Krista McGee are two leading authors in the young adult space, and it has been so exciting to watch them support each other's work. Krista and Shannon are not only colleagues but friends, and both share a passion for working with young adults. They each believe in the power of story and its ability to inspire and touch readers and wanted to offer a free gift to you within the pages of their books.

We hope you enjoy reading the following excerpt of *Anomaly*, the first in a new trilogy by Krista McGee.

Happy Reading!
Your Friends at HarperCollins
Christian Publishing

An Excerpt from *Anomaly*
by Krista McGee

PROLOGUE

Fifteen minutes and twenty-three seconds.

That's how long I have to live.

The wall screen that displayed the numbers in blood-red letters now projects the image of a garden. The trees are full of pink and white blossoms, the green grass swaying a little in the wind. I hear the birds as they call to each other. I smell the moist soil.

But the countdown still plays in my mind.

Fourteen minutes and fifty-two seconds.

It isn't really soil I smell. It isn't really the garden breeze I feel on my face. That is simply the Scientists' "humane" means of filling my bloodstream with poison, of annihilating a member of the State who has proven to be "detrimental to harmonious living."

The wall screen is beginning to fade. The colors aren't as bright. The blossoms are beginning to merge together. They look more like clouds now. I don't know if the image is changing or if it is the effect of the poison. I could try to hold my breath, to deny the entrance of this toxic gas into my body. But I would only pass out, and my lungs would suck in the poison-laced oxygen as I lie here unconscious.

No. I will die the way I finally learned to live. Fully aware. At peace. With a heart so full of love that even as it slows, it is still full.

Because I know something the Scientists refuse to acknowledge.

Death is only the beginning.

CHAPTER ONE

I suppose I've always known something was wrong with me. I've never quite been normal. Never really felt like I fit. Don't get me wrong. I've tried. In fact, I spent most of my life trying.

Like everyone in Pod C, I was given a particular set of skills, a job I would eventually take over from the generation before us.

I am the Musician of Pod C.

My purpose is to stimulate my pod mates' minds through the instruments I play. I enable the others to do their jobs even better.

And that is important because being productive is important. Working hard is important. I have always been able to do that. But being the same is also important.

This is where I have failed.

I started realizing this in my ninth year, the year my pod mate Asta was taken away. We were outside in the recreation field and our Monitor had us running the oval track. We ran nine times—one time for each year of life. This was part of our daily routine.

Sometimes, I would like to say no. To just sit down, not to run. Sometimes I want to ask why we have to do this. And why we always do everything in the same order, day after day. Why couldn't we run ten laps? Or eight? Or skip laps altogether and do something else? But I knew better than to ask those questions, to ask any questions. We are only allowed to ask for clarification. Asking why is something only I would consider.

I am an anomaly.

So was Asta. But I didn't know it until that day. She always did what she was told, and nothing in her big black eyes made her appear to be having thoughts to the contrary. She was training to be our pod Historian, so she was always documenting what we were doing and what we were discovering. Her fingers could fly over her learning pad faster than any I'd ever seen. But that day, when we were running, she stopped. Right in the center of the track. I was so shocked that I ran right into her back, knocking her to the ground.

"I apologize." I reached for her hand, but when she looked up at me, I saw a yellowish substance coming from her nose. I had never seen anything like it. Her eyes were red and she was laboring to breathe—all of this was quite unusual. I pulled my hand back and called for the Monitor to come over and help Asta.

But the Monitor didn't help her. She looked down into Asta's face and her eyes grew large. She pressed the panel on her wrist pad. "Please send a team to Pod C. We need a removal."

The Monitor motioned for me to finish my laps. No one else had stopped to see what happened. The rest of my pod mates simply ran closer to the edge of the track, eyes forward, completing the circuit.

I stood and tried to run, but I did not want to run. I wanted to stay here, to help Asta. She looked . . . I do not know how to describe it. But whatever it was made my heart feel heavy.

Berk ran up beside me. "You will never beat me." His grin shook me from my thoughts. I was determined to beat Berk. He always thought he was faster, but I knew I could outrun him. So I picked up my pace. Berk did the same.

We were on our fifth lap when I saw a floating white platform with four Medical Specialists land beside Asta on the grass inside the track. "Where will they take her?"

"I don't know." Berk slowed a little. He was watching the medics lift Asta onto the platform, then wrap her in some sort of covering. "Maybe take her to the Scientists. They will help her."

Berk was going to be a Scientist. One of *the* Scientists who govern the State. That made him different—but in a good way. The Monitors never corrected him, and he was allowed to study any subject that interested him during the time the rest of us worked on improving knowledge in our specialty areas.

I didn't say anything else, but the image of Asta being taken away—removed—stayed with me. And somehow I didn't think she was going to be helped. The look on the

Monitor's face was not the look she gets when one of us falls and scrapes a knee on the track. It was the look she gets when we do something we shouldn't. But Asta hadn't done anything wrong. She just had something wrong inside her.

Like me.

A few days later I asked the Monitor if Asta would be coming back. I had worked on how I would phrase that question for days. It could not sound like a "why." It had to sound like I simply wanted information, clarification. I had to sound like my pod mate Rhen. Logical. Not emotional.

"Excuse me." I tried to ask with an air of indifference. "Will Asta be returning to Pod C?"

The Monitor did not even look up from her communications pad. "No."

And that was all. I had to bite my lip to keep from asking why. I imagined all kinds of reasons. None of them made sense, and none of them, I knew, could ever be voiced.

In the quiet of our cube, I asked Rhen, "What do you think happened to Asta?"

But Rhen just looked at me like she did not understand the question. "She was removed."

And that's all she needed to know.

When I still couldn't stop thinking about it, I asked Berk. We were back on the track several days after Asta's removal. "If she went to the Scientists, why don't they fix her and send her back?"

Berk slowed his pace a little before answering. "Maybe they will keep her with them."

"But she's our Historian." I could argue with Berk. He actually enjoyed it, liked questions. "They already have one of their own."

"Whatever they are doing, it is right." This is what we have always been taught. And, of course, it is correct.

"But I want to see her."

"When I leave to live in the Scientists' compound, I will tell her that."

That made me feel better. And worse. Better because I knew Berk would do what he said. Worse because I knew that when he did, I would lose another pod mate. I would lose Berk.

I did not want to think about that.

"I will win this time." I pushed all thoughts of Asta from my mind and ran as hard as I could to the line marking the end of our circuit.

I won.

:::

About the Author

Author photo by Amy Schuff Photography

Shannon Dittemore is the author of the Angel Eyes Trilogy and has an overactive imagination and a passion for truth. Her lifelong journey to combine the two is responsible for a stint at Portland Bible College, performances with local theater companies, and a focus on youth and young adult ministry. When she isn't writing, she spends her days with her husband, Matt, chasing their two children around their home in Northern California.